HOMETOWN
FAVORITE

HOMETOWN FAVORITE

A NOVEL

Bill Barton and Henry O. Arnold

Foreword by Chris Sanders

Revell
a division of Baker Publishing Group
Grand Rapids, Michigan

© 2008 by Bill Barton & Henry O. Arnold

Published by Revell
a division of Baker Publishing Group
P.O. Box 6287, Grand Rapids, MI 49516-6287
www.revellbooks.com

Printed in the United States of America

Library of Congress Cataloging-in-Publication Data
Barton, Bill, 1966–
    Hometown favorite : a novel / Bill Barton and Henry O. Arnold ; foreword by Chris Sanders.
        p.   cm.
    ISBN 978-0-8007-1914-2 (cloth)
    ISBN 978-0-8007-3286-8 (pbk.)
    1. Football players—Fiction. I. Arnold, Henry O., 1966– II. Title.
PS3602.A84226H66 2008
813′.6—dc22   2008016702

Published in association with the literary agency of Fedd & Company, Inc., 9759 Concord Pass, Brentwood, TN 37027.

To Gerald and Jeanie,
two of my real-life heroes because they get out of bed
and face the world every day.
Bill Barton

———————

To Kay, my closest companion, who never stopped believing.
Henry O. Arnold

Foreword

> It was impossible, so it took a little longer to accomplish.
> —Wally Byam, Airstream founder

All of my life people have told me what I cannot do. In high school, I was told I could not play college football. After a successful career at Ohio State, I was told I could not play in the NFL. After being drafted in the third round by the Houston Oilers, naysayers told me that I would not make it, and even after being in the league for a few years, I still had my share of doubters as well as moments of self-doubt.

Just like everybody else, I have had my share of "Job-like" experiences. Some of these were on the playing field where it is just a game, and others have been in the game of life that have left me "sitting in the ashes," wondering if it was worth it to go on. Still, I have learned over the years that the Rodney Atkins lyric is true—that when you're going through hell, you've got to keep on going.

When Bill first approached me with the idea for this book

and asked for my help authenticating the life of a professional football player, I did not hesitate. Although fiction, the story in *Hometown Favorite* is an inspiring example of how people get through difficult times. It demonstrates something I have seen over and over—with God's help and a lot of work, anything is possible.

Chris Sanders
retired Tennessee Titans wide receiver

P A R T

One

1

The lemon yellow Hummer skidded to a stop in front of Dewayne Jobe's house, the hip-hop music vibrating the vehicle's insides with percussive explosions. Jesse Webb, owner and operator of the pulsating vehicle, blew his horn to the rhythm of the beat.

The front door of the house swung open. Cherie Jobe stepped out onto the porch and planted her free hand on her hips.

"Jesse Webb, I'm gonna call the police if you don't turn off that yellow tank and stop raising the dead."

Jesse's grin transformed into a look of mock hurt. "Miss Cherie, we're just celebrating." Conceding to her trumped-up scold, he reached over to lower the volume.

"You got that thing so loud I couldn't hear Gabriel's trumpet." No longer able to hold a scornful expression, her face gave way to a bright smile. "Get in this house, both of you. My boy's not ready."

Riding shotgun with Jesse was Sylvester "Sly" Adams, quarterback for the Springdale Tigers and record holder for throwing the most touchdowns in the high school's history—due in large measure to his best friend Dewayne, Springdale's star wide receiver.

"Still trying to make himself look pretty for the cheerleaders." Sly opened his door and bounced off the front seat.

Jesse came around the front of his Hummer. "He could spend all day in front of his mirror and still not look as pretty as Sly."

"My man," Sly said, and the two boys pounded fists.

Cherie smiled at the antics of her son's friends and ushered them into the house.

Springdale had only one recreational offering for its citizens . . . high school football. As soon as young boys showed the least bit of interest in the sport and displayed a reasonable measure of aptitude and competence, they were absorbed into the peewee league for early training and experience. Jesse, Sly, and Dewayne were born in the same year, signed up for the peewee league in the same year, and grew into the rhythm and flow of the game together, perfecting their skills and at times showing true genius. Tomorrow the three friends would play their final game of high school football for the Mississippi state championship.

Sly sauntered toward Dewayne's bedroom, with Jesse at his heels.

"Jesse, could you come here a minute?"

At Cherie's request, Jesse started turning back toward the living room, but not before throwing a playful punch at Sly's shoulder. He flashed a boyish smile of surprise when Sly wheeled to smack him back. The boys traded a few good-natured slaps before Sly dodged the last backhand and disappeared into Dewayne's room.

"My boys. What am I gonna do without all your craziness!" Cherie said.

Jesse gave Cherie a quick peck on the cheek and then settled his thick frame into a well-worn Webb factory recliner. In spite of his fireplug physique, Jesse was swift on his feet. With his agility, he had racked up an impressive number of tackles as a linebacker for the Tigers.

It would have been easy for him to stay with his kind and class growing up in Springdale, Mississippi, but the team sport of football worked a strange magic on Jesse's impressionable psyche, and he had instead chosen two African Americans to be his best friends. It went as far back as those first years in the peewee league when kids recognized different skin shades only as colors from the same palette and not with any overtones of bigotry. The mutual respect the three boys had for each other's talents closed the deal on a permanent friendship, and their trust for each other on and off the field made them inseparable.

Cherie perched on the sofa near the young man she considered an adopted son. "I'm in a quandary, Jesse." She smoothed the wrinkles out of her dress with agitated fingers.

"About what, Miss Cherie?"

They ignored the playful jive coming from Dewayne's bedroom.

"My boy and his future," she said. "God has given him a gift, and I don't know what's the best way for him to use it. You're going to college, I know, and I want that for Dewayne, but I don't know the best choice for him."

"I envy him." Jesse's head drooped. "I don't have choices, Miss Cherie."

Heir to Webb Furniture, a fourth-generation business, Jesse had every intention of accepting the CEO mantle as soon as he fulfilled another Webb tradition of attending Ole Miss and playing football, if not exceptionally, at least honorably.

"Ole Miss, Webb Furniture, and the rest of my days in Springdale are laid out for me. I couldn't change that destiny if they offered me the moon."

Cherie reached her hand over to Jesse's thick leg and patted the firm muscle above the knee. "There's pride in knowing who you are, where you come from, where your future's headed. It will be a comfort to me knowing you're close by."

Jesse gave her hand a quick squeeze. Her motherly tenderness seemed to ease the sting of resignation that came from having his future set in stone.

Cherie sighed. "But my boy . . . it's the moon they seem to be offering," she said.

"How's that?" Jesse leaned forward in the easy chair.

Cherie stretched herself over the arm of the threadbare sofa and reached behind it. She pulled out a battered shoebox with a rubber band over the top that tried to keep the stack of letters tucked inside. The lid pushed upward as soon as she removed the rubber band, and the top letters popped up and spilled onto the floor. Cherie bent over to retrieve them from the faded carpet.

"Colleges and big-time universities wanting Dewayne to come play for them and offering to pay his way," she said as she collected the letters and displayed them for Jesse to behold.

Jesse moved over to the couch to look at the pile and gave a whistle. "You need a bigger box." He picked up a few of the envelopes. "Guess folks all over have figured out how good our boy is."

"I don't know where to begin. Robert and I never went to college."

Cherie Turner and Robert Dewayne Jobe met on the assembly line of Webb Furniture, each one thinking the other a thing of beauty. They began spending as much off-hour time together as possible, and months later, neither of them could think of any reason why this relationship should not become permanent.

Cherie had never remarried after her husband's death . . . a tragic accident of a fatigued husband working double shifts to provide for a new wife and their soon-to-be child. Early one morning a police officer spotted the rear bumper of Robert's car sticking out of the water of Deer Creek. With no evidence to the contrary, the coroner ruled it death by drowning, probably due to falling asleep at the wheel just as the car came upon the precarious curve onto the bridge over the creek.

The likes of Robert were not to be found again. Rather, Cherie raised her son by herself, believing the good character of his father was installed at birth and trusting God's mercy would make up for all human deficiency. The quantity of inquiries displayed before Jesse's unbelieving eyes was evidence enough that character and talent flowed in Dewayne's bloodstream.

Dewayne's size, dexterity, and quickness defied reason. By his seventeenth birthday, he had topped out at six feet six inches, weighing two hundred forty pounds, all muscle, bone, skin, and functioning organs to sustain this young man under the grueling training regimen he endured from his coaches. The grocery bill for the two of them would have fed a family of six. By his last season of high school football, he was a good head taller than anyone on his team and most of the boys from all opposing football teams who lined up against him. Add another three feet of arm span to his six-six height, and any player assigned to cover Dewayne would need a miracle to stop a pass completion or bring him down. Double coverage and gang tackle were about the only defense a team could use to stop Dewayne, and even then, he would drag his tacklers along like Gulliver dragging the Lilliputians for a few extra yards. His proficiency at offense applied to defense as well. He and Jesse were a formidable pair of linebackers who knew the game and each other's moves so well, it was not often they were duped by another team's offensive play. And each time Sly came onto the field with his all-star quality at quarterback, it was hard for the hometown fans not to expect a touchdown. Being undefeated their senior year was not a cakewalk, but it never was in question either. By midseason, everyone in Springdale knew their team would play in the state championship, and they were the odds-on favorite to win.

The clamor of Sly's entrance broke the spell cast over Jesse and Cherie staring at the queries for Dewayne's talent. Sly burst into the living room as though pursued by tacklers. He gripped a football and pumped his arm in several directions, looking for would-be receivers as he provided his own sports commentary.

"The offense has collapsed and the blitz is crashing in on the Sly. He fakes right, then left. He stiff-arms one three-hundred-pound tackler. He leaps over the second one like a gazelle. No one can sack the Sly."

"Somebody shut him up," Dewayne said as he entered the living room.

"He dashes across the field, waiting for a receiver to get open." Sly danced sideways. "He lobs the pass over the heads of the opposing team"—he pump faked toward Dewayne, then turned and pitched the ball—"dropping the pigskin into the outstretched hands of the receiver."

Jesse caught Sly's pitchout without ever taking his eyes off the stack of letters Cherie held in her hands.

"Another touchdown for the Sly." Sly acknowledged his imaginary cheering crowd by waving his hands in the air.

Sly might have had an exaggerated view of his skills, but on the football field, he lived up to them. He was fast enough to evade most defensive players who got past his front line, and he enjoyed dancing around the field, dodging tacklers, almost as much as throwing touchdowns. Orphaned at a young age and raised by a doting grandmother, Sly had created an image of himself that required a belief that he was superior to most other humans. In spite of a fawning public, Jesse and Dewayne were the only ones allowed into his narcissistic bubble, and to his credit, Sly did not mind his two best friends taking him down a notch or two when the preoccupation with his ego got out of control.

The three boys were rarely apart, except when the social norms kept Mississippi's blacks and whites separated, but the trio pushed even those boundaries. They sat in the pews of each other's churches or went to a single-color restaurant or attended a public function with a young lady of the opposite race. These small challenges to social traditions raised eyebrows and stimulated behind-the-back conversations, but as long as the Springdale Tigers kept winning, the boys could do no wrong and all was right with their world.

When Cherie cleared her throat, Sly redirected his attention from his fantasy fans to the letters in Cherie's hands. "Is that D's fan mail, Miss Cherie?"

"I guess you could call it that," Jesse said.

"What did I tell you about throwing the football in my house?"

Cherie's mild scold made Sly fidget and produced a rare sheepish grin on his face. "Sorry. Too excited about State tomorrow."

"Dewayne, you never told us about all these letters," Jesse said, waving a stack of letters in front of his face like a fan. "You sure been secretive."

Dewayne shrugged. "Nothing to tell really."

"Nothing to tell," Sly said, taking a handful of letters out of Cherie's hand. He began to flip through the stack, discarding each one into the shoebox after reading the letterhead. "D, you got Penn State, Michigan, Ohio . . . too cold for your black Mississippi blood. The University of Tennessee . . . you just volunteer yourself onto the next one. It looks like the entire SEC is coming after you. You got your cowboy colleges, and finally your elite West Coast Rose Bowl contenders. That's an impressive list . . . almost as good as mine."

"What are they offering?" Jesse asked.

Dewayne shrugged his shoulders again, looking more uncomfortable. "Full rides."

"Don't be hanging your head, my brother." Sly slapped Dewayne across his broad shoulders. "This is a proud moment."

"So what should he do?" Cherie asked.

Quiet settled over the boys. Jesse stopped fanning himself and handed Cherie the letters. She shuffled them into a neat pile before returning them to the cardboard box.

"What do you want to do, D?" Jessie said, and he picked up the football in his lap and began to pass it back and forth from hand to hand. The thump of the ball smacking Jesse's hands as he played his own game of pitch and catch dominated the sounds in the room.

"I want to score touchdowns," Dewayne said.

"That's right." Sly went from slap to embrace. "My man here wants to catch himself a boatload of touchdowns and a fat NFL contract."

"Mama and I have been doing a lot of praying about this," Dewayne said. "We need God's direction."

"What do you think, Sly?" Cherie asked.

"As long as God don't send him to Miami, he can go anywhere that pays to let him play."

"You never told us you decided on Miami," Jesse said.

"Strong program that made me the best offer, eighty-degree winters, and women as far as the eye can see."

"Careful now in front of your mama," Cherie said.

"Ain't any of them ever going to replace you, now." Sly leaned over and gave Cherie a kiss on the cheek.

"Don't be playing with me." Cherie waved him away, unable to resist a smile. "Be serious now. Where should my boy go to college? The coaches have been talking. The recruiters have been calling. But I want to hear from his best friends."

"Miss Cherie, D needs to get as far away from Springdale as he can," Jesse said. "I think a West Coast school might be his best bet."

"No lie, Miss Cherie," Sly said. "With our boy's hands he can pull in those passes. The sports pages like to see that kind of beauty and that is what gets the attention of the NFL."

Sly intercepted the ball from Jesse, stopping the hypnotic rhythm of the passing. He stretched out his passing arm dramatically and pretended to throw a "Hail Mary" out the front window in the westward direction. "Go west, young man."

Dewayne just smiled and then patted Cherie on her shoulder. "We need to go, Mama."

"Don't want to be late for your last pep rally," Cherie said.

"No, ma'am," Jesse said, springing from the recliner. "We win State, I'm buying you a new recliner." He kissed Cherie on the cheek before bounding out the front door.

Sly repeated Jesse's farewell on Cherie's cheek with an extra "You know I love you," and Cherie added her own tender pat to his face.

"You coming?" Dewayne asked.

"Of course I'll be there," she said.

Like his friends before him, Dewayne kissed his mother on the cheek.

"You know the Lord is gonna steer us right, Mama," he said.

"No doubt, son, no doubt," she said. "Now go on. Don't be late."

Dewayne squeezed his mother's arm before walking out the door.

Cherie picked up the few letters that still lay on the floor, folded them, and replaced them in the shoebox. Before sealing the box, she laid her hand on the letters and closed her eyes.

"Lord, we need thy wisdom," she whispered. "Let the right one rise to the top."

The only location large enough to accommodate the town of Springdale for the pep rally was the Webb family farm. The level of play, the team's competence, and the town spirit had not had a simultaneous appearance before in Springdale, and talk was that it would be another generation before the convergence of the three would happen again.

Neighboring counties could spot the three blazing bonfires. The multitude roared as the head coach introduced each starting player, accompanied by a blast from the marching band's brass section as the player dashed into position facing the crowd. Cherie had maneuvered onto a small rise a short distance from the center of the celebrations. This bond of humanity had one goal in mind: to unite their individual desires and energies into a force powerful enough to win the support and blessing of the gods of football, and to raise the town of Springdale out of the universal plainness of small-town America.

Jake Hopper, the receivers' and quarterbacks' coach for the Tigers, did not like standing with the other coaches and staff and the team for these football rituals. He preferred anonymity. He preferred the controlled discipline of the practice field or the blood rush of the game. He accepted these chaotic traditions as a necessary evil.

He ambled through the crowd until he spied Cherie. Here was a friend, a calm in the maelstrom. He moved toward her, but a group of teenagers bolted in front of him, blocking his path and nearly trampling him as they rushed to get a better view of their heroes. He waited for the herd to pass and then made steady progress toward his goal.

Jake stepped up beside Cherie. "And what do you think of our pagan rites?"

"It's loud enough to bring down Jericho's walls," Cherie said. "I should have brought my OSHA earplugs from the factory."

"That assembly line working you hard?"

Cherie cupped her hands over her ears. "Hard enough, but I don't think it ever gets as loud as these kids."

"Humanity changes little, I'm afraid, except through calamity, and then reluctantly," he said, approving his pithy statement with a smirk.

Jake Hopper gave of himself body and soul to taking the God-given talent of each player and molding it. In his heart of hearts, he considered himself a sculptor of living, flesh-and-blood models, shaping and perfecting the fluidity of speed and motion of the human body. And a well-executed, unrepeatable moment on the field brought a bigger smile to his face than a touchdown or even a win.

Jake prized the singular bond between player and coach, a bond of souls when competitive physical play brings out a special bliss between men. Jake and Dewayne had that bond, an idealized bond of a father and son, free of responsibility beyond the rules, discipline, and training necessary for the game. Dewayne had no father. Jake had no children. Yet the two men provided for each other what was missing in their lives.

"Excuse me for being forward, but if all our sons had mothers such as you, the world would be whole," Jake said, a bold statement, especially from someone unaccustomed to making them. Perhaps the sips of vodka before arriving at the pep rally inspired the boldness. He felt a pang of regret, a flushed embarrassment at the compliment. He was thankful for the darkness. It helped conceal his chagrin.

At that moment, the music from the marching band raised its decibel level, and the cheerleaders, shimmering pom-poms stuck to the top of each raised arm, began their escort of the senior boys to the front of the team.

"Hush now. They're about to introduce my boy," Cherie said.

Jake turned his eyes away from Cherie and wondered how life might have been different had he met Cherie in their younger days. She might have spoken the same words just now but substituted them with "our boy." The thought produced in him a pang of regret.

2

Half a dozen buses hauled the Springdale Tigers, the cheer-leaders, the marching band, and most of the student body to the state championship game. Like a large military convoy, the citizens of Springdale followed the buses for the two-hour drive to the stadium in Jackson, Mississippi. Sly, Dewayne, and Jesse sat in the very back of the team bus. There was no boisterous behavior or extraneous noise. The players had slipped into their game zone. The season's preceding games had already made the history books. This last effort would define the team and the character of each individual player.

"I ain't accustomed to losing, you know that?" Sly's voice was louder than necessary. "I get my way on the field."

"Your way on the field is the only way," Jesse said.

"I am the way," Sly said, and he and Jesse pounded fists in front of Dewayne.

"Be careful now," Dewayne said. "Save it for the field."

They had faced nothing like this before, a threshold into a new phase of life. It required a form of courage they could not understand, a courage that would provide the resolve to move beyond tonight into manhood regardless of the outcome, and the bus sped them toward that end.

Jake Hopper ambled down the center aisle to the rear of the

bus and sat down on an armrest. He had refrained from drinking before this game, although he had yielded to a swallow of mouthwash before leaving home. He scanned the faces of the three boys sprawled out on the extended seat in the back.

"You guys have fun tonight," he said, and the boys nodded. "Dewayne, you and Sly play like always . . . pitch and catch . . . nothing's different, nothing's special . . . Dewayne, just let the ball come to you. Sly knows how to place it. This is your moment, and I'm . . ."

The eyes of Jake's audience diverted above his head. He turned around to see the head coach standing behind him, and he yielded to his superior.

"Jesse, you and Dewayne got to remember what this team always does in a bind. They pull out their quick pitch. You got to be ready for that. The running back will line up behind the tight end instead of the gap between the guard and tackle. That's the sign for the play. Heads-up for you, Dewayne . . . you've got the read. When you see that lineup, shout, 'Judas!' three times, and then widen out a little more and rush up the field to force the running back inside. Jesse, you come in and clean his clock. Put a chokehold on this team . . . force them to use the Judas play, then finish them off with some smashmouth tackling. No overtimes. Just a clean game and we're out of there with a championship."

He slapped Jake's back as a signal that the speech was over and that Jake should return to the front with him. Jake rose and took one last look at the trio. Words failed him, and he had to trust they understood his pride in them as he lumbered back to his seat.

In the stadium, no one was left sitting in his seat. All were on their feet. Dewayne had scored two touchdowns: the first,

24

a down-and-out pattern where he outran his coverage; the second, a leaping catch in the end zone. Sly had scored one with a quick dash into the end zone from the five-yard line. Jesse recovered a fumble and ran it back sixty-five yards for his touchdown. He had never run so far and so fast in his life. In spite of these scores, the Tigers were still up by only four points.

The Red Devils from southern Mississippi, a team with equally impressive players and an undefeated season coming into this game, had come back to score every time the Tigers had made it into the end zone. The last time, however, the Tigers had held the Devils in the red zone and forced them to kick a field goal from fifteen yards. With less than two minutes remaining on the clock and a score of 28 to 24, the Devils kept the Tigers from getting a first down, forcing them to punt. The return was a twenty-two-yard gain, leaving a mere forty-four yards from the Devils' line of scrimmage to the goal line. The first play Dewayne had blocked the expected pass. On a blitz in the second play, Jesse had sacked the quarterback for a three-yard loss, his third sack for the game.

From the Tigers' side of the stadium, there was chaos, enough noise to travel through the cold and damp night air like a howling army. From the Devils' side, there was an overwrought silence except for mumbled prayers for divine intervention and jinxes against the Tigers. For every soul on their feet, life outside the confines of this stadium had ceased to exist.

Dewayne spotted the play as soon as the Devils came to the line on third down. The running back had taken his position out behind the tight end.

Dewayne whirled around to the team, shouting, "Judas! Judas! Judas!"

The defense made the instant adjustment.

Dewayne looked at Jesse one last time to make sure he had heard the call and saw his teammate stepping toward the outside and giving him a thumbs-up. It was a short count, and as soon as the center snapped the ball, Dewayne rammed into the tight end, forcing the Devils' running back toward the hole.

After the quarterback had made the quick pitch to the running back, he began to sprint in the opposite direction. When the running back caught the ball, he hesitated, and from the corner of his eye as Jesse dashed toward the open hole made by the Devils' tight end, he saw the quarterback moving away from the action to the open field. The unexpected move surprised him.

Confident it was a pass option off the pitch, Jesse made a snap decision to follow the quarterback, expecting the Devils' running back to pass it to the quarterback for a clear shot to the end zone. When Jesse changed his route and followed the quarterback, the Devils' running back saw the clearing ahead of him and sprinted through the scrambling bodies into an open field.

Dewayne managed to touch the running back's heel with the tips of his fingers as he fell to the ground from the tight end's forceful resistance, but his touch had no effect. He watched from his helpless position on the ground, the weight of the tight end draped over his stomach, as the Devils' running back raced toward the end zone, outrunning a helpless Jesse not fast enough to chase him down.

Within seconds, the pent-up anxiety on the Devils' side of the stadium over a sure defeat erupted into pandemonium. On the Tigers' side, the vision of a silver-and-gold-plated trophy encased in the main hall of the high school was shattered glass. Screams meant to confuse the Devils became cries of horror and lamentation. The town of Springdale had performed all the proper rituals and offered all the right prayers to prevent this outcome. Where had the system broken down? A cruel joke had been played upon them. Now all that remained was the mourning.

Time enough remained on the clock for a Devils' kickoff and a Tigers' return. Springdale fans were delirious with momentary hope as the kickoff return placed them at the thirty-yard line, but the Devils' defense solidified. Two desperation passes from Sly to Dewayne, each one blocked by the Devils' triple-team coverage of Dewayne. Then a final forty-seven-yard field goal attempt. The ball nicked a Devil's helmet and never had the chance to fly toward the uprights. It bounced to the ground and lay dead until snatched by a jubilant Devil, who tossed it into the air. The coveted game ball seemed to float for a few seconds above the field, buoyed on the Devils' euphoric shouting. The fact that this object would forever be in possession of the Devils was too bitter a consequence for every Springdale citizen.

The trip back to Springdale was like that of a routed army returning home after a long and exhausting war. All movement was painful, not from the punishment of combat, but from the ache of defeat. Discreet tears flowed only when the bus had pulled away from the stadium, and in its dark and silent interior boys hid their faces and allowed disappointment to flow from their eyes. This time could never be repeated, only replayed again and again in their memories, a continual loop of heartbreaking highlights.

There were great moments to revel in, but the Tigers could enjoy only the minutes leading up to the final two. Up to that point their lead had never been overtaken, their potential victory not in serious jeopardy. But to a player, breaching the memory threshold of those last two minutes was perilous, a thorny punishment with a difficult recovery. The head coach stood in front of the bus hoping to pour the balm of comfort on his broken team with some reassuring words, but he needed comfort in order to give it. Silence was best. He simply waved into the darkness of the bus's interior and sat down.

Surrounded by empty seats, Jake sat alone, staring into the melting ice in the plastic cup he held. He had finished one drink in the privacy of a locker room toilet and picked up a second cup of ice as he left to board the bus. He opened his briefcase and used the lid to screen the odorless, colorless vodka he poured into his cup. After draining his drink in short, rapid swallows, he closed the lid on all the physical evidence.

When Jake's wife had left him because she was craving a bigger city with more opportunities—at least that was how she'd described it in the note Jake found when he came home from a late practice—he turned to alcohol. Only sips at first to aid with sleep, to deaden the pain of loss, the feelings of rejection and inadequacy, and to bolster false courage. He was not sure when his use of alcohol for medicinal purposes had become an addiction.

Jake pulled himself out of his seat and into the aisle, pausing long enough to make sure he could maintain his balance. He held on to the seats as he made his way past the players slumped down and dejected, quiet and still as though tossed in these positions by a heartless fate.

When he arrived at the back of the bus, only Dewayne looked up at him. Sly and Jesse kept their eyes on the images flying by their windows. Jake needed to make this fast. The alcohol was making its ascent to his brain, and he would need to return to his seat. He leaned over and patted each boy on the knee before he turned around. The gesture brought Sly and Jesse to their senses, and they turned their heads from the windows. All three watched as Jake descended back into the darkness toward his seat.

Each boy knew the pat on the knee was a gesture of departure. Their friend and mentor was releasing them to future success or failure with the hope that what paternal wisdom he might have provided them through his coaching would be remembered with fondness.

The three boys had been the first on the bus after the game and had retaken their seats in the back, each clutching his duffle bag to his chest like a protective shield. They had slouched across the seat like rag dolls, motionless, no one willing to speak, all three cross at even having to breathe. When the silhouette of Coach Hopper disappeared into his seat, Jesse broke the barrier between them.

"I swear I thought it was a pass option off the pitch."

"You thought. You thought. You thought," Sly repeated in a contemptuous mantra.

"The running back hesitated and I thought—"

"You thought. You thought. You thought." This time Sly's voice was louder, and his hand sprang into the air, flapping his fingers together to mimic a bird talking.

"We played a full game, not just two minutes," Dewayne said.

"Don't defend this chump," Sly shot back.

Jesse's mouth pulled back in a grimace as though a large hand was squeezing his gut, but he put his hand over his mouth to cover it, to stifle any words he might blurt out in his defense.

"I dropped some passes," Dewayne said. "You fumbled once."

"And I recovered it. Two-yard loss. Big deal," Sly said.

"The game is forty-eight minutes, Sly."

"And it was lost in two. Stop taking up for him. All he needed to do was play by the rules. We know all the plays. We know where each one is going to be. He broke the trust, man. He didn't have your back. Where was he? Where was he? Chasing rabbits."

Jesse pretended to be invisible. It was better to hear a friend say these things so he would not have to suffer hearing his own voice repeatedly cast these accusations against him. It was better that his friend try to deflect the slings and arrows so there would be no additional wounds to compete with the self-inflicted ones. Dewayne's defense relieved him from having to speak, from having to move.

"Lay off now before you go too far," Dewayne said.

"Too far," Sly said. "The rules of life are made for people like him, but he don't have to play by the rules. The white boy makes his own kind of rules."

Jesse kicked out his leg, as though trying to kick off his shoe, his first sign of life in several miles.

Dewayne shifted in his seat. "Careful, Sly . . ."

"You be careful. He has every advantage while you and I have to fight for everything we get."

"This ain't the time or the place, Sly," Dewayne said, looking into Jesse's trembling face.

Sly began to shake his head, starting a swaying motion in his body. Dewayne laid his hand on the back of Sly's neck, but Sly knocked it away with his arm.

"I can't believe you're taking up for him," Sly said, leaning forward and pointing his finger at Jesse. "You and I are going places, D. We're leaving Springdale, and we're shaking the dust off our feet. We're leaving this fool behind."

Jesse twisted his head from the window to look at Sly, tears streaming down the solemn-stoned bust of his face. In Sly's cruel words, Jesse saw his immediate and distant future play out before him: he would be scorned and despised by the good people of Springdale for a time, though most of the citizens would hide the true face of their contempt for his split-second decision that cost them their coveted state championship behind a strained but civil mask. The *Springdale Leader* would write about the play that lost the game, and every reader would fill his name in the blank. Who would remember that Jesse Webb had been the best linebacker in the history of the Springdale Tigers? In time, the town's disdain would pass; the population would find new reasons to hold a grudge, new people to scorn, and this spirit of disparagement would pass from everyone—except perhaps from Jesse, a compartment of his heart holding the contemptible memory like a cold stone, creating an invisible deformity every bit as real as a clubfoot or withered hand.

"We could have had it, man," Sly said, his head hung low. "We could have had it."

The Webb bloodline might have sealed Jesse's future profession, but his friend's words would coat every decision, every thought process, every emotional impulse, that Jesse would ever have.

3

Jesse and Sly caught the smell of fried chicken coming from Cherie's house as soon as they opened the doors of the yellow Hummer. They were late. Dewayne had stationed himself at the top of the steps, his arms crossed over his muscular chest like a menacing bouncer. Sly and Jesse pointed the finger of blame at each other.

"Come on now," Dewayne said. "I saved you each a drumstick."

This was the boys' last meal together. Dewayne would be leaving in the morning for California to play for USC, where he would continue to perfect the wide receiver skills that Coach Hopper had nurtured and developed. In the next few days, Jesse would leave for Ole Miss, and Sly would catch a plane to Miami. Their daily involvement, their daily sharing of dreams, of boasts, of secrets, would end with this night. The meal Cherie prepared was a unanimous favorite of all three. Cream-style corn, mashed potatoes covered in redeye gravy, three-bean salad, and homemade biscuits fought for room on the plate with the mound of panfried chicken. Between mouthfuls washed down with sweet tea, the boys joked with Cherie with the respect and familiarity that came from the years of caring attention she had given them. Dewayne was her flesh and blood, but she freely disciplined and loved Sly and Jesse as if they were her own. She never begrudged the cost or the time required to prepare the mountains of food.

Cherie would not sit down with the boys while they ate. Her place was to monitor the kitchen—to see that one of them had prayed a proper blessing before a single bite was consumed, that all plates were sufficiently supplied, and that the sweet tea in their glasses never went below the halfway point. She would not let them lift a finger to help her. A future liberated wife might resent her indulgence in the kitchen with this trio.

For as long as the boys could remember, Cherie had always worn the same raggedy apron at every meal. Threadbare and stained, it was one of the few gifts Robert Jobe could afford. He had given it to her while she was pregnant with Dewayne. The boys had found a catalog from a kitchen design company out of New York, opted for the most expensive designer-autographed apron among the nine selections, and pooled their resources to have it shipped to Jesse's house in time for them to add their own special artwork.

There was no big ceremony. Sly simply forced her to sit at the table in his chair, and Dewayne put his hands over his mother's eyes as Jesse presented her with a beautifully wrapped package.

"It's too pretty to open," Cherie said, and squealing like a child intimidated by the splendor of the presentation, she pulled the apron out of the box. Her eyes widened as if she beheld a sultan's treasure. "Ohhh . . . it's beautiful!"

She savored each second it took her to unfold the apron. There were the decorative floral patterns painted on by the professional in New York outlining the edges, but inside the floral frame were three drawings done in multicolor Magic

Marker by each boy, with the number of his football jersey painted on his chest and each in a dramatic pose: Sly poised to throw a pass, Dewayne leaping to catch a pass, and Jesse crouched down ready to make a tackle. When the apron had arrived in the mail, the boys gathered at Jesse's house and went straight to work.

Cherie did not attempt to restrain her tears as the boys put the apron on her and tied it in the back, like servants dressing the queen. Between rounds of kisses planted on the boys' cheeks, she extolled the apron's beauty and what it must have cost and how she would cherish it all her life. The boys congratulated themselves on the success of their surprise.

As much as Cherie loved her boys and appreciated their thoughtfulness, she could not spoil the moment by exposing them to the deep truth. One month into their marriage, Robert Jobe had given her the apron she always wore. Robert's apron was the first thing she put on when she came home from work, and she kept it on until time for bed. Its closeness was like a soft impression of Robert always against her skin. And though she would wear the new one for the rest of the evening, careful to keep it spotless, it would go back into the box the moment the boys departed.

After final hugs, the boys left to revisit a few old haunts, and once alone, Cherie could not resist examining her gift. She cleared the table and wiped it clean before laying the apron on the bare top. She fondled the luxurious fabric, bringing it to her cheek, and then ran her finger over the floral outline, her eyes squinting in admiration of its detail. With the apron stretched out before her, she laid a hand on each rough-drawn image of her boys and implored God to bless the men they were becoming.

The boys' drive through town was brief before heading out to the Webb farm, its five hundred acres a natural destination. After one summer of working with men three times his age, Jesse had talked his father into hiring Sly and Dewayne, and throughout high school all three spent their summers mending fences, hauling hay, herding livestock, and clearing forests. For Sly and Dewayne, it was an opportunity to make some money; and even though Jesse did not have the same financial needs as his best friends, there was still within him the pride of earning his keep from the sweat of his brow.

Before getting out of the car, Jesse pulled three Romeo and Juliets from the glove compartment. As a last hurrah the boys lit their cigars, each puffing the smoke into the tranquil air like small signal fires and gazing over the field at the Charolais cattle bedded down for the night, their white hides reflecting the moon's full light.

"You remember that first summer when we shot the bull between his legs with your BB gun?" Dewayne said, hearing the bellows of the enraged victim in his mind.

"Hard to miss a target that big," Sly said.

Jesse chuckled. "I thought he would charge us for sure."

"I found out that day just how fast I could run," Dewayne said.

Each cigar dissolved into ash as the experiences of past summers flew out of the boys' communal memories and brought stabs of laughter or moans of vexation: Jesse driving a tractor into a tree, Dewayne trying to "break" a three-hundred-pound sow and being bucked off into the muck, and Sly shinnying up a post in the barn and screaming at the sight of a six-foot-long rat snake slithering in his direction—each boy trying to defend his actions to an unsympathetic jury of his peers. And when the memories turned to silence, the flashing rumps of the lightning bugs, the lingering hoots of a barn owl, and a sharp coyote's yap at the silvery moon provided the sights and sounds for the boys' private thoughts to drift unencumbered.

The knock on the front door interrupted the raspy humming of a favorite hymn. Cherie shut off the water in the kitchen sink and picked up a dishtowel to dry her hands. Through the glass of the storm door, she could see Jake Hopper swaying unsteadily on his feet, holding a gift in both hands. His perspiring face gave off an incandescent glow beneath the porch light.

"Coach Hopper," Cherie said as she opened the door. "You just missed the boys."

"That's fine."

Jake shuffled his feet backward as the door swung toward him. He kept his head bowed, only bobbing it up now and then as if gasping for breath above some invisible surface line. Cherie slung the dishtowel onto her shoulder and leaned against the doorframe. She would be polite because this man had been good to her boy, but she did not feel like a visit. She had spent her entertainment quotient on her boys.

"I got something for Dewayne . . . a little going-away something . . . I thought I'd . . ."

Jake could not finish anything he started. He never should have had that last drink before he left the house, or maybe he should have had another drink. It was a tough call. He could see that Cherie didn't know what to make of his rambling, the nervous gestures, and the subtle dancing feet.

Jake almost dropped the gift, swinging it in her direction, then pulling it back into his stomach like a fake handoff.

"Coach Hopper, are you all—"

36

"Please, just Jake. Just call me Jake. I like Jake. I'd like for you to say my name. My parents didn't name me Coach. Just Jake."

When he saw the surprise and wonder on Cherie's face, he laughed to try to deflect his nonsensical, verbal bumbling.

"I'm sorry. I haven't seen you much . . . or seen Dewayne much since graduation. I just wanted him to have a little something . . . a memento of all the years . . ." His voice faded out, but he steadied his arm enough to hand the gift to Cherie before an involuntary muscle spasm jerked it back.

"I know you have meant so much to him . . . Jake," she said, taking the gift from his wobbly hand.

"I want to stay in touch . . . to stay connected to you or to him through you . . . you know . . . keep in touch."

"That would be good." Cherie dropped her head in a failed attempt to conceal her embarrassment for Jake.

"Good night, then."

Jake turned around and hurried down the steps of the porch. If he could get to the car and back to the house and consume another drink or two or three, he would fall asleep and wake the next morning and never remember what a fool he had made of himself. The number of those mornings of not remembering had increased over the last several months. He managed to finish out the school year without raising suspicions, and since he lived alone and ignored all social contact, there was no one curious enough to check on his well-being. His secret life remained secret.

Then some force greater than the craving for a drink stopped him on the return to his car and whirled him around, and the words exploded out of his mouth.

"May I take you to dinner sometime?"

But Cherie had closed the door; the click of the latch was the only response he heard.

Mother and son stood in the outdoor terminal with passengers moving behind them and boarding the bus. A shy pride had taken both of them. Unable to look very long in the eyes of the other, neither were willing to finalize the end of this phase of their lives and take the step of faith into independence now required of them.

"I packed all the leftover fried chicken from last night," Cherie said, handing him a paper sack full of chicken pieces wrapped in wax paper.

Dewayne frowned, knowing there would be a long hiatus before he could enjoy this kind of cuisine again.

"Two things to remember." Cherie reached into her skirt pocket. "Your judgment is good. I trust it and so should you. And I'm gonna pray for you every day." Then she pulled out five one-hundred-dollar bills and gave a quick account of the number before she placed them in her son's hand.

"Mad money," she said.

Dewayne started to resist, but Cherie raised one finger in the air, halting any budding quarrel.

"Now hug your mama before she starts making a fool of herself and says no to this college nonsense."

The embrace was eighteen years' worth of gratitude and thankfulness for a life that could not have been lived with any other parent-and-child combination. Cherie ended it by taking Dewayne's hulking shoulders in her petite hands and pushing him away. He accepted the gesture as the signal from the stronger of the two that there was no turning back now, and he took that first step onto the bus.

"What was the present Coach Hopper brought you last night? I put it on your dresser."

Dewayne paused at the top of the steps. "I forgot to open it. Next time I'm home I'll get it. Thank him for me."

Those were his last words before the bus driver closed the door. Dewayne stepped into the center aisle and found an empty seat as the bus pulled out of the dock.

With a final wave to each other, their independence was complete.

PART
TWO

4

As the new BMW 325 convertible raced along a winding road through the Hollywood Hills, Dewayne watched the expensive homes whizzing past. They were nothing like the houses in Springdale, Mississippi. Even the pricey homes where he had grown up did not compare to the size and opulence he now passed. He never could have imagined coming so far in just a few years, but he swore never to forget the humble life he had left behind in Springdale and those qualities of character that had shaped him.

In this new world where cultures from all over the globe gathered for higher education, free expression of every kind was an accepted practice, and it was displayed in a variety of ways that never would have been dreamed of in Springdale. Even after two and a half years of living in the midst of the liberated society of the university campus and achieving success playing football for USC, Dewayne still felt like a stranger in a strange land. Were it not for the letters Cherie wrote twice a month keeping him informed of Springdale's comings and goings—from time to time including a fifty-dollar bill from Webb Furniture overtime—and reminding him there was no doubt of his worth in her mind, he might have faltered along the way and slipped from the foundation of his faith.

A rust-colored haze had settled over the San Fernando Valley.

"It's gonna be all right, baby," the sweet voice said from the driver's seat.

Rosella Caldwell shifted the BMW into a lower gear as she approached the sharp curve before starting another steep ascent. She lifted her hand from the gearshift and gave a reassuring squeeze on top of Dewayne's left leg that bounced from nervous energy. He scooped her hand into his and stroked each finger before he kissed the back of her hand.

Dewayne had declared himself a business/finance major his first year and had met Rosella, also a business major, in an English class that first semester. Her sparkling obsidian eyes caught his attention when he looked up from scanning his textbook as she took her seat beside him on the first day of that class. They were now in their fifth class together, and it was early this semester when a partnership for a class project finally prompted them to yield to the natural chemistry between them as they began to date.

It was not just the dazzling beauty of Rosella's eyes arresting his attention that first day of class but the formidable intention behind them, a confidence reminiscent of his mother. In Mississippi, a confident black woman was a rarity. The inequality among races and genders there made Cherie's inner confidence all the more impressive in Dewayne's realm of experience. These two women might have come from different worlds, but both had a depth of self-assurance Dewayne respected and valued. Rosella knew what she wanted. She valued the opinions of others and gave the proper respect to professor and student alike, but she never lost herself in the process of absorbing other people's ideas.

With each business class the two of them had taken together, their attraction had grown. But each of them had priorities and commitments, and neither had been willing to allow a romance to derail those goals . . . until this semester, in Entrepreneurial Finance, where their professor had drawn the names of each team from his country gentleman's walking hat. The project for team Caldwell and Jobe was to decide what to do with an ailing movie studio: spin it off by selling it as separate businesses, or produce a genre of film that has a track record for success and thus save the studio? The project required viewing a number of different types of films and conducting an unscientific poll of audience reactions to determine genre tastes, then settle on the type of film the troubled studio should produce to save it from Chapter 11. It was a winter semester class, so Dewayne's schedule was more flexible, although he still had to maintain a strict conditioning regimen.

In the beginning, going to the movies was solely for educational purposes, but their drives to the theaters had given Dewayne and Rosella the intimate time necessary to build a relationship beyond what academic, athletic, and film class dialogues had accomplished so far. This was a significant raise in the bar of personal interest. An early sign that this classroom partnership had moved to the next level was the number of romantic films compared to the other genres they viewed. The ultimate shift from class project to full-blown romance came when they forgot to conduct the survey after the movie. The blame could lie on an extraordinarily sad film that flayed bare the human condition, involved the death of one of the lovers, and was a sure Oscar contender. Their efforts yielded only a B from the professor, but their own Hollywood romance made up for the average grade.

Dewayne clicked off one three-story mansion after another as they traveled the meandering road. He was a kid, staring wide-eyed at palatial spectacles he had only seen in magazines or on television. *Were there that many people in the world who can live like this? And how can people live in these places and not get lost?*

The car slowed as they turned into a well-manicured entry. Rosella keyed the numbers on the pad that unlocked the gate.

"My heart is beating like a sledgehammer on a steel door." Dewayne massaged his chest, trying to relieve the pain.

As they pulled up the drive, he stared at the extravagant three-story house with its Corinthian-style columns stretching the length of the front porch. Dewayne had been adjusting to three stories as the normal height for the houses in this neighborhood. However, Rosella's home not only rose up three stories, it also spread out from north to south, wings on a great domiciliary bird. "I think I might be sick."

He felt Rosella's fingers digging into his side. She must have thought a brief tickle might relieve some of his angst, but it only made it worse. The big tough football man was having a mild panic attack.

"You know my mama gave birth to me on the floor of a furniture factory," Dewayne said, shaking his head at the sight of this mansion he could only imagine as a heavenly reward. "You are so out of my league. I grew up in an outhouse compared to this."

Since the tactic of tickling had failed to dissipate Dewayne's anxiety, Rosella took a different approach.

"It's not too late. I'll call them right now and tell them . . . what do I tell them?" Rosella lifted her cell phone out of her purse, flipped it open, and set her index finger on the speed-dial position.

Dewayne had not expected such a quick resolve and felt ashamed by Rosella's stone-faced demeanor, but getting his legs to move out of the car seemed a near impossibility.

46

He gritted his teeth. Even though he would rather face two charging three-hundred-pound linebackers, Dewayne knew showing weakness was not something he wanted Rosella to remember. So he opened the door and set one foot on the driveway, and said, like a fire chief leading his men into a burning building, "We're going in." His confidence waned, however, as they walked down the path.

Rosella's parents watched their approach through the glass door from inside the house.

"Look at that. She's dragging him along like a pet zombie."

"Franklin Caldwell, not another word."

High school sweethearts Franklin and Joella Caldwell had been married for thirty-five years, both of them LA born and bred. Both had taken personal vows never to return to their former neighborhoods once they discovered the way out. They were the first in their families to go to college, and both became instant high achievers: Joella ran her own successful high-end interior design company, and Franklin was the founder and CEO of Caldwell & Associates, an architecture firm with buildings and complexes across the country.

"Another football player," Franklin mumbled.

"How many times do you have to be warned?"

"From Mississippi, no less."

Joella stomped her foot on the floor, rattling the glass figurines on the antique table in the foyer.

Rosella had kept the fact that she was dating a football player from them as long as she could. But when she realized there was no turning back from the swift pace of this relationship, she knew she'd best broach the subject sooner rather than later.

"You've probably read about him in the sports pages," Rosella had said, hoping a star buildup might make the idea more palatable. She had prepared the dinner the night she asked her parents if she could bring him home, a softening tactic. "He was the number one guy in his position in the conference last season."

"Honey, you must have a short memory." Joella's response came as she sliced into her leg of lamb and Franklin chewed his asparagus spear much longer than necessary.

"It's not like before."

"Like before" was a hot button, a code word for a Bonita catastrophe with long-term familial consequences. The Caldwells' first daughter, Bonita, had arrived just nine months into the marriage and never felt she could measure up to the high standards set by her parents. By high school, she had embraced a full-throttle rebellion to the point that her father and mother dreaded answering the phone or the doorbell for fear of bad news.

"Like before" was during the disastrous college semester when Bonita had hooked up with an older college football player who cared only about sleeping with as many women as he could. There was little sympathy once Bonita informed the father she was pregnant. His way of dealing with it was to seize the opportunity to turn pro at the end of his junior year and join a team on the other side of the country.

Franklin had taken several gulps of merlot before he exploded.

"No! And not only no, but have you lost your mind?"

"My mind is not what I'm losing." Rosella stabbed at her food with her fork. "It's my patience."

Twelve years after Bonita's birth, Rosella made her entrance. The Caldwells had not planned to have more offspring because they feared the child could be a repeat of the first. Nevertheless, they regarded a pharmaceutical mishap as a redemptive act, a second chance for parenting skills tested by fire to produce a better outcome. Rosella was the antithesis of Bonita. She had embraced the model child challenge at an early age, going the extra mile in everything to make up the deficits of her older sister.

Franklin was firm. "You forget that besides grief and shame, the only thing the first football player that came into our lives left us with was your niece."

"A child we've barely seen since she was born," Joella said.

"Are you pregnant, Rosella?" Franklin snapped his napkin. "Tell me now and let's get it over with."

The meal ended with Rosella in retreat, steam still rising off the untouched four-course meal.

"You stepped over the line with that one, Franklin," Joella said, shaking her head in disbelief. "I'm going to leave you now to pull your size 11s out of your mouth and chew on your sock while I try to salvage this dinner. When you come to your senses, an apology will be in order."

Rosella had accepted her father's grumbled apology even if it lacked much conviction, and wasted no time in setting the introductory dinner date.

Now three weeks later, the reception was pleasant, hugs for Rosella, firm handshakes for Dewayne. Small talk over cocktails—designer water for Dewayne—was kept to stories behind the eye-catching collectibles gathered from numerous trips abroad, and a room-to-room tour of the four thousand square feet that made up the first floor dominated the opening hour of the evening. Dewayne's only requirement was to contribute genuine reactions of interest and amazement to Joella's design of each spacious room, which he did.

When the second hour began in the expansive dining room,

the French cuisine illuminated by a crystal chandelier, Dewayne inquired about the Caldwells' professions. In reply, Franklin pointed out the two coffee table–sized books on display in the glass bookcase behind Dewayne that depicted all the structures his firm had designed, and Joella treated Dewayne to meticulous descriptions of the homes of celebrities, politicians, and business tycoons whose millions she had spent enhancing their luxurious interiors. Rosella was attentive to her parents' favorable reaction to Dewayne, and as she watched his evident pleasure in hearing their accomplishments, she was thankful for this positive sign.

The final hour of the evening drifted toward an optimistic finish. After a three-course dessert of a variety of chocolate pastries, the women risked the chance to leave the two men alone and took it upon themselves to clear the table and remain in the kitchen. Dewayne and Franklin nodded and smiled, each man a little perturbed at this abandonment. After Franklin took his final swallow of brandy, he suggested they step outside and view the backyard, a real source of pride for him.

A large deck overlooked two acres of manicured flora that included a small grove of lemon and orange trees, and a waterfall cascading into a pond stocked with koi. Thrown in for good measure, one could view a slice of Los Angeles between clusters of cypress trees in the valley below.

Franklin opened a marble box ornamented with a bas-relief of a serpent and pulled out two cigars. Dewayne declined the offer, so Franklin returned the rejected cigar to the box, then clipped the end of his own and lit it.

"She won't let me smoke in the house," Franklin said through the exhale of a long drag. Franklin had hoped if the women were going to ditch them, perhaps a change of scenery would spark a new flourish of conversation. He wanted Dewayne to make some comment about the beauty before him, lighted well enough to be a film location, so he could begin another rambling monologue about what native species of plant life filled the gardens and the extraordinary care each variety required.

Dewayne waited for Franklin's lead as the conversation between the two men waned.

As Franklin watched his latest cloud of cigar smoke dissipate, he said, "I've been all over the world, but I've never been to Mississippi."

Dewayne instantly detected the disdainful coating in Franklin's voice. It stung, but he forced himself to stay calm. He kept his antennae raised for the slightest shift in tone. "Yes, sir," he said.

"Ever been outside of Mississippi?"

"No, sir, not until I came to Los Angeles."

"Just a good old country boy," Franklin mused. "I was a ghetto boy myself, and I have no desire to remember those days."

"I'm thankful for my roots." If Franklin was going to get personal and maybe pass judgment, then Dewayne was going to deflect as much as possible with his own individuation.

"Roots . . . you can have all that Alex Haley nonsense." Franklin spit a fleck of tobacco off his tongue, making it impossible for Dewayne to know whether it was an act of hygiene or a way to punctuate his words with derision. "I'll make my own history, thank you."

"You have, sir. And it's very impressive."

"I'm glad you see that. We worked hard and didn't let our past or our skin color keep us from accomplishing anything we set our minds to."

Dewayne sensed this was Franklin's way of pointing out the superior means of using one's brains over brawn.

"We've raised Rosella to think and act the same."

"I know she'll make you proud, sir."

"I expect her to."

Dewayne was not sure where Franklin might be directing this conversation, and he glanced back toward the double doors off the deck for any signs of rescue.

"Your parents, are they proud of you?"

"My daddy died before I was born, but the way my mother describes him, I believe he would be proud of me. I know my mother's proud of me, and that's what counts."

"Rosella tells me your mother works in a furniture factory."

"She does. And I'm proud of that."

Dewayne did not want this conversation to turn hostile, but he was not willing to allow the threat of an insult to go unnoticed.

"I hear there is talk about you not coming back for your senior year. That professional opportunity might entice you away."

"I've got my reasons for finishing what I started."

"So you come from Mississippi to the Promised Land to seek your fortune." Franklin waved his cigar like a baton over his own fortune. "I can admire that."

"Sir, I came out here for two things, to get an education and to play football."

"I'm glad you mentioned only two things. You're not thinking to add to that list, are you?"

Franklin had issued the challenge. By standing up for his own personal history and showing pride in his roots, Dewayne felt the tidewaters were rising. Before he could answer, Franklin filled the void.

"Rosella might not have told you that she has an older sister."

It was a news flash to Dewayne.

"She was a rebellious child, but precocious and plenty of brains. We were hopeful when she started at UCLA until some hotshot Bruin got her pregnant and disappeared into the world of professional football. Bonita and my granddaughter disappeared as well . . . out there somewhere. We thought she'd come home, but she never did."

Dewayne detected in Franklin's voice a disgust at a wasted life, yet still mourning the loss of a child and grandchild.

"The last we heard . . . and it's been several years now . . . she had a second child by God knows who and is living in some godforsaken part of LA."

Franklin paused to take several hasty puffs off his cigar, creating a tobacco cloud around his stern face. It was a long moment before he turned from his pensive gaze over his backyard landscape to focus an intense stare on Dewayne.

"Mr. Jobe, I'm not too fond of football players. I lost my older daughter to one, and I don't intend to lose another. So what are your intentions with my daughter?"

Dewayne bowed his head. No one had ever spoken to him in this way. No coach. No teacher. No one had ever challenged Dewayne to state and defend his intentions. His mother had not prepared him for people who would question his motives and try to tear him down, but it was still the thought of his mother that inspired him. The sum of the Caldwell fortune could not buy or compromise the strength of character or deep wisdom of such a powerful and humble woman.

Dewayne raised his head, his eyes latching on to Franklin's piercing stare. "First, let me say I'm sorry for the loss of your older daughter, and my prayer is that God might bring her back to you. As for your other daughter, my intentions are to never lie to her, to always honor and respect her. I'm a poor boy from Mississippi, which you have pointed out, and only God knows what the future holds for Rosella and me, but I'm not trying to compete with you on any level. You can say I'm not good enough, and you'd be right. You can say our families are from different worlds, and you'd be right about that too. But what I have been given and what experiences I've had in my life, I wouldn't trade for anything you've got or anything you've done. You do not need to fear me. History will not repeat itself. I can only promise you one thing, Mr. Caldwell: I will never steal your daughter away from you or compromise her in any way."

Franklin remained at a standstill the entire time Dewayne spoke. Dewayne noticed the steady, descending burn of the smoldering tobacco of Franklin's cigar. If he remained motionless much longer, the fire would singe the flesh around his fingers. When mother and daughter came through the double doors to join the men on the deck, Franklin relaxed his rigid stance and adjusted the stub of the cigar in his hand.

Dewayne could not help but smile at Rosella's expression, bright with the hope that father/boyfriend time had passed without incident. He reached out his hand for her.

"You two solving the world's problems?" Joella asked.

"Just admiring the view," Franklin said, and in the illumination of the garden spotlights, Dewayne thought he could see a faint smile curling over Franklin's lips.

5

Dewayne collected their luggage from the conveyor belt, and he and Rosella went outside the terminal of the Memphis airport to wait for Cherie. Dewayne had a few days before he had to start summer school for his last year at USC. He had gone every summer to make up for the light academic load he took during football season, and because of the distance and the expense, Dewayne had made the journey home only once. It was time to come home again, but this trip held more at stake. This trip was not the casual return of the hometown boy to visit family and friends. This trip was to introduce Rosella to the reality of Dewayne's life.

Their first argument had come when Rosella paid for their plane tickets. Even though she never played up her affluence or purposely made Dewayne feel second-class, he still struggled with the fact that he could not compete with the lifetime of wealth she had known. They settled the argument by agreeing Dewayne's ticket was simply a loan.

The couple stood next to their luggage waiting for Cherie to arrive. Dewayne had tried to prepare Rosella for the two extremes of their upbringing, and though she reassured him that it did not matter, Dewayne expected her to have a similar, queasy "what-have-I-gotten-myself-into" reaction to seeing his house in his humble neighborhood in his humble community as his own when she had driven him to her house that first time. It would be either a painfully long weekend full of forced conversations and sham, pleasant reactions or one that might exceed his wildest expectations.

The exhilaration at seeing her son after such a long time was a shot of adrenaline. Cherie felt like a young woman. She bounced out of the car as though the seat had ejected her, and mother and son held each other for so long, the airport police got impatient and instructed them to move along. Dewayne tossed the bags in the trunk while Cherie and Rosella hugged and cackled like newfound sisters. From the beginning, Dewayne had written Cherie the details of this growing romance, and the way Dewayne had portrayed Rosella, Cherie was predisposed to like her. Cherie knew her son would bring home only a woman of quality. The two women did not stop talking the entire drive until Dewayne complained about his isolation from the conversation.

"Rosella and I need to make history," Cherie said. "Pay attention to the road."

When they pulled in front of the house, there sat a tricked-out black Tahoe with Sly inside.

"Can I ask for more blessings?" Cherie jumped out of the car.

Sly braced for the hug he had come to expect from his surrogate mother, as though he was about to be sacked. When Cherie released him, Dewayne took her place, both men shouting as if they had won a big game. Dewayne introduced Rosella, and Sly scooped her into his arms like an Old World lover, leaving Dewayne shaking his head at his dear friend's ability to surprise.

"Girl, it's a good thing my man is keeping you out of my sight on the West Coast, 'cause if you were on my side of the world, you'd be under lock and key."

"You ain't got a lock and key big enough," Rosella said, sticking her finger into Sly's chest and pushing him away from her.

"My man, you have got first prize here." Sly finished the cuddle with a kiss to Rosella's cheek. "It's a wonder you can concentrate on football."

"I manage." Dewayne pulled Rosella from Sly into his own embrace.

Cherie chuckled at the boys' competition for Rosella's attention and directed them inside so she could start supper. She took Rosella out of Dewayne's grasp and led her up the front steps, as over her shoulder she instructed the boys to get the bags.

Sly could not remove his admiring gaze until Rosella disappeared into the house.

"She is one fine-looking—"

"That's enough."

They fought over who would carry Rosella's bag, and Dewayne gave in out of fear that the leather strap might break in their tug-of-war. With a first round settled and nothing left to distract them, Dewayne took in Sly's Tahoe.

"Where'd the ride come from?"

"It's a loaner, my man," Sly said, polishing the hood with his shirtsleeve.

Dewayne began an easy pace around the vehicle, admiring all the bells and whistles inside and out.

"How does a poor boy get a set of wheels like this loaned to him?"

"One plays football and one plays really well. You must be a slacker."

"So you don't mind testing the rules." Dewayne kicked the left front tire. His foot recoiled from the tight inflated rubber indifferent to the abuse.

"Rules are flexible when nobody's paying attention."

"There's always somebody paying attention, *my man*."

"Listen to Mr. Clean. I win games and the school I play for is making money off me, so why shouldn't I get to eat at the table?"

"Looks like you're eating well," Dewayne said, finishing his inspection with the slam of the passenger side door. "And speaking of eating, I'm starved."

Dewayne headed toward the front door, leaving Sly staring a hole into his friend's back. He refused to feel intimidated or ashamed for enjoying a few undisclosed benefits given him by generous people willing to show gratitude to high achievers. *You can be born with nothing, but you sure do not have to live that way*, he reasoned. Sly had made Miami's program exciting, bringing national attention to the university. Proud he had earned this windfall, he rubbed the hood ornament. It was not a handout, and no one would hear him apologize for it.

After one plateful, Rosella said she knew why Dewayne had grown so big with such good cooking. It would have been hard to pay Cherie a higher compliment. Even with three people around the table and Cherie at her traditional place of chef and server, it was obvious a part of the boys' trio was missing.

"No word from Jesse?" Sly asked. "Why isn't Jesse here?"

"Needed to work late," Dewayne said.

"Work late?"

"You don't stay in touch with your homeboy?"

"What are you talking about?" Sly asked.

"He's at the factory now, learning the business. He dropped out of school."

"How do you know so much?"

"I have my sources," Dewayne said, winking at his mother. "You knew Jesse broke his leg in a game."

"Broke his leg," Sly repeated.

It was obvious that when Sly left Springdale three years ago, he had never looked back, never thought about looking back.

"Got clipped midseason his first year. He tried to come back the second year, but he had lost the passion for the game, I guess. Don't know for sure what happened to him."

"He told me the pain just would not go away," Cherie said. "I see him at the factory from time to time, favoring his right leg, but I think he tries to avoid me. He never comes over anymore, and I hear that . . ."

Cherie's voice faded as she began to pour more sweet tea. She was afraid she might be going too far with information she could not substantiate with a firsthand account, so she hoped the splash of tea over the ice in Rosella's tall glass would obscure her last words.

"Hear what, Miss Cherie?"

Rosella's polite innocence forced Cherie to finish what she had begun.

"Well, I shouldn't have even started," Cherie said. "I mean, it's like I've never seen him do what they say . . ."

"What are you talking about, Mama?"

"It's gossip. It could just be gossip," Cherie said, frustrated she had been compelled to participate in a vice she detested. "But I worry about him."

"You haven't told us anything to be worried about yet," Sly said.

Both boys glared at her with a "come clean" look, and she could not escape the inquisition.

"Word is he's drinking a lot. That's what they say, but like I said, I've never seen him take a drop of anything but my sweet tea. All I know is when I see him at the factory, he's not the same boy who used to eat at my table."

Sly and Dewayne halted their consumption of food. Sly let the prongs of his fork rest on his plate, and Dewayne leaned back in his chair and slowed his chewing. Cherie's news had interrupted a happy reunion, and the two of them needed a second to process the startling information, be it hearsay or truth.

"You boys can't leave here without seeing your friend," Cherie said, not giving them much time to reflect.

"But I've got to leave for Miami bright and early in the morning," Sly said.

"Then you find him tonight," Cherie insisted.

With Cherie's word as their mandate, Sly and Dewayne cruised the streets of Springdale in Sly's Tahoe in search of Jesse. They had left Rosella and Cherie to their girl talk.

"This fool could be anywhere," Sly said, unable to keep the tone of complaint from influencing his words. "I mean, why do we have to do this?"

Dewayne looked at him as if he'd had a moment of temporary insanity.

"You forget who gave us the order? We'll find him," Dewayne said. "Springdale's no bigger than the way we left it."

If Jesse was working late at the factory, then they would go

60

there first. As they circled the town square and headed out the highway leading to Webb Furniture, they saw the yellow Hummer dominating a long line of cars and pickups in front of the Rebel Rouser Sports Bar. Sly swung the Tahoe into the first open space in front of the bar, and they went inside.

It was hard to ignore two strapping African-American football players striding into a bar, and the habitués recognized the local celebrities at once. The owner of the Rebel Rouser had framed pictures on the wall of each senior the year they had gone to the state championship game, and circling a large group shot of the entire team and coaching staff was a drooping banner painted in school colors that read SPRINGDALE TIGERS DISTRICT CHAMPIONS. It was the owner's way of remembering the glory. The two boys responded in kind to the warm greetings as they passed through the crowd on their way to the shooting gallery where Jesse was playing pool.

The back room was cramped, the atmosphere soured from years of cigarettes smoked and alcohol consumed. REBEL ROUSER in bright red neon and the green glow of shaded bulbs over the pool tables lighted the space. Photographs of Mississippi veterans from the Civil War to the wars in Iraq and Afghanistan interspersed with posters of scantily clad women posing with automobiles and handyman tools haphazardly plastered the peeling walls.

Dewayne grabbed Sly's arm, stopping him from interrupting Jesse while in the middle of a game. From a distance, unnoticed in the murky light, they watched their friend run the table in a game of eight ball surrounded by a juiced crowd fascinated by the wonder of Jesse's skill. Between each shot Jesse gulped down a swig of beer, his bottle held for him by a former Tigers cheerleader. Even in the diffused illumination, the friends could see that Jesse had lost significant weight, and indeed, he did favor his right leg as he maneuvered around the table. When Jesse sank the eight ball with a hard smash as though he had fired it from a gun, the cheerleader performed a Tiger acrobatic leap and a ludicrously extended kiss. Sly was ready to walk out the door and willingly lie to Cherie, but Dewayne led him out of the shadows into the smoky, muted light.

Jesse was about to light a cigarette when his friends appeared at the end of the table like black apparitions staring at him with a prophet's insight. The cigarette dangled off his lip and fell to the floor. Were he not in a public place, he might have burst into tears at the sight of his friends. Instead, he covered the impulse with a loud guffaw and hobbled toward them, falling into their arms like a penitent.

"Man, it's good to see you boys," Jesse said, a strength returning to him that had not pulsed through his body for a long time.

"Yeah, yeah, you too, my man," Sly said.

Dewayne said nothing. He nodded to the crowd, who waved and smiled in return but did not want to participate in this private moment, and they dispersed to other tables and other games. Even the cheerleader knew there would be no invitation to join this trio, and she became a part of the human stream keeping their distance from this privileged encounter. Jesse was unable to release his friends. It was as though the power he received from their touch had brought him back to life.

"Is this your idea of working late?"

Jesse knew it was a subtle chastisement for being a no-show at dinner. "Yeah, it was lame. I just . . ."

He wanted to explain, but the truth remained aloof and he released the grip on his friends.

"We missed you, that's all," Dewayne said, rubbing a hand

down Jesse's side, his friend's weight loss noticeable to the touch. "You know you never need an invitation."

"Yeah, I know that." Jesse was careful not to make direct eye contact.

"You missed meeting D-man's girl," Sly said, giving Dewayne an elbow. "He not careful, that girl is gonna end up in Miami."

Dewayne returned the elbow to Sly's ribs and laughed. "He's all talk. Nothing's changed with this boy."

"I keep up with you in the papers and the sports channels," Jesse said. "You're superstars. You're making Springdale proud."

"We miss seeing you, brother," Dewayne said.

"Yeah . . . ancient history." Jesse fumbled his cigarette pack out of his shirt pocket. "I guess you heard about my bad luck."

"I thought you'd get back in the game once your leg healed," Dewayne said.

"I thought so too." Jesse rubbed the spot on his thigh where the femur had been shattered. "The game had been knocked out of me. I saw no reason to keep going."

Dewayne nodded his head toward Jesse's leg. "I see you're still hobbling."

"Never fully healed. Guess I'll be a gimp the rest of my days."

"You drop out of school and come home to this?" Sly said, indicating the room with his hand.

Jesse had secured a cigarette from his pack, and in the time it took to light it, he found the backbone to look Sly in the eye.

"Nothing changes with you, man." Jesse smiled and pointed his finger toward Sly's face. "You know how to cut through it. I came home to this because this is my place, and I know my place."

"Hey, ain't no judgment allowed between us." Dewayne gave Sly a second jab with his elbow—but this time he didn't accompany the playful gesture with laughter. "We're here just to encourage you, brother."

"I'm encouraged, my man. Let me buy you a beer."

Jesse lifted his hand toward the bartender, but Dewayne shook his head.

"Not tonight, Jesse. Maybe next time."

Sly begged off because of the next day's early departure, and Dewayne allowed the snub to cover his own desire to exit. The pair dared not confront Jesse with the truth of how they saw the downfall of a best friend. Neither of them had a magic solution. They had not left Springdale to become miracle workers. And they could not join him to drink from his fountain of anguish. The agony would have to curdle in Jesse's gut alone. So after another group embrace and the exchanged lies of promised future reunions, one last plea from Jesse accompanied their exit.

"Hey, if you stick around, you might see Coach Hopper," he said, his cheerleader friend returning to his side with a fresh beer. "He's here most nights."

But the cry had come from too far away. The faintness of its echo failed to register on ears that had gone deaf to the past. Sly and Dewayne gave a last wave of recognition as though Jesse was a mere fan, and they faded out of his sight as startlingly as they had appeared. Sly backed out of the parking lot in his Tahoe and mumbled a bitter critique of their onetime inseparable friend.

"Jesse never did have the sense God gave a turnip," he said, and Dewayne offered no rebuttal.

———

Cherie and Rosella had spent their evening together sitting on Dewayne's bed as Cherie gave a rambling saga of Dewayne's life represented by specific objects: painted handprints from elementary school—God's first visual sign of his future in football; a piggybank of the Bible where he squirreled away his coins; a picture of his father with a collage of pictures of Dewayne at different ages, cut out and glued in a circle around Robert's smiling face; an African mask he had made from beans, beads, buttons, and safety pins, revealing a creative side of Dewayne that Rosella never suspected; a Best Sportsman award given in his junior year in high school and the only one on display in the room, the other trophies boxed up and hidden away in his closet; a bronze casting of a cross with the inscription "No Greater Love" at the base, given him on the day of his baptism. Rosella absorbed it all in rapt attention, and by the end of the evening, Cherie told Rosella that if she ever heard her son was not treating her with proper respect, she would be on the first bus to California prepared to visit upon him divine wrath. Rosella assured her such a trip would not be necessary.

When Dewayne got home, he heard the ladies cackling before he unlocked the door and followed the laughter into his bedroom to find Rosella modeling his high school helmet and shoulder pads. Both women screamed when Dewayne said hello, and Rosella, her adrenaline racing, charged him with lowered head, only to bounce off his laughing abdomen like a coin off the head of a drum. Dewayne and his mother were laughing so hard, neither could help Rosella to her feet.

Dewayne gave a minimalist explanation of his time with Jesse, avoiding any details of how he and Sly had found him or any mention of the disquieted feelings he was still trying to process. Given the late hour, Cherie had not pried, so after the exchange of "good nights," Rosella was the first to climb into bed and turn out the light in Cherie's room. Dewayne came out of the bathroom and saw his mother spreading her blankets across the sofa. He looked under Cherie's bedroom door to be sure it was dark before speaking.

"What do you think?" he whispered, nodding his head in Rosella's direction.

"I believe you wouldn't have brought her home if you thought she would not have met my approval," Cherie said.

"You approve then?"

"What I approve of is your heart and your mind and your God-given ability to make a good decision. I trust your judgment, just like I trusted mine when it came time to decide about your father."

"But I want your blessing too. Rosella just might be . . . just might be your daughter-in-law."

"Son, my blessing is freely given."

Cherie approached Dewayne and wrapped her arms around him. When she pulled away, she invited him to sit down in the recliner, and she took her place on the sofa.

"In your letters you've been talking about being in love with this girl, and you said that Rosella comes from money. It's all right she comes from money 'cause from what you've said and from what I see, money hasn't corrupted her. I can tell when folks are condescending. I got the intuition to know when people can't see beyond the end of their nose. She's not trying to hide any airs, and I got no sense she was just doing the time so she could impress the boyfriend's mother. She's real."

Dewayne released a sigh of relief. Cherie's appraisal of Rosella was vital, and in this case, welcome, because it matched his own.

"Now as for her daddy, don't let him get you riled. You keep on loving his daughter like the gentleman you are, and you'll win him over. You want her parents' blessing. You want that spiritual covering when you start your own life together. That's God's way of handing down blessing from one generation to the next. You must not take that for granted. Are you hearing me?"

"Yes, ma'am."

"So have you broached the subject yet?"

"We've talked about it, but I haven't asked her. I think she's ready, but I wanted to talk to you first, and I was thinking once I got your blessing, I might ask her here, where I grew up, where I'm most comfortable."

"I approve, and I got one more thing to add. Have you got something to offer her?"

"What do you mean?" Dewayne asked, eyeing her with playful misgiving.

Cherie pulled a black jewelry box out of the pocket of her bathrobe and waved for him to move closer. Dewayne slipped out of the recliner and knelt beside his mother.

"You've never seen this until now," she said, opening the lid to reveal an engagement ring encircled with diamond chips. "It's not fancy or pricey by today's standards, though it set us back a couple of house payments back in the day, but if a man is going to ask a lady to marry him, he should offer a token of his love."

"Mama, this is beautiful! But why don't you ever wear it?"

"I wear the band, and that's enough. I figured when this day arrived, I would make a bequest along with my blessing. That is, if you like it and think Rosella might."

"I love it, and I believe she will."

Cherie dropped the box into his open palm. He looked at the ring as if he'd been handed Solomon's treasure.

"I held her hand tonight as we said the blessing and felt her ring finger . . . should be a perfect fit."

Dewayne's jaw dropped with a short guffaw. "Mama, I should start calling you 'Sly.'"

"Conniving for a good cause is the way I look at it."

They had to hush each other so as not to wake Rosella with their laughter and be caught in their conspiracy. Then Cherie took her son's face into her hands. Her laughter had subsided, replaced with an earnestness that silenced the last of Dewayne's laughter.

"Son, one last thing. I too think Rosella is the type to cherish this small ring, but it's a test." She gently patted the sides of Dewayne's face to assure him she did not mean to hurt him or insult Rosella. "This is not a judgment. There is nothing wrong with being raised in a high-dollar lifestyle, but it's a world where you will have to find your feet. You'll grow into it, and Rosella will be your guide. This ring will link you to your past and your future."

"Thanks, Mama," Dewayne said, and then kissed Cherie on the cheek before going to bed.

Cherie had taken a personal day from her job so she could spend it with Dewayne and Rosella touring the sights of Springdale. It was another test Cherie had concocted. She wanted to appraise the authenticity of Rosella's reactions when she saw the disparity of upbringing between Dewayne and her. It began at Webb Furniture.

"The place of my boy's birth," Cherie said, her air of pride evident as they walked across the factory floor. "Most babies are born in a hospital. Mine came on a conveyer belt."

Cherie pointed to the spot beside her workstation, the one

she'd had for over twenty years. A drop of sweat bubbled to the center of her forehead and trickled down to the bridge of her nose. She wiped it away.

"It was as hot a day as today, and I felt like I was roasting my baby. The heat was stifling and nobody seemed to know how bad I was feeling."

Rosella scanned the workers—human humidifiers performing their assigned tasks with mechanized precision.

"Making recliners for the fat man is what we do."

Cherie nodded at her girlfriends around her workstation. It was near break time and the ladies were ready for hugs and introductions.

"It's what we do, and we do it well," Cherie said, and the bell for the ten-minute break clanged and the amplified sound of the mass assemblage of cheap recliners for furniture outlet stores all across America shut down.

Cherie introduced Rosella to her co-workers, and she greeted each of them warmly, with no politician's glad-handing. It was Cherie's friends who embarrassed her, going on about what a fine catch Dewayne was, all the time rubbing and patting him as if he was some mammoth pet with Rosella standing in plain sight.

Amused by the gushing feminine affection given Dewayne, Rosella said with a smile, "The man is taken."

In Cherie's mind, Rosella was passing her covert test.

They circled the town square three times to give needed focus for points of interest. They saw the church where Dewayne grew up and Cherie was still a faithful member—it remained unlocked day or night, for who knew when God might call a sinner to his house to repair a relationship. They ate lunch at

69

their favorite diner, where many of the locals were happy to see the hometown boy, and ordered a meat and three-vegetable combination for Rosella whose refined palette was unaccustomed to such southern cuisine. It took a few moments for her taste buds to accept the unusual flavors, but the food went down smooth.

Their final stop was the cemetery to pay their respects to Robert Dewayne Jobe.

"I don't come as often as I should," Cherie said, linking all three together with an arm around each one. "A part of me just never wants to accept he's gone. I don't believe the good Lord is a thief, but from time to time, in the dark quiet moments, I do believe I was robbed of this man."

Rosella laid her arm over Cherie's shoulder, and Cherie raised her hand to brush her fingers over Rosella's cheek.

"Except for his size, you're looking at the spitting image of his daddy," Cherie said. "No scientific explanation as to why he's so big, but I love every ounce of him."

"Me too," Rosella whispered.

The drive home from the cemetery was quiet until they passed the high school. Rosella wanted to see where Dewayne had played, and he promised to take her there in the evening when no one would be around. Dewayne inquired about Jake Hopper.

"There's talk he may retire," Cherie said. "Jake was hoping the athletic department would see him as a natural choice to replace the head coach when he left two years ago, but the job went to someone downstate. I think he's just doing his time."

"You never told me that. Do you ever see him?" Dewayne asked.

Cherie could not answer. She had heard Dewayne but was staring out the window, posing as though lost in thought and hoping he would not repeat his question. The timing of just returning from the cemetery seemed like the truth of her answer would be a betrayal. Jake had eventually gotten the courage to ask Cherie to dinner, and though flattered by his initial offer, she did not accept. She thought that would end any future invitations, but she was wrong. By the fifth time, she had run out of excuses. They had driven to Memphis for dinner, the couple not ready to deflect the stares and gossip from a Springdale populace that would follow a public appearance of an interracial couple. It had been a pleasant experience, which brought pangs of guilt that she might be happy with someone other than her first love. However, these secret trysts continued—strictly honorable with never a hint of alcohol on Jake's breath—and Cherie had to admit there was a furtive enjoyment in his attention. When all of Springdale knew the position of head coach had been offered to another, Jake's invitations became infrequent until they stopped altogether.

Cherie was disappointed as this platonic companionship had fizzled out, but she accepted it as another unexplainable consequence of life.

"Mom, do you ever see Coach Hopper?" Dewayne repeated, cutting off all of Cherie's escape routes.

"From time to time . . . in passing," she said.

"Well, tell him I said hello."

Cherie nodded to acknowledge her son's request, but she kept her gaze on the familiar terrain passing outside the car window.

After supper, Cherie shooed the couple out the door for some alone time, so she could clean the kitchen before she caught

71

her ride to the trustees' committee meeting at church. Rosella had insisted on helping, but Cherie would have none of it.

"You two go on, now. It's a lovely evening, so go enjoy it."

When Dewayne pulled into the school parking lot and drove around to the stadium, he saw the field was vacant with only a couple of low wattage security lights shining on the fifty-yard line. Dewayne helped Rosella climb over the fence, and they walked onto the field.

"So this is where you set all those records," Rosella said.

"This is the place," he answered as they reached the forty-yard line.

"What's it like to be back here?"

With that, he broke into a sprint as though her voice had terrorized him. When he reached the end zone, he threw up his arms in the signal of a touchdown and jogged back to Rosella waiting for him on the fifty-yard line, casting a faint shadow in the security lights.

"Just had to get out some energy," he said, dancing around Rosella and teasing her by fluffing her hair with his hands.

"Boy, you are some kind of crazy tonight," she said, trying to rein him in.

"Blame it on the moon. Blame it on love. Blame it on being on the fifty-yard line with the woman I want to spend the rest of my life with," he said.

Rosella captured his hand and brought him to a stop.

"What did you just say?"

Dewayne fell to one knee and kept his head lowered until he got full control of his breathing.

"I need to do this now while my blood is up."

He reached into his back pocket and retrieved the black jewelry box.

"From USC to Springdale, Mississippi, is a long journey,

but I see it as the hand of God. I'm only good at one thing—catching passes and running fast—and I believe it's what I'm supposed to do with my life. But I don't want to do it alone, and I don't want to do it without you. I believe you are the one for me. My love for you consumes me, and I feel for the first time in my life I am a whole man."

Dewayne raised his head and looked into Rosella's face. She had closed her eyes as if meditating on the words Dewayne was saying, words she desired him to speak, words that were a communion of mutual love, words spoken like a tender prayer. He kissed her hand, then opened it and placed the jewelry box on her palm. Rosella gasped and fell to her knees. She stared at the box as if she might open it by force of will alone. Dewayne placed his long fingers on the lid and pulled it back. To anyone but Rosella, the ring would not realign constellations—it was a ring of the heart, and the only hearts that mattered were the two beating on the fifty-yard line of Tiger Stadium.

"If you will have me, Ms. Rosella Caldwell, I would like to be your husband for the rest of my life. I would like you to be my wife. Will you marry me?"

The power of such love expressed was an ephemeral fracture in the night's sky. Rosella pressed into her future husband and laid her cheek upon his.

"Yes, I will marry you," she whispered. "And love you with all my heart."

6

The Caldwell backyard had been turned into a wedding cosmos masterminded by the daughter of an architect and an interior designer: decorated tents and booths, each with a sampling of finger-food cuisine from numerous cultures; arbors covered in flowers; tuxedoed musicians; multicolored banners hanging from manicured trees; large framed photographs of the happy couple mounted on easels and scattered throughout the pristine gardens; a wedding altar constructed like a cathedral's nave at the far end of the yard with the city of Los Angeles in the background. The multitude of guests rambled through this wonderland, drinking and eating their fill.

The list of highly favored guests was lopsided. Cherie, Sly, and Jesse were all who had made it out from Springdale, and a few of Dewayne's USC teammates who had not gone home during this short break between summer school's voluntary workouts and the beginning of the season. The rest of them represented the Caldwell side. Rosella and Dewayne had decided against bridesmaids and groomsmen. When the musicians began to play the wedding music, the bride and the groom entered from separate sides of the patio and then were joined by their families. The group began a casual march through the backyard, flowing like a fresh stream through the guests with the Caldwells and Cherie flanking the couple's sides. The procession came to rest before the altar for a ceremony of prayers, blessings, Bible verses, and original vows under the minister's guidance.

Cherie had flown to Los Angeles to enjoy the days of parties and preparations leading up to the wedding. The Caldwells treated her like royalty, insisting she stay with them. At first she was intimidated, fearful she might get lost in the vast square footage or get in the way of the armies employed for this affair, but just two days before the wedding, she had confided to her son that she was putting in her order for a heavenly mansion modeled after the Caldwells'.

When Sly and Jesse flew in the day before the wedding, Sly told Rosella it was not too late, she could still come back to Miami. "Dewayne will be nothing but grief and trouble," he said. "And only I can make you a happy woman."

Cherie put the kibosh on such jive talk. "What God hath joined together this fool will not tear asunder," she said and reinforced the paraphrased quote with a slap to the back of Sly's head.

Jesse looked a little better than the last time Dewayne saw him. He had gained some weight, but his face was ashen and haggard, and his movements were fidgety, almost spastic. He kept disappearing during the pre-wedding socializing and never seemed to be able to settle down. Dewayne pulled Sly aside and asked if he noticed Jesse's unusual behavior, but Sly said all he was noticing was the beautiful bride.

Before the evening concluded, Franklin instructed the waiters to supply every guest with a glass of champagne, and while the waiters carried out that order, he led Joella and Cherie by their hands onto the highest point of the patio where they could be in full view of the wedding party. When three glasses of champagne appeared on the railing in front of the trio, Franklin waved his hand for everyone's attention.

"What a pleasure it is to have you in our home. Thank you for joining Joella and Cherie Jobe and me in witnessing the union of our children and the creation of a new family."

He had to pause to hem in his emotions. He had not anticipated the sudden reminder of the absence of his older daughter and two grandchildren. Joella slipped her arm around her husband's side, and Cherie placed a hand on his shoulder. The two matriarchs brought Franklin's attention back to the moment.

"When Dewayne first showed up on my doorstep, I played my part as the skeptic. What father doesn't assume that role when it comes to his daughter? Has God ever created a man good enough for a father's daughter? Apparently so or the human race would have come to a quick end."

A murmur of amusement passed over his audience.

"From the moment we met, I knew he was a cut above the standard; yes, in physical size and in the quality of his character . . . all credit due to Cherie Jobe. So the peaceable war of attrition began that first night here on this patio when he spoke so eloquently and without shame about his personal history. About his profound respect for my daughter. In pursuing Rosella's love, you could say he was pursuing her parents' love as well, and the three of us yielded to his gentle persuasion. This was not a situation of conqueror and conquered. In all honesty, I say Dewayne Jobe's entry into our lives was a victory for us all."

Sly and Jesse burst into applause, inspiring the wedding party to join them and giving time for Franklin and the women at his side to raise their glasses of champagne.

"I must confess until now I had not paid close attention to the game of football; no personal prejudice, just a lack of interest.

But things have changed. Joella and I are looking forward to this last season of Dewayne's college career, and I expect to be in the stadium doing my part for the home team. And it's nice to think we might have a potential Heisman Trophy winner as a son."

A second round of applause began, but this time without Sly's instigation.

Dewayne looked over at his friend and smiled, fluttering his glass of champagne in his direction.

Sly shook his head and waved him off. "That's father-in-law talk," he said, just loud enough above the applause for Dewayne to hear him.

"Join Joella, Cherie, and me in saluting this new couple with an ancient Jewish blessing: 'May the Lord bless you and keep you; the Lord make his face to shine upon you and be gracious to you; the Lord turn his face toward you and give you peace.'"

All glasses rose in the air. All champagne was consumed. All heaven seemed to be focusing its benevolent attention on this blissful couple.

A horde of reporters, girlfriends, fans, and family had gathered in front of the team's entrance to the USC stadium, waiting for their particular player to emerge from the locker room. It would take Dewayne time to work his way through the masses, speaking to those demanding a quote for a paper or an autograph, and waving off the disappointed females who hoped to score their men by their power of seduction. The oversized wedding band on his finger was a big deterrent.

Because the team had won its first home game, Rosella knew it would take longer for Dewayne to run the gauntlet, so she sat under a tree studying her textbook while she waited. Dewayne was taking his usual light load, and because he had gone to school through the last four summers, he would only have to take a couple of classes the last semester of his senior year, allowing him time to train for the spring combines.

Without being rude, Dewayne passed through the mob like he was parting the waters. When he saw Rosella under the tree absorbed in her textbook, he slipped behind the tree, giving her a fright that elicited a squeal and a smack on the chest. He scooped her into his arms and stretched out the kiss so all single females who thought they might have some future chance with him could see his heart had been subjugated.

The walk home would take ten minutes, and when one lone female approached with a paper in her hand, Rosella was prepared to allow a brief pause for Dewayne to sign her paper, but she hooked her arm through Dewayne's and drew him closer, a visible sign of ownership.

The woman had the emaciated face of an African refugee with a tipsy expression, and as she drew near them, she gabbled in a strange tongue. Her hair was a nest of windblown street trash. The shapeless clothes she wore outsized her shrunken frame, and the odor rose from her body like heat waves off hot pavement. She became a roadblock on the sidewalk, forcing Dewayne and Rosella to stop. Dewayne reached for his wallet, and the woman unfurled the discolored and wrinkled newspaper she was carrying. On the front page of the society section of the *Los Angeles Times*, above the fold, was a half-page random collection of some of LA's finest celebrating the Caldwell/Jobe union.

"'USC Football Star Marries Caldwell Daughter,'" she said, looking into their annoyed faces. She had memorized the headline. "You don't look so happy today. You don't look so happy to see me."

The creature's voice had the croaky sound of an old hag who had stepped out of a fairy tale. She tapped the image of Dewayne's face in the picture of the newspaper.

"You don't look like a gold digger to me," she said. "Looks like you didn't need to marry her for the money."

"Excuse us," Rosella said and began leading her husband with an end-around move away from the creature.

"Don't be in a hurry now," the creature said, trying to counter the couple's sweep. "I'm just happy for you is all. Not every day you get married and make the society page."

Dewayne and Rosella sidestepped the creature and quickened their momentum. The creature wadded the paper and kicked it like a soccer ball over their heads.

"Not every day you get to see your family either."

Rosella stopped dead in her tracks. She released Dewayne's arm and turned around.

"I guess you bought into the crap that I was dead."

"Bonita?"

The last time Rosella had seen her sister was on a street corner with two children, one just a baby crying in her arms. Her mother had picked Rosella up from school to run errands, but they drove through a part of town that was not the normal errand route, and by its rough environs, she knew it should be off-limits. But Joella traveled the different streets at a steady school-zone speed, looking at every human they passed for any sign of recognition, while strangers glared at them as though they were foreign invaders.

Joella sped up when she spotted a woman on the street corner with two children, but drove past them and stopped a half block beyond the corner where they were waiting. She ordered Rosella to stay put before she scooted out of the running car and jogged back toward the huddled trio.

Rosella turned around in her seat to see her mother open her purse and hand the woman cash, brush her fingers once down the right side of the little girl's face, stroke the forehead of the crying baby, and return to the car, all without saying a word to any of them. She would not have even known she had seen her sister, niece, and nephew had she not overheard Joella tearfully telling Franklin what she had done when they thought Rosella was asleep in her bedroom.

"Back from the dead," this haggard woman now said, raising her arms to support her point. "Never really died except in the minds of the Caldwells."

"Bonita . . . Bonita," Rosella said, as if repeating the name would confirm she was not looking at a ghost.

In the depth and rustle of her heart, Rosella felt as if she was waking from years of slumber, unsure of the altered landscape and vivid characters. It seemed one night long ago she fell asleep and was told her sister departed to a world from which she would never return nor Rosella could ever visit.

"So why didn't I get my engraved invitation to the big event?"

"Bonita," Rosella whispered, restraining the impulse to touch her sister. She could not decide on a slap or an embrace, so she locked her hands behind her back and felt relief when Dewayne came behind her and took her hands into his.

"Is 'Bonita' all you can say?"

Rosella's inability to articulate anything beyond the mention of her name brought a hostile expression to Bonita's face.

"I guess it's been so long you'd need a DNA test to prove I was your sister."

"Calm down, ma'am," Dewayne said.

"Well, the jolly green giant is not just pretty to look at. He talks too."

"Don't, Bonita, please."

"Don't what, sister dear? Don't admire the pretty addition to the family? Don't speak to him? Don't what?"

"I don't know what to say," Rosella said. "I don't know how to deal with this."

"Ma'am, is there some way I can help you?" Dewayne started to reach for his wallet. "I've got a little money—"

"He's pretty, he talks, and he's willing to help. Looks like you hit the jackpot, girl." A grin appearing on Bonita's withered face exposed a number of chipped and missing teeth. "Yeah, I need some money. My kids are hungry."

"No. No money. We're not giving her any money," Rosella said, beginning to gain some control over this shock to her ordered world. "If you're real, if you're really my sister, then tell me where you live. Give me an exact address, not some street corner. I'll get you some groceries. I'll buy some food and bring it to you tonight. If you're there, you'll be real to me. If you're not there, then you're still dead."

Neither woman moved, their eyes locked. Rosella's brain was in overdrive searching for identity and meaning to this unexpected discovery.

"Do I still have a niece and nephew?" she asked.

Bonita nodded.

"You have them there. I want to see them. I want to touch them. Now what's your address, and it better be real, not some shelter."

Dewayne was dumbfounded as he watched the two sisters. Never in his life would he have imagined a scene like this. He couldn't help but look for similarities between his wife and this disheveled woman.

Rosella flipped open her textbook and clicked on her pen.

She looked at Bonita as if daring her to offer a lie. Bonita coughed and swiveled her head as though she might be casting around for a fake address, but the address she gave seemed legit. It was in East LA, a numbered apartment in a recognizable complex off a main street. No phone number—there was no money for a phone.

Rosella snapped her textbook closed. "I'm coming to this address. I'm knocking on a door, and I'd better see you there. I'd better see two children with you. You had better not be messing with me."

With that, Rosella turned and strode away without her husband.

Like a lost child, Dewayne stood before Bonita. He turned to leave and saw his wife on her forced march, then reached for his wallet and removed two Andrew Jacksons and handed them to Bonita before starting his jog toward Rosella.

Bonita's whisper was just loud enough for Dewayne to hear as she stuffed the bills in her pocket.

"He's generous too."

The brisk wind scuttled the litter along the street and around their feet as they unloaded the groceries from the car. Since he carried the lion's share of the sacks, Dewayne was thankful his sister-in-law's apartment was on the first floor of a two-story complex. This was a place he did not want them to be after nightfall. There was no grass except the weeds growing through the cracks in the sidewalks and concrete courtyard, no foliage except a few withered bushes at each end of the complex, no views except straight up into a smog-filled sky, no vistas except the empty lot across the street—an apocalyptic playground of abandoned cars and rusting home appliances. Undernourished dogs, rodents, and scavenger birds lurked through the rubbish of the ailing terrain, searching for any nutritious scraps. Random clusters of human life moved through the city blocks like spies of nature on the lookout for an escape route. No life, human or animal, showed any comprehension of the world outside this wretched cubicle of a neighborhood.

The groceries got heavier and heavier as Dewayne and Rosella endured the long wait for the door to open and listened to two stories of gangster artists and domestic squabbles at different levels of volume conflict. A beautiful young girl with skin as black as ink opened the door and slouched in the entry as though daring them to gain admittance. She was dressed in shorts and a loose halter top, her thin body pierced in the nose, in the right eyebrow, and in stair steps up each earlobe, and she was chewing the life out of a stick of gum. The music coming from the inside was at concert level.

"Who are you, honey?" Rosella asked, studying the young girl's face for any Caldwell features.

"No, honey, who are you?" The girl's voice dripped with mockery accentuated by popping gum sounds inside her mouth.

Her sarcasm was a slap in the face, but Rosella smiled and continued.

"I believe I'm your aunt Rosella. I believe . . . I mean, your mother is my sister—"

"I know what an aunt is. I ain't stupid."

"No, you're not . . . you're definitely not," Rosella said. "I'm sorry. Is your mother's name Bonita Caldwell?"

After a brief, nondescript look, the girl slammed the door and began shouting at someone. Dewayne was thankful for all the weight conditioning he had done over the years, but he still had to set the twenty-pound ham on the concrete to lighten his burden.

A moment later, the door opened, but the girl still blocked the passageway.

"What you want?" The music level had dropped but only by a few decibels.

"I saw your mother today. I told her we'd bring some groceries." Rosella shifted the sacks in her hands and pointed to the ones overflowing in her husband's arms.

The door slammed in their faces once again, followed by more muffled shouting. When the door reopened, the music was playing at a manageable level, and the guard at the door appeared ready to allow admission.

"My mama's sick, but she says you can come in." The girl stepped back.

Rosella handed her a couple of sacks and picked up the ham at Dewayne's feet. They followed the girl into the kitchen. Dewayne and Rosella gave a cursory glance to the other people lounging on the broken secondhand furniture in the cramped apartment before they dumped the sacks of food onto the table in between the dirty dishes. The kitchen pass-through gave them a view into the living room. A young boy about twelve years old and three teenage boys stared back at them, bobbing their heads to the beat of the music as if hypnotized. The leader of the older boys wore a sleeveless shirt, dreadlocks scraping along his shoulders; his arms covered with frightening tattoos of satanic power, and his demeanor reflected the art on his arms. None offered a greeting. They seemed to be waiting for Dewayne to make the first move to know if this colossus would be a friend or foe. He did, but only a slight nod, not enough to elicit a response from the muted quartet sprawled over the room.

"We should help you put these away," Rosella said, waving her hand over the mound of groceries, and the girl gave an indifferent shrug.

That was enough for Dewayne. He was ready to leave, and this was the fastest way out. When he opened the first cabinet, the surprised roaches scattered for the nearest dark nook, and Dewayne took a step back.

The girl gave Dewayne a look of amused disgust at such a big man acting like a sissy when it came to roaches. She picked up a can of green beans and tossed it to him. He caught it with one hand and placed it on an uninhabited shelf.

"What's your name?" Rosella asked, hoisting the ham into her arms and opening the refrigerator, as devoid of food as the cabinets were.

"Sabrina," she said, picking up another can and tossing it to Dewayne, which he caught like a pass from a quarterback. This playful action brought Sabrina's scowl up to a smirk, a step in the right direction.

"You have a brother, right?" Rosella asked.

Sabrina nodded without suggesting that her brother might be in the next room or showing any intention of an introduction. She kept tossing cans to Dewayne, her interest maintained by him showing off the skills that had made him a star. The pitch-and-catch game Sabrina and Dewayne were playing helped make Rosella's interrogation run smoother. If Sabrina had any idea who was catching her passes, she gave no indication.

"Is he here?" Rosella arranged the ham on the lower shelf in the refrigerator before she started filling it with other perishable items.

Unexpectedly, the loud music dropped a few decibels.

"Hey, baby, ask her if she's a lawyer." The raspy voice paused to wait for Sabrina to carry out the request. She did not.

"'Cause if she ain't a lawyer or a cop, she sure is asking a lot of questions . . . questions you ain't got to answer."

Sabrina's cocked arm dropped to her side. Dewayne kept his arms in position to receive her pass. When she did not throw the canned peaches, he dropped his arms and stepped around the column that was blocking his view of the living room. All heads were lowered but one—the tattooed, dreadlocked one—and Dewayne knew he was looking at the chief of this small tribe.

"He's in there with my boyfriend and his crew," Sabrina said. She set down the can on the counter and folded her arms in front of her.

"What's your brother's name?" Rosella said.

"Lady, whatever you do, you must be getting paid by the question," the boyfriend said.

The heads of the followers bobbed as they snickered at their chief's joke.

"Hey, Bruce, come here," Sabrina said, summoning her brother from the living room.

The youngest and smallest member of the foursome got out of his seat.

"Little man, you ain't got to go nowhere."

The boyfriend stretched his legs across the filthy coffee table and rested his hands on his flat stomach, the easy posture of one who is convinced of his own power.

Bruce dawdled into the kitchen and stood in front of Dewayne, a dwarf to this giant. His voice cracked as he spoke, the sound of boy-to-man transition.

"Don't you play football?" he asked, his glum visage brightening at the prospect.

"I play a little," Dewayne said, and he leaned against the wall, keeping a fixed stare upon the boyfriend.

"You play for USC, don't you?"

"Guilty as charged," Dewayne said, and he extended his hand to the boy. "You must be Bruce. I'm Dewayne Jobe."

"I know who you are." Bruce's small hand was swallowed by Dewayne's mammoth one. Then he pointed to Rosella stuck halfway into the refrigerator. "She your ho?"

Rosella banged her head on a refrigerator shelf before she pulled out altogether and whirled around to face the boy. Bruce was sure his rude remark would gain him favor with his sister's boyfriend and his gang. There were spontaneous whoops of approval coming from the living room, which would have pleased Bruce except that Dewayne's clench of his hand suddenly became painful. Dewayne stepped around the corner into the living room—Bruce in tow, his hand in a vise grip, his efforts to break away fruitless.

Dewayne growled. The sound was so unexpected, it silenced all derisive laughter, although the kid who appeared to be Sabrina's boyfriend kept a glare of defiance on his face.

Dewayne pulled Bruce back into the kitchen. "You want your hand back?"

The strength had drained from Bruce's arm and hand, and he had given up his endeavor to escape. He nodded his head.

"Then you tell this lady, my wife and your aunt Rosella, that you are sorry."

No one had ever spoken to Bruce in this way. No one had ever confronted him about what was considered unacceptable words or behavior. His role models lay slouched over the living room furniture, boys just a few years his senior who had only provided Bruce with the knowledge and the skills to survive in their hostile, insular world.

This new model had broken into his life; a new model causing physical discomfort and finding no humor in his remark; a new model demanding different behavior, a different mind-set, and a new vocabulary that had never crossed his lips.

Bruce looked from Dewayne to his newfound aunt. "Sorry," he said. He felt the pressure consuming his hand ease, and he quickly withdrew from the giant's grasp.

As he covertly massaged his hand, it occurred to him that this giant was his uncle, but he had no idea what that should mean to him.

"Where's your mother?" Rosella asked, too upset by the combination of the squalid conditions and the treatment from her own relations to accept the apology tortured out of her nephew.

Once she thought she might be confronting her sister and her children, Rosella had kept her expectations low, but the moment Sabrina let them into the apartment, and she beheld the flesh-and-blood family resemblance, an element of hope began to work in her heart that there could be a future with these strangers.

"I told you she's sick," the girl said. A sour attitude had returned to claim her face and voice.

"I want to see her," Rosella said. The tone of her voice made it obvious that the only way to get rid of her was to grant her wish.

Sabrina gestured toward one of two closed bedroom doors with a bathroom in between. Rosella blustered past Dewayne and Bruce. Someone turned down the music so the only sound in the apartment was Rosella rapping on the bedroom door.

"Bonita. Bonita, are you in there?" Rosella said. A moan came from behind the door, and Rosella took that as a cue to enter.

Bonita lay stretched out on her filthy bed wearing nothing

but a pair of panties and a T-shirt stained with vomit and blood. Beside the bed was a milk crate with a piece of jagged plywood for a tabletop. On it were a lit candle and all the paraphernalia required for shooting heroin into one's veins.

Rosella stormed over to Bonita and began to slap her face in an attempt to make sure she was still alive. Enough disgruntled resistance came from Bonita to assure Rosella she was among the living. Though she never opened her eyes, Bonita began to thrash around, angered by this harsh treatment, until Rosella grabbed the wrist of Bonita's right arm and caressed her hand. This calmed Bonita, and Rosella stretched out her sister's arm and examined the heroin tracks on her skin, their condition ranging from the stale signs of partially healed wounds to the freshest of punctures.

"How long has she been like this?" Rosella asked, but knowing her sister had been like this for years, she clarified her question. "I mean today? She wasn't like this when I saw her earlier. What happened?" The fury in her voice got a quick response.

"She came home this afternoon, said she was gonna take a nap," Sabrina said. She and Bruce stood in the doorway with Dewayne towering above them, taking in the scene.

Dewayne could not help feeling an immediate rush of guilt at the thought that his gift of forty dollars had contributed to Bonita's current state. He watched Rosella fold Bonita's arm over her stomach and tiptoe out the door. He and the kids cleared the way for her to pass, and he followed her to the kitchen. Rosella rummaged through the detritus on the bar counter between the kitchen and the living room, found a pen, and began to write her phone number on a piece of paper. She thrust it into Sabrina's face.

"This is my cell. You call me . . . you call me if . . ." She could not finish her sentence and walked out the door.

Dewayne took one last look at his niece and nephew and followed his wife out the door. The last words he heard coming from the apartment before he was out of range were, "Girl, cook that ham." It was a command from the boyfriend.

On the way home Dewayne asked if they should go back, if they should call an ambulance, if they should get Bonita to a doctor, get her into drug rehab, do something for the kids. All Rosella could do was shake her head, pausing long enough to wipe the tears from her eyes. Dewayne gave up, laid his hand upon her shoulder, and kept it there the rest of the silent drive home.

7

Jake Hopper polished the tip of his cue stick with some chalk, blew off the excess, and then eyed the eight ball.

"Corner pocket," he said, and he bent over the table. It was a gentle shot with the cue ball just grazing the eight ball, sending it on its slow roll that won him the game. The crowd whooped their rebel yells as the losers tossed tens and twenties onto the pool table.

This game advanced Jake to the Rebel Rouser's final four, which would pit him against the owner of the Tiger Mart, a local Springdale gas station. Jesse sat in the second row of bleachers lining the wall in front of the competition table. He would play against one of the Rebel Rouser's own bartenders. The winners of those two games would battle it out for the championship.

Jake gawked at the cash strewn across the green felt. "I'd have quit coaching earlier if I'd known I could make this kind of money," he said, setting his stick on the table.

He liked looking at all the cash waiting for him to collect, like manna gathered by the children of Israel. He began to ramble around the table, picking up each bill and smoothing it out before stacking it on the table's rail.

Jake glanced over at Jesse, who had paid no attention to

Jake's victory lap. Jesse's jittery hand sloshed the booze into the air, and it splashed onto his fingers. His focus was on the two TV sports commentators recapping Sly's final triumphant game of his senior year, a coup for Sly, who had gotten his team into a prominent bowl game and positioned himself as a top contender for the Heisman Trophy and the first pick in the draft come spring.

Jake paused from amassing his money and walked over to Jesse.

"You can't be defined by one moment in your life," Jake said, but Jesse paid no attention, deaf to any words from anyone other than those coming from the television.

When the show cut to a commercial, Jesse killed off what remained in his glass.

"Go easy on that stuff," Jake said. "You've still got the bartender to go before you have to face me." He laughed, hoping to make his words not seem like a scold.

"Don't tell me what to do, Coach," Jesse said and slipped out of his seat. "I can beat anyone in this town drunk, stoned, and one arm tied behind me."

Jesse headed toward the bar for a refill, and Jake continued his solemn collection like a church usher. The Rebel Rouser scheduled the pool tournament on the weekend of the last games of the college football season for maximum customer appeal. Jake had entered the competition as a lark, never expecting to have made it to the final four.

Since his resignation, he had found a new community. Jake had become careless: leaving liquor bottles on top of his desk at school, arriving late to practice, being ill-tempered with students and colleagues alike. All were signs the people in authority could no longer ignore. The student body applauded him in the final school assembly, and the Tigers' athletic director gave him a cheap plaque for his contributions to the football team, which he threw in the Dumpster behind the school along with mounds of other trash his desk had accumulated over the years. He had decided it was time for a fresh start, putting all the past behind him, and he invested his savings into the soon-to-open Hopper's Barbecue. He would put whatever money he might win from this pool tournament into the business.

Jake's thoughts turned to the former Tiger all-star linebacker. True to his word, Jesse had annihilated his opponents, giving them no more than a couple of shots apiece after the opening break. The Rebel Rouser had grown to love Jesse. His fun-loving antics always drew a crowd—Jesse's trick shots and victory dances were hits with the locals—and it never hurt his standing to buy his fans a round of drinks from time to time. But it was discomforting for Jake to watch the former Tiger linebacker put on his show, and those nights when Jesse had drunk himself into a stupor, Jake drove the boy home and put him to bed. On those nights, Jake stayed close to sober.

When Jesse returned from the bar, fresh drink in hand, his entourage, anxious to see the master in action, followed him. At the same time, Dewayne's last game as a Trojan was about to begin. No one begrudged the pauses between shots to watch Dewayne play on the wide screen mounted above them, and when Dewayne took it into the end zone after seven plays, the boisterous reaction resulted in Jesse's missing his first shot.

The commentators were quick to bring up Miami's conquest earlier that day and the relationship between Sly and Dewayne. When they mentioned the boys were former teammates in Springdale, Mississippi, the reaction in the bar was deafening. For a second time Jesse missed his shot, but his opponent had also missed his two opening shots, so the game was still even.

Jake noticed the negative effects of the commotion on Jesse's concentration as the game progressed. When his opponent was up by two balls, Jesse called a time-out to go to the bathroom. He blamed it on the level of alcohol he had consumed. When he exited the bathroom, Jesse responded with more hyped energy, which Jake took as an attempt to psych out his competitor and get his own wandering attentiveness back in tune with the game at hand. With each deliberate step around the table, he huffed and grunted, holding his pool stick above his head like some primitive warrior. It appeared the Rebel Rouser's court jester had returned in full possession of his charms.

Jesse had just enough time to sink one shot, a dazzling combination netting two balls at once, evening the score and extracting from the crowd a vocal counter that rivaled the cheers for the hometown boy on the screen. Then someone shouted that the network was showing film clips of Dewayne playing for the Springdale Tigers. The commentators gushed that Dewayne's raw talent for catching passes and scoring touchdowns in high school was being perfected in his college career, and now the wide receiver was establishing his position as a rival for the Heisman and a contender for overall pick of the draft.

Once again, Jesse lost his audience. Each quick shot of a pass thrown from Sly to Dewayne brought eruptions, and Jake saw the frustration spread over Jesse's face, replacing the renewed buoyancy that had been there seconds before.

Like a blind Cyclops, the sports commentators had no comprehension of the power they wielded. In their enthusiasm to establish Sly and Dewayne as phoenixes rising from the ashes of defeat, the commentators showed the video clip of the Tigers' heartbreaking loss to the Devils four years ago when the Devils' running back had scored the winning touchdown. The commentator added, "Springdale anticipated the play based on the running backs' alignment, but the linebacker failed to pick up on it."

No one in the Rebel Rouser shooting gallery heard anything else after that statement. The sporadic boos that popped into the stale air could not push back the tide of humiliation. The telecast and commentary bordered on torture, and no one was more tortured than the one who had absorbed all the blame for the defeat. It seemed to Jake that Jesse began to shrink, as though Jesse's spirit had fled from his body like a ghost fleeing dawn and leaving behind a debilitated corpse. Jesse finished off the contents of his glass in loud gulps, drinking to replenish himself, drinking to quench a desperate thirst, drinking to fill the darkest hole that was his tomb.

The Rebel Rouser crowd had made a silent pact not to watch the television but to pay deliberate attention to the hometown boy who walked among them and had not forsaken Springdale for the lure of fame and glory in the world beyond. The infinite dark inside Jesse's skull shattered his ability. He scratched his next shot, something no one had ever seen him do. As though he were suffering from shell shock, Jesse rubbed the tip of his stick with more chalk and watched the bartender sink three balls in a row. When Jesse shot again, he knocked the cue ball into the pocket, another historical moment never before witnessed.

The bystanders were cowed as they watched the steady disintegration of their friend. They felt no animosity toward the bartender who was now running the table. They worshiped him for his skill of mixing the perfect drink, but even the bartender knew this harsh victory would be bitter. When lining up his last shot before moving on to the eight ball, he purposely added too much English to the cue, and ball number six bounced from rail to rail, coming to rest dead center of the table. He wanted to give Jesse one more chance, and everyone in the room, including Jesse, recognized his generosity.

But Jesse was no longer with them. His body was going through the motions. Whether or not it was intentional, no one would say, but when Jesse hit ball thirteen, it careened off a rail, glancing the eight ball and knocking it into a side pocket, ending the communal angst.

The bartender was obsequious, saying his win was the dumbest of luck, but Jesse shrugged it off with a fragile smile, saying everybody has an off night. The crowd congratulated the bartender but saved the heartiest backslaps for Jesse and consoled him with offered drinks as they broke ranks to watch a little more of the football game. Jesse unscrewed his pool stick and placed it inside the case Jake held open for him.

"I don't think I'm gonna stick around and watch you play, Coach," Jesse said, tucking his trembling hands in his jean pockets. "Hope you don't mind."

"Jesse, a man is not defined by one event in his life," Jake said.

"That's your favorite line, Coach; best to use it now on somebody else."

"Let me drive you home."

"You got a game to play."

"I never expected to get this far," Jake said. "No way can I beat Tiger Mart."

Jake placed his hand on Jesse's shoulder, but Jesse deflected it as if it was an incoming punch, and then pretended it was an accident by scratching the back of his head.

"Sorry, Coach, but I don't need your pity," Jesse said.

"It's just an offer of a ride home. No harm meant."

"No harm done." Jesse's hand had gone from alleviating a

pretend itch to rubbing the back of his neck. "You play your game. I'm good."

When the owner of the Rebel Rouser decided the crowd had ordered a sufficient number of drinks to keep them going for the next game in the competition, he called for a return to the tournament table.

"Rack 'em up," the owner shouted. "It's Tiger Mart vs. Barbecue Man in the second round of the final four."

"I got to go to the john," Jesse said and slapped Jake on the arm. "I may get to feeling better and stick around."

"I wish you would," Jake said. "I need your support."

The bar's congregants took their places around the table, and Jesse slipped through the circle toward the men's room.

When the last man left the lavatory with an encouraging word to the Rouser's favorite son, the favored son locked the restroom door, set down his case, turned on the faucet, and splashed some water on his face. After wiping the excess off the metal counter above the sink, he pulled a plastic bag from his pocket and sprinkled the powdery contents on the dry metal tray. He cut the cocaine into two thin lines, took a straw from a shirt pocket, and snorted both lines in quick succession, one through each nostril. He peered into the mirror and saw the water trickling down his skin like clear blood. He listened to the sound of his ragged breathing, like new tires on wet asphalt, and longed for the blessed trap of sleep.

8

Dewayne opened his Bible as he stood before the grave site surrounded by family and friends of Jesse Webb. Cherie had called her son to tell him of Jesse's death. The Hummer had flipped over an embankment and smashed into a tree, and the black box in the Hummer had revealed that the vehicle was traveling at an excessive rate of speed. Jesse had not been wearing his seat belt.

Cherie also told him about the rumors speculating between accident and suicide, considering the condition Jesse was in when he left the Rebel Rouser that night. All Dewayne could think about as he listened to his mother rattling off the details through her tears was how his dear friend had died the night of one of the best games of his life—three hundred twenty-seven receiving yards, four touchdowns, two school records—clenching the conference title and the honor of leading his team to a bowl game that might win them a national championship. It was a mystery how life orchestrated those two events on the same day, at the same time. Why had Death been so near at hand for Jesse and so far away from Dewayne?

And where is Jesse's spirit floating now, Dewayne wondered as he stared at the text of the Twenty-third Psalm. *In what unnameable white light does my dear friend float?*

"The Lord is my shepherd; I shall not want," he began. He read at a tedious pace, not ready to watch the internment of Jesse's body. "He maketh me to lie down in green pastures, he leadeth me beside the still waters. He restoreth my soul . . ."

Couldn't God have restored Jesse's soul . . . kept him from ending his life this way? Dewayne almost spoke his thoughts aloud.

"He leadeth me in the paths of righteousness for his name's sake. Yea, though I walk through the valley of the shadow of death . . ."

The shadow that devours, the shadow that has no conscience, the shadow that indiscriminately chose my dear friend and not Sly or me, who stands behind me, or my wife, who stands beside me, or my mother, who stands on my other side, or any of the billions of other people Death could have plucked from the living.

"I will fear no evil . . ."

But there was evil and evil was hungry to suck up another soul.

"For thou art with me; thy rod and thy staff they comfort me . . ."

Where were you in Jesse's desperate hour—and, yes, God, where was I? Where was your rod of protection, your comforting staff?

"Thou preparest a table before me in the presence of mine enemies; thou anointest my head with oil; my cup runneth over . . ."

No bountiful table for Jesse to feast upon, no healing oil for his head, no cup overflowing with joy.

"Surely goodness and mercy shall follow me all the days of my life; and I will dwell in the house of the Lord for ever."

Goodness and mercy were too slow; they followed too far behind Death, and, yes, Lord, he is in your house now, at peace, at rest, leaving us here to wonder where evil might collide with our lives.

"This is the Word of God for the people of God," he said, and a few amens echoed in response. "Jesse's stay here with us was too short; a good soul was taken home too soon."

Dewayne extolled Jesse's virtues and praised his family for giving Springdale the gift of their son. He admonished the graveside community not to forget Jesse, and to hold those dear to them a little closer, to listen to them a little longer, to see them a little clearer once they would depart this hallowed ground. But when it was time to pray, he had run out of words. He did not know how to speak to God. What was he to say to a God whom he acknowledged a faith in, a God with whom he had had such insignificant communication, a God who had presented him with the challenge of treading the dark of his own mortality?

The reverend from the Webbs' church sensed Dewayne's spiritual exertion and stepped in. Once they lowered Jesse's body into the grave and the line of family and friends had passed the opened earth, pouring handfuls of dirt onto the casket, the crowd set off in deferential silence.

Jake Hopper had come in late and sat in the back of the chapel at the funeral home for Jesse's service. He had not followed the procession to the graveside in his car. Instead, he stumbled along a garden path through the cemetery and waited at a distance, half hidden behind an obelisk, listening to Dewayne eulogize his good friend. Jake had been the last one to have a conversation with Jesse, perhaps the last one to take full notice and discern his fragile state before he got into his Hummer.

Jake had not been sober since he had defeated the Tiger Mart man at the pool tournament that had pitted him against the bartender for the championship. This was his first public appearance, and he braced himself against the obelisk and took another drink from the flask concealed inside his coat pocket. They never got to crown the Rebel Rouser's King of the Cue. The police had arrived at the bar right after the bartender had made his opening shot. Jake had seen Jesse come out of the bathroom and hurry from the bar. The demands of the game had kept him from obeying a drunk's instinct to protect a brother addict. Hadn't he tried? Hadn't he offered?

Now in the rise and fall of the soul's mercury, in the pool of its lowest red depths, he tried to drench the theory he might now be a murderer. He might be the cause of an innocent death.

A collective of sports news reporters had gathered on the main road cutting through the cemetery but had kept a respectful distance from the grave site as they waited for the end of the service to interview Sly and Dewayne. Two college football stars, each leading his team to a conference title, each headed to a major bowl game, each a contender for the Heisman Trophy and leaving for New York City for the ceremony in twenty-four hours, and each returning home for the funeral of a best friend—it was a news story that could not go untold. Dewayne insisted they go to a neutral location to hold this impromptu press conference, and he led them to the parking lot of the high school. Out of respect for Jesse, both Sly and Dewayne kept all comments about their years playing for the Tigers on a positive note, even though one intrepid reporter asked if either of them thought there might be a connection between Jesse's death and their state championship loss their senior year.

"We lost as a team," Dewayne said. "There is never one play that loses a game or one player that makes a team lose. You win or lose as a team. End of story." And the moment he heard those words come from his mouth, he felt a rush of regret. He could have provided a stronger buffer to shield the hurt feelings of his friend when Sly was raging against him after the Tigers' defeat to the Devils, but he had wimped out. His defense had been lame.

Why had he never looked Jesse in the eye when he was alive and said the words he had just spoken to an anonymous reporter?

Jake remained in his car behind the reporters and curiosity seekers in the parking lot, unable to see or hear much of what was happening, but that was not the point. He wanted only to be in proximity to Dewayne and Sly, for being near them was easing some of the pain and assuaging some of the confusion. For the moment, he did not have the reckless need to soak his fears in alcohol. By focusing on the importance of Dewayne and Sly to his life, perhaps to his survival, he would not have to drink again for that minute, that hour, that day, for who knew how long.

Jake followed them to Cherie's after the interview and then waited until nightfall before leaving the refuge of his car and walking to the front of the house, walking carefully so as not to stumble, holding his hands out from his sides to maintain an awkward balance. He stood at the end of the path leading to the front porch, placed his hand on the mailbox, and peered through the windows at the dinner preparations going on inside the house. It was like watching a play on a set that enclosed the actors. He wished that he could breach this set, that the characters would invite him onto the stage to be a player in this story, to contribute to the action, to add to the depth of each character from the wellspring of passions and desires swimming through his own heart. But he could not force his legs to inch his body forward to the light, toward the life inside the bright set. He feared they would have a moral limit as to who could enter and no invitation would be issued.

"Coach? Coach Hopper, is that you?" said the voice that

snapped him out of his dream. He stepped back, and the lucent glow of the streetlight brought recognition.

Dewayne stepped off the porch and bounded toward Jake, like a child dashing toward a favorite uncle. Sly was at his heels, and both men shook his hand and pounded his shoulders. It was the admission he had hoped for, yet dreaded.

In the light Dewayne and Sly saw a hollow-chested man whose hair was thinning on top of his bowed head; the pallid face of an alcoholic with papery skin and an expression of constant mourning. Gone was the robust confidence that had once inspired them. Dewayne asked him to come in, but he declined, citing an urgency he would not identify. He just needed to feel their touch, to hear their strong voices, to have them say his name to remind him that he was still among the living, that no one held Jesse's death against him.

He was doing fine and about to open his own barbecue restaurant, he told them. "Hopper's Barbecue," he said with excitement, almost as if he thought man had never before attempted the concept of offering barbecue to the public. Then came the request out of the blue, from the giddiness of the moment. He had not wanted to burden these Heisman nominees, but could they help their old coach with this new phase of life? Would they come to the grand opening of Hopper's Barbecue at noon tomorrow? Their enthusiastic yes surprised and pleased Jake.

Sober now from head to toe, he walked backward to his car, talking to the boys the entire way, not wanting to lose sight of them. Maybe they could wear their old Tigers' jerseys and pass the football in front of the restaurant? They would draw the crowd in, and the *Springdale Leader* would be sure to take pictures of him flanked by these future superstars. He would call in a favor at the high school and request several of the current football players who would love to be in the presence of two former

106

Tigers, and throw in some of the cheerleaders as a bonus. He would ask the police chief for an escort to the restaurant, maybe even block off the street to give the boys plenty of room for a little pitch and catch. Dewayne and Sly would just show up, sign some autographs, take a few pictures, throw a few passes, and eat the best barbecue ever made since man became a carnivore—all before getting on the plane to New York and arriving in the Big Apple in plenty of time for the award ceremony.

Jake had found himself, and he called in many favors that night. No one wanted to miss this opportunity to exploit the return of two Springdale heroes, especially on the heels of such a sad day as this one had been. Everyone agreed it would help bring the town back to life. Jake did not touch another drop the rest of that night. He did not drink again until the following morning when he turned on the television to watch the morning's sports news as he made his coffee and prepared to eat his cereal, the first bite of food he had had since he could remember.

"So which of you will win the Heisman tomorrow?" the newscaster asked.

Both Sly and Dewayne pointed to themselves before starting to laugh.

"Well, not to put the other nominees down—they are all excellent players—but all our polling numbers show the race to the trophy is between you two."

Jake chuckled, wondering where in Springdale that All Sports Network had set up this interview with Sly and Dewayne. If he had known in time, he would have tried to finagle the interview in front of Hopper's Barbecue.

It wasn't until the commentator encouraged the viewers not to change the channel—when they returned from commercial, they would play highlights of Sly's and Dewayne's college football careers—and stated that the show was live from New

York, home of the Heisman award ceremony, that Jake realized Springdale's only luminaries were now separated from him by several states. The grand opening of Hopper's Barbecue was no match for the publicity of national talk shows surrounding all things Heisman.

The reality came as a sucker punch to his empty gut. Instead of pouring milk into his cereal bowl, he unscrewed the pint bottle of whiskey he had neglected the night before and saturated the flakes in its intoxicating warmth. The phone began to ring. It rang as he ate his cereal and watched his boys exchange playful banter with the commentator. Had not the three of them had such an exchange just last night? How had they gotten to New York? The network television showed highlights from their college games, but for Jake it was a broadcast of personal humiliation for America's entertainment.

He dropped the bowl and spoon in the sink, put on his overcoat, and stepped outside. He looked into the bright blue sky. *Perfect day to travel toward a horizon . . . any horizon*, he thought. He opened his trunk and retrieved a pint of whiskey from a cardboard case. As he eased his car onto the road, a convincing proposal occurred to him: maybe this was God's way of punishing him for being a murderer.

Had he answered the ringing phone instead of going out the door, he would have heard from Cherie that All Sports Network had flown them all last night on the company plane to do a live studio interview that morning from New York, put them up in a four-star hotel, and shuttled them to the studio the next morning in a stretch limo. Hopper's Barbecue could not compete with such superstar treatment.

Jake broke the seal off the bottle with a twist of his wrist. He began to sing an old hymn, "What can wash away my sins . . . ," before he took a long pull from the fresh pint.

9

"Sly, you put on a clinic in the championship game against Tech," Robert Hickman, host of *This Week in College Football*, said. Hickman, a former college running back for Texas, was unable to contain his delight at being in the presence of the top two contenders for the Heisman Trophy.

"Sly brought Miami back from the brink," Dewayne said, grinning at his friend and slapping his large hand into Sly's open palm.

"I'll say he did," Hickman said. "With twenty-five of thirty-eight passes for four hundred thirty-two yards—"

"And no interceptions." Sly could not help himself and gave the camera a quick smile and wink.

"I was going to get to that," Hickman said. "In fact, I think you had the fewest interceptions of any quarterback in college football this season."

"What do you mean, you think?" Sly expanded his chest in mock indignation. "I thought the great Robert Hickman knew all things."

"I do. I most certainly do." Hickman pointed to the earpiece in his left ear. "And my little magic earpiece tells me that indeed I am correct about that stat."

"Yet another record for my man," Dewayne said, punching Sly's arm.

"Ah, yes, but hold your Heisman horses," Hickman said. "Because one Dewayne Jobe has conked out the college record for the number of touchdown catches, USC's record for the number of receiving yards, and the conference record for receiving yards. And when you add the jaw-dropping performance of his last game, three hundred twenty-seven yards, four touchdowns—"

"I'll tell you who's gonna get conked out," Sly said. "I'll tell you whose jaw is gonna drop, and that is my man here, when they announce my name as the winner."

Dewayne laughed and shook his head, knowing that when Hickman had laid down the gauntlet, there was no way Sly would ignore it.

"Rumor has it you were the best man at the D-man's wedding."

"I was the best man all right, and his poor wife knew it. It was the saddest day of my life . . . and hers," Sly said, hanging his head in mock sorrow and wiping a fake tear.

"Just for the record, Mr. Hickman, I had no best man at the wedding," Dewayne said, not willing to allow Sly's inane comment to obscure that special day. "If my father had been alive, he would have been my best man."

"Here's a dream scenario for you," Hickman said, steering the conversation back to the topic of sports. "On the same NFL team, I'll give you Sly at quarterback. I'll give you the D-man as wide receiver—"

"And I'll give you a championship every year," Sly said. "We would show the world who rules, plus I get the girl."

"It'll take more than a championship, a Heisman, and some fast-talking fool to take her from me," Dewayne said, and this time the punch to Sly's arm was less playful.

"My man, careful of the throwing arm." Sly rubbed the spot

of contact before he cocked his arm and pretended to throw a pass. "The Heisman Trophy arm."

"Do I detect a little tension here . . . a little rivalry thing going on?" Hickman said, goading the possibility.

"Only in your mind, Mr. Hickman," Dewayne said.

"Well, there is plenty of room for a little rivalry. All the polls say this Heisman race is as tight as a Texas tick on a bull's rump." Hickman turned from Sly and Dewayne and looked into the camera. "But like all races, they must come to an end. And so it shall be tomorrow when the winner will be announced right here on All Sports Network with yours truly hosting the event. Many thanks to my two special guests, Sly Adams, quarterback for Miami, and Dewayne Jobe, wide receiver for USC, locked in a neck-and-neck race for the Heisman Trophy. Folks, the votes have been cast, the ballots have been counted, but no matter who goes home with the trophy or how their bowl games go in a couple of weeks, these two young men have a very bright future in professional football. For *This Week in College Football* I'm Robert Hickman. Be sure and join me tomorrow on ASN for full coverage of the Heisman ceremony."

After the theme music for the show was over and the bright lights in the studio were turned off, the handshakes and autograph requests began from the All Sports Network tech crew and staff. Everyone knew that the value of one autograph would skyrocket after tomorrow's ceremony, and no staffer would let Sly or Dewayne get away without securing both signatures.

When they did escape the building, Rosella was waiting for them in the limo. She had watched the whole program from the comfort of the car's backseat.

"So how'd we do on our first appearance with the Hick Man?" Sly said, leaping into the limo and throwing his arm around Rosella's shoulders. "Were we stars?"

"In your own eyes," Rosella said, and she slipped out of Sly's loose hold and sat next to Dewayne in the seat opposite Sly.

"Oh, what coldness comes from the sister." Sly began to shake like his whole body was freezing.

After a short sightseeing drive, Dewayne and Rosella got out of the limo in Times Square and told Sly they preferred to walk back to the Hilton. They ate their New York kosher hot dog on a park bench with a steady cavalcade of pedestrians providing free entertainment. Drug dealers peddling escape; prostitutes peddling pleasure; preachers peddling paradise; bewildered, abandoned kids sliding along, their eyes glazed with loss; the confused homeless lurking in and out of corners; punks on Rollerblades flying by, oblivious to anything but speed—all passed in front of them, an exotic human stream.

"I can't stop thinking about Jesse," Dewayne said, stretching out his long legs after finishing his hot dog. "I just let him go."

"I've been thinking about my sister and her kids. I don't know which is worse, dying once or dying every day."

"Jesse and your sister . . . we can't do anything about, but maybe her kids."

"What are you saying?"

"I'm thinking out loud. I'm saying nothing. I'm saying everything. They're kids. They could have a future. Maybe we can do something."

Dewayne and Rosella ambled back to the hotel, holding on to each other in a reassuring embrace, aloof and untouched by the world around them, seeing no one but each other, hearing no sound but the soft tones of solemn whispers and longings.

In their four-star room, Dewayne and Rosella could see the world as fruitful, inviting them to taste the sweet wine offered, and in the darkness, they came together—comfortably, slowly, in the pace of confident and permanent lovers. To this room and to this bed, they brought a mind and body intact like a sturdy vessel able to withstand any destructive power. The changing shapes of the world would flummox them. The people in their lives would reveal the riddles in their souls regarding human nature—those questions that would rise to challenge their beliefs and either inspire action or hamstring the best of intentions. But one thing remained certain—a love that was fluent in any language, a love that was solid and clear as transparent iron, and they would cleave to it and to each other as if they had been asked to write the final chapter of mankind.

Dewayne got out of bed and slipped from the room, leaving his wife to stay in bed as long as sleep would keep her there. The aroma of the breakfast buffet filled his nostrils as soon as the elevator doors opened onto the mezzanine. A half-dozen chefs and servers stood at their stations ready to serve Dewayne and a handful of other early risers. When Dewayne passed the juice bar, he saw Sly and another man in the corner of the room almost concealed by a tall fern. The man finished scribbling something on a piece of paper and then stood up, stuck his pen in his suit pocket, gave Sly's hand a vigorous shake, and walked toward Dewayne. A half smirk on his face, the man dressed in a thousand-dollar suit left behind the heady scent of expensive cologne after he disappeared around the corner.

Dewayne approached Sly's table, the breakfast dishes pushed aside, leaving an open space for the papers left behind by the man. Sly did not look at his friend. He kept his concentration on the written figures and statements.

"You're up early this morning," Dewayne said.

Sly said nothing; his head remained lowered, eyes fixed in their downward focus.

"Who was the suit? He looked familiar. Was he—"

"Why don't you pile your plate with some food, my man, and sit down?"

"Was he an agent?"

"My man is getting into my business." Sly folded the papers in a neat half fold and creased the middle with a slow swipe of his thumb.

"You know we're not supposed to be talking to agents yet."

"Are we going to eat breakfast together or not?"

Sly's challenging glare into his friend's eyes was now Dewayne's focal point.

"We've still got our bowl games to play. Agents aren't even supposed to start sniffing around till after that."

"We're not always in control of our lives." Sly raised his hands in a gesture of helpless submission to life's whims.

Dewayne looked around the room, annoyed at Sly's disdain for the rules and his cocksure attitude. The check in his gut would not let him reply, and Sly took that to mean breakfast together was not in order, so he slid around the table and stuffed the papers into the inside of his coat pocket as he stood.

"My man, I got it covered." Sly laid his hand on Dewayne's shoulder. "There's only me in this world to back me up. I don't have a mama or a pretty wife looking after me."

"You've got a friend."

"I got a friend forever in you, my man, but I'm making new friends," Sly said, patting the papers inside his coat. He took Dewayne's hand and placed it on his chest where he could feel those papers. "You feel that? You're touching the promise of the moon, my man. You are touching the brightest future this boy has ever dreamed of."

114

"Just be careful."

"The Sly-man is always careful."

Sly's bright smile broke the mask of seriousness on his face.

"Now, if you'll excuse me, I've got to write my Heisman victory speech."

———————

The complaining began the moment Rosella adjusted Dewayne's tie and made him stand in front of the full-length mirror for a final inspection. Everything was too tight, and no amount of adjustments and tweaks would satisfy. The carping over the ill-fitting monkey suit continued even when they were ushered into the crowded ballroom and the cameras began their click and flash and the reporters lobbed their questions. The complaints stopped when Rosella kissed him for luck and gave his bottom one last smack before handing him over to the ushers who would guide him to the row of nominees seated before the beautiful Heisman statue.

Dewayne and Sly squeezed each other's head with macho force and counted out three gentle head butts, the ritual they performed before each high school game, the incident that morning forgotten. Dewayne then shook hands with each candidate, praising each for his success. No matter who walked out with the trophy, this moment would be a highlight in their lives and put all of them in an advantageous position when it was time for the draft.

The stage manager announced to the room they were about to go live, and he began the final countdown like a NASA scientist. Robert Hickman got a final spritzing, took a last swallow of bottled water before tossing it to an awaiting assistant, and was all smiles ready to welcome folks in TV land tuned in to watch the Heisman ceremonies as soon as the red light blinked on the camera and the theme music faded out.

Dewayne turned to look for Rosella, the very thing his mother scolded him for when he would turn around in church to look at the people behind him. He spotted her and she blew him a kiss. Sly had to nudge him to refocus his attention. When he turned back, he saw himself on the monitor stretched vertical, flying into the end zone in slow motion just as the football sailed into his hands. These displays of virtuoso performances of each contender lasted several minutes while Hickman read a brief biography. But when Hickman was to announce the winner, he was unable to finish saying the name before Sly and Dewayne leaped from their seats and pressurized each other with their arms before a national television audience. The other players stood on their feet and dutifully applauded.

"You deserve it, buddy. I'm so proud of you. You totally deserve it."

Dewayne pulled Sly from his arms and gave him a slight push toward the podium.

Sly reached out to shake Robert Hickman's hand, but eyed the trophy like he wanted to grab it and start jumping up and down.

Dewayne looked back for Rosella. It was more difficult to spot her because people were scrambling for better positions to see the newest Heisman winner. When he found her, she was dabbing her eyes with a Kleenex. When he caught her eye, it was his turn to blow her a kiss.

"When Mr. Hickman announced my name, my best friend gave me a big hug and said that I deserved this. Well, now that I've got this beautiful trophy in my hands, I kind of have to agree with you, my man. This does look good on me."

Sly took the pause for polite laughter, more forced than spontaneous.

"I'll start by thanking my teammates and the coaching staff at Miami. All props to you for giving me the opportunities I needed to make the plays. I thank my hometown of Springdale, Mississippi. The Springdale Tigers rock! And I thank my best friend, Dewayne Jobe. I felt the East Coast guys have been supporting me this whole season. They've given the team and me some great coverage and early on were holding me up for this award. Props to them all around. I knew the West Coast would go to my man here on the front row with me, and he deserves every vote he got. So my thanks especially go to the sportswriters in Middle America for swinging their votes my way. Thank you for honoring this small-town boy who always had big dreams. You have made one of his biggest dreams come true today."

Dewayne and Rosella could not get to each other fast enough. By the time the ceremony was over and Robert Hickman had signed off the air, Rosella was happy to be held in the strong arms of her husband. They were unmindful of the cameras flashing all around them, snapping their strobe light pictures as if they were some celebrity couple.

"Stop this now. You're hogging my camera time," Sly said.

He stepped in between them, giving Rosella a kiss on the cheek and slapping Dewayne's arm.

The cameras continued to click and brighten the room with their constant blaze. Rosella wanted to flee, but Dewayne scooted around Sly and locked his arm around her waist.

Sly kept pumping the air with his trophy and muttering under his breath, "This is my night."

Reporters began to ask their questions.

"You two say you are best friends, but you're both pretty competitive. Does that have any effect on your friendship?"

"There is nothing wrong with healthy competition," Sly said.

"Not at all, but it has never hurt our friendship," Dewayne said. "Remember, we grew up together. That's where the bond grew strong, and nothing will change that."

"You two looking forward to the combines and the draft?" another reporter asked.

"Bring it on," Sly said.

"Yeah, I'm looking forward to both, but I've got a bowl game coming up and that's my focus," Dewayne said. "We'll cross those bridges when we come to them."

"Dewayne, are you disappointed not to win?"

Dewayne could feel Rosella grow tense, and he just pulled her closer to him.

"It is always nice to be honored with awards and especially to receive college football's highest honor like Sly here. But my friend will go home tonight with a hard, cold bronze statue, and I will go home with a warm, loving wife. Now, you tell me who the real winner is."

This time the laughter from the crowd was authentic and unprompted, nothing polite or forced because of a lame comment, but genuine and sustained for several seconds with some reporters punctuating the laughter with applause. Before departing, Dewayne threw his arm around Sly and kissed him on the side of the head, then let him go. He and Rosella began to move toward the banquet room, giving Sly time with the press to revel in his night alone.

10

Bruce stared into the flame of the candle on the coffee table. He had closed the blinds and drawn the curtains so the tiny flame was the only light holding back the darkness in the filthy living room congested with trash, half-eaten food, and beer bottles. He had complained of stomach cramps and parlayed this into an excused absence from school.

Sabrina had gone to school. She maintained her commitment to get an education if for no other reason than to be away from the apartment. The only thing keeping her from leaving altogether, other than her love for her brother, was her boyfriend, Tyler Rogan. He provided masculine comfort, steadiness, and affection that could be brutal at times, but still made her feel needed. He was a male presence in her life who would say "I love you" at unexpected times and in such a way that made her believe he meant it. So she tolerated the chaos Tyler brought into her life, tolerated the drugs he gave her mother and sold out of the apartment for the cash it provided . . . and she tolerated the sex Tyler demanded and the occasional bruises he left when his temper got the best of him. It was the price she paid to have a family.

Bruce watched Bonita tie the rubber tubing around her arm, then lean back in an easy chair that Tyler and his crew had found in a Dumpster. Bruce's gut tightened. His mother was leaving him again. How many times had she left him before? He had lost count, and when she came back to the world, she was always on the edge of falling off at any moment. He could call out to her, but she would not hear. He could touch her, begging for attention, but she would not respond. Whenever she departed on these drug-induced journeys, she left behind a wretched, breathing corpse.

It felt like a punishment, Bonita's frequent escapes, but what had he done to deserve this? He tried hard to be good. He tried hard to deserve his mother's love. He did not want to do anything to drive her away. What had he done to make his mother leave him behind again and again?

Tyler was slow roasting the crumbs of heroin in the table-spoon over the flame of the candle. When the chunks boiled into liquid, he set the spoon on the coffee table and brushed a cockroach onto the floor that had been feasting on food particles before he smashed it with a ferocious stomp of his foot. He examined the smashed cockroach on the grimy carpet and cursed it before he kicked the small carcass under Bonita's chair.

"Hey, little cockroach," Tyler said. He snapped his fingers just inches from Bruce's hypnotized face. "Little cockroach, someday you can have a taste of this. Go bye-bye with your mama."

A wicked laugh burst from Tyler's mouth, causing Bruce to grip the sides of the easy chair.

"Hurry up, baby. Mama's ready," Bonita said.

The demand to feel the immediate ecstasy was making her anxious.

Tyler filled the syringe, and with the precision of an expert caregiver, he tapped the inside of Bonita's arm to raise a deflated vein and injected the drug.

Bruce had seen enough. He began to pace as he watched his mother descend from reality like a deflated balloon. Tyler shouted that Bruce's frantic pacing was annoying, but the adrenaline rushing through Bruce's body would not allow him to keep still. For not obeying the order, Bruce dodged a beer bottle hurled at him by a volatile Tyler, and he ducked into the kitchen just as the crew came through the door, flush with cash from the latest drug sales.

After brooding on the perennial emptiness of the open refrigerator, Bruce spied some cash on the kitchen table. He slammed the refrigerator door, stuffed the few dollars in his pocket, and then slipped out of the apartment. No one noticed him go. No one called out after him. No one cared whether he stayed or went, whether his stomach was empty or full, whether he lived or died.

Dewayne had completed his eighth and final week at the Sports-Plex in downtown Los Angeles, a premiere facility devoted to taking young college athletes who were in line for the draft and getting them into optimum shape for the combines held in Indianapolis. By going to school year-round, Dewayne had worked out with his faculty advisor a way to have only one class his final semester in order to graduate. The easy economics class that he and Rosella took together required minimal study so he could have the time to train at the SportsPlex in preparation for the combines. Even though USC had won its bowl game and Dewayne had received the MVP award for the game, he chose not to snub the combines. He was looking forward to meeting coaches and managers from the different franchises so when it was time for the draft, he would know who was talking about him and whom he would deal with during negotiations about an offer.

After winning the Heisman and leading Miami to victory in its bowl game, Sly had put himself in the elite category of those who skip the combines. Dewayne just laughed at his friend's inflated self-importance when he told Dewayne to be prepared for yet another disappointment when the sport's world heard Sly's name called as the number one draft pick.

Dewayne and Rosella agreed they would not rush into making a decision about whom they might hire as a sports agent, even though several agencies were making inquiries. Rosella proved a perceptive negotiator when she worked a deal with the SportsPlex management to cover Dewayne's training expenses. Once drafted, Dewayne would pay the costs of his training, and as a bonus to the SportsPlex for its kind treatment of him, he would be a representative for the center for one year.

This success began to build a confidence that they could handle many of the business decisions regarding Dewayne's career. They knew the value of athletes endorsing a product or a company, and the millions that come with it, but they also knew that unless they were generous to those people who had helped him along the way, no amount of wealth would be worth it.

The couple had not purchased a second car. They were trying to live off Dewayne's scholarship stipend, so Dewayne often took the bus to and from the SportsPlex. Part of their agreement with the SportsPlex was to do interviews with sports news outlets whenever requests came in, which was often.

One day Dewayne was surprised to enter the lobby from the training center and find no reporters waiting to ambush him. The receptionist stopped him as he headed out the door, however, and pointed to a little boy sitting in the corner.

"He says he's your nephew," the receptionist whispered.

Dewayne went over to the boy, who kept his eyes focused

on his shoes. He did not recognize this undersized, ragged kid at first. There was a sports magazine in the boy's lap with a picture of Dewayne on the cover. He thought this kid might have used the uncle ploy to sneak into the facility and get an autograph.

"You want me to sign that for you?" Dewayne asked, expecting to see the boy's sullen face transformed into elation.

"You really my uncle?" the boy asked. "Do I really have an aunt Rosella?"

Dewayne took a step back as he recognized the boy.

"Bruce? Is that you, Bruce? Is your name Bruce?"

"Yeah, don't wear it out," he said.

With Bruce's sullen answer, Dewayne knew immediately he was the smart-mouthed kid who lived at Bonita's apartment.

"How'd you find me? How'd you get here?"

"I can read the newspapers. I know how to catch a bus."

Dewayne looked back at the receptionist, who was busy talking on the phone.

"You hungry?"

The boy gave Dewayne a look of desperate expectancy.

"Come on."

Bruce followed him through the double doors back inside the training center. Several tables filled with food were set up on both sides of the hallway. Dewayne pointed to the tables, and Bruce attacked, stuffing handfuls of food into his mouth right off the trays like a starving animal. A couple of trainees walked by, and Dewayne explained that Bruce was his nephew. Bruce paused from gorging himself and an odd look of surprise crossed his face.

The reaction mystified Dewayne, but only for a moment as it occurred to him that Bruce was shocked to hear him admit to being his uncle. There was hope in the boy's eyes.

Dewayne watched the boy satiate his appetite until he was out of breath.

"You need to leave something for the players," Dewayne said with a half smile.

The sight of the lavish spread had deafened Bruce to Dewayne's casual joke. He was in shock from this new experience . . . the shock of a full stomach. Dewayne told him to grab some granola bars and fruit for the road.

"You got bus fare?" Dewayne asked as they walked outside the SportsPlex.

"Spent it all getting here," Bruce said.

Dewayne stretched out his hand toward Bruce before they crossed the busy intersection to get to the bus stop. For Dewayne, it was an automatic response to care and protect a child in his custody, but Bruce flinched before the giant paw.

"You hurt my hand the last time you took it," he said, with no hint of resentment for the pain and mortification Dewayne had caused him months ago.

"You're right, sorry about that," Dewayne said and returned his hand to his coat pocket.

They crossed the street to the bus stop and watched the traffic in silence until the arrival of the city bus. Dewayne paid their fare, and they took their seats in the middle of the bus.

Passengers stared at the unusual sight of this well-dressed, well-built high-rise of a man and this diminutive boy in frayed clothes who had gotten on the bus together, and sat together, but acted as though they did not know each other. Several stops passed before Dewayne could think of anything to say.

"What am I going to do with you?"

Bruce shrugged. He was as disoriented by the impulse that had brought them together as Dewayne was.

Dewayne was used to turning heads in public, but not under

these circumstances, and all he knew to do was smile and wave to travelers who kept blinking in disbelief, dying to know the story behind this unusual couple.

"Is it rough out there?" Dewayne asked, which could have meant any number of scenarios, but Bruce took the question to mean his specific situation.

"Yeah."

The discussion Dewayne and Rosella had regarding further involvement in the lives of Bonita's children had been put on hold, but now it had shown up on his doorstep, hungry, reeking of body odor, and bewildered as a refugee.

"I think we need to get you cleaned up," Dewayne said.

Bruce's forehead creased, as if weighing sides of an argument in his mind. Finally, he looked up at Dewayne and nodded.

Rosella returned from school with a load of groceries she bought on her way home. She kissed Dewayne on the cheek, thanking him for doing the laundry, but he had to explain as he pulled the clothes out of the dryer that he was not doing their laundry. These were her nephew's clothes.

While Rosella stared at him, dumbfounded by this news, he explained how Bruce had come to the SportsPlex and he had not said much about what was going on at home, but it must be bad or he would not have tracked him down.

"He's in the bedroom watching TV, waiting for his clothes."

"He's in my bedroom?" Rosella asked.

"He seems scared, and I don't know the next move," Dewayne said as he snapped out the wrinkles from Bruce's shirt and laid it on the dryer.

Immediately Rosella began to put dinner together. Dewayne put Bruce's clothes just inside the bedroom door and went to help Rosella put the groceries away. When he started to open a bag from the pharmacy, Rosella snatched it out of his hand and told him the contents were a woman's business. She marched toward the bathroom, returning a few moments later to put dinner on the table.

Through two helpings of spaghetti, Rosella drilled Bruce about the conditions at home, but he was not forthcoming with abundant detail. He admitted to the chronic scant amounts of food and little money. He admitted Tyler was a constant presence who used his street smarts for drug transactions. He admitted his mother still took drugs, but lied about the rate of recurrence. And he admitted Tyler and Sabrina were a couple.

Bruce searched the faces of his aunt and uncle for signs that these admissions had increased their anxiety. He was fearful of what they might do, afraid if they heard too many terrible things, they might not want to have anything to do with him.

By the time Rosella had filled his bowl a second time with a mound of ice cream, Bruce tried to reassure them that he could handle the situation, he could find the help his mother needed, and he could deal with Tyler. He was not asking for any help, did not need help; he just wanted to know if the two of them were for real. He never knew they existed. His mother had never spoken of Rosella, Dewayne, or his grandparents until she had pointed out their pictures in the society page of the *Los Angeles Times* covering their wedding day. From then on whenever he could steal a newspaper, he looked for articles about Dewayne. It was the first time all day he had strung two sentences together, and he talked nonstop, an unbroken monologue, trying to sound like a man capable of self-reliance.

They spent the rest of the evening shopping for clothes, an expenditure not in the Jobe budget, but one demanded by conscience. Dewayne took charge. Bruce had never made a selection of clothes in his life. From time to time Bonita would arrive home and toss him some underwear, socks, and a bag of used clothes with well-worn looseness gathered from large bins at Goodwill. The clothes Dewayne handed him came wrapped in plastic, folded, with no wear and tear. It was not an extravagant shopping spree, the clothes fit in two bags, but as they left the department store, Dewayne noticed that Bruce was walking upright for the first time that day.

All three sat in the car in front of the apartment complex, no one willing to concede the night had ended; no one willing to admit to being stumped about what the next step needed to be. Dewayne reached into his wallet and pulled out some cash.

Bruce looked at the tens and twenties coming in his direction but did not reach for them.

Dewayne snapped the money a couple of times, encouraging Bruce to remove the bills from his hand, but Bruce looked away, then grabbed his clothes bag and opened the car door.

"I don't want your money," he said and slammed the door behind him.

Rosella rolled down her window and was about to speak as Bruce stormed off toward his apartment, but when Dewayne touched her arm, the words in her throat iced over. They watched him walk through the gate into the complex, never looking back.

"Should we go in?" she asked.

"No," he said, stroking the back of her hair. "We'll see him again. I don't know when or how, but—"

"We should call the police. We should do something," Rosella said, her body trembling with rage and guilt.

"This is beyond us," Dewayne whispered. "This is . . . this is beyond me."

Rosella took an unusually long time in the bathroom after they got home. Dewayne dozed off a few times, trying to stay awake so they could talk before they went to sleep. When she finally came into the bedroom, she was smiling and holding something behind her back. He could not imagine what she might be smiling about but was happy to see her mood and countenance had improved since dropping off Bruce.

"What's going on?"

She climbed into bed beside him and showed him the four-inch white wand she had been concealing from him. In the middle of the wand, he saw the color blue.

"What's this?"

"You remember that night in New York . . . the night of the Heisman? Sly wasn't the only one to get a trophy."

"What are you talking about?"

"You're going to be a daddy. I passed the pregnancy test."

It had been a day when life had thrust itself upon him; a day that had been routine for billions of people and had seemed to start in similar fashion for him when he kissed Rosella good-bye that morning and caught the bus to the SportsPlex.

All bets were off.

His reaction to Rosella's announcement was joyous; he needed to express joy; his wife needed to hear his joy, see it in his face and eyes, and feel it in his exhilarated embrace.

But the performance belied a disquieting visceral groan. What would he do with a child? His one moment to act like a father to a despondent boy had slipped through his fingers. He had done little for the child—some food, a few clothes, almost nothing in comparison to the need. Fatherhood existed for millennia with all levels of success and failure. This could work, this mysterious role called a father, but it required him to fall humbly into God's merciful grasp, even though he questioned the evenhanded judgment of a heavenly Father who would give and take away, who would allow life to cast the one who had been sent to him that day back into a world of hurt and uncertainty.

11

The sprawling lobby of the Marriott adjacent to the RCA Dome in Indianapolis was teeming with college football players, sports agents, coaches and staff from the professional teams, and sportswriters and television reporters from all over the country.

For the league, the annual combines provided a one-stop shopping event for the coaches and general managers to measure the abilities of the incoming rookie class who would soon be eligible for the upcoming draft. For the three hundred college players talented enough to get invited to this event, it was like going to a very specialized job fair where they could show off their physical and mental skills in various designed tests and workouts in front of all the representatives of the teams, and if they performed well, they could move up their potential standing in the draft.

For someone of Dewayne's physical size and notoriety, it was impossible for him to check into the hotel, collect his combine itinerary, and go to his room unnoticed. He would have preferred to avoid the attention. He was happy to see some of the star players from teams he had played against during his college career. He shook hands with coaches and general managers but did not want to get too cozy early in the process. He was going to be assessing them as much as they were him, and there were some teams he wanted no part of their program. He kept his comments polite but terse to the media as he made his way to the elevators. One aggressive sports agent kept the elevator door from closing with one hand, made a quick sales pitch, and with the other hand, stuck his card inside Dewayne's front coat pocket.

When the elevator doors opened onto a quiet thirty-fifth floor, Dewayne pulled the sports agent's card from his coat pocket and dropped it through the slit between the carriage and the hallway floor. He smiled as he walked to his room at the thought of the agent's card spinning end over end as it floated the thirty-five floors to the lowest level of the hotel.

The light was blinking on the phone when he stepped into the room and threw his bag on the bed. He went through the list of messages, jotting down the names and numbers of those coaches who expressed a desire to set up a private meeting. He knew the next several days would tax his mental and emotional strength more than the physical demands on his body. His daily workouts at the SportsPlex would prove their worth in this setting.

After the official opening remarks in a special dining area, the hotel served a buffet dinner. He tried to eat alone, but staff members from the front offices of different teams kept sitting down beside him and asking him inane questions about his personal life: What kind of car did he drive? How long had he been married? Did he have any hobbies? What jobs—if any—did he have as a kid growing up in Springdale? Did he prefer one type of weather to another? Was he a "dog person" or a "cat person"? When he replied, "Dog person," the next question was, "What kind of dog would he be?" Dewayne reacted with a severe look of scorn, and the questioner excused himself. Dewayne did not bother with dessert and went back to his room. After calling Rosella, he told the front desk not to put calls through, messages only, and he went to bed.

"Let the slave trade begin," whispered a quarterback from one of the Big Ten teams who stood beside Dewayne. They were in the large room at the RCA Dome designed for the weight and measurement induction on the first day. It was the only portion of the combines opened to the media, and sportswriters and network television crews filled every square inch not taken up by the players and coaches.

Like cattle, players formed groups according to their positions, and designated handlers herded each group onto the stage. They weighed each young man to the half pound and measured him to the quarter inch. Within seconds, the results of each player's height and weight flashed onto a giant screen for the teams to record and the media to broadcast.

When the receivers took the stage, Dewayne was a good two inches taller than any in his group. The numbers of 6′6″/265 pounds flashed on the screen, and the coaches and staff kept their poker faces as they recorded Dewayne's numbers. No one was showing any interest in anyone.

After a series of psychological tests, a marathon of physicals began with an evaluation of the players' general skills. They did a vertical jump and a standing broad jump. Each player was required to bench-press two hundred twenty-five pounds as many times as he could. Then in their position groups, they had to do a twenty-yard shuttle drill. All of this happened before going through a workout specific to their position.

Team doctors and trainers twisted, pulled, and bent all the joints in Dewayne's body. Next he went through head-to-toe

X-rays and a dental exam. They questioned him repeatedly about any personal injuries on or off the field, and he reported that there were none. By the time the day ended, Dewayne felt as though he understood the experience of the auction block, the intrinsic worth of his physical and mental merits appraised by all those come to evaluate their future purchase. He described his humiliation that night to Rosella, but she did not have a great deal of pity since she was lying on the sofa in their apartment with a plastic bucket next to her.

Early the next day the running backs and receivers sprinted onto the Astroturf of the RCA Dome and were put through their paces with a series of running, jumping, and agility drills before the quarterbacks appeared to test them on their running routes and catching ability. There was no small talk among the players, each one mentally committed to his best performance and not wanting the slightest distraction.

An unusual quiet came over the field when Dewayne's name echoed through the sound system to prepare to run the forty-yard dash. It was the day's shortest event, but the most critical. No other statistic carried more influence for any NFL prospect; no single number had more impact on a player's draft fortunes. Dewayne's speed was legendary, but there was always a higher margin of error with on-campus workouts plus the penchant for hyperbole within the world of sports, and these coaches wanted to see for themselves under the scrutiny of electronic timing machines whether he was capable of living up to the advertising. The businesslike atmosphere of players shuffling from one station to the next ended as Dewayne approached the starting line. Scouts, players, spectators, the media, coaches, staff, and the league-sanctioned film crew snapped to attention as Dewayne crouched down in his start position.

It is impossible to understand the mystery of a time of 4.28

seconds. How many times can someone blink his eyes in 4.28 seconds? How many words can you say? How many times can you tap your foot, snap your fingers, or clap your hands in 4.28 seconds? Coaches who had clocked Dewayne with their personal stopwatches kept looking back and forth from their clocks to the timer display. Even with the millisecond of human error that factored into a handheld stopwatch, the margin still made little difference in the outcome. It was the fastest time of all the players at the Combine, and the fastest time that had ever been seen by a man his size.

In slightly over four seconds, Dewayne had become the combine media story. All Sports Network broke into its morning news programming with a live shot of the RCA Dome and replayed several times the tape of Dewayne running the forty-yard dash and the 4.28 seconds flashing on the electronic board with commentary explaining the observable fact ranging from clock malfunction to performance-enhancing drugs. How could the experts explain this phenomenon any other way? The buzz of reaction took awhile to subside, and Dewayne kept his attention on the three-cone drill that was coming up. He would not allow the commotion of his forty-yard dash to distract him.

That night in his room, he scrambled through the calls from agents, team reps, and media, deleting most of the inquiries. The last call was from Sly: "My man, who was chasing you today, or were you trying to outrun one of my passes? Love you, my brother."

Rosella was in bed, bucket at her side, when he called. "Baby, you've been all over the television today," she said, her throat raspy from dehydration. "They must have played your forty-yard dash a hundred times."

"I figured the faster I ran, the quicker this combine thing would be over and I could get back to you."

In hopes of cheering her up, he said his impressive time would change their lives in a positive way when it came time for different teams to make their offers.

In response to his suggestion that they celebrate soon with a big steak dinner, Rosella dropped the phone on the floor and put her head in the bucket.

Dewayne proved he had speed, but he had to prove he had the hands to go with it.

The next morning, the players ran a series of routes: the ten-yard-out route, a fifteen-yard curl, a corner route, and a deep route. His footwork and route running were on the money, and he caught everything thrown to him. The quarterbacks were also under the microscope, evaluated in this drill for their accuracy, so most of the passes were direct hits and even the ones that were either high or low were still well within Dewayne's wingspan.

The afternoon drills were even more taxing. All the receivers lined up between two quarterbacks. The first quarterback would be fifteen yards in front of the receiver. The second, fifteen yards behind, with five more quarterbacks stretched out across the field on each side. The receivers had to catch the ball, get rid of it, and turn around and catch the next one as they ran the width of the field for a total of twelve catches—all on the run. This drill was fast and unforgiving. If anyone dropped a pass, it was almost impossible to catch up. Dewayne's strategy was to keep his thumbs and index fingers touching, with his fingers flared in a wide circle always ready.

This worked for the first six passes. The seventh pass was low, and Dewayne had to go down to his knees to catch it. He caught the ball, but when he spun around, out of the corner of his eye he saw the next ball about to sail past him. He reached up with one hand and snatched the ball out of the air, like a baseball pitcher reacting to a line drive hit right at him. He spun back in the other direction and was from that point on ahead of the quarterbacks.

After the drills were complete, the final days were devoted to formal meetings, with coaches and general managers talking to players considered good additions to their organizations. These gatherings gave a player and the staff an early look into the chemistry factor. Everyone wanted Dewayne to explain the unexplainable: the exceptional combination of his size and speed. The query was always the same, and it began to feel like a series of ominous interrogations right out of *The Twilight Zone*—same question, different faces. He had lost count of the number of urine samples he had supplied the doctors, but the most powerful performance-enhancing drug they could find flowing through his bloodstream was Gatorade. Through it all, he never lost his cool or felt as though he was unjustly accused or harassed. His reputation was all he had, and he never forgot its importance.

On the last night of the combines, Robert Hickman snatched Dewayne on the way to dinner and requested a live interview. Dewayne had avoided giving any in-depth interviews throughout the combine process, but he thought it would be easier to do an interview with one person and quell the rumors flying through the world of sports.

Hickman led Dewayne down the tunnel and onto the on-location set constructed in the middle of the football field.

"This is Robert Hickman live from the RCA Dome with special guest Dewayne Jobe who just this week at the annual combines here in Indianapolis has fired the shot heard round the sports world.

"The combines separate the men from the supermen. It is a rite of spring and the rite of passage for top players from college football teams to go through a succession of grueling physicals and psychological tests, and if that weren't enough, to then be put through a punishing progression of specialty drills that leave a player in total exhaustion at the end of each day. When you add these activities to all the meetings with the coaches and their staff, the week goes by faster than Halley's Comet. I suspect my special guest broke the record this week for having the most meetings. Wouldn't you say, Dewayne?"

"I had my share, but so did many other players," Dewayne said.

"Modesty is not acceptable in one so young and talented." Hickman grinned before he looked back into the camera. "It's the combine's shortest event. It's the combine's most critical event. No other statistic carries more punch. No single number has more impact on the future of a prospective draftee. It's the forty-yard dash. To be the fastest at the combine each year, well, somebody has to do it, but to be the fastest and come within a millisecond of breaking a record, that's when you get people's attention. But to be the fastest at the combine, nearly breaking a human land speed record, and be six foot six and weigh two hundred and sixty-five pounds, now that's a feat that could only be performed on Mount Olympus."

The network ran the footage of Dewayne's forty-yard sprint repeatedly as Hickman continued his commentary.

"No, TV land, that was not played at fast speed. That was actual speed, and the time of four point twenty-eight seconds is documented and in the books. Raw speed . . . that's what fascinates every coach and athlete. Raw speed fascinates us all. Not every athlete can say he is fast. Speed is that one thing that's out of reach for many athletes. Speed is the one elusive

137

quality a coach can't give to an athlete. It's all in the DNA. It's all in the genetic codes. Or is it? So, my friend, look me in the eye and answer the question that has been flying around the RCA Dome like debris in a tornado. Are you taking any performance-enhancing drugs of any kind?"

"No, sir," Dewayne said.

"Simple enough answer, but would it hold up in a court of law? Some people are saying you need a lawyer."

"What I need is for people to believe me. I don't need to lawyer up. I've got nothing to hide. What you see here is God's gift to me, and all I'm trying to do is glorify him with that little bit of talent."

"Again with the modesty. Well, your little bit of talent displayed so brilliantly this week has boosted your chances to be the first overall draft pick, something your good friend, Sylvester Adams, could not keep quiet about. I caught up with him in Miami."

Footage of Sly wearing sweats and holding a football outside a training center appeared on the screen.

"I've known the D-man all my life, and that Dewayne Jobe doesn't know what a steroid looks like. He doesn't even take an aspirin. He'll tell you he's gotten this far because of God, and who am I to argue, but he backs up his talent with a great work ethic. Anyone who has played with him knows that. The talent my man has cannot be stopped by lies and rumors. He's the best."

"You heard it, folks, from this year's Heisman Trophy winner. You don't get better street credibility than that," Hickman said as the image of Sly disappeared from the screen and the camera returned to Hickman. "So, Mr. Jobe, does this drug story have legs, or could this be the end of it?"

"No team has anything to fear when it comes to drafting me.

I have submitted and I will continue to submit to a drug test anytime and anywhere. I say bring it on 'cause none of it will keep me from playing my best game every game."

"Thus endeth the statement from Dewayne Jobe as he attempts to put the kibosh on the rumors of drug use to increase his speed. And when we return, we'll see highlights from this year's combine and performances from other star college players trying to make their case for a career in the world of professional football . . . We're back after these messages."

12

He had planned his attack for days, going over varied strategies in his mind, adjusting and readjusting based on the different responses of his foe. He even drew out an assortment of scenarios on his school notebook paper, and when he felt he was ready, he took his baseball bat and rehearsed his best plan, taking swings at his phantom enemy. He thought of nothing else night and day. He had to rid his family of this evil. He had to be the hero.

Bruce squatted down behind the shrubbery inside the apartment complex not ten feet from the entrance of his apartment, slapping the bat in his hand in a steady, rhythmic beat. He knew his adversary. He knew his plan. He closed his eyes, reenacting his victory in his imagination and the glorious restoration of his family to health and prosperity. It was worth the risk. It was worth whatever pain and suffering he inflicted . . . whatever pain and suffering he himself might have to endure. His plan was the only way to end the nightmare . . . the *only* way. But there was one flaw, a flaw he never considered in all the outlines he had drawn . . . his sister.

Why was she with him tonight? She had told him she would be spending the night out with girlfriends. He had waited to execute his perfect plan when she would be absent. He had hidden his mother's secret stash of drugs—leaving her with an ample amount to keep her incapacitated long enough to carry out his mission—so she would have to call her dealer and get him to come to the apartment to replenish her supply. He had calculated the time to be late at night when darkness and surprise would be his allies. Now his sister was in the mix.

He knew Tyler would not come alone. He was never alone outside the protection of Bruce's apartment; he required the company of like-minded minions at his beck and call, ready to obey the master's every whim. In his well-rehearsed preparation, Bruce would use a single, deft swing of his bat to fell each member of Tyler's crew, destroying his support system so the two of them would face each other alone.

And that was precisely how it worked up to the point that Sabrina grabbed him from behind. He never anticipated his sister trying to stop him, working against him, aiding and abetting the enemy. There had been only two members of Tyler's crew, and an energetic blow to the stomach of one and the knee of the other rendered them useless.

Bruce took advantage of the element of surprise, pausing after each blow to be sure the strike felled its intended target and for a split-second to enjoy the cries and even the curses from the wounded enemy. Sabrina grabbing his shirt brought him back to reality—that and condescending threats to send Bruce to meet his Maker.

Bruce yelled at Sabrina to let go of his shirt, and he strained against her resistance, like a workhorse trying to pull a load too heavy for its strength.

Sabrina struggled to hold on, to stop her brother's craziness ... until Tyler jerked the bat from Bruce's hand and smacked him across the side of his head with it. She released the shirt and staggered back when she saw the squirt of blood projected into the air like a geyser. Horror now held her captive.

With each curse followed a blow to Bruce's body until Tyler grew tired or bored from the lack of response, except for the muted groans.

A few lights came on in the apartments. One annoyed inquiry about the racket echoed within the enclosure, to which Tyler responded with a vicious threat. The inquirer closed the door, and the lights went out.

Tyler threw the bat on the ground and stormed off, his wounded comrades hobbling behind him. Sabrina knew Bruce was still alive because the blood gurgled in his mouth when he took a breath. She dashed inside their apartment and tried to rouse her mother, whose system was overwhelmed by heroin. She refused to budge off the sofa.

Sabrina ran back outside and dragged her brother to the street, hoping Tyler would be there, take pity on this bloody wreckage, and drive them to a hospital, but there was no sign of him.

She screamed for help in all points of the compass, but there was no response. Her neighborhood was too accustomed to screams, too accustomed to noisy, vicious chaos, to come to her aid. Her loyalty to Tyler was supposed to make her and her family immune from danger, but instead, it had brought it to her, laid it at her feet, and expected her to take the blame.

No longer able to prop up her brother's limp body, she crumpled onto the sidewalk, sobbing. She wrapped her arms around Bruce, searching the darkness for any help that might emerge.

The call came at 2:37 a.m. Rosella heard her niece's hysterical voice on the other end of the line, giving her a jumble of information: Bruce was hurt bad, almost killed. A police officer had come by their apartment, making his rounds, and driven them to County Hospital. She was calling from the emergency room, and come fast, Bruce was bad.

It took some coaxing on Rosella's part to get Sabrina to turn in her boyfriend as they sat in the emergency room waiting for the doctors to put the finishing touches on repairing the damage to Bruce.

"I tried to protect him," Sabrina kept repeating, but it was unclear whom she was trying to protect until she had calmed down enough to tell Rosella, Dewayne, and the police officer what had happened. Her effort to keep Bruce from attacking her boyfriend had saved Tyler the pain of a blow from the bat, but had brought unholy destruction upon her brother, something she thought she could prevent if she had just kept Tyler out of Bruce's range. But Tyler had proven too formidable.

The judge's head tilted back against his chair, signaling that if he had to listen much longer, he would have to take a nap. He listened to Bonita make her final plea to keep custody of her children, but he had witnessed too much harm under her care. Her drug addiction had impaired her ability to be a mother, and to listen to her own children testify to that fact was a knife in his own heart.

From his place on the bench, he could view the plaintiff's mother constantly wipe the flow of tears from her eyes, while the father's eyes were vacant, looking away at anything other than the scene before him. He did not blame them for their conflicting reactions as they listened to the demoralizing history of a lost branch of their family that reappeared without warning to overwhelm them.

He observed Rosella's distraught face as she dug her nails into Dewayne's hand, and held onto Sabrina's arm with her other hand. Her husband had his free arm draped over her nephew's shoulder, his fingers lightly tapping the bare skin between Bruce's shirtsleeve and the cast that went from his wrist to above the elbow.

He watched Bruce, who kept his eyes focused on the images of baseball bats he had doodled onto this new cast. The healing for the rest of his wounds—the fractured skull, the busted eardrum, the concussion, the black eyes, the one broken rib, and numerous bruises—had accelerated because of his youth.

As the story unfolded, the judge acknowledged the one benefit to come from this painful mayhem. Bruce had played the role of protector and removed the evil that had leached into his family. Tyler would spend the rest of his life as a juvenile behind bars, wearing a wardrobe of orange and not given the rehabilitation opportunities to become a productive member of society until he turned eighteen.

The judge kept his poker-face expression through Bonita's impassioned arguments and promises to reform. How many times had he seen a family united in this way by one member's destructive behavior? He could not recount the number of times this type of case had appeared before his bench, and he was thankful that this time he did not have to separate the children or place them in foster care. He would see them removed from a squalid and dangerous environment and given the care and protection they had never received. He was impatient to pronounce his verdict.

He brought down his gavel with a hard snap of his wrist. The ruling was final. Bonita would go to a court-ordered rehab program, and after six months, if she proved a model citizen, showed a consistently drug-free bloodstream, and gained some level of steady employment, he might consider reuniting her with her children.

But Bonita did not make a good first impression on the judge with the new beginning he had offered. Instead of thanking his Honor for the prospect of redemption, she castigated him for separating her from her children, accusing him of practicing the evils of slavery. Then she turned on her family, condemning them all to eternal damnation.

The judge did not hesitate. The restraining order was instantaneous, and it took two bailiffs to hustle her out of the courtroom. When the sound of Bonita's curses became a faint echo, the judge stood behind his bench and dismissed the court. He looked at the family and whispered brief words of encouragement before disappearing into his chambers.

The judge had concurred with Franklin and Joella that they should take the children to their home and try to establish some level of normalcy. They would regroup after a few days and figure out where they would go from here.

Dewayne and Rosella followed her parents back to their home in the Hollywood Hills.

"They have no idea where they're going, do they?" Dewayne said.

Rosella had to smile at the culture shock that awaited her niece and nephew.

"Maybe now is the time we ought to be more intentional with those kids."

"What are you saying?" Rosella asked.

"I don't know. What am I saying? It scares me to think about it . . . us just starting out, making our own family."

Dewayne patted Rosella's belly, and she held his hand there for its soothing touch.

"Once I'm drafted, we'll get settled in that city, and maybe we can get a big house. I don't know what we'd have to do legally, but . . ."

Rosella reached over and touched her husband's lips with her fingers. The man she loved never ceased to amaze her.

"We'll talk to the kids. See what they think."

13

The only two people in the green room not talking on cell phones and BlackBerrys were Dewayne and Rosella. The conversants paced the room, wildly gesticulating, enveloping the couple in a forest of bizarre creatures and technological sound. They sat at a table for two, eating brunch from the mounds of food provided for this elite group of college football players and their agents for the first day of the draft. Rosella's appetite was beginning to return, although she ate at a snail's pace, allowing time for each bite to register whether it would dissolve into nutrition or create havoc.

Sly passed by their table as he worked his phone and poked at Dewayne or stole a piece of fruit off his plate. Once he even kissed the unsuspecting Rosella on her cheek, then dodged the swipe of her fork as he continued without pause his latest fast-talking with whatever general manager from whatever NFL team he was conversing with at the time.

Since the combines, the discussions with agents had been polite and short, but the interviews with representatives from over half the teams in the league had been long and often tedious. Dewayne wanted Rosella present at each interview, which had been difficult to schedule, what with their final semester at school, her job, her time helping her parents with

Sabrina and Bruce, and her recurring nausea. Most interviews took place in Los Angeles, but a few were flyaways and Dewayne had to go without her.

All morning leading up to the live broadcast of the draft from Radio City Music Hall, All Sports Network featured interviews and highlights of the leading contenders of those who would be chosen by a team in the first round. Of those players, the network had invited the top ten prospects to attend the draft live. Dewayne and Rosella had considered all the information and knowledge gained from the multiple team interviews, and discussed the situation with Franklin, Joella, Cherie—and even Sabrina and Bruce, who said to take the team that would pay the most.

That issue was the most disturbing to Dewayne. How would he react to the imminent offer of millions of dollars? How would it change him? He called Cherie and asked his mother's advice.

"I'd apply it to my debts as far as it would go," she said with a chuckle, and then told him the same thing she said the day she put him on the bus for Los Angeles four years ago. She trusted his judgment, and she'd pray for him. "If you didn't have character before money comes to you, then you won't be able to buy character no matter how much you get."

He had no idea where he would fall in the order of the draft, he had no idea what he might become the instant he became a wealthy man, he had no idea how much his life might change, but he and Rosella had finally placed the matter in God's hands and were at peace.

Next to the oversized clock on the wall was a digital time clock, ticking off the minutes like a rocket countdown until the draft began. Dewayne checked his watch against the official time. It would not be long. Each team had set up a war room back at its facilities in each city with a representative at Radio City who would hand the name of the player to the commissioner to announce on national television when the two parties reached an agreement.

Once the clock started, each team would have fifteen minutes to announce its choice. During the critical opening round, every team would contact its first choice to avoid an embarrassing and costly mistake, should that player object to playing for that franchise.

At their island table for two, Dewayne and Rosella had remained aloof from all the preshow phone activity as players and teams tested each other to determine the level of commitment. It all boiled down to the financial: How much would a team invest in a player? How much would it take for a player to become a member of an organization?

What Dewayne wanted to hear was the passion in the coach's voice more than any astronomical monetary lure.

"So it won't come as a shock, Mr. First Pick . . . that would be me, of course . . . will be asking for a forty-million-dollar five-year deal with a twenty-million-dollar signing bonus," Sly said, making one of his sorties by their table between phone calls.

"Your deal . . . chump change, my man," Dewayne said while buttering his toast.

Sly shook his head, disbelief written across his face. "Maybe you are on drugs after all."

"It's all about the endorsements. They can last longer than your football career, and the best thing about them—they are injury free." Dewayne took a bite of his toast.

Sly's BlackBerry started to vibrate, and he backed away from the table before he answered the call.

The Houston Stars had been a championship favorite two years ago, until the salary cap purge killed them. The first of this two-year rebuilding effort had put them near the bottom; this second year the bottom was where they were. When Dewayne's cell phone rang, he looked up at the official clock and saw that the blinking digital lights were at zero. The draft had begun, and he was speaking to George Gyra, the head coach of the Stars.

"Dewayne, we're on the clock, and we'd like to name you as our first pick."

Dewayne glimpsed "Mr. First Pick" and could not help the grin. He then reached over and took Rosella's hand. Her strength was vital.

"Coach Gyra, I'm honored that you would name me the first pick of the draft for this year. I'd love to play for you, sir, and the Houston Stars. When we spoke a month ago, you impressed me with your vision for the team and your passion."

"I want to win, Dewayne. Don't ever doubt that. I want the championship, and with your help we can build a winning team. You're a difference maker, and I intend to give you every opportunity to get into the end zone. But more important, I want you and Rosella and your future child to feel as if you are being welcomed by family. We want you in Houston."

Dewayne had not anticipated such an impassioned speech, but it was enough.

"You want to live in Houston, baby?" he asked, squeezing Rosella's hand. She responded with a kiss on his hand and a beaming countenance.

"Coach Gyra, by the official clock here in the green room, we still have twelve minutes left and I don't want to waste your time, so let's talk the terms of the contract."

"I don't normally handle that, Dewayne, and we've got plenty of time for—"

"Sir, I want you to sleep well tonight. I know you're in the war room with the staff and the GM."

"We're all here."

"Put me on speakerphone, please. Let me speak with Mr. Thomas."

Rosella removed the dirty breakfast dishes as Dewayne pulled some papers out of his coat pocket and spread them on the table. He stole a look over at Sly and saw him in a heated debate with his agent. Through the phone, Dewayne could hear the Stars' war room becoming quieter by the second.

"Dewayne, it's Sam Thomas," the general manager said. He waved his arm above his head to settle the last of the noise. "We don't need to talk contract now, do we? That could take months, and we've got less than twelve minutes."

"That's why I'm going to make it easy. What was last year's number one contract worth?"

A staff member had the figures in front of him and handed the numbers to Sam.

"It was a six-year deal," Thomas said. "Twenty million salary, signing bonus . . . twenty million, and with incentives it tops out just over fifty million."

"Every team takes a chance on a player, and I'm honored you're taking a chance by making me the first pick." Dewayne's voice came across the speakerphone loud and clear. "So let's take it slow. Instead of six years, let's make it three. Instead of fifty million in salary, let's make it ten. You pay two point five million as a signing bonus and two point five for the next three years. If you want to extend it, put a clause in there at your option that after three years we can repeat the same numbers. This should free up salary cap money to keep most of your older, more experienced players, bring in some of the other new ones you want, and start building the winning team everyone wants."

No one had moved while Dewayne laid out his terms. Only

the GM's assistant had the presence of mind to jot down the numbers. Everyone else had turned from the speakerphone to gape at Sam. The room was silent.

"Mr. Thomas?"

"We're here. We're here. We're just a little confused. This is unusual. Don't you have an agent?"

"My wife and I don't feel that's necessary at this point."

To be sure Sam Thomas heard the correct figures, he repeated the numbers Dewayne had quoted him, and then looked at Gyra and the other staff members for any reason not to accept this deal. There was no dissent, only bewildered expressions.

"Dewayne, I believe we are all in agreement on the principal terms," Thomas said. "But it will still take some time to get the contract ready and have you and your lawyers look it over before it's signed."

"Just write the contract based on the wording your first pick signed last year," Dewayne said. "Change the numbers and the name, and we're good to go."

"We can do that." Thomas began snapping his fingers and pointing to the lawyers to get to work.

"Sir, if it's all right with you, I'd like to walk into the studio, shake hands with the commissioner, and hold up a Stars jersey as soon as your rep gives him the word."

"He is about to get the word even as we speak."

Sam Thomas and Coach Gyra looked at each other, stunned by this good fortune. It was all they could do to restrain themselves from cheering like wild fans.

Dewayne directed Rosella's attention to a monitor. The camera had zeroed in on the Stars' envoy seated at his desk, talking on the phone, and writing on his notepad.

Dewayne covered the mouthpiece of his phone and whispered, "That's my name he's writing."

"It's done then?" Rosella asked, and Dewayne nodded his head. He could not help but enjoy causing such consternation back in Houston, but it was all for a good cause. He and Rosella had planned this for some time. It was a concept that would rumble through the sports world like constant aftershocks for who knew how long. The best way to effect change was not necessarily to start small.

"Mr. Thomas, I'd like to do something a bit unusual," Dewayne said.

"More unusual than the deal we've just struck?"

"Yes, sir. I'd like your permission to announce our deal on national television."

A period of silence followed. Rosella and Dewayne watched as the Stars' delegate stepped away from his desk and made his way toward the podium where the commissioner waited to receive him.

"This is a first." The general manager sounded as if he was talking more to himself than to Dewayne.

"So's my deal," Dewayne said. "I'm the first draft pick. I'd like to shake things up, maybe set a precedent. I'm part of a team, and I want people to hear that message."

"How soon can you get to Kennedy airport?"

"We need to pack and check out of our hotel. About three hours tops."

On screen, the commissioner shook hands with the Stars' delegate and turned the podium over to him.

The hustle and flow in the green room stopped. A pause came in the frantic deliberations. Everyone pressed in closer to the monitors, all eyes watching, all ears tuned, except Sly. He was looking around the room to see who still might be talking. His eyes widened when he saw his best friend with his cell phone to his ear.

"We will have the company jet pick you up and fly you and your wife back to Houston for a press conference and signing all before the six o'clock news. Keep your phone handy. I'll have someone on this end get back with you to give you the flight details and what private hangar we arrange for you to meet our plane."

Dewayne and Rosella rose from the table and began to walk hand in hand out of the green room. Sly caught up with them at the exit just as the commissioner announced that Dewayne Jobe was the number one draft pick. Voices in the green room erupted. Dewayne had his cell phone cocked to his ear as they moved past Sly.

"Cat got your tongue, baby?" Rosella said, and she patted Sly's cheek as they breezed out the door and into the backstage area of the Music Hall.

"Make them pay, my man," Sly said, shouting above the noise in the green room. "Make them pay."

Dewayne paused beside his friend and swung his cell phone behind his back. "It's not about making them pay, it's about getting paid. It's a process, baby, and what I'm about to do is going to make me the richest man in pro football. Watch and learn."

Dewayne slapped Sly's shoulder and proceeded out of the green room.

Rosella stopped at the edge of the stage and stood beside the first row of stage seating for VIPs. Dewayne was ushered down the aisle between the thirty-two desks, one for each team, toward the podium, his cell phone still plugged into his ear.

"I'll have your contract ready when you arrive in Houston,"

Sam Thomas said. "Make the announcement and then get to the airport."

Dewayne disconnected the phone and slipped it into his suit coat pocket.

Sly knew something was up when his agent took his BlackBerry away from his ear long enough to slap him on the back and told him to shake it off and be glad he wasn't playing for last year's worst team in the league. Sly clicked off his phone, forgetting there was an NFL coach on the other end, and watched Dewayne hold up his Stars jersey with the number 1 written on the back and front. His friend was going blind from the white light of all the cameras flashing in his face, and he felt the envy in his gut for not receiving this honor, even if it was last year's worst team. He wished he were holding up the jersey, the first to shake hands with the commissioner, the first to go blind from the lights of the cameras. He needed to be happy for his best friend. In time, he would get over the snub.

But the next newsflash made the sting to his feelings irrelevant.

What made Sly's blood turn cold, what muted every cell phone and BlackBerry conversation in the green room, what brought the world of professional football to a standstill, was Dewayne's announcement.

"I'll be—" were the only words heard in the green room before the entire place detonated.

The flight down to Houston on the Gulfstream G5 was smooth, and for Dewayne and Rosella, it was not long enough to enjoy the luxurious comfort and the pampered attention from the two flight attendants who indulged their every whim. Sam Thomas and Coach Gyra along with several of the Stars staff were there to meet the couple when the limo whisked them into the private entrance of the stadium past the gathering press corps and diehard fans who wanted their first glimpse of the man who had stirred up so much excitement. The public relations office thought the stadium was the perfect backdrop to parade the new star before the press and the city of Houston. The draft in New York had just closed, so Thomas and Gyra gave Dewayne the nickel tour of the locker room and workout center while Rosella looked over the contract before they all sat down to go over the simple terms of the agreement. Thomas commented on how exceptional it was for Dewayne's wife to be so involved in the business side of things, and not some agent.

"She's an exceptional woman with an exceptional mind," Dewayne said.

When they toured the locker room, a few veterans of the team about to leave for the day got the surprise of their lives with this unexpected visit. Gyra introduced the vets to their new teammate, and Gyra and Thomas passed Dewayne off to Harrison Barrow, a three-hundred-pound offensive tackle. Harrison gave Dewayne a tour through the maze of state-of-the-art rooms, from a small medical center to a relaxation room equipped with a kitchen and minibar, oversized leather chairs and sofas, and a plasma television covering most of one entire wall. Before Harrison gave Dewayne back to Gyra, he stopped him in the relaxation room.

"Been in the league a long time. Never seen anything like what you did," Harrison said. "They're calling this the deal heard round the world."

Harrison placed his meaty hand on Dewayne's shoulder.

"Me and some of the old-timers were talking. We probably

would have been casualties of the salary cap this year, but thanks to your deal, we might get to stay in Houston."

Dewayne was hoping for this kind of result, and he might have made his first friend out of the deal.

"This approach makes the most sense to me," Dewayne said.

"Anything you need you let me know," Harrison said, patting Dewayne's shoulder a couple of times. "You'd better go. Sam gets grumpy when he's off schedule."

Harrison pointed him in the direction back to the main locker room.

"Hey, Jobe. You gonna finish school?"

"I wouldn't want to get on the bad side of my mama now, would I?" Dewayne said as he went around the corner.

Sam Thomas took the first few minutes of the press conference to extol Dewayne for his athleticism and his character, and he gave the general outline of Dewayne's deal, just signed . . . only waiting for the ink to dry before being given his signing bonus check and playbook and put on the plane to Los Angeles. Thomas ended his comments by saying in all his twenty-seven years in the league, he thought he had seen it all until today.

When Dewayne took over from Thomas, no reporter had the standard questions about his size, his college history, his alleged use of steroids, and his loss of the Heisman. The *why* of today's decision trumped those questions.

"It's simple," he said. "When it comes to the salary cap every year, you see great players who've paid their dues to a team and the league being forced to renegotiate smaller contracts just to stay employed and help their team. I'm not a proven commodity. Those guys are. For a team to be successful, we need their experience and dedication. I look up to them. I'm just doing my part now because I plan to be around for a long time and be part of a winning team."

Rosella and Dewayne stared at the check for $2.5 million propped against the binder of the Stars' playbook sitting on the tray table in front of them. The Gulfstream would have had to be flying at full throttle to have kept up with their speeding hearts.

"Ten percent goes to God," Rosella said.

"No argument," Dewayne said.

Dewayne reached out and ran his finger over the embossed bumps along the cut check that outlined the total, as though he was reading Braille. "I want to pay off Mama's mortgage."

"No argument."

Rosella took her turn swiping the raised sum with her finger. "I'll pay off the SportsPlex, and then maybe I should buy a car."

"Good. I'm getting tired of driving you everywhere."

They both started to giggle.

"You should agent my endorsement deals. Keep it in the family," Dewayne said.

"How much you pay me?"

Dewayne's bright face went pensive as though descending deep into thought. "How about minimum wage and all the lovin' you can handle?" he said, his face as straight as a union negotiator's.

"I've seen what happens when I have all the lovin' I can handle." She patted her belly. "I think I'll just take the money."

Their laughter vaulted above the roar of the Gulfstream's engines.

Four

Within forty-eight hours of their return from Houston, Rosella hired a lawyer to advise her on the first endorsement deals offered Dewayne. This was no Monopoly game or college assignment. Jobe Enterprises, Inc., was established with Rosella as president so any and all who requested Dewayne's commercial talent would deal with a professional company. In everything Dewayne did he wanted to establish a reliable reputation in this nascent stage of his career, and he did not mind manipulating the commercial world of advertising to make up for what was universally considered a salary deficit when it came to his football contract. His gravy train had left the station and was building a full head of steam.

Dewayne settled his account with the SportsPlex the moment the Stars' check cleared the bank. On the same day, he paid the organization its fees and each personal trainer a thousand-dollar bonus and shot his first photo session for SportsPlex print materials, which would recruit prospective college athletes destined for the NFL, touting the excellent facilities and personal attention. For a business barely in operation, the success was marvelous.

Cherie's second visit to Los Angeles was for another celebration. She sat between Sabrina and Bruce with Joella and

Franklin behind them in the bleacher section for the families of all the graduates. When the names of Rosella and Dewayne Jobe were announced one after the other, Cherie ignored any embarrassment she might cause by her jubilant display of shouting, waving flags from USC and the Houston Stars, and hopping in the stands like her shoes had hot coals in them.

Bruce had embraced every aspect of his new life. Sabrina rebuffed every kindness. It had been an odd and painful adjustment for Franklin and Joella since the kids had moved in with them. To begin with, they did not know each other. Sabrina reminded her grandparents of Bonita. They felt her rejection from the beginning, as though Sabrina had picked up where Bonita left off. Sabrina seemed to carry the wounded memories of her mother's rages against her family; her mother had spoken in the vilest of terms about her upbringing and how her parents treated her and never understood her, and how, by God, she was never going to raise her kids that way. But Sabrina also held the tender but hazy memories of a grandmother who made rare visits to street corners to deposit sacks of food, clothing, and cash for Sabrina, her brother, and her mother. It was like a visit from a fairy godmother who drove up in a fine carriage, delivered her gifts, and then disappeared until the next surprise visit.

Her rusted parenting skills in need of retooling, Joella tried to stay out of Sabrina's way. Much like the days when she left a cache of goods on the street corner, Joella would leave purchases and gifts with personal notes in Sabrina's room or on the table in the foyer. It was as if Joella was trying to coax a wild animal to trust her with enticing treats, but Sabrina's hardened exterior was tough to crack.

Bruce was polite and ate the scheduled meals with them while Sabrina usually ate alone in her room or outside. He loved his own room, although the technical gadgets that came with it beset him. Exposure to such things had been limited, and his skills at activating a computer, a TiVo, and an iPod were untried. When Franklin took the time to show him how to operate the equipment, it was as if Bruce had entered a new world. Within a short time, he was a master engineer, even showing Franklin tricks with remotes he never knew existed. These shared times created a male bond sorely needed in their lives. Franklin needed a way to connect with the lost life of his daughter, and Bruce was the way to get in. Bruce needed male relationships free of danger that allowed him the opportunity to find out what it might be like to be an innocent little boy.

For Sabrina and Bruce, having Cherie in the Caldwell house for the days around graduation added an extra dimension of stability. Each night she and Joella joined forces in the kitchen, and the infectious mirth and contentment shared between the two as they went about preparing food were like the main attraction on the entertainment bill. Bruce would sit on a bar stool and watch them organize and assemble each dish, listen to their stories of exotic travels or the simplicity of small town life, and accept their knowledge and counsel when they were dispensed as if he were hearing words from great sages.

Sabrina was a harder nut to crack even by this charming, female duo. She usually shut herself in her room when she came home from school each day, but gradually she ventured into the kitchen for the last half of dinner preparations. When Joella asked if she would be willing to set the dinner table, Sabrina inquired about where she kept her dishes. Joella offered a muted prayer of thanks for this fissure in Sabrina's durable exterior.

So this was their introduction to normalcy. This was their view of how a family could function without chaos, uncertainty, bloodshed, and violence. This was what a full stomach felt like. This was what love had to offer. The first great question Bruce and Sabrina had to ask themselves was, how had their mother walked away from all this?

Dewayne and Rosella made every effort to be a part of their lives, and they decided a new start for everyone in Houston was the best thing. When asked if they were ready to take on the parental responsibility of a seventeen- and thirteen-year-old when both were in their early twenties, Dewayne and Rosella said it felt more like big brother and big sister stepping in. Rosella added that it would be good practice for when their own kids became teenagers. Franklin and Joella would make frequent visits for Stars home games, but would remain in Los Angeles to stay involved in Bonita's progress. Perhaps if everything went well, they could all have Christmas together.

At the prospect of a real Christmas, even Sabrina brightened. Both children had had very little experience with the holiday, but since their mother's trial, their new life already felt like Christmas.

Departures were tearful. Cherie first, and she did not mind hugging a little boy because it might embarrass him or a teenage girl because she exuded a "don't touch me" attitude. None of that mattered. They were near blood and would be treated as such, and having these children a part of their lives was God's will, she told her son as he drove her to the airport in his new vehicle—a Denali loaded with the bells and whistles and a bench front seat to accommodate his size and growing family.

The departure for Houston brought emotional trauma for mother and daughter due to the affecting upheavals of pregnancy and because Joella was now losing the one daughter she had been close to her whole life.

Sabrina volunteered a squeeze to Franklin and then to Jo-ella, but did not linger with either of them. Bruce gave Franklin a manly handshake, but could not pull that off with his grandmother. She trapped him, soaking his head with another round of tears, until he could break free and take shotgun in Dewayne's Denali.

The foursome took only what the two cars would hold. They would buy new furniture for a new house. It would be a fresh start. Rosella had already established business and personal bank accounts in Houston and made an appointment with a Realtor. As soon as her feet hit the ground in Houston, she would start seeing the houses they had selected from the virtual tours they had taken on the computer. They packed the trunks with the goods Bruce and Sabrina received in the short time of living with their grandparents. They had not brought so much as a toothbrush from their former dwelling; they sought to create all things new for these dear children. What trepidation they felt as they pulled out of the Caldwell driveway, heading east, was minimal compared to the expectancy they had for their future.

They built some extra time into their journey before they had to get to Houston for Dewayne to start camp. Dewayne wanted his family to see places like the Grand Canyon and to go to an Indian reservation. This adventure began to build a unit, began to create a team and establish lines of communication and trust. Sabrina's face began to carry more smiles than scowls; her demeanor became more compliant and calm. Everything excited Bruce. The world kept getting larger and larger so that his thirteen years of inner-city life began to feel like a dream, its hold on him beginning to fray.

When the city of Houston came into sight, Dewayne took the interstate that went by the stadium so the kids could see where they would be spending their Sunday afternoons for the Stars home games.

They rented a couple of suites at a hotel near the Sports Park where the Stars Training Center was located, and each day while Dewayne was at minicamp, Rosella and the kids looked at potential houses, checked out school districts, visited churches, and familiarized themselves with Houston's metropolis.

Since the trial, all references to Bonita diminished. Early on, Sabrina had sworn she would leave and go find her mother, but those threats soon ended. Although Bruce never mentioned her, it was obvious to those who observed him when he was pensive, staring off into space, that he was thinking about Bonita.

Without them knowing it, Rosella made a copy of a picture of their mother when she was a teenager still living at home and wearing her all-girls' prep school wardrobe, her face pinched in a goofy expression, her hands scrunched up on the sides of her head like deformed ears, a scarce moment of glee Joella had caught on film, and she presented it to them in a cherry wood frame as they stood in the kitchen of the empty six-bedroom house they had decided to call home.

With each house they had toured, Rosella realized the kids were thinking perhaps Bonita would be coming to live with them and they would need a room for her. Rosella did not want to spoil any illusion they might have, and she played along with the fantasy.

To keep faith with Bruce and Sabrina and to strengthen their growing bond, Rosella and Dewayne encouraged Sabrina and Bruce to think well of their mother, imagine her as that young, full-of-crazy-life teenager in their picture, pray for her, and start writing letters of encouragement to her at the rehab center in Los Angeles. In time, they would all know what to do.

The money Dewayne had already made from his endorsement deals financed the purchase of the house. The private and business accounts with a prominent Houston bank would enable Rosella and Dewayne to keep track of all their funds and move portions around for investment purposes. After purchasing the house, the next expenditures went toward furnishings for fifty-seven hundred square feet and computers, supplies, a communication system, and accessories for the offices of Jobe Enterprises, Inc., set up in an expansive room just off the kitchen.

Rosella offered summer jobs to both kids. The thought of making money was beyond their comprehension. Sabrina would be Rosella's assistant, gradually taking more responsibility as she learned the business. Since Bruce was becoming quite the computer wizard, Rosella put him in charge of designing a program to keep Dewayne abreast of all the football statistics he would want and updating his weekly itinerary. Dewayne thought at first that it might be stretching the kids' abilities, but Rosella countered with, "These kids are bright and have never been challenged. If you always give them something easy to do, they'll never learn to trust themselves to reach for something difficult." He trusted her judgment and knew she would be a hands-on manager, and he was curious to see if her experiment with giving Bruce and Sabrina so much responsibility would work. Besides, she wanted her house and the business to be up and running smoothly by the time the baby arrived.

Dewayne had a short window of time before training camp, and he wanted to take the family to Springdale to see Cherie and show the kids where he grew up. He would be shooting a credit card commercial in New York with Sly two days before training camp and it would be the last opportunity for them to travel as a family before the start of school and the arrival of the baby.

―――――――

Cherie acted as silly about Bruce and Sabrina as if they were royalty but without all the hands-off formality. It was as if she was a kid herself—always in grandmotherly physical contact with both of them, a pinched cheek, ruffled hair, a gentle pat, or a vigorous hug—and Dewayne was surprised not only by her behavior but also by the sting to his heart.

"You never treated me this way when I was a kid," Dewayne said after he had witnessed more doting than he could stand—a "yes" to every request, never a "no" to anything the kids wanted or wanted to do. "You're gonna spoil them."

"Stop acting like an old coot," Cherie said, throwing an elbow into his ribs for emphasis. Then she added for everyone to hear, "That's because you were more trouble than these kids ever thought about being."

Dewayne shook his head in dismay at being the victim of Cherie's exaggeration of how life was growing up under the maternal rule of Cherie Jobe, just to impress Bruce and Sabrina.

Even though it was all for fun, deep down the kids loved how someone was standing up for them, believing in them, honoring them, stating to the world they had value. This collective effort by the whole family to allow Sabrina and Bruce the opportunity to start over—not on a clean slate, but on a brand-new one—was creating a new belief system in their hearts. When Cherie talked them through her house, pointing out the special objects—Dewayne's trophies, the picture of her husband, the hand-painted and autographed apron hanging in a place of honor in the kitchen unsoiled because of lack of use, endowing each with a mystical power by its supporting stories and her enchantment as the teller of the tale—it was as though she was offering Bruce and Sabrina a brand-new history. She was giving them a picture of life as it could or should be and not how it had been.

Except for the trip from Los Angeles, Bruce and Sabrina had little exposure to the outside world beyond the sprawl of city dwelling. Experiencing rural, small-town life was like stepping into a foreign country. The morning devoted to sightseeing in Springdale did not take long. The highlight of the tour was the walk onto the Tigers' football field and Dewayne and Rosella's reenactment of his proposal.

While Rosella, Cherie, and the kids ate vanilla ice-cream cones dipped in chocolate at the Dairy Freeze on the town square, Dewayne signed autographs and chatted with local residents about this new phase in his life. Winston Garfield, a bow-tied, buttoned-downed, first-class small-town editor and reporter for the *Springdale Leader*, spotted Dewayne as he came out of the paper's offices. Winston had been covering Dewayne since his first days as a Tiger, through his college career, and now to his current status as first-round draft pick for the Houston Stars. Dewayne always appreciated his support—Cherie was faithful to send her son Winston's articles while he was away.

Dewayne talked with Winston like the old friends they were. He had not really sat for an interview since signing with the Stars, and Dewayne gave Winston a sports story worthy of a journalism scoop. Dewayne had to purchase another round of ice-cream cones before the interview was over.

Rosella drove them around the town square, and when Dewayne saw the bank where Cherie had her accounts, he asked her to stop. He said he needed to cash a traveler's check for the trip home tomorrow, and he instructed Rosella to circle the square while he did this quick bit of business. It would have been a waste of time to talk to Cherie about the other reason for the stop. Within ten minutes, Dewayne paid the balance of his mother's mortgage and was back in the car. Cherie was none the wiser, but did comment on how long it had taken to cash a traveler's check. Dewayne covered his subterfuge by commenting on how busy the tellers were for this time of day. He knew soon enough the truth would be discovered when the bank sent her the "paid in full" notice, and he would receive the scolding phone call. Houston would be a much safer distance to handle Cherie's brief but grateful anger.

"Don't cook tonight, Mama," Dewayne said as they pulled in front of Cherie's house. "I want to see Coach Hopper, and I'll buy us some barbecue for dinner tonight."

A little bell rang when Dewayne opened the door into Hopper's Barbecue. The store was empty. Dewayne looked over the counter in the back but saw no one. He stepped back outside, ringing the bell once again, and looked at the hand-painted sign to make sure he had gone into the right place. The wire holding one side of the sign had rusted out, and it tilted to one side. He glanced up and down the street . . . few cars, fewer pedestrians . . . and he stepped back inside. Once more, the bell rang.

"Coming! I'm coming, for Pete's sake," a voice grumbled.

It was almost a minute before Jake stumbled out of what looked to be an office off the work area behind the counter. He was trying to tie the strings of his grimy apron behind his back. There was a shared moment of wonder when the two men looked at each other.

Dewayne couldn't believe that this dissipated, droop-eyed man was the same one who had shaped his talent in those critical formative years of high school and had treated him with the kindness of a loving father. As Dewayne's eyes swept over the dingy interior—the place needed a good scrub—Jake quit trying to tie the apron strings and let them dangle.

"How's business?" Dewayne asked, and he regretted this question the second he said it. Why couldn't he have just said hello?

"Ain't it obvious?" Jake spoke much louder than was necessary as he threw his arms wide open, taking in the expanse of emptiness. Immediately, he too regretted his strident response. Why couldn't he have just said hello? Why couldn't either of them act as if this unexpected reunion was a pleasant surprise?

Dewayne looked tentative about moving closer, but after an uncomfortable pause, he stepped forward and extended his long arm over the counter.

"Can't shake your hand. I just washed up," Jake said, nervously rubbing his hands across the smudged apron.

"I understand." Dewayne snapped back his hand like a cop directing oncoming traffic.

"Wouldn't want you reporting me to the health department now." Jake tried his best to make light of the rebuff by holding up his hands to prove their cleanliness.

"We're in for a quick trip to see Mama, and I wanted to see you and get dinner for everyone tonight. Just wanted to see how you're doing."

"That's good. That's good. I'm good." Jake struggled with his emotions. There was no sense in telling him the truth, no sense in opening old wounds, was there? "So what's your pleasure?"

When Dewayne placed his order, Jake stood there as if he had not heard it correctly. Dewayne explained the increase in the size of his family and said that it would be good to have leftovers for the trip home tomorrow.

Jake seemed disoriented by Dewayne's order, and he looked about the work area as if it were unfamiliar territory. Finally, he spotted a side of meat in the stainless steel meat slicer and moved toward it as if deciding it was the best place to start work. Jake slipped on a pair of plastic gloves and went to work.

The two men did not speak throughout the process of preparing the order. Dewayne could see the progress of Jake's life since the last time he had seen him. Jake had kept up with Dewayne's success through the media. So what was there to talk about?

When Jake had sacked up everything, he laid the food on the counter and shuffled over to the register.

"That's, ah . . ." Jake paused and rubbed his moist forehead with a plastic-gloved hand as though scratching an intense itch. He sighed, redoubled his efforts to focus on the key pad, and then punched in some numbers. "That's thirty-seven dollars and forty-five cents."

Dewayne pulled out a hundred-dollar bill and apologized for not having a smaller denomination.

"That can happen. That can happen . . . when things change . . . overnight," Jake said. He looked at the bill but did not take it from Dewayne. "You know, you're a little late."

Dewayne looked at his watch as if somehow Jake was privy to his schedule. He shrugged, waiting to be enlightened.

"My grand opening of Hopper's Barbecue," Jake said. "Half the town came to see you and Sylvester pitch and catch in front of my shop and you were a no-show. I expected something like that from Sylvester, but not from you."

"I'm sorry. I don't even remember it." The sweat glands on Dewayne's back began to push the pores open.

"So insult me some more . . . don't even remember it."

"I'm really sorry. Really. I'll try and make it up to you. Whatever it takes."

"Forget about it."

Jake pushed the order toward Dewayne, who kept waving the bill at him.

"Look, just keep the change. It's okay. I don't need—"

"I'm sure you don't need it. What you need is character, character I remember you having when you were a kid, character your mother has."

"Yeah . . . yeah," Dewayne said and laid the bill on the counter. He scooted the sack into his hands and enfolded it over his chest like a protective covering.

Just before Dewayne's exit, they stood looking at each other once again, just like they did after he had entered the shop, yet both more informed from the heart's revelations.

Regret filled them on multiple levels, but neither could express it: regret for old wounds, regret for surprise entrances, regret for promises broken, regret for spoken words coated with bitterness, regret for flustered apologies.

Dewayne just nodded his head, and Jake returned to irritating the itch on his forehead. If Dewayne could have kept the bell from ringing at his exit, he would have. If Jake had never paid attention to a meddlesome customer's suggestion to hang the bell in the first place, neither one of them would have had to endure the sound of this departure . . . a last mutual regret of both men.

15

"My man, Dewayne Jobe, needs a big credit limit because he signed such a small contract," Sly whispered and then winked into the camera. "But don't tell him that."

The camera widened out from a close-up of Sly's face to reveal a football field under a blazing hot sun. Sly took a few steps back and hurled the football downfield. The ball flew high just in front of Dewayne, requiring him to leap into the air to catch it. He caught it with one hand, went into a forward roll, and came back onto his feet. The director shouted, "Cut!" and the entire film crew began to cheer.

"That's the money shot," the director said as he waved for Dewayne and Sly to come to the monitor bank under the tent to watch the replay from the different camera angles. The pass from Sly to Dewayne had been a multicamera master shot.

Dewayne was shooting his last commercial before training camp began, and the largesse coming from this endorsement would be the most lucrative to date. It was Sly's first time in front of the camera, but he took to it like the star he knew he was and would always be. It was a perfect combination of people and events: high school friends who had played for the same team, college superstars, rivals for the Heisman, first and second overall draft picks. And now the national attention each one had gotten over his contract—Dewayne's for its low figures, Sly's for his not having signed yet with New York because he and his agent were still haggling over the dollar amount. He could not attend training camp until his deal was done.

The national credit card company loved this convergence of player and circumstance and intended to play it for all its worth. They would get at least three commercials out of this two-day shoot, and Dewayne would prove his point to Sly that the quickest way into the winner's circle was doing this dog-and-pony show for the highest bidder.

"That's cold, bro," Sly said as they sat side by side in their makeup chairs.

"That's cold hard cash, bro," Dewayne said. "You remember how hard your life was before you left for Miami? You want to go back to that?"

"I don't want to go back to nothing except your mama and her cooking. Case closed." Sly slid off his chair. "Now let's go warm up for the camera."

Once they were on the field, throwing the football, and out of earshot of the director and the crew who were setting up for the shot, Sly started ragging his friend.

"You know the press has cut loose on me because I'm hold-ing out. My agent says I can't get the deal I deserve because of your lowball contract. I should be getting Heisman Trophy money, but you screwed everything up."

"It's a system failure . . . been going on for years," Dewayne said. "I just thought I might see what I could do to correct the problem."

"Don't sell your crap to me," Sly said, adding extra muscle to his throw. "You Mr. White Knight? You saying you can be greedy for endorsements but not in football?"

"The way I see it, they are all making money off us, but it's different with the team. We all need each other to win. Just like back in the day."

"Back in the day . . . you and me." Sly held on to the ball. "D-man, we're not the same, you and me. We're difference makers. We need us a team, but we're leaders, and we should be paid for it."

"I agree, but not when you have to cut the pay of good players that have been on the field longer, or cut them altogether just so you can buy your bling."

After the director and cinematographer had analyzed the master shot from every camera angle, Dewayne slung his arm over Sly's shoulder and took the football out of his friend's hand as they slipped out of the tent where they had been watching the replays.

"These guys talk way too long," he whispered. "Guess that's how they earn their money. It's a whole lot of hurry up and wait."

"You guys make it look so easy," the vice president for marketing from the credit card company said as he burst out of the small canvas tent, elated with what he had seen. The top of the VP's perfectly coifed and frosted hair came up to about Dewayne's middle, which made him look like a little boy running to his daddy as he jogged toward Sly and Dewayne. He was all designer made, down to the embossed two-tone sunglasses.

"We're the pros from Springdale, Mississippi, remember?" Sly said.

"Serendipity shots like that one-handed catch with the forward roll could get you a fat multiyear deal with the company," the VP said, taking the football from Dewayne and tossing it from hand to hand as if he were trying to be a player.

Dewayne's face brightened as though electrified. "Just pleasing the man," he said with false humility.

Sly bent over as though he was about to be sick. The VP pretended he caught the joke.

"Now, let's get set up for Dewayne's close-up coming out of the forward roll and trotting to the camera," he said, and the crew went to work.

"Hey, there wouldn't have been a forward roll had I not led him with my pass," Sly said, taking the ball out of the VP's hands and reenacting the throw onto an empty field. "I put it right where it needed to be . . . pinpoint precision . . . Sly's laser beam."

"I expected no less from a Heisman Trophy winner," he said. "You are the man."

"So I get that fat multiyear deal too?"

The VP had already turned his back and was heading onto the field to have his confab with the director.

When the shot was set up and Dewayne had gone through rehearsals for sound and camera, the director called for quiet. Sly took a fresh cold bottle of water from an assistant and sat in his actor's chair to watch the action in the monitor. This shot was just a one-camera setup. When the director shouted, "Action!" Dewayne did another forward roll—he had to stay in character, he told Sly later—and stepped to the camera, looked right into the lens, and delivered his line flawlessly.

"That was perfect," the director said. "One more for safety."

Dewayne repeated the action again without error, and the cinematographer nodded his pleasure.

"That's a wrap," the director cried, which the crew greeted with surprise and elation.

Sly shook his head in amazement as he watched the replay of his friend's work on the monitor. He had to admit, it was perfect. Sly's close-up had required eight takes, half of them for flubbing his line, but Dewayne had nailed his in two. He watched the replay once more: forward roll, step to camera, lean into frame, big smile, and "My man, Sylvester Adams, needs a big credit limit because he hasn't signed his contract yet," Dewayne said, winking to the camera. "But don't tell him that."

Dewayne Jobe is right out of a fairy tale, Sly thought and poured the rest of his water over his head as the film crew began to break down the set.

Like a scene out of an old western, defensive linebacker Colby Stewart marched into the locker room. He wore flip-flops and baggy gray sweatpants cut off six inches above his knee, nothing else. The fluorescent lighting burning through the mist in the locker room reflected off Colby's bald head, giving him an aura of a Byzantine saint. A chiseled, muscled landscape covered his six-foot frame with identical medieval beasts in attack mode tattooed on each forearm and given a name: "Death" for the right arm and "Mayhem" for the left, twin companions in the fight against touchdowns. The tour de force was upon his V-shaped back: the god of the underworld driving a four-horse chariot in the viewer's direction with fire and brimstone raging in the background, the colors of the conflagration scintillating off his white skin. An arched caption written in monkish script above the masterpiece read "And Hell Followed After Him."

Colby's modus operandi was high-octane rage—all the better to wreak havoc upon his opponents—but too often his fury did not remain on the field. He was a usual suspect in any Houston barroom brawl, and once a season Colby made the headlines with a domestic violence arrest for doing some harm to a current girlfriend. This reputation had not hurt the jersey sales with his name and number or kept him off the cover of several football video games, *Smash/Cut* being his number one bestseller.

He had been the Stars' first draft pick five seasons ago, and despite his being the leading defensive player in the league, the Stars had not had the success they had hoped for with such a high-rated player. This fact only fueled his anger and a determination to leave the team after this season, but the Stars had made him a restricted free agent and stuck a "franchise" tag on him, underpaying him, in Colby's mind, at $8.8 million a year.

The salary was well above average for a player at his position, but way below the stature with which he esteemed himself. Lifestyle and attorney's fees ate up most of what he had collected each year, and he was looking to hit the jackpot of free agency. The franchise sticker kept him from his end of the rainbow gold for another year, and instead of holding out, he was smart enough to stick it out, proving to potential buyers he was a team player and a constant terror on the field. A few players called out to Colby as he strutted toward his locker, head bobbing from the heavy metal pumping into his brain from his iPod, but his only acknowledgment to the courtesies was to grunt.

The first week of training camp was shoulder pads and helmets only, full pads came later, and in the Houston heat, the least amount of clothing a player had to wear, the better. All the rookies bonded into a tight group before matriculating into the team. Most egos were checked at the door, and even though the veterans pulled some locker room pranks on the rookies, it was all in good fun and rarely carried onto the field. If the rookies showed respect and deference and maintained a proper work ethic, the older players would take them under their wings and offer nuanced advice about what to expect from other players and their on-the-field eccentricities and tricks. This was invaluable help for the new kids, and it made them feel more at ease with themselves so they could concentrate on their jobs.

Because Dewayne had created such a controversy with his contract deal, everyone was sizing him up on and off the field. He refused all requests from the press for interviews, giving them only locker room sound bites that always flattered his coaches and teammates. He gave no response to any rumors of drug use; he good-naturedly submitted to all drug tests by team doctors or surprise visits from league physicians entering the door, cup in hand, and always with the same results . . . negative. The newest rumor began to circulate not long after his arrival in the city about how many children he had fathered since coming to Houston. It was true that women gathered outside the lobby of the hotel where the team stayed during training camp and used their charms to entice the players as they got on and off the bus each day for practice. Dewayne always pretended to be talking on his cell phone as he walked the Siren gauntlet, a trick he learned from his friend Harrison Barrow. But a very pregnant Rosella squelched that rumor in an interview for a Houston newspaper when she allowed her picture to be taken, hoping to prove that she was the only claim on Dewayne's heart.

No one was sure how to take Dewayne. Coaches and players, press and public were wary at first. Was this guy a real saint, or was he coming in with a savior attitude, trying to make everyone like him before he took off the appealing mask and insisted the universe revolved around him?

Dewayne knew the charm offensive was the best approach, one person at a time, but Colby was always on the lookout for a chink in the armor. The Stars was his team; the sixty-foot full-color banner of him hanging outside the stadium proved it, and his standardized fuming attitude backed up the bluster.

This alpha male would not relinquish his dominance without stiff resistance.

Each day held its routines of stretching and conditioning, followed by players working with specialty coaches and focusing on drills unique to their positions. Defensive and offensive drills, special teams practice, and specific lineups designed to break in the rookies and give the veterans back their groove. A part of each day, defense and offense would line up opposite each other and run plays. It was a time for rookies to be humiliated or show their stuff. It was a time for veterans to break them in without breaking them. Colby preferred the breaking part.

A rule of practice was to keep physical engagement to a minimum. No one was supposed to hit the ground, but Colby wrote his own rules. Dewayne was always third in line for the outside receiver position, allowing the veteran receivers to take the first throws. He paid close attention to the defense and watched how they adjusted to the play as each player ran his route. The mental concentration was more exhausting than the physical as he tried to read the overall defense as well as evaluate the moves of the individual player in front of him.

When Dewayne ran his routes, Colby was always the one closest to him, whether it was man coverage or zone, and the more Dewayne improved, the angrier this tattooed beast became. Colby was the designated trash-talker, and Dewayne was surprised that the coaches allowed it to go on. Harrison Barrow pulled him aside when he came back from running one of his routes, having once again ignored Colby's verbal abuse.

"You're getting a free education," Harrison said. "Referees would never let it go to this extent in a game without throwing a flag, but if you can handle Colby's trash talk, nobody can rile you."

Dewayne's next route was a crossing pattern downfield, cutting toward the middle. The quarterback threw the ball behind him, and as he turned to grab it, his field of vision suddenly changed. Instead of being eye level with backfield defensive players, he was looking at blue sky and bright sun. Dewayne lay on his back, listening to a distant voice become steadily louder.

"You are a Jobe steak on my plate," Colby shouted as he strutted around Dewayne's prone body lying motionless on the ground. "You been grilled and charbroiled. You are well done and dead. My fork and knife are cutting you up."

A hand came into Dewayne's view, diffusing the sunlight in his eyes, and a voice asked how many fingers he saw. His correct answer recharged Colby.

"And the boy can count. The boy has himself an education. He can count all the way to four, matching his IQ."

Dewayne jumped to his feet, as though refreshed from a power nap, and realized only then he had retained possession of the ball. Colby received no reprimands from coaches or players as Dewayne made his way back to the huddle; he knew it was a test, and to pass the test, one endured and struck back with equal force or pure cunning when the opportunity presented itself. Dewayne knew everyone expected a volatile reaction, knew his metal was hanging above the fire. When it was his time to go to the line again, he asked the offensive coordinator if he could run the exact same route as before. The coach nodded his approval, amused and curious to see what might happen with the exact same call and matchup.

The quarterback got the ball off quicker this time with a more accurate throw. Dewayne reached for the ball and caught a glimpse of the Colby locomotive coming right for him. Dewayne snatched the ball out of the air in front of Colby, but instead of lowering for impact, he spun away and headed up-field. Dewayne gave a quick look back and saw Colby doing his Superman impersonation through the air but finishing with a bumpy landing, bouncing across the turf on his stomach, each hit knocking a little more air out of his lungs. Unlike Dewayne, he did not lie on the ground for a beat. He was up on his feet, cutting a broad circle, silent except for the rapid gasps for breath. Dewayne jogged back, bouncing the football in his hands, thinking maybe now Colby would have to capitulate some of his power attitude.

Colby cut off his forward progress. "Nobody in the NFL will hit you harder than I can."

"Then my rookie year should be a cakewalk," Dewayne said and tossed Colby the ball.

Coach Gyra waved Dewayne off the field, and he approached the head coach, expecting a warning to save it for the first game and for the other team.

"The hospital called," he said. "There's no panic. Everything is fine, but your wife is there and she has gone into labor."

———

Robert Dewayne Jobe III was born at 5:32 a.m. three weeks ahead of schedule but quite healthy and sporting a full head of curly hair. During training camp the team remained seques-tered, but Dewayne had been in constant phone contact with Rosella, and he had forewarned the staff the baby might arrive at any time. Joella had moved in a few days before Dewayne left for camp, and Cherie was just about to take her two-week vacation to come to Houston and relieve Joella when she got the call she was now officially a grandmother. By the time Franklin arrived, little Robert was out of the incubator and in his mother's arms with only another few days left in the hospital.

Dewayne still showed up for camp every day, but for the first few nights after Robert was born, Coach Gyra allowed him to stay at the hospital instead of the forced team retreat in the downtown Plaza Hotel. He loved the game, but the separation from his family at this time was harder than any hit Colby could deliver.

16

"Split right . . . three sixty-seven, and let the fun begin," the quarterback said, and the huddle began to break. "The ball will be there."

The last statement was directed to Dewayne. It was his first play in the first game of his first NFL season, and he was going to get the ball. Special teams had taken the touchback, and the Stars were starting on their own twenty-yard line. He jogged out to the right side of the field.

All Dewayne could think was, *Do not drop the ball*. It was a simple one-step up, one-step back route. He just needed to make a big target and catch the ball, just catch the ball, no heroics necessary. He did not want his first pass to slip through his fingers. Seventy-eight thousand people filled the stadium, millions more could be watching the game at home, bookies had made their odds and taken their bets, Cherie and Franklin had brought the kids to the game, while Joella and Rosella stayed home with the baby and watched it on television. All he needed to do was to get this first play behind him. He did not need to do anything fancy or score a touchdown, and by all means he didn't want to jump offsides. Just a solid catch, a few positive yards, and that would be enough.

Out of respect for his speed, the Chicago cornerback assigned to cover Dewayne was playing about ten yards off the line of scrimmage. The center snapped the ball, and as Dewayne completed the step-up, step-back routine, the ball was already hurtling through the air to him. Everything slowed down as he watched the point of the ball sail right into the large diamond shape he had made with his thumbs and index fingers.

The second it touched his gloves, his fingers gripped the ball tight enough to make it squeal, and he spun around upfield. Mission accomplished until the cornerback buried his helmet into Dewayne's chest, stopping his forward progress and robbing him of the one yard he had gained.

With the ball tucked into his right side, Dewayne grabbed the back of the cornerback's shoulder pads with his free hand and tossed him aside like an annoying branch hanging over a trail. The cornerback waved his arms and his hands tried to grasp any part of Dewayne to slow him down until help arrived, but he fell empty-handed to the ground.

The safety had a good angle of pursuit, but by midfield, he gave up the chase and watched helplessly as Dewayne outran him. By the time he reached the ten-yard line, he pulled back his engines like an airplane preparing for descent and glided into the end zone.

When he saw the officials raise their arms to signal his first NFL touchdown, it was as though he had crossed into a madcap Wonderland, and he did not know what to do. The stadium was on the verge of collapse from the exploding fireworks, the rock music booming from the speakers of the JumboTrons on either end of the field, and the announcer screaming his name over and over. He went down on one knee and said a short prayer of gratitude, and by the time he got to the amen, the gang tackle the defensive team had hoped to use on him eighty yards back was now administered by exultant teammates who escorted Dewayne to the Stars bench without his feet ever touching the ground.

The offensive linemen dropped Dewayne beside the bench after going through the cheerful slaps of coaches and players to his head and shoulders. He took off his helmet, waved to the fans behind him, and then found his family twenty rows back on the forty-yard line.

Bruce and Sabrina obviously appreciated Cherie's revelry for her son's accomplishment and made an equal spectacle of themselves. Even the internationally renowned architect, once disdainful of what he considered low forms of entertainment, who had refused to watch a collegiate or professional football game until Dewayne came into his life, was now on his feet straining his vocal cords, adding to the dissonant sound rising out of the stadium.

Colby waited for Dewayne to stop waving to thousands of his new best friends and step off the bench before he slipped up beside him.

"That 'going down on one knee, praying in the end zone' thing . . . nice touch," he said before he pounded Dewayne on the shoulder with his fist, a gesture that was far from congratulatory. "So I guess I'd better get used to seeing you do that little humble-pie act every time you score, huh?"

"I'd like to think so," Dewayne said, turning away from the fans and grabbing a cup of Gatorade off the table.

"Well, well. My man has himself a direct line to God," Colby said, his derisive chuckle a slight to Dewayne's pleasure of this moment.

"I do." Dewayne took a swig of Gatorade, sloshed it around in his mouth, and spit the backwash at Colby's feet. "And I'm not your man."

Colby looked at the splatter on his new game shoes and

sneered as he stretched his helmet over his bald head before heading onto the field. He was smart enough to expend his displeasure at Dewayne's comeback upon the opposing team, and it was a good investment. Chicago scored only field goals, two of them, both in the second half, while Houston added three more touchdowns to their score.

When Dewayne returned to the bench after a repeat of his pious end zone ritual, Colby folded his hands in front of him and bowed in mocking reverence. But Colby's ire was raised to a new level when he watched Dewayne in the locker room for a postgame television interview and heard him acknowledge how he had incorporated his faith into his whole life. When the reporter tried to single out his first NFL stats, Dewayne deflected the credit to his teammates and singled out Colby for "leading a great defensive effort by holding Chicago to six points." Colby could not bear to receive praise from someone he believed to be so self-righteous, and he stormed out of the locker room, rejecting all requests for an interview.

The season progressed much as it started. In ten games, Houston lost only twice, and with the schedule of remaining games, the Stars were confident that going to the play-offs was a sure thing, a prospect that had eluded them the past two years. This fact was not lost on the public or the media, and Dewayne Jobe was usually the first name out of everyone's mouth about why the Stars' fortunes were beginning to turn. He had been named "player of the week" twice since the first game, an unusual feat for any player but rare as hen's teeth for a rookie.

Not all was perfect in Jobe-world, however. His image of faith and integrity had a polarizing effect on people. For most Houston fans, as long as the Stars were winning, Dewayne could believe in fairies and dress like one. For fans of other teams, it was easy to dislike someone who sprinted by his defenders as if they were running through tar on his way to the end zone, then did his "going to the chapel" kneel, as some sports commentators had dubbed it, each time he crossed the goal line. There were those in the media and even within the Stars organization who felt he should go easy on the God speak, but Rosella and his mother reminded him how he had gotten this far with God's help and it was not smart to take him out of the equation now.

Even if his public image suffered a bit from his expression of faith, it did not damage the number of offers for product endorsement that flooded into Jobe Enterprises, Inc. Often Dewayne was on the phone in the locker room discussing the particulars of deals with Rosella. Most advertisers were able to accommodate the demands of his schedule and shoot a commercial with a crew in Houston. But there was that rare trip to Los Angeles or New York, and Rosella had him in and out of a location within thirty-six hours. He never missed a practice and his health never suffered under such a demanding schedule, nor did his bank accounts. By midseason, what he had made in endorsements and investments was ten times what the Stars had paid in a signing bonus.

What did suffer was the level of respect and goodwill Dewayne had gained with his teammates early in the season. His "Bull Durham, Ah Shucks, Glory to God" public oratory was beginning to wear thin on many players, and it did not help that his fame and business deals were increasing week by week. Dewayne was oblivious of the general resentment until none other than Colby pointed it out to him.

After a second straight loss, which put their record at ten and four—not bad enough to jeopardize their play-off chances, but not conducive to building strong momentum going into those last two games—Colby strode through the locker room and went over to Dewayne, sitting on the bench in front of his locker heedless to the volume level on his phone as he debated the price of a national car rental company endorsement with Rosella. Colby got within inches of his face and glared at Dewayne until he told Rosella he needed to call her back.

"You and me," Colby said. "We're going for a drive."

Dewayne thought it would be a good idea to have some one-on-one with Colby away from football. They pulled out of the stadium parking lot in Colby's SL500 Mercedes convertible and headed toward downtown Houston. The drive was befitting Colby's reputation as a linebacker, weaving through traffic at NASCAR speed, and Dewayne was glad he buckled in the second he shut the door. When they pulled into the parking lot of the End Zone Bar & Grill, Colby spoke to him for the first time since leaving the stadium.

"No need for you to take a knee thing once you walk through that door." Colby pointed to the sign. "It ain't the same kind of end zone."

It was, however, the only smart investment Colby had made with his Stars money. He was the majority owner of the eatery, and his reputation brought in a large and loyal clientele of those who identified with Colby's personality or were just wannabe bad boys. Everyone spoke to Colby, none to Dewayne, as they followed the hostess sashaying her way through the tables in her too-tight, too-short skirt to Colby's back corner table where he could observe and be observed. Two ice-cold beers and platters of Colby's favorite appetizers appeared on the table almost as soon as he and Dewayne had taken their seats. Dewayne requested the waiter trade out his beer for a cranberry juice, and it was gone as quickly as it had appeared.

"I'm gonna make this quick and painless," Colby said before guzzling a third of his beer. "The locker room is tired of hearing you go on about God and your endorsement deals. You got a life outside the locker room . . . ," he waved to the universe, ". . . keep it there."

"Are you a spokesman for one, or do you speak for others?" Dewayne asked and nodded his head in thanks to the waiter who had brought him his cranberry juice.

"I speak for me, but I know my team. I know what they're thinking when they listen to your God crap during interviews or you haggling about what endorsement you're going to do this week. Am I making this easy enough for you to understand?"

Dewayne was in a public place, and worse, it was not a neutral place. It was Colby's territory, and it was well marked, so any outward display of the turmoil flaring inside his gut would not have been the correct path to follow. He wanted to smash Colby's face into the spinach dip appetizer, but thought that was not a suitable turn-the-other-cheek response to this plotted entrapment and verbal abuse.

"I think I get it," Dewayne said. He sipped his drink but refused to eat any of the food set in front of him. "Yet one thing I don't get . . . that it's your team."

"It's my team until I decide different," Colby said. "You can keep your God and your endorsements, but you're not taking the team from me."

Dewayne looked into the restaurant at the bustling crowd. They were Colby fans, and Dewayne felt the isolation. He dropped his head and looked at his folded hands, folded not for prayer, but fingers locked to keep him from taking his drink and pouring it over Colby's bald head. Still, Colby's harsh words gave him pause. Perhaps he had been naïve and insensitive toward his teammates.

"You know, Colby, I'm hearing you," Dewayne said, deciding to submit to the dominant male. "I'm sorry if I offended you or any of our teammates."

"I just love this religious crap, the way you sling it around," Colby said, his scarcely disguised anger coming out in a blast of laughter.

"You're angry, Colby, and I'm sorry, but I don't see God as the culprit."

"Fancy words for a jock, but I got no use for God. I don't waste my time with God. There's nothing God can do for me I can't do for myself."

"God could give you peace and make you happy," Dewayne said.

"Save it for church," Colby said and finished off his beer.

The hostess approached the table to check on the progress of consumption, and Colby rose from his chair and threw his arm around her waist, pulling her into his side.

"Guess what? This is the only piece that is going to make me happy," he said, biting her ear, which got him an affectionate reaction. "I'll get the manager to call you a cab as I leave."

Dewayne finished his drink and watched Colby and the hostess work the room as they made their way toward the exit, making his fans feel appreciated for keeping his bank accounts flush.

———

After their conversation at the restaurant, Dewayne had steered clear of Colby for the rest of the season, but he did take Colby's advice about the endorsements. He told Rosella to put all endorsement deals on hold until the season was over. He did not need the distraction as the team approached the play-offs, and he wanted to be sensitive to his teammates. That gave Rosella free time to develop her skills at investing their current assets in profitable portfolios. With the help of a New York firm she was able to increase their wealth by 27 percent, take care of the baby, work at their church, and get Bruce and Sabrina all the places they needed to be on any given day.

The biggest challenge Rosella had to face during this more relaxed time was the Houston traffic with Sabrina at the wheel. Sabrina had been complaining that she was well beyond the legal driving age, and Rosella agreed. So in the evenings, Rosella gave Sabrina her first driving lessons while Dewayne watched the baby, helped Bruce with his homework, and studied his playbook. Dewayne breathed a sigh of relief each time he heard the garage door open and the ladies return from their adventure. It meant they had survived the streets, but after the women were inside the house, he always slipped into the garage and walked around his Denali inspecting it for any scrapes or dings.

One night when Sabrina bounded into the kitchen and lifted the car keys off the key rack, all excited about testing her driving skills for the first time on the freeway, Rosella begged off.

"Robert Jr. has a slight fever, and I just don't want to leave him," she said.

Homework covered part of the kitchen table with Bruce and Dewayne bent over it, pretending to solve a difficult math problem by mumbling some bogus figures. Dewayne knew the silence in the kitchen meant that both women were staring a hole into the top of his head, and he did not want to look up. He had no desire to get into the front seat of his Denali with his teenage niece behind the wheel. If he were going to the hospital, it would be for slamming into another player on the field and not colliding with a vehicle on the street.

Rosella cleared her throat and called his name. It was a summons, and Bruce started to laugh. Dewayne raised his head with a "do I have to do this" look plastered on his sullen face.

"I'm thinking you need a little uncle/niece bonding time," Rosella said.

"But do we have to do it on the freeway?"

"I'm really careful, Uncle Dewayne," Sabrina said, which made Bruce laugh and caused a harsh glare from his big sister.

"I'll help Bruce with his math. You two go on."

Dewayne had to admit that Sabrina was careful and displayed a confidence and poise behind the wheel that he had not expected. As a reward for her excellent performance and for not frightening him, he took her to dinner at the family's favorite steakhouse. They had barely ordered their drinks before fans began to come up to the table asking for autographs or taking cell phone pictures of Dewayne and Sabrina out on the town. When they got home that night, the way uncle and niece joked about their driving experience, and the way Sabrina bragged of how cool it was to have dinner with someone famous in a restaurant, it was obvious to Rosella and Bruce that they had missed a good time.

"We've been slaving over math while you two were out having fun," Rosella said with only a minor hint of envy.

Dewayne agreed to make himself available for the next couple driving lessons. A week later when Sabrina announced that the school would soon be offering a driver's education class, both Rosella and Dewayne were relieved. They were ready to pass off the responsibility of teaching Sabrina the finer points of driving to an expert.

Dewayne's declining endorsement deals so he could focus more on the final games before the play-offs did not prove to be much of an advantage for the team. The Stars split their last two games, giving them an eleven and five record. They only won the first game by a field goal—no touchdowns for Dewayne—and lost the second by fourteen points, with only one touchdown for the rookie receiver.

It was a sloppy way to end the regular season, Coach Gyra admitted to the reporters at the press conference after the second game, but he pointed out that the Stars had made it to the play-offs, something not achieved in several years. He was grateful for the dramatic turnaround within one season and promised to make Houston proud in the upcoming games.

"I don't know what happened. The offense didn't adjust to what the Chicago defense threw at them," Colby said. "How do you get confused this late in the season? I don't know. Ask Bible Boy Wonder over there." He wiped the perspiration off his head. "He always has an answer for everything."

The locker room atmosphere was morose. The Stars had gone into the play-offs with an eleven and five record that won them home-field advantage for the first game, but Chicago had returned to Houston with a grudge against the Stars for their demoralizing defeat at the beginning of the season. The final score was 17 to 13, and Dewayne had scored the only touchdown late in the third period. The defense had done their homework and shut him down. Chicago had given back their previous humiliation.

Before the Houston television reporter moved on to Dewayne, he asked Colby if this would be his last year with the Stars since he would now be a free agent. Colby finished the interview by giving the reporter several options of where he could stick his microphone.

"I wish I could tell you why we lost," Dewayne responded to the interviewer's question. "I agree with Colby. I didn't make the right adjustments to Chicago rolling out a linebacker in double team coverage. Chicago came to play the full sixty minutes. They were at the top of their game, and I can't take that away from them."

"So what are you going to do with your time off?" the reporter asked, casting a cautious glance over his shoulder at Colby.

"I'll be back in the weight room later this week," Dewayne said.

Five

She dropped her Bible and screamed the moment she recognized him. It took a few seconds to be sure her eyes were not playing tricks: no dreadlocks, no exposed muscled and tattooed flesh, no crew to flank his stride. A bright smile replaced his permanent scowl.

When he spoke, there were no hard, clipped phrases, no profanity, especially not in the sanctuary of the Lord. From what she could tell, on the surface there were no more vestiges of the former life. Even his voice was different as he told her that he had met Jesus and Jesus had forgiven him. Jesus had given him a new perspective. Jesus had given him a new life. Jesus had helped him get out of jail shortly after his eighteenth birthday because Jesus had helped him become a model citizen while in juvenile detention. And once free, Jesus had given him a new location in which to live, and a marketable skill in computers had gotten him a job so that he could have an apartment and a car—both modest in price.

There was only one thing Jesus had not given him yet, and that was Sabrina. That would be the last request he would make of Jesus. That was the last fleece he would lay out before the Lord to prove his goodness to him. If Sabrina came back into his life, then it would be complete. As God had proven himself to Tyler Rogan, so Tyler would prove himself to Sabrina, to her family, and to the world.

He had been able to say all this to her in the back of the church where the Jobes were members.

That Sunday, Dewayne had given the testimony of his life, and while hordes of people had surrounded him after the service, wanting to be close to the aura and catch a glimpse of the favored one, Sabrina had detached herself from the throng and gone to the ladies' room in the vestibule. When she had exited the bathroom, she was stunned at the sight of her former boyfriend. Her Bible fell to the floor and her hands went to her mouth to stifle her scream.

"How did you find me?" Sabrina asked, her words muffled by her hand.

Tyler stooped down and retrieved the Bible. He smoothed out the crumpled pages while he spoke. "Everyone in the country knows Dewayne Jobe. I just happened to see in the paper where he would be speaking at Quail Valley Church. I was here last Sunday and saw you, but . . . ," a slight choking in the throat, the misting of his eyes—a marvel Sabrina never thought possible—"after what happened back in LA, I figured you and your brother would be living with them. At least that's what I'd heard, and I just had to see for myself. I just had to take a risk and see if there was any chance for us. After all I've done, I don't expect you to forgive me, but I could never live with myself if I didn't try."

"You . . . you nearly killed my brother. You gave drugs to my mother. You made me love you," she said in choking whispers as she hit him on the chest with her fist.

"I was an evil son of a—" and there he remembered the ground upon which he stood. "I was evil, and I am unworthy to ask for your forgiveness, let alone hope I might receive it.

But if I'm lucky, if God grants me my last wish, and you can give me your forgiveness, then after that, maybe I can get your trust. After that, maybe your love."

Across the lobby, Bruce waved for Sabrina to join them as they went out the doors into the church parking lot.

As Sabrina moved to rejoin her family, Tyler stopped her, laying his hand gently on her arm. He gave her his card—an actual business card with his name listed as an employee of a professional company specializing in website design for up-and-coming hip-hop artists to help market themselves and their music on the Internet—and told her not to tell her family that he had gotten this new life and moved to Houston. He wanted to prove himself to her first. If he could win her back, then he would take the next step to win her family. One step at a time, he had told her, no need to rush, and no need to let her family know they had met; it would be their secret until it was time to be revealed.

"Call me," Tyler said. "There is so much I want to tell you, so much I want to do for you." And he disappeared back into the sanctuary.

When the family was piling into the car, the first question asked was who the young man was in the lobby. Sabrina said it was someone from the church, new in town, working for a website design company. When Dewayne commented on the "clean-cut" quality of the young man's appearance and Rosella mentioned the cuteness factor of his overall countenance, Sabrina could not hold back the smile that insisted on having its way on her face. She fiddled with Tyler's card inside her purse all the way home, studying it like a forensic scientist and rubbing her fingers over the embossed lettering. It was no cheap card with its high-quality paper stock, nice lettering, and a phone number. She memorized it, dialed it on her cell phone, and let it ring once before she clicked off the connection. The number seemed legit. When Bruce asked who she was calling, she told him it was just a friend.

For the next test, he would need to answer the phone. She delayed this test until she got home, and implemented it in the privacy of her bedroom. She still disconnected the call once he answered, but his "Hello's" were a small validation. It only took seconds for him to return the call to the mystery number and to identify himself on Sabrina's voice mail, and say perhaps the other party had misdialed or gotten the wrong number . . . or perhaps not. In any case, he would be happy to speak with them about any professional or personal needs they might require. This made her giggle. How did Tyler get so professional? When did he get to be so polite? Maybe it was Jesus.

———————————

"You believe people can change?" Sabrina asked her family one month, five dates, and multiple phone conversations after the epiphany on the Sunday morning. "I mean, Jesus can change anybody, can't he?"

"What are you talking about?" Dewayne asked, home from doing the latest in a series of television commercials for the national credit card company. The company had built a six-spot campaign around Dewayne that would air next season and had signed him for $1 million per spot with a $5 million signing bonus before the first sixty-second advertisement was even in the can.

This was Sabrina's first test to see how the family might react to the entry of a former villain into their lives. It had taken some serious persuasion on Tyler's part. Persuading Sabrina to continue to see him after their first date had not been so difficult. They had to keep their encounters brief and semisecluded. He drove her by the downtown office building where he worked and pointed to the fortieth floor. The company he worked for was expanding into the record business, he told her, with a recording studio in LA, and he would be required to make regular trips to the Golden State with new artists he had discovered. Twice he took her out to dinner—modestly priced restaurants, the first time they had ever eaten out somewhere that wasn't fast food, the first time they could hold a menu in their hands instead of read from a lit-up billboard hung above a cashier's head, the first time for a real waiter who brought food to their table and didn't speak through a mechanical voice box. When she asked about any obligations he might have to the juvenile justice system in Los Angeles, he showed her his most recent round-trip plane ticket—Houston/LA for a monthly check-in with all the appropriate people who were monitoring his progress. They were all very pleased with his new life, and six months from now, if he stayed out of trouble—and it was very important to him to stay out of trouble, to show the fruit of a reformed life—these trips would be business-only excursions that would not include visits to his probation officer.

These were all impressive selling points for Sabrina, but she still could not tell her aunt and uncle the truth about whom she was seeing. The lies were simple, she was meeting with friends from church, friends from school, but she knew she could not keep up the subterfuge and the subject would soon see the light of day. Every time they were together, he treated her with the utmost respect. There was never any hint of drugs. There was no demand for sex; they went no farther than holding hands and the good-night kiss when he dropped her off by her aunt Rosella's borrowed car at the suburban park where they always met.

Tyler and Sabrina always kept a safe distance from each

other at church, not wanting to arouse suspicion. Even though she thought it a bit unusual that he didn't seem to have many friends—only the few people she saw him speaking with at church or the fellow workers he spoke of at his job—Sabrina was grateful his former LA posse was out of the picture.

In spite of all these positive experiences, Sabrina had still been reluctant to raise the subject of Tyler's transformation with the family. What convinced her to move forward on the matter was her own mother. Even though no one had laid eyes on her in more than six months, Bonita had begun to communicate with the family by letter four months into her rehabilitation. She allowed no visitors—Franklin and Joella could not have even five minutes with her, and this was Bonita's choice. There was never a phone call. She said that to be seen or heard until she was truly ready would retard the positive changes she was making. She did not confess to a "come to Jesus" moment nor did she refer to the sins of her past and ask for anyone's forgiveness. She just said she was making positive changes in physical health and general well-being that the doctors and social workers confirmed, and she would continue to remain in contact with infrequent and short epistles of her improvement.

When Tyler inquired after Bonita and Sabrina commented on her mother's recent correspondence and improved condition, he mentioned that after his release from detention, he had gone to see Bonita at a halfway house where she was staying. He could authenticate the status of her change for the better.

"She never mentioned seeing you," Sabrina said.

"We talked about not bringing up any bad vibes from the past," he said. "I wanted a fresh start."

That was all it took to convince Sabrina now was the time. So before Tyler left to return to Los Angeles for a juvie check-in and a major Web design presentation of two new artists to the marketing department of his company, he made Sabrina promise to discuss the possibility of reentry into the family. She had finally decided on her approach.

"It happened in the Bible all the time," Sabrina said, running her fork through the pile of peas on her plate like a blind mole. "You know, God changing people."

"Yeah, well, so it can happen." Rosella shoveled a spoonful of pureed carrots in Robert's mouth. "You're talking about your mother?"

"Yeah, her, but anybody," Sabrina said. "God can change anybody, right?"

"What's impossible for man is possible for God," Dewayne said. "Or something like that."

"And if they changed, we'd have to forgive them and love them, right?"

"Of course, we would," Rosella said. She gave Sabrina an inquisitive frown, her hand suspended in the air with another spoonful of pureed carrots. "Where are you going with this, girl?"

Sabrina was smart enough not to tell the whole truth. Telling about meeting Tyler at church on Sundays was all the information they needed to know at this point. Rosella's hostile and Dewayne's skeptical reactions to the news that Tyler had appeared on the scene bore out the wisdom of her choice not to tell them about their clandestine rendezvous. She spent the rest of the evening fielding the same questions she had asked Tyler, and where Sabrina had been satisfied with his answers, her aunt and uncle reserved their judgment.

Dewayne seemed a little more receptive than Rosella to the idea of a new Tyler, and Sabrina saw a reason for hope and a confirmation in her own ability to size up a person. Her uncle treated her like an adult. Her aunt was much more protective

205

. . . overbearing. She appreciated both reactions and knew that in the not-too-distant future she would be able to tell them all about their relationship. A meeting at church could be arranged, just a chance to talk to him, hear in his own words what new life he had embraced, and from there the family would know how to proceed.

It was Bruce who shut down the discussion at the dinner table with an "I don't want to ever see him again." What followed was a prolonged silence as the family quietly but hastily finished their supper. The matter had to be settled later that night in Bruce's bedroom. Sabrina was kind. She did not try to force the issue or give her brother an ultimatum. After all, his attack on Tyler and his gang had been out of love for her and their mother, and under the circumstances, it felt justified.

"It took a lot of guts to do what you did," Sabrina said. She leaned on the door frame into his bedroom, hesitant to enter without permission. "You stood up. You were a man, and I didn't appreciate it at the time."

Bruce had been silent while he listened to his sister, his face buried in his pillow. He now rolled his head over to look at her. "You never said that before."

Sabrina took that as an invitation and sat on the edge of the bed. "I wouldn't let anything or anybody drive a wedge between us."

She patted his back gently, knowing it was her brother who had suffered the most because of Tyler; it was her brother who had been the innocent one and endured the corporal pain and mental distress of a punishing defeat at the hands of a monster allowed into his life by a wayward mother and a delinquent sister. But could not this onetime monster be regenerated by God? Does he not deserve another chance? Was he completely unlovable?

Bruce raised his head off the pillow. "Do you really love Tyler?"

Sabrina did not have an immediate answer. She was wading into deeper water. Both of their lives had been lived in extremes . . . extreme chaos and destruction, extreme peace and blessing. Tyler had been a major contributor to the former; her uncle, the provider of the latter. They were the only two men she had known. In the examination of her heart inspired by her brother's question, she expressed all she understood to this point in her young life.

"Our mama didn't teach me anything about being a woman. Tyler did, and even though he was mean sometimes, he always said he loved me and he always was around. I guess I'm like those baby animals that love the first thing they see once they open their eyes. Tyler was the first person I saw who acted like I was somebody that had value. I guess I loved him for that."

"And you want to give him another chance?" Bruce asked.

"He's different now. I know that. I can see it in his eyes and by the way he treats me. Don't tell Aunt Rosella, but we've been seeing each other besides at church, and he's changed. He's really changed. He is really trying to start his life over, make something of himself. I'm not saying we're gonna get married or anything. I'm just saying he's sweet to me, and I want to give him another chance."

Bruce laid his head back on the pillow, but this time not face-down as if hiding from past shame and future uncertainty. He laid his head on its side, which Sabrina took as a hopeful sign. It was not an outright rejection of what she was proposing.

Bruce did not want to hurt or disappoint his sister, but he wondered whether he could trust her. Was she about to invite a demon back into their lives, or had Tyler become a real miracle

207

story of God's intervention? Was Sabrina insightful enough to discern Tyler's nature? Was she safe with him? Was any of the family safe with him? He looked at her.

"If he hurts you, he won't take the bat away from me next time," he whispered.

Sabrina smiled and pinched Bruce's cheek.

"We'll both have us some bats."

Dewayne and Rosella never thought they would see Tyler again, but if they did, they knew it would be on the evening news, some correspondent reporting about his latest crime spree and his arrest. They never expected to see him in church, sans dreadlocks and T-shirt, dressed in a three-piece suit.

He was not just in church, but also in front of the whole church, introduced by an associate minister as one of the newest members of the community to join, and not just any pew-warming member, but one who would be contributing his talents to help promote the music ministry of the church. There was even the possibility of signing the church's worship band to the record division of the company that employed Tyler.

Would that all new members follow this young man's example, the associate minister admonished. Amens and hallelujahs popped into the air like verbal popcorn as the minister gave a brief and sanitized history of Tyler's former ghetto life and how God had done his Damascus Road thing on Tyler while in juvenile detention.

Here was a bona fide testament to the power of God, the minister said, and all God's children said amen, all God's children except Bruce. He withheld his judgment. Rosella and Dewayne shook their heads in disbelief as they added their amens. Sabrina beamed as she enthusiastically said her amen.

And so the experiment began. The rebuilding of trust was the first order of business, and Tyler was very careful not to force his way into the family. Life remained normal in the Jobe house, except there was a new addition to the dynamic. Even though he was a frequent topic of conversation, Tyler did not receive any invitations to dinner nor was he invited to accompany them on any family outings.

In the initial weeks, discussion of Tyler still caused tension; no one was able to altogether shake the memories of a sullen Tyler slouched over the sofa in Bonita's apartment, the knowledge of his drug business, and the horror of seeing his handiwork on Bruce's body. Rosella and Dewayne wanted to observe Tyler, and they were not willing to push Bruce into a relationship in which he did not yet feel comfortable. To help buy this new image of Tyler, Bruce needed time.

In the beginning he was allowed to sit with Sabrina and the family at church, and they could date, so the sneaking around ended—much to Sabrina's relief. But Bruce always sat on the opposite end of the pew and made sure Dewayne was between them.

Once while Dewayne was out of town for a weekend shooting another commercial, Bruce bumped into Tyler coming down a hallway at church. The fight-or-flight syndrome began to pump up Bruce's heart rate.

Before he dropped his head, Bruce saw Tyler tuck his Bible under his arm while he spoke to a couple in the worship band of the church. Bruce inched his way along the wall, eyes cast down, listening to Tyler spout off some of his promotional ideas for the band. As Bruce walked by, the couple thanked Tyler, took one of his business cards, and departed. Bruce could hear Tyler's footsteps coming up behind him, and he froze.

"You don't need your big bad uncle to protect you, little brother," Tyler said. "Why you always hiding behind him?"

"I don't hide behind him."

It was just the two of them in the hall.

Bruce had no bluster of confidence. He pressed his body into the wall.

"You're looking at the new Tyler. That old Tyler is gone. Ain't nothing to fear, little brother, but fear itself."

"I'm not your little brother." Bruce looked up and down the hall for a friendlier face.

"You're my little brother in Christ," Tyler said. "Can we be friends?"

Tyler extended his hand, but Bruce just stared at it as though it were an unrecognizable gesture. Tyler bobbed his hand up and down to indicate an urgent desire for a handshake that could be the representation of forgetfulness, to let bygones be bygones, to press on to a new future. Bruce was not buying it. A handshake was not enough to forget what it felt like being beaten with a baseball bat within an inch of his life, to forget the time in the hospital, to forget his battered image he observed in the mirror for months after the altercation. Sabrina got a confession and a request for pardon from Tyler.

Where was his?

"There you two are," Sabrina said as she scooted down the hall. "Come on, church is about to start."

Bruce sidled up beside his sister and put his arm around her waist, starting a forced march toward the sanctuary with Tyler trailing behind them. It would be weeks before the two of them would have another opportunity for a private conversation.

Rosella had negotiated a new national endorsement deal with a power drink distributor for Dewayne during the off-season that netted him another signing bonus of $7 million and $1.5 million per commercial—six commercial commitments over the next two years—and an additional $1 million for print ads. Between his conditioning regime and workouts at the Stars' facility and his flying to film endorsement obligations, the kids in school, and Rosella running their business, there was little time for vacations.

If the family was to see each other, Franklin and Joella had to come to Houston. They made a brief visit and brought encouraging reports of Bonita's recovery: she would soon be out on her own, she had gotten a job while still in the halfway house, and there was a picture proving positive signs of her upturn—weight gain, a new coiffure, clothes that appeared to be purchased for professional work, and a smile. As for Cherie, she preferred to come when football season was in full swing and the Houston temperature was not so severe.

When the church announced back in the winter the intention to take a mission group to Dominical, Costa Rica, to work in remote jungle villages, no one in the Jobe clan thought much about it, even though the planned trip would occur during Sabrina and Bruce's spring break. But when Sabrina mentioned Tyler had signed on to go, she began to encourage the idea as an option for a family vacation. The group from church would spend the week building an orphanage during the days and holding a vacation Bible school in the evenings. In spite of Tyler's presence, Bruce took to the idea of having an adventure to some exotic place and being a part of a mission they could do as a family along with other kids and their families at church. Dewayne said he would be willing to take time from personal training, and Rosella agreed to go when Joella said she would come and take care of Robert Jr.

What struck the group of short-term missionaries as they traveled three hours by bus from San Jose to Dominical were the extremes: extreme poverty, extreme wealth.

They spent each day at the construction site in a jungle village working on the orphanage. It was part of a broader ministry outreach from the local church in a village not ten miles from this wealthy resort area in Dominical, with homes carrying million-dollar price tags—and much, much higher ones. Impoverished villagers lived in structures they made from scraps of plastic, tin, tree limbs, and discarded materials "borrowed" from the wealthier neighborhoods.

Seeing such poverty was a first-time experience for most of the group. Dewayne and Rosella shared the conviction that the wealth they were accumulating could find a benevolent use. They discussed establishing a foundation to support similar mission programs on a year-round basis, and they dreamed of sponsoring events back home to raise people's awareness of the plight of these people.

Bruce took to the work as though he were born to do it. He knew nothing about building a structure, but with minimal instruction from a team leader, he tackled his assignment and finished it before anyone else. Then he asked what else he might do. By the middle of the week, he was assisting the crew supervisors on the more difficult tasks of raising walls and installing windows. At night after vacation Bible school was over, he sketched ideas for different rooms within the orphanage that were modeled after his own room—a budding architectural skill straight from the bloodline—and began to dream of ways he could raise funds to equip the orphanage with the technology to which he had become accustomed in a short time. He understood the poverty of these Costa Rican kids, and if they were anything like him, most would excel, given half the advantages given him.

Tyler and Sabrina had not had so much concentrated time together since they parted company in Los Angeles. These new circumstances and the new life each had started in Houston had kindled something in each of them neither could define except to name it as an awakening of love for the other. Sabrina had been shrewd in questioning her aunt about how to know it was real when love came knocking, and Rosella gave a mysterious answer: "You know it's love because you never felt it before."

It had never really been love before with Sabrina and Tyler. It had been lust, convenience, nothing better to do, status symbol, or all of the above. With the role models of her aunt and uncle, Sabrina saw what love could do for a person, and she began to believe there might be a real future with Tyler. The way Tyler and Sabrina had conducted themselves prior to this mission trip had achieved a level of trust from Rosella and Dewayne that had made Sabrina feel that she was gaining in maturity. Now working side by side with Tyler for the good of humanity, Sabrina felt strong romantic feelings rise to new levels.

Although Tyler did not take to the backbreaking labor as readily as most of the others on the mission team, he responded to the attention he was getting from Sabrina and returned her affections with equal fervor. Each day the group was given free time in the early afternoon when the heat of the day was at its peak, and a couple of times Tyler would take the opportunity to go into Dominical on his own, telling Sabrina he was on scouting missions for future work projects. He returned with tales of poverty and ideas for extended mission trips that thrilled Sabrina's budding spiritual nature. Who would have thought this young man could make such a transition? Nothing was impossible with God.

In the late afternoons when the local children went home after vacation Bible school and the mission group had had its evening devotional, most in the group went into the city on sightseeing tours and shopping sprees. Tyler and Sabrina went once, but then opted for the chance to be alone. With no transportation available and the beaches only a short distance from their compound, the option was clear.

After a mile of amble under a moonless sky, Tyler and Sabrina lost connection from all human association, and with an additional twenty minutes of strolling in and out of the tide, they happened onto a lagoon that became their mystic hideaway for the rest of their missionary experience. After the city lights vanished behind the northern curvature of the beach and rocky outcroppings, how separated from human sight the couple felt. The touches began as gentle tests and discoveries, lying prone on the soft sand, and grew with intensity. This was love, they protested against any hesitation or hint of guilt. It was not like the past, the destructive past so far behind them now, but the present with its new understanding, its new commitment to the new life that had dawned in each one's heart.

Each night this sea and sand and forest enclave became an illusion of love, a hidden place that burned in their minds during the scorching hours of orphanage construction, on through the afternoons of teaching the children the virtues gleaned from Bible stories, and into the evenings of group devotions, until they could dash to this tropical finish line and consume themselves in the images they had conjured in their minds during the day.

Two months later the consequences of their passion were evident. Sabrina called Tyler and asked him to meet her at the city park near his office. Couldn't it wait until tonight? he asked. His day was slammed. The response was an emphatic no. School had been out only a few weeks, and Sabrina was deep into her job at Jobe Enterprises, Inc. Because of a poor high school scholastic record while she lived in Los Angeles, she needed to go to summer school to fulfill her academic requirements in order to graduate and begin college in the fall. Her days were equally slammed with work and school, but this issue required immediate attention.

Tyler was not waiting for her at the bench beside the fountain in the middle of the park where they had always met before he reentered the Jobe family picture. She spied a suit coat, shirt, and tie draped over a laptop on the bench, and after determining these clothes belonged to Tyler, she scanned the park for him. The sound and vibrations of the vocals coming from the street caught her attention, and she moved toward the metallic two-toned shades of a blue and gold low-riding, high-sheen chromed vehicle. A male form leaned on the outside of the car, his head in perfect synchronization with four other heads inside the car bobbing to the beat of the music pounding from the console. The passenger in the front seat had to point her out before Tyler noticed Sabrina standing behind him.

The startled look on Tyler's face was like a small poke in her already tight stomach, and his face did not recover fast enough to satisfy her or remove the invisible finger that punctured her belly. He turned back around and leaned inside the window of the car, exchanged a few words, and suddenly the normal street noises were back in the air again. The driver of the car removed the CD and handed it to Tyler. He needed a few days to finish the transaction, he told them, and he would call to make the next appointment. Praise for Tyler's taste in women came from the passengers inside the vehicle before it moved into the flow of traffic.

"You're early," he said as he stepped toward the bench and removed his do-rag.

"Why are you not wearing your suit?" Sabrina asked, following behind him.

"It's hot, baby. It's Houston hot. It's Costa Rican hot," and he turned around, threw his arm around her waist, and kissed her hard.

That was the first time she had felt any aggression from Tyler, reminding her of the old days, and she pulled back and licked her lips. She tasted alcohol.

"Have you been drinking?"

"It's nothing. My homeboys are clients. Just showing some respect. It's business, baby." He returned to the bench where his wardrobe and laptop lay.

"It just surprised me not seeing you in your suit."

"I gotta dress the part . . . when in Rome, baby." Tyler began to slip into his shirt. "Suits make these guys uncomfortable, and if niche music retail keeps growing like it is, I'll start my own clothes line and put P. Diddy out of business."

"Well, you might want to think about starting a clothes line for kids," Sabrina said, folding down the upturned collar of his shirt.

"I hear you, baby. That's a great idea. I'll put you in charge of designing—"

"We can start with our kid."

Her words put an abrupt halt to Tyler's redressing. Sabrina was smiling. She did not want to frighten Tyler with this announcement or give him any reason to plot a hasty retreat.

She wanted one outcome, and she wanted Tyler to want it as much as she did.

The scenario she had worked out in her mind after she had taken her pregnancy test was sound and logical. Tyler just could not go off, she had to keep him from going off, she knew the brutal results when Tyler would go off, and this information was as much of a sucker punch as that from Bruce with his baseball bat. She was testing the hypothesis of God's transformative power within another human being.

"Are you saying you're gonna have a kid?" Tyler threw his tie over his shoulders, slinging one end around his neck like a scarf.

"I'm gonna have our kid."

Tyler began to hyperventilate. Sabrina placed a hand on his shoulder, but he shifted his weight and slipped out from under it.

Sabrina took that as a good sign; Tyler had not knocked her hand away. She had to be patient and understanding. She must remain calm and positive. This was dramatic news for anyone to hear, and she needed to keep the focus on all the potential good that could come from this.

Tyler jerked the tie off his neck and wadded it up.

"You're telling me this is my kid?" Tyler asked. "I mean, it never happened before when we were in LA."

"We weren't ready then. Maybe it's God telling us we're ready."

"Ready for what?" Tyler threw up his arms and dropped onto the bench.

"It happened while we were in Costa Rica," she said. "Isn't that romantic?"

It was obvious from his expression, his body language, that he did not quite see the romantic implications.

"You got one choice," he said. "Get rid of it."

Sabrina pretended not to hear his retort. It was an impulsive response to unsettling news. It was not the reaction from someone changed by God. It was the reply from the old Tyler, and she was not going to let the old Tyler reemerge and swallow up the new Tyler.

"Baby, my aunt and uncle, my grandparents, they are all going to be happy for us," Sabrina said, sitting down beside him. "Even my mama will be—"

"You think your family is gonna be happy when they find out I'm the one who did this? You think they won't throw my past right in your face?"

"But that's just it. Your past is in the past."

Tyler bounced off the bench and up onto his feet. He began to pace back and forth in front of Sabrina, expelling blasts of air from his mouth. He was a locomotive building steam for the long climb out of this valley.

"This is it. Your family . . . it'll never work. You best get rid of it. They'll never accept me. They'll never accept this baby."

Sabrina watched his vigorous gait. At points he seemed about to explode and threw out an arm or kicked a leg to release the swift buildup of energy. She could not watch and had to avert her eyes. There was too much truth to what he was saying. There had been too much realism in their history for her family to react to an unplanned pregnancy with joy.

"I've got some money saved," she said. "We could go somewhere . . . maybe."

"Maybe I should just leave," Tyler said.

She feared these words most. Her father left, and her brother's father was never there to leave. He had appeared long enough to impregnate her mother and disappear like some phantom. This, Sabrina could not tolerate. She was not like her mother.

Tyler was not like those other men, like so many other men who refused to accept responsibility. Yet she could not lose this baby. If she panicked, she could lose them both. If she was wise, she might keep them both.

"You love me, don't you?" Sabrina was only semiconfident of his answer.

As he continued to wear out the pavement in front of her, that confidence began to wane, and the quicker the decline in her confidence, the more she began to realize she might be facing this situation all by herself. The family could reject her as they had rejected her mother. The family would not allow a second generation of shame. Was she just like her mother? Would she walk the same path now that she was pregnant? Would the account of her mother's ruinous actions be a version of her future?

She thought since her aunt and uncle had entered her life, her future had changed, life had been generous and kind, and in its generosity, it had brought Tyler back to her. He had to love her. He had to be committed to her and to this child. God had to be a part of this whole plot. In her mind, all the signs of his participation were there.

Tyler came to an abrupt halt in front of her. "Do you love me?"

Surprise and relief flooded Sabrina's face. Of course, she loved him. Had she not proven it to him?

"And you want to keep this baby?"

Of course, they should keep this child. Their love had created this child.

"And you know down deep your family would never agree to us getting married? They would never let me see you again."

Of course, she knew there was the issue of her family. It would hit the fan when this news came to the light.

"And you don't want to do this alone; you want to do this together."

Of course, they must be together for this. There was no one else in the world with whom she wanted to walk into the future.

All of this confirmed, he sat down beside her.

"I love you, and I want to keep this child," he said.

Sabrina surrendered to the burden of her overtaxed heart and the sobs came in rippling drifts. Tyler tucked Sabrina's head into his shoulder and brought his other arm around her for support.

People rambling by cast snooping looks in their direction. When she became calm, Tyler wiped her tears and kissed her face. She had been frightened that the old Tyler might have won the battle.

He placed his hands on either side of her face and spoke in a calm, reassuring tone. "I have a plan to make this work."

Yes, the new Tyler had won, and the vice grip inside Sabrina's heart began to loosen its hold.

18

Dewayne had been gone three days, pretending to catch passes and run around tacklers in a studio for a series of football video games, the first of which would debut in the fall. Technicians wired his body from head to toe to record all his moves in front of a green screen so the computer designers could draw his likeness and make his image do far more amazing things on-screen than he could ever do on the playing field. He hated to be gone so long, but the company needed to shoot enough action footage for animators to use in the first three videos; the price paid for this level of success. There would be no words of complaint.

Rosella had arranged for the plane to leave early that morning so he could get home and make it to the Stars' training facility for a half day's workout. Dewayne felt good about the team for this coming season. During the early summer minicamp, the veterans and rookies were acting like family at a reunion. The biggest factor for the improvement in team spirit was the absence of Colby Stewart.

Two days after the Jobe family had returned home from the mission trip, all the sportscasters were talking about, in a thirty-six-hour sports news cycle, was how Colby had signed with Baltimore and was now the highest paid linebacker in the league.

When Dewayne heard the news, he had to admit he was relieved. There was no love lost. He thought he might call to congratulate Colby, make a gesture of kindness, but the hectic pace of his life swallowed up the half-hearted intention. He assumed he might see Colby in the locker room before he left, but when Dewayne came to practice after the mission trip, Colby's locker was empty.

Dewayne opened his locker and found a message written from Colby: "If your God loves you, then you better pray our teams don't meet up." Dewayne had decided to keep the note. If the two teams did happen to meet in the coming season, Colby's memo might be a real motivator.

The day Dewayne left for the three-day trip to New York to shoot his football video games, Tyler was traveling to Los Angeles. Rosella had shuttled them together to the airport, dropping Tyler off at his airline gate before taking Dewayne to the private jet service that would fly him to New York.

Tyler's plan called for the three of them to be together, the entire Jobe family in full knowledge of his itinerary.

On the afternoon of Dewayne's return, Rosella packed her husband a comfortable change of clothes and blended his favorite smoothie, iced down in a cooler in the backseat of the Denali. Before he had left for New York, he had encouraged Rosella to go to the spa, said she deserved such pampering and the baby would be fine with Sabrina and Bruce. She was reluctant, but he was insistent. Had not Robert survived without her for a week while they were on the mission trip? Rosella finally conceded when Sabrina had offered to pick up

Dewayne, telling her aunt not to worry; she would be sure to have Uncle Dewayne call her cell as she drove him to the training center from the airport.

Sabrina had earned a new level of trust as Rosella had given her more and more responsibility with the business after closing several new endorsement deals for Dewayne. This rapid increase in their business required creating computer accounts for each new client and tracking expenses specific to each, and Rosella had trained Sabrina how to monitor all this client information as well as cash flow. It wasn't unusual for Sabrina to spend several hours a day on these tasks.

Once Rosella repeated for the umpteenth time where she would be if the kids needed anything, she left for the spa for eight hours of physical indulgence with a group of players' wives from the team. Bruce played with Robert on the floor in the office while Sabrina sat down to finish some business on the computer.

When Sabrina heard the garage door close and saw Rosella back out of the drive and pull away from the house, she took five minutes to be sure her aunt would not return for some forgotten item, then dropped the bomb on Bruce that she was going to get Tyler.

Bruce took the news that he and Robert Jr. would be alone in the house with Tyler while Sabrina picked up Dewayne and delivered him to the training facility with disgust.

"Why does he have to come here?" Bruce said. "I'm old enough to take care of myself and the baby."

Sabrina needed to be patient. She needed to stay calm. She did not want Bruce to see anything unusual about this news and make him apprehensive.

"Tyler is coming to help me with some new computer software Aunt Rosella bought, and he can be putting it into the system while I'm gone."

She did not expect Bruce to understand what she was doing, what she was going through. Understanding would come later with the revelation of the truth, and she hoped his forgiveness, everyone's forgiveness, would follow. Forgiveness from her family was a part of her plan, the part she had not discussed with Tyler.

She began her note to Rosella, scribbled on Jobe Enterprises stationery:

> Aunt Rosella, I hope you can forgive me someday. I didn't want things to work out this way. I didn't intend to fall in love or get pregnant. It's best for us to leave. We took some money from the company for two plane—

Her cell phone rang. Tyler was headed to their rendezvous point. Time was running short, and she needed to leave now to keep the plan on schedule. She folded the note and stuck it in the desk drawer. She would finish it when she returned.

One of Tyler's associates had dropped him off in a parking lot of a gargantuan shopping mall close to the Jobe house, where he was to meet Sabrina. When Tyler strolled up to the Denali in the mall parking lot, Sabrina was perturbed with his tardiness, but was soon placated once he embraced her and told her all would be well. She steadied her nerves, cleared her head, and refocused. The thought of being in Costa Rica in twenty-four hours with her future husband was all the incentive she needed to continue with the plan.

They dashed back to the house, and before Sabrina pulled out of the garage to head to the airport for her uncle, she watched as Tyler dropped the Roofies in the smoothie drink. If he had calculated the correct dosage for a man Dewayne's size, he would be out for several hours, and Tyler swore the drug would burn through the bloodstream so fast his system would be clean enough for a drug test in a few hours.

Tyler removed his gloves after closing the lid on the cooler and getting out of the car. He kissed Sabrina.

"Baby, you call me as soon as your uncle is asleep. Meanwhile, I'm going to be buying us two first-class tickets to paradise and get the numbered account set up for the money transfer."

Sabrina reached her hand out of the window and took Tyler by the collar.

"This is just a loan, right?"

"Yes, baby. Just a small amount to carry us through until the baby gets here. Once we get ourselves set up and I get some things working, we will pay back that loan."

"With interest."

"Better interest than any bank would offer. I promise."

Tyler took her hand away from his collar and kissed it. The promise and the kiss satisfied her, and she pulled out of the garage.

———————

Half an hour later, Sabrina sat in her uncle's Denali and worried the computerized sound system with her index finger, impatient to find a song on the radio to calm her down or at least distract her attention as she waited for Dewayne to emerge from the private air fleet hangar.

In spite of her edginess, so far the plan was going well. At any moment, a Ciga Games Lear jet from New York would taxi Dewayne across the tarmac. Rosella had always insisted on this form of travel when she negotiated any of his endorsement deals that took him out of Houston, and it had not taken long for Dewayne to become accustomed to the specialized perks. The jet would deposit him in front of the hangar's small, luxurious lobby. Rosella had left him a message that she had decided to go to the spa and Sabrina would take him to the Stars' training facility from the airport.

After Sabrina left for the airport, Tyler had gone to work on the computer. There was very little talk between Tyler and Bruce once Tyler was in the house.

Ever since the mission to Costa Rica, Tyler had been a frequent guest in the house, and everyone but Bruce was growing more comfortable with him around. Bruce kept his distance, observing Tyler's polite and restrained behavior with the family. He knew Tyler's quiet circumspection was not normal. He did not buy the "new Tyler" line his sister kept using, and why not? If the old Tyler had nearly beaten him to death, why should he expect an authentic spiritual makeover?

Bruce played with Robert in the room next to the office and was happy to be out of Tyler's sight, but when the baby started to get fussy, Tyler appeared at the door.

"Can't you keep that baby quiet?" he said, his voice weighted with exasperation.

"He's a baby," Bruce said, lifting his little cousin off the floor, cradling him in his arms, and bouncing him to stop the crying. "They make noise."

"Yeah, well, put a cork in him or something. Just shut him up. I'm working."

Bruce recognized the new Tyler had been unable to restrain the old Tyler. Perhaps he would soon tip his hand for the others to see that the old Tyler was the real Tyler now and forevermore.

"I thought you were supposed to be in LA for a week," Bruce said.

"In my line of work things move fast, little man, and you got to keep up. Go where you gotta go. Do what you gotta do."

"Why you wearing plastic gloves?" Bruce asked.

Tyler looked a little surprised they were on his hands. "Germs . . . Now shut that baby up," and he disappeared from Bruce's view.

Bruce took Robert into the kitchen, set him in his high chair, and gave him a cracker and a bottle of juice, which kept him occupied until Bruce could prepare him some real food. He did everything he could to keep from banging around in the kitchen so as not to disturb Tyler. He swore he would never again allow himself to be in this position.

Bruce opened the microwave door before the beeper went off signaling the cereal for the baby was ready. He closed the microwave door and poured the cereal into a bowl, and just before he was about to bring it over to the high chair, he could hear Tyler talking to someone in a low voice.

He set the bowl on the counter, gave the baby another cracker, tiptoed to the door into the office, and stuck his head around the corner. Tyler had his back to him with his cell phone cocked to his ear, held in place with his shoulder. Bruce watched as he opened the desk drawer where Rosella kept a small antique box filled with cash, and while he talked on the phone, he counted out a thick stack of one-hundred-dollar bills and then stuffed them into an envelope and put it into his travel bag.

There never had been a new Tyler. Bruce was right all along.

When Tyler reached over to zip his bag closed, he turned around in the desk chair and looked at the door. No one was there. He finished zipping his bag and returned to typing on the computer as he continued his phone conversation.

"You're doing great, girl," he said, speaking just above a whisper. "It's just like taking a nap. Listen to me. I've got everything set up, and I'm about to buy our plane tickets. Tonight we're gonna be flying south of the border and . . . hold on. Hold on."

Tyler heard the baby starting to crank up into a full-blown squall from the kitchen, and he did not want Sabrina to hear the noise in the background and turn her anxiety into full-blown panic. He swung the chair around and saw Bruce standing in front of him, holding a nine iron.

"I'll call you right back, baby," Tyler said and closed his phone and set it on the desk. "That was your sister. Says your uncle's not feeling well and she's bringing him back to the house."

Bruce stood his ground and waited for Tyler to move. The crying intensified.

"Ain't you gonna do something to keep that baby quiet?"

But Bruce did nothing, said nothing. He was waiting. It would not hurt Robert to cry.

"So is history gonna repeat itself, my little brother?"

It would repeat itself but with a different outcome. Bruce was not going to wait until the others got home. He was going to finish it now, his way. He was going to finish what he started in Los Angles outside his apartment door, and this time there was no posse to eliminate. It was man-to-man, and he was determined to rid his family of this evil for the last time.

"You know when I get out of this chair, you're gonna die," Tyler said, drumming his fingers on top of the desk. "Do not go to the hospital. Do not collect two hundred dollars. Go straight to the morgue."

Thus saith the old Tyler. If Bruce had only spoken up sooner, if he had only expressed his fears about Tyler from the beginning, perhaps this moment might never have arrived. But it was here. It was real. And it would be over soon.

The crash in the kitchen and the ensuing shriek from the baby were the distraction Tyler needed. He leaped out of the chair the second Bruce turned his head toward the noise. Bruce recovered enough to make one swing with the club, hitting Tyler in the rib cage, but did little to stop his momentum. Tyler grabbed the iron with one hand and slammed the heel of his other hand into Bruce's nose, knocking him backward into the glass coffee table.

The glass exploded, and Tyler turned away, squatting down to shield his face and body from the flying glass.

When the glass settled to the floor, Tyler stood and raised the golf club in preparation for a second assault, but there was no counterattack. Bruce lay motionless on his back. A shard of glass had pierced his neck.

Bruce felt a current pulsating through him like a small electrical charge. His impending death did not frighten him. He accepted it. What he struggled to accept was the failure of his second attempt to prevent this malevolence from overtaking his domain. He saw the blurry image of Tyler standing above him, resting the nine iron on his shoulder.

He closed his eyes, feeling the strength flow out of him. He knew it was time to rest. He had done all he could do, and he felt a peace replacing the loss of vitality, a peace that brought knowledge—a knowing that the world would someday recognize what he had know all this time.

Tyler watched until the last flicker of life had departed, and then he went into the kitchen to quiet the shrieking baby. The baby had knocked the bottle off his tray, spilling juice on the floor. Pure rage merged with the adrenaline coursing through Tyler, and within minutes, he had silenced the baby's cries. Permanently.

He surveyed the kitchen like a dissatisfied artist trying to determine what brushstroke he needed to complete the picture. Tyler listened. The only sound was his own breathing. A cluster of fresh ice cubes dropping into the ice container in the freezer startled him, and he raised the golf club, prepared to strike. He opened the door to the freezer just to satisfy his curiosity and then slammed it shut.

He reviewed the murder in each room and realized it was not quite the plan he and Sabrina had discussed, nor was it what he had envisioned in his private contingencies, but after pausing long enough to contemplate what had been accomplished, he felt as if he could live with this alternative. In fact, this scenario would be better for the future at large. He had crossed a line from which there would be no turning. He had made irrevocable choices, and it would require a few innovative brushstrokes before the canvas was complete. But he could see the big picture. He could do the simple math and figure out this reduction in the population would give him fewer responsibilities down the road. Nothing like a little pandemonium to help clear the mind and bring everything into focus.

If he was committed to this altered plan and would see the upcoming challenges through to the end, this could very well evolve into the master plan that would make him famous. He had raised the bar. The criminal world would marvel for years to come about this day and what he pulled off. But he had to be very, very smart.

Tyler's cell phone started ringing, and he saw it was Sabrina's number. He returned to the office, leaned the golf club against the desk, and unzipped his bag. He peeled off the latex gloves, put on a fresh pair, and then removed a nine-millimeter Glock and zipped the bag closed. After securing a round in the chamber, he stuffed the weapon into the back of his pants and took a few deep breaths. He decided it would be best to shield her eyes from the calamity in the kitchen as he guided her from the garage through the house to the office. He had to keep the visual trauma to a minimum, and there was no time to clean up the aftermath. Besides, leaving things as they were might work well in his master plan, he thought. He trusted his instincts to improvise. Still, it was going to be hard to keep Sabrina focused on the task at hand on the computer with the bloody scene just a few feet away.

He figured Sabrina was calling to tell him she was almost there, so he glided through the kitchen and opened the door into the garage. The moment he silenced his phone, the door to the garage started opening, and he stepped back into the kitchen until he saw Sabrina driving Dewayne's car into its slot. The car flew into the garage, and she stopped it just before crashing into the back wall. Sabrina catapulted out of the car as if a snake had just slithered out from under the seat, her arms waving as though sending a distress signal.

"I can't believe we're doing this. I can't believe we're doing this," she said, skating in circles over the paved open space where Rosella parked her car.

Tyler pushed the button in the kitchen to close the garage door, then scooped Sabrina into his arms and pressed her close, encouraging her with words of praise and comfort while covering her face with multiple kisses until she was able to gain control.

"We're going to see this through, baby. It'll be over soon," he said as he looked over her shoulder at Dewayne's slumped body in the front seat.

After making sure Sabrina was calm enough to release, he reached into the front seat and unbuckled Dewayne's seat belt. He grabbed Dewayne by the arm and leg and was surprised at how easily the dead weight of the big man slid across the leather bench seat of the Denali. Maybe the pulsating adrenaline rush had given him superhuman strength.

Once he positioned Dewayne in the driver's seat, Tyler tested which posture looked more natural to his master plan: would it be more natural to have Dewayne slumped over, his head resting on the steering wheel, or would it be better if they found him leaning with the back of his neck on the headrest?

He asked Sabrina for her opinion and immediately regretted it. He knew from her response he needed to be direct in all his requests, so he grabbed her arm, pulled her over to the opened door, flattened out the fingers of her right hand, and scraped her nails down Dewayne's left cheek, which left his head leaning to one side, a position Tyler had not considered but liked for its ordinary pose.

This simple task reinvigorated the hysteria from minutes ago when Sabrina leaped out of the car, so Tyler decided it was time to let her know the original plan had advanced into a master plan much greater than the sum of its parts. The master plan required him to downgrade her role.

With one hand, Tyler covered Sabrina's mouth, and with the other, he placed the barrel of the Glock against her temple.

Her eyes widened to take in this incomprehensible universe as she sucked air through the mesh of Tyler's fingers. What horror had befallen her? What had happened to change the dream of paradise?

In a whisper as gentle as the breath of a sleeper, he told her it would be best not to scream, and if she did everything he asked of her, then all would be well. He kissed her head and her eyes and then moved his hand from her mouth and kissed her lips. When he felt some of the tension begin to subside, Tyler placed his hand over Sabrina's eyes and led her out of the garage, through the kitchen, and into the office.

The second decisive moment was at hand. When he sat her down in the desk chair, he spun it around so she would see the gravity of her situation and cooperate with him.

"It was an accident," Tyler said before spinning the seat around and pinning her shoulders against the high back of the leather chair to keep her from attacking him if she was so inclined.

Sabrina's eyes began to throb as if to reject what she just saw, but her eyes failed to protect her and the image of her brother's death registering on her brain like a massive weight. She felt her head sinking into her shoulders unable to support the heaviness. She saw Tyler's lips moving, but she had to concentrate to hear the words.

". . . he just fell," Tyler said. "We were messing around . . . the fool tripped . . . I'm telling you . . ."

What was he telling her? What was he saying? Sabrina heard the words, but she could not understand them.

". . . And when that baby wouldn't shut up . . . I tried, you know . . . I tried to calm it down, but things went bad . . . I picked it up and things went bad . . ."

Sabrina protectively moved her hands over her abdomen. She felt her heart and lungs burst into flames. *This must be what hell is like*, she thought. *This is what it is going to feel like inside my body. I'm going to hell when this is over*. For her part in this tragedy, she was convinced she deserved nothing less.

Tyler pulled out the drawer and saw the taped, laminated sheet of the log-ins and passwords for the different business accounts. He blocked Sabrina's side vision and pressed the tip of the weapon against her head while she worked on the computer. He thought it best that her brother's body should not visually distract her as he pushed her to work in haste.

Through the magic of SWIFT codes, Tyler was becoming a wealthy man. He could feel the tingle in his spine as Sabrina typed in each password for a Jobe Enterprises, Inc., business account, and he watched the millions depleted from each account into his own. Tyler had set up a numbered account in a Caribbean bank for the transferred money.

Using the office computer to establish the account as well as to book the airline tickets was a stroke of genius, he thought. It would all make logical sense to those who would come upon the aftermath of this event and have to interpret and make sense of this bedlam.

With the click of the keyboard, millions disappeared from one account and appeared in another. In a matter of only a few minutes, Tyler had fulfilled his rags-to-riches American dream. But he must not become giddy or careless here at the end, he reminded himself. He must remain focused and not be sidetracked from what he had set in motion.

Sabrina had not spoken a word through the entire computerized banking process. The only account that did not have a log-in and password on the sheet was the Jobe personal checking account, which, she swore, contained only a few hundred thousand dollars.

It was a paltry sum compared to the millions waiting for him. Tyler would not be a greedy man. Let them say of him when people recited this story that he had not left this family in destitution, that he had shown restraint.

"I thought you had changed," Sabrina said, and she covered her mouth to stifle the sob bubbling from her throat.

"I changed my address," he said, checking the last of the numbers on the screen to make sure they matched the numbers he had printed off when he set up the account.

"But your job . . . and church, the things you told me . . . how you treated me . . ."

"You can read about it in my autobiography," he said, and once he was assured that all the numbers checked out, he had her shut off the computer. "I'd like to thank the academy for this award for best actor in a leading role in bringing down the house of Jobe," he said as he caressed Sabrina's swollen face with the tip of the gun.

In the final terrifying moments as Sabrina felt the cool end of the gun slide over her skin and she looked into Tyler's grinning face, one lucid thought came to her. She had opened the door of her heart and this house to the devil. There could be no forgiveness for what she had done, only punishment and death.

Sabrina knew what was coming and she would not go without some level of resistance. Tyler grabbed a fistful of her hair and yanked. She released her grip of the armrests and rose to her feet. He kept the tension on her hair, lifting her almost off her feet as he jammed his weapon inside his pocket and clutched the nine iron leaning against the desk.

Sabrina realized she still had her bag slung over her right shoulder as she was marched into the kitchen. She grasped her bag and swung around, striking Tyler in the side of the face with this newfound weapon. The heroic burst of energy to change fortune only amused Tyler, and Sabrina stared at him in wonder at the ineffectiveness of her strike.

The blow to the side of her head was so swift, it did not have time to register in her brain.

Tyler watched Sabrina crumple to the floor, a human rag doll among the scattered contents of her purse. This could not have been a more perfect outcome. He would not have to move her body at all. He bent down, picked up Sabrina's cell phone and passport, and slipped back into the office.

One final sweep of the desk netted him another twenty-five hundred dollars and Dewayne's passport. This luck felt orchestrated, but he would never admit to it. No, when his criminal peers told this story, they would speak of him as the architect of this master plan. The glory belonged to him alone. He dropped the extra cash, Sabrina's cell phone, and his weapon into his bag, and then laid Sabrina's and Dewayne's passports on top of the fax machine next to the E-tickets and travel itinerary sent over from the agency—one-way flights to Argentina departing that afternoon.

He needed to delay the admiration for his work. A few more details needed his attention. Satisfied with the condition of the office, he threw his bag over his shoulder, snatched the golf club—he may actually take up golf, he thought, once he had settled into a new location—and returned to the kitchen. Sabrina had not moved from the point on the floor where she had fallen, but to be sure she had indeed expired from the deft strike to the head, he placed two latexed fingers on her neck in search of a pulse. He found none, so he tiptoed out of the kitchen, careful to avoid contact with the bodies.

Once in the garage he quickened his pace. After removing the smoothie containers from the cooler and dropping them into his bag, he decided he liked the door of the Denali to remain open. He then counted out five thousand in cash from what he had lifted from the desk in the office, leaving him a balance of just over ten thousand, and stuffed the money into Dewayne's coat pocket. He wrapped Dewayne's hand around the leather grip of the nine iron and set the end resting on the garage floor. Finally, he reached over the steering wheel and turned on the ignition.

The master stepped back to the kitchen and took one last look before closing the door. Then the master reviewed all the steps he had taken to implement his plan, those calculated and those spontaneous. He almost hated to leave the scene, considering how perfectly everything had gone. He wished he could be here when Rosella arrived, followed by the paramedics and the police. He wished he could hear their interpretations of the gallery of scenes laid out for them, gloat as they deduced the wrong conclusions, even muster a level of false sympathy for the accused.

Yes, he would write this story of exactly how it happened. He would not leave this masterwork for lesser mortals to write. His account would be definitive.

"This is OnStar. My name is Martha. How may we assist you, Mr. Jobe?"

The voice startled him out of his reverie. Martha had to ask the question a second time before Tyler was sure of the voice's origin. How did that happen? He did not move. He held his breath, his mind racing with new alternatives to this unexpected twist. Martha asked the question a third time with a slight edge of impatience, and Tyler realized he must have hit the OnStar button when turning on the ignition to the car.

"Due to lack of response, OnStar is disconnecting."

No one would believe this ending except the aficionados of pulp fiction. It was a detail even the master planner had to admit he would never have chosen to tempt fate's whims. It was brilliant, and the master planner filled the enclosed darkening atmosphere with uproarious laughter.

19

Just hours before the Jobe calamity, Cherie had left Webb Furniture early, complaining of some pains in her chest and an upset stomach, a delayed reaction to last night's Chinese takeout, she explained. She took a half day of sick leave, a rarity in Cherie's professional life. On her sofa was where she wanted to be, watching Dr. Phil and Oprah, shows she never saw because she was stretching sheets of simulated leather over the metal frames during daylight hours.

The flat screen that hung in her living room was like a memorial to her son's kindness. When Cherie had found out her son had paid off her mortgage—he did receive that scolding he had anticipated—Cherie had taken a portion of the money she had in a savings account and bought herself the flat screen to watch her son play football. Now, the reminder of his thoughtfulness toward her brought a wave of emotion as she turned on the TV and settled in to rest.

She was frustrated when a special news bulletin interrupted Oprah's interview with a celebrity promoting the release of her new movie, one she had no intention of seeing. The screen cut to a reporter standing in front of a chaotic scene. Something about being in an upscale, residential neighborhood outside Houston, the reporter said. Cherie thought the house in the background looked so much like Dewayne's, but she could not understand the reporter's words. The masses of people—firefighters, police, reporters, and general onlookers behind the police barricades distracted her. But when she heard the reporter say her son's name, she rose from the sofa and began to shuffle backward toward the bathroom, her eyes riveted to the screen. Paramedics were coming out of the Jobe house pushing gurneys loaded down with black bags and depositing the contents in waiting ambulances. As the ambulances began to drive away, Cherie tumbled into the bathroom, voiding everything inside her stomach.

When she returned to the living room, she held on to the back of the recliner to keep from collapsing and listened to the police spokeswoman give an account of what was known so far. An OnStar representative had received a call from the owner of the vehicle, an occupant who resided in the house, but there was no response. She became suspicious and alerted the police. Four people found inside; Dewayne Jobe was the only one found alive, and he had just been taken to an undisclosed hospital suffering from carbon monoxide poisoning.

Cherie returned to the bathroom to ride out a second wave of convulsions in her abdomen and chest. The persistent ringing of the phone in the kitchen pulled her out of the bathroom, and as she passed through the living room to answer the phone, Oprah and the crowd convulsed in laughter at the story the celebrity had just told. Cherie could not believe they were laughing. How could they be laughing at a time like this?

She stumbled over to the television and turned down the sound. She could not abide hearing laughter. She answered the phone, thinking it might be Rosella, but instead it was Jake Hopper. Yes, she did have the television on. Yes, she had just seen the report. Yes, it was unbelievable. Yes, she was also in shock. And why were they even having this conversation?

"I'll close up the store and be right over," Jake said.

Cherie did not reply but carried the phone with her to the television, stretching the cord to its full length. She took the remote in her hands and began to back away from the screen, not wanting to be too close to the horror it had reported. The TV had become an enemy, forcing its sick, repulsive, sanitized news into her home, her life, her heart.

Her son. Her only son.

She flipped the remote and found another cable channel covering the story.

All three children were dead, the reporter said.

Cherie dropped the phone on the floor, and the taut cord yanked the receiver back into the kitchen.

All three were brutally murdered, the reporter continued.

Cherie dropped the remote, and when it hit the hardwood floor, the plastic case broke open, scattering the batteries.

The reporter ended the segment by saying they could not confirm it, but police were saying Dewayne Jobe was the number one suspect who may have perpetrated these heinous crimes.

The only thing left to drop to the floor was Cherie, and she collapsed in an agony of broiling pain.

"My son," she whispered. "My only son."

Rosella had commented to her friends how strange it was that Dewayne did not call on his way to the Stars' training facility once he landed, and had she not been in the middle of a mud bath, she would have called him. There wasn't even a message from either Sabrina or Dewayne when she checked her voice mail after showering off the medicinal dirt, and when she called them, she left a terse message on each of their voice mails. He and Sabrina would get a mild reprimand from her at dinner tonight.

But the police were waiting for her in the parking lot of the Mediterranean where she had spent an invigorating day with her friends. She would not be going home to prepare the family dinner.

The two uniformed policewomen who escorted her to their car and drove her to the hospital were very polite, but they gave Rosella little information about what had happened at her house. In an act of benign deception, one policewoman asked for Rosella's cell phone, explaining the battery in her phone had died and she needed to check on her child in day care. In all innocence, Rosella gave it to her. The officers did not want her to receive or make any calls that might give her a concrete idea of what disaster had befallen her family. They tried to keep Rosella from panicking by telling her there had been an accident, people were hurt—to what extent they weren't sure—and she didn't need to go home. They would take her straight to the hospital.

The policewomen would let someone above their pay grade tell Rosella who was dead and who was still recovering. They had not been at the scene, so they could not comment on the small army of people who had descended upon Rosella's neighborhood, and the reason for the police escort was to avoid the crowds and media that always show up when a celebrity of any kind has an accident.

All this seemed to reassure Rosella for the duration of the drive, so much so she forgot she had loaned the officer her phone. After the phone call, the officer turned off the phone and concealed it on the seat between them.

When they arrived at the hospital, television trucks were camped outside the front entrance and a crowd of people moved in and out of the lobby. The driver of the police car spoke to someone on the radio, then drove a few blocks farther down the street and entered a loading dock at the rear of the building. A Detective John Hathaway met Rosella and the two officers at a back entrance leading to the lower floors. Rosella took her phone without noticing it was off, and she dropped it into her purse as the officers told her good-bye.

John Hathaway and Rosella walked together down the long hall in the lower floor of the hospital. Hathaway had worked as a uniform for four years and in homicide for the Houston Police Department for the last twenty-three. He had been successful at cracking many difficult cases for which he was honored with awards and citations and mayoral handshakes, none of which he cared about. What he did care about was the case, and what he did not like was people telling him how to do his job, people who talked too much and knew even less. He walked with a limp courtesy of a fleeing suspect who did not like the fact of Hathaway's pursuit and so fired at him. In turn, Hathaway did not like the suspect's reaction, especially after he had taken a bullet, so he returned fire and stopped the suspect's escape. That was when he got the handshake from the mayor.

In twenty-seven years, Hathaway had gone through three marriages, all of them childless, and a couple of girlfriends between each divorce. The job needed him to be sharp, and he feared the comforts of domestic life would make him soft, so a pair of twins, null and void, occupied his current love life. When it came to keeping a steady partner, he was no more successful with his fellow detectives. His leaving-no-stone-unturned method of case building and a zero tolerance for sloppy work meant he was in constant conflict with anyone who labored beside him, but in spite of his sour personality few would say that time spent with Hathaway had not made them better detectives.

"Is my husband here?" Rosella asked.

"Yes, ma'am, but he's unconscious at the moment. They'll let us know as soon as he wakes up."

"Unconscious? Why is he unconscious?"

"Carbon monoxide poisoning," he said.

Rosella stared at him in complete disbelief.

"That's exhaust from a car."

"I know what that is," she said as they walked into a small seating area.

"Yes, ma'am. Why don't we take a seat here and I can walk you through this. Would you like some coffee . . . something to drink?"

"I just want to see my husband. I want to know what happened."

When Rosella sat down in the red fake-leather chair with metal armrests, she did not notice where she was. She did not notice the other detective and the coroner talking in low voices off to the side in the seating area, an attorney from the DA's office speaking with a uniformed policeman, or a coroner's aide chatting it up with a custodial worker. She did not notice the sign above the double doors that read "Hospital Morgue" or the large viewing window with its drawn curtain concealing two covered bodies on stainless steel tables on the other side. She could not see the two assistants ready to unveil the corpses when instructed.

What she did see was John Hathaway sliding the wooden coffee table in front of her and taking a seat on the edge. He had her complete attention. Her eyes were fixed on the man whose skin hung from his face in a perpetual 3:00 a.m. sag. He would unlock this mystery.

"When was the last time you spoke with your husband, Mrs. Jobe?"

"Last night . . . yes. He called from New York."

"What was he doing in New York?"

"Filming a football video game. Why can't I see my husband?"

"What I'm about to tell you is going to be very painful, Mrs. Jobe."

Hathaway was not devoid of compassion. He never found this task of delivering bad news an easy thing. Policemen and doctors were always telling people bad news, it was part of the territory, and long ago he had lost count of how many times he had to be the message bearer for the Angel of Death. He thought it best to keep direct eye contact while communicating dreadful news. It made the listeners feel as though they were getting the complete truth. If he looked away, they would feel he was hiding something.

If they ever looked away, which they normally did—as did Rosella, covering her newly cleansed face with her hands and bathing her skin in a cascade of tears—he still kept his eyes in direct contact with the listeners. And once he delivered the words, he was prepared to answer any questions to the best of his ability and offer comfort with a hand to the shoulder and a word of sympathy.

Hathaway never faked his words or his gestures. It was his way of building trust and relationship. He had grown accustomed to raw distress in times of extreme trauma, but he had not grown calloused to the experience. Each human emotional wreck was

244

different, as was each crime scene, and he treated each with respect and compassion. He offered Rosella tissue after tissue throughout his monologue—sanitizing the gruesome parts and not offering his interpretation of all the evidence he had observed at the scene—and when she could hear no more, he stopped and laid his hand on her bent, convulsing back. Touch in the midst of anguish was a sublime form of empathy.

But it was not over. He had just opened the doors to torment. Hathaway was a prophet, and there was no turning from his story. He helped Rosella to her feet and guided her to the window. The policeman and the attorney followed and, like muted ghosts, took their stations behind them, alert to every possible reaction from Rosella. It was best to get as much done in the early stages of shock as possible, and so it was critical for Rosella to identify the bodies of Bruce and Sabrina—and if she was able, Robert Jobe III.

Hathaway knocked on the glass, and the curtain flew back. Rosella refused to look, and Hathaway placed his arm over her shoulders and held her in his firm, supportive grasp until she raised her head. He cocked his head toward the assistants, and they pulled back the sheets covering her niece and nephew. Hathaway squeezed her shoulder as a fresh wave of grief consumed Rosella when she confirmed these children were her kin, but she had not buckled. Hathaway decided to gamble and show her the baby.

With her head buried in Hathaway's chest, he nodded again, and an assistant rolled a small table into view. He gripped Rosella's arm with his other hand, but it was not enough to support this final wretchedness. In a paroxysm of misery, she jerked back from the vision of her son and almost out of Hathaway's arms. The policewoman came to Hathaway's aid and wrenched her out of his arms. She motioned for the custodian to help, and together they carried Rosella back to her seat and held on to her while her screams echoed down the hallway. Hathaway signaled to an assistant to close the curtain and then looked straight into the attorney's face.

"She is innocent and she knows nothing," he said, a pronouncement he had never made about a potential suspect this early in the investigative process when a thousand questions still needed to be asked and all the details analyzed.

The attorney only nodded and kept his opinions to himself. The coroner suggested getting a prescription for Rosella from the hospital pharmacy before departing the hospital and offered to facilitate that course of action.

As they stood in front of the doors of the doctor's private elevator waiting for it to arrive, Hathaway signaled for the other detective to step forward and hand him the ziplock plastic bag.

"Do you recognize this handwriting, Mrs. Jobe?" Hathaway asked while he held up the corners of the bag in his fingertips for Rosella to read.

Rosella leaned forward and stared at the words made slightly out of focus by the plastic. She blinked to see through her watery eyes. Regardless, the handwriting was immediately recognizable.

"My niece . . . my niece wrote that?" It was a question and a statement. "When did she write this?"

"It appears it was written today," Hathaway said. "Further tests will make it conclusive."

"My niece was in love with my . . ." She violently shook her head as if to sling away that horrible thought. "And she was pregnant?"

The elevator doors opened, and Hathaway handed the bag back to the detective and waved for him to wait for him there until he returned. He watched Rosella step into the elevator and slowly turn to face the doors. Her motions were rigid, her expression, stoic. He stepped in and punched the button, wondering how much more this woman could take.

On their ride up to the floor where Dewayne waited, Hathaway explained to Rosella she would not be able to return to her house for several days while they were going over the evidence and making their reports. He suggested that she make a list of personal items she might need during that period and a female officer would collect them and bring them to wherever she would be staying. Did she have any friends she could stay with, any other family who would take her in? Or would she prefer a hotel? They would be happy to make any arrangements. Rosella made no indication she heard anything Hathaway said.

The doors of the elevator opened, and they stepped into white light and a cadre of reporters. The two uniformed officers went into defensive action, pushing the reporters and camera operators back against the wall, clearing a path for Hathaway and Rosella.

"Was your husband having an affair with your niece?" a reporter shouted as Hathaway hurried Rosella down the hall to Dewayne's room. "She was pregnant at the time of her death."

Hathaway swore under his breath and vowed that if he found the officer who had leaked the information, he would have his badge—probably some rookie at the scene who could not resist the temptation of payola from a tabloid. But he couldn't lie to Rosella when she asked for an explanation. He was going to need her to build this case. He needed her trust, and the truth was the only way to get and maintain it, no matter how painful the news.

"There was a pregnancy test found in the trash, Mrs. Jobe," he said. "It was inconclusive and partially destroyed, but we're running tests."

It took a second for Hathaway to realize their forward progress had ceased.

Rosella stopped in the middle of the hall and jerked her elbow out of the detective's grasp, wondering what other devastating news would come to her today. She felt as if she was devoid of choices, her decision-making capabilities stripped from her. The ability, the will, to put one foot in front of the other had departed.

"She was pregnant . . . ," Rosella whispered—a question, a statement, a bewildering confirmation of a truth that devastated her.

Hathaway reclaimed the tender hold on her elbow. His reassuring touch felt as if he had been a friend for life and not a stranger she had known for half an hour who had spent the time force-feeding her with nothing but horror. He led her to the door of Dewayne's room.

Rosella stood at the doorway and looked at a husband she no longer knew. When had he changed? What kind of a monster had he become right before her very eyes? An oxygen mask strapped across his face, an IV stuck in his arm, and the other arm handcuffed to the bed. A nurse told Hathaway that Dewayne had been conscious earlier and spoken to the doctor, but he was still not sure what had happened. She would call the doctor and tell him the patient's wife was here.

In his semi-dream state, Dewayne must have sensed the presence of people, and his eyes flickered open. When he saw Rosella, he reached out his hand to her, but the handcuffs kept him from stretching the full extent of his arm. She started to turn away, but something kept her from moving from the door and it was not Hathaway's body blocking her exit. It was a raging impulse to wreak havoc, to destroy the source of all her pain, to bring down swift justice, and she spun around and rushed toward the bed.

Hathaway was so surprised, he was unable to move for several seconds, and he stood in awe at this woman pummeling her husband with her fists and cursing him to the lowest points of hell.

Jake had banged on the door for several minutes and called her name, but Cherie did not answer. He could not see anything through the window because of the closed curtains. He could hear the television, but it did not sound loud enough to mute his pounding. Her car sat in the drive. He went over to a neighbor's house; they had not seen her, but told him she kept a spare key under a flowerpot on the top front step.

He told them to call the police, dashed back to the house, found the key, and went inside. The phone was still off the hook and the remote was in pieces. Cherie lay crumpled on the floor. The cable channel was carrying the news of the Jobe family tragedy and announced that soon the district attorney would be making a public statement live on the air.

He knelt beside Cherie's body and touched her. He felt no warmth. There was no reflexive response. He whispered her name, raising the volume level each time he spoke it, but there was no reply. He laid two fingers on her moist, cool neck and whispered her name again. There was no sign of life. He stood and studied the room. He wanted to be sure he could remember to tell Dewayne exactly the way he found it and exactly the way he had found his mother, as if she had decided to take a nap on the floor and never woke up. He knelt back down to wait, to pray, to regret, to ponder, to plan, and as all these thoughts tumbled through his mind, he heard the sirens in the distance.

20

John Hathaway refused to appear with the district attorney, the police chief, and their entourage at the press conference. It was not his style, especially when he believed there was a rush to judgment. Before the press conference had begun, Hathaway went several rounds with the DA, disputing his haste to call this an open-and-shut case.

"There is still the boyfriend," he argued, though he had to admit the evidence was weak.

Tyler's name had come up when Rosella provided Hathaway with all the names of close family and friends. Hathaway called in an LA detective to track him down. The detective found him looking haggard and drawn in the control room at a recording studio, evaluating the latest cut from a local hip-hop artist. He had been in the studio 24/7, he said, and had not seen or heard any news from the outside world. When the detective apologized for having to pass on such distressing news, he noted Tyler's distraught reaction at hearing of the death of his girlfriend, along with the fact that the dates on the plane ticket checked out—he had yet to use the return portion of the ticket and probably would not, given the terrible circumstances. Through his tears, Tyler said, "Why return to Houston now? Why even live?" The corroboration from multiple associates who swore Tyler had been a workaholic for the last several days worked in his favor to persuade the LA detective that Tyler had a convincing alibi.

The police chief, a former partner of Hathaway's, was sympathetic to John, but sided with the DA. It was an election year. The DA was running for the U.S. Senate, the police chief for mayor of Houston. The national focus this case had sparked would continue to hold the country's attention and keep them in the spotlight for a long time. The free media hype was too tempting, and Hathaway lost the argument to delay a public declaration of the results in the preliminary investigation and the state's judicial intentions.

All the evidence pointed to Dewayne Jobe as the killer—he had certainly been tried by the public, the majority of Americans believing him guilty and worthy of the death penalty, which was sweet news for the DA. But Hathaway had a gut feeling on this one. It felt too hygienic, too sanitized for a crime of spontaneous passion, and his gut reaction had kept him going back to the scene and to the lab, searching for clues, looking for the missed fingerprint, any carelessness a murderer might leave behind. Yes, Rosella had told him Tyler had been in their home many times over the last few months so, of course, there would be physical evidence of his presence, evidence that would be hard to attach a date and time to, but still there was his gut feeling.

Hathaway's final plea was that he had not yet submitted a full report, they were still recovering and analyzing records from the computer, but the DA countered with the tide of public opinion being all that mattered and he should hurry up with his report.

"I won't have another O.J. travesty on my watch," the DA said, which ended the conversation, and Hathaway left for his favorite watering hole. If he was going to watch a press conference, he might as well do it with his drink of choice in his hand.

The bar patrons reflected national opinion . . . the judicial system could not try and execute Dewayne Jobe fast enough. Prior to the press conference, the network interviewed the owner of the Stars, and he did agree that based on the startling revelations so far by the press and the statements leaked from the DA's office, the circumstances did not look good for his star player. Yet his steadfast position was, unless and until they proved the man guilty, he would remain innocent. This statement brought a chorus of boos and profane comments from the horde.

The DA outlined the working theory that would make his job a cakewalk, citing the alleged improper relationship between Dewayne and Sabrina as the catalyst setting all the circumstances in motion. Sabrina's note to her aunt was at the top of the list as evidence of Dewayne's guilt.

"They had even recently been seen in public," the DA exclaimed, barely concealing his confidence of the open-and-shut quality of this case.

The undeniable evidence of purchased one-way plane tickets and passports substantiated the DA's conclusions. In addition, the girl's fingerprints on the computer's keyboard and the depletion of funds from private accounts were added support to the hypothesis. The unfortunate deaths of the child and nephew were accidents of an apparent struggle between Sabrina and Dewayne, which ended in the death of the young woman, and once he realized that the horror of the aftermath he had created was all too real, he tried to commit suicide. Yes, the state was confident that with all the documented evidence, they could expedite this case swiftly, no, the state had no other suspects, and yes, Mr. Jobe remained on a suicide watch.

In a final tragic twist to the story, the reporter turned to the camera at the end of the press conference and announced that Dewayne Jobe's mother had died of a heart attack in her home, apparently the result of hearing the news that her son was the primary suspect in the multiple homicides of his own family.

Just as the reporter was signing off, Hathaway got a call on his cell phone from the lab informing him Sabrina had not been pregnant at all. The test must have been . . . what? What must it have been? Hathaway wondered. Rosella had told him she was not pregnant, but had she thought she was and taken the test? He had not thought to ask her that question. Then had Sabrina thought she was pregnant and confronted the father with inaccurate information? Whoever had taken the test with its ensuing result, look at what madness this false positive may have wrought. When Hathaway considered all the possibilities swirling in his head about the old and new circumstances of this case, he killed his drink, tapped his empty glass on the Formica top, and ordered a bottle.

Rosella was isolated from herself. She felt an infinite distance from God, an infinite distance from light and all goodness, an infinite distance from any traces of human consciousness. She was a raw wound of complete loneliness. It was impossible to speak, impossible to pray, impossible almost to move or think, impossible to summon a memory. The loss was so palpable that to force a memory to the surface of her conscious, any memory of any of these people who were once her family, was a task beyond her capabilities. Were it not for her parents who had come the second they heard the news, Rosella would have been incapacitated. The limo had picked up Franklin and Joella on the tarmac outside a private hangar of the jet service they used to get to Houston and whisked them away to where their daughter was in hiding. In the past few days, she had been able to reach a point of lucidness only to make two decisions: she would bury the children in Los Angeles, and she would see her husband before she departed.

The officer came to the door of the holding area and indicated to Rosella that it was time to see Dewayne. Her parents warned her against such a move, but she refused to heed their advice. It made no sense to face him at this point, but face him she would, just to prove to herself that she was capable of standing opposite an evil she had never dreamed would demolish her life. The officer led her down a hall and took her into another square chamber where another uniformed officer sat at a desk.

When she entered the room with her escort, the officer at the desk pushed a button, triggering the automatic lock on the door that would lead her to Dewayne. She hesitated, the tiny level of confidence to face her husband now draining out of her. The officer at the desk reinforced her doubt by informing her she did not have to go through with this, but Rosella's momentary vacillation passed and she signaled she would continue. The first officer pulled open the door, instructed her to take a seat at the third booth, and said that her husband would be coming any minute. When her time was up, he would return to get her. If she wanted to leave sooner than the allotted time, she need only wave in his direction. She sat in the chair and took the phone in her hand.

The first thing Rosella noticed was that Dewayne seemed to have shrunk in size. The shackles on his arms and legs reduced this erect human tower of strength and superiority into a docile, shuffling creature, one who lived on the streets and slept in shelters. Her last image of him was in another weakened state, supine on a hospital bed, weeping into the oxygen mask as she beat him with her fists. His face and neck still bore the marks of her assault. His uniformed guide secured him in his chair by connecting his manacles to a lock beneath the table of his booth. These once long arms, the wingspan of a condor, which had caught impossible passes and had wrapped their length in a warm embrace around the inviting body of his wife, were appendages of the deformed.

The officer lifted the phone from its receptacle and placed it into Dewayne's hand.

They breathed into their phones and stared into each other's swollen eyes. What personal and moral injustice had brought them to this place? What had either of them done to deserve the insanity visited upon them? What reasonable explanation would either of them have to offer that might hold a clue to what had happened? Could they speak any solace to each other? For a time, looking at each other through the opaque glass shield and listening to the raspy breaths of struggling life through the earpiece of the receiver seemed to be the only choice. Dewayne did not appear desperate to declare his innocence.

Rosella did not feel the wrath of days before. Her heart was shut inside a barren, caged booth with no image or memory to provide an ameliorating buffer that might soothe the open wounds. She glanced over at the officer who had escorted her, and when he thought she might summon him, she held up her hand to stop him. This simple distraction loosened her tongue: her parents had come to take her back to Los Angeles where she intended to bury their son, unable to bear the thought of leaving him in Houston with his murderous father, and they would return the bodies of her niece and nephew to their mother.

"Rosella, I am innocent," Dewayne said, but she would not allow him to interrupt her, to divert her with false claims.

"Your mother is dead," Rosella said. She let the news travel the length of the telephone cord and register in Dewayne's brain, and when he asked how and why, she gave him the information with a dulled sense of pleasure that this news would make him suffer. Why shouldn't he suffer? His suffering would never measure up to the ocean of her desolation. *Add the death of your mother to the list of your murders*, she thought, and Dewayne bowed his head, sobbing in anguish. She told him Jake Hopper had made all the funeral arrangements, but there was no compassion in the telling.

"I am innocent." He choked out the words as he wept, tears dripping off his chin and spotting his orange jumpsuit. "God is with me."

"Like he was with my baby," Rosella blurted, unable to restrain her fury. "Like he was with Sabrina and Bruce. Like he was with your mama. Well, it's good he's with you, because there's no one left in this family he can be with."

"Don't say that, Rosella, please don't," he said. "I need you to pray for me."

She slammed down her phone. She could not bear to have the receiver pressed against her ear and hear the sound of his voice any longer. She laid her hands flat on the table and bowed her head. Was this a pious gesture? Was she going to respect his request? Would she, in fact, pray for the murderer of her family? The sparkle of her wedding rings caught her attention, and she resolved at that precise moment she would shed no more tears for her husband. She would spend all remaining grief on her blood family.

Rosella raised her hands in front of the glass as if she were about to direct a vehicle into a parking space. She looked into Dewayne's bloated face, and with her right hand, she removed the diamond ring, followed by the wedding band from the ring finger on her left hand. She shook them in her hand as if they were cheap dice as she kicked her seat against the wall behind her. Rosella inhaled a deep breath and hurled the tangible symbols of her vows against the glass.

Dewayne reacted as if the glass would not protect him, and he jerked back, releasing the phone in his hand. The phone crashed onto the table, and then slid off, the receiver swinging from side to side like the victim of a hanging. He had enough slack in his chains to allow him to lay his forehead on the table in the booth, unable to bear any more of his wife's severe denunciation.

Rosella did not wait for the officer. She yanked the chair out of her path and ran toward the exit, leaving Dewayne howling her name with the deepest cries of animal torment.

The officer who escorted Dewayne from his cell returned to the booth and the man slumped over in his chair. He pulled him back so he could unlock the chain that had connected him to the booth, and then helped him rise to his feet. Dewayne's body started to tremble during the long walk back to his cell, and the guard requested assistance to help him hold up this broken colossus. Once the cell was unlocked and the shackles unwrapped from Dewayne's body, the lack of weight seemed to release the tremors. The guard tried to help him to his bed, but Dewayne went into full-blown convulsions and fell to the floor, his body writhing in his soul's hemorrhaging sorrow.

21

Salvador Alverez stepped out of his beachside bungalow in Quepos, Costa Rica, just ten miles north of Dominical, and stretched his limbs. His eyes squinted from the glare off the crystal blue sea of the late afternoon sun. The only thing he wore was his new Rolex, the one indulgence he had allowed himself just before he left the United States. The markup on stolen goods was always 100 percent profit, but the deal a member of his gang offered was too good to ignore. The five hundred he had given for the watch was in and of itself a steal since its value would be in the mid four figures. Salvador was anxious to begin his new life, and this was the first evidence of transformation.

He leaned back inside the front door and told his female companion still lying in bed, it was time for her to go; he had business to take care of. She had five minutes. Then he sat down in the lounge chair and stretched his legs over the railing of his front porch.

Everything had fallen into place for Salvador. There had been no glitches in his plan. The most important lesson he had learned in life was to be patient. Patience was a virtue, and by practicing it, he had seen that patience was profitable. By being patient, he had gained knowledge. By being patient, he had become a wealthy man. By being patient, he had transformed himself into a man of power, someone with whom the world would soon reckon.

In the brief time since his arrival, he had been establishing himself as a citizen in this new land, exchanging currency, creating accounts in local banks, making inquiries about property with some local Realtors, and letting it be known that the music business in America had been good to him. He had not been flamboyant, throwing around cash like trinkets tossed by a Mardi Gras king. That was not his style, and besides, the serious money had not yet arrived that would inaugurate his kingdom, a kingdom that would have no end. The money would arrive soon, and he would be patient, but these initial steps were laying the foundation of his credibility among the locals, a valuable commodity in his conversion process.

Salvador had had several conversion experiences in his short life, but this new one would be his final revision. It took a person several tries to get life right, and he was pleased he had found a version that would fit for a long time. He had not come to this new world solely to spend the fresh wealth he had acquired. His vision for the future was far too grand than to become sluggish with self-indulgences, something his prosperity could provide him for years to come. He was much too ambitious. He had come for the investment opportunities, seeking ways to expand his kingdom, ways that would bring the world to him, ways that would demand respect from equals and inspire fear from those beneath him. And ways that would relieve him of the memories of his years on the street, his time in jail, his brief con as a model Christian, his foray into the darkness of murder.

Tyler Rogan, born again as Salvador Alverez, had vision, he had connections, he had venture capital to back his inspirations, and he had a plan he had begun to conceive as he rode in the car from Houston to Los Angeles while his associates slept. Tyler was always making plans, a skill he developed whiling away the long hours of incarceration.

His companions for the long drive had been his business associates in Houston, the crew Sabrina had happened upon the day she informed Tyler he was the father of their child. When Tyler had walked out of detention in LA after serving his time for beating Bruce with the baseball bat, he had no commitment to rehabilitation, no interest in anything other than a return to the old life, and his time behind bars had been a real motivation to move up the ranks among the members of his gang.

Imprisonment had been time well spent. Tyler had taken a couple of online business classes and had learned to build websites; he was not about to waste the hard-earned taxpayer investment into his rehabilitation by watching hours of television and pumping iron in the yard each day.

Two things helped him gain independence and veneration when he returned to civilian life: jail time enhanced his status with the gang's rank and file, which, in turn, had developed a deeper level of trust for him within the leadership, and he had come back with a solid plan to expand the power, influence, and assets of the gang. They needed a legitimate business to shield their profits, the first chapter out of any organized crime handbook, and so they purchased the recording studio. He would then use his skill as a website designer to attract prospective recording artists. With this legitimacy as cover, Tyler would be the liaison for the drugs sold on any street corner in any city in America.

Tyler was the most qualified and willing person within the gang to take the business to the next level, and when his plan received the unanimous approval from the leaders, Tyler told them that Houston would be a great location to test out their expansion program. He would need capital, product, and associates to support his street cred, and he promised that within two months he would turn a profit for them. Tyler had been a man of his word. In one month's time, he was sending revenue back home, garnering further respect and goodwill; but this success did not satisfy Tyler. He had not chosen to relocate in Houston by default or by pulling the name out of a hat. When he watched the Stars play on the television in the detention center's recreation hall, heard Dewayne's interviews about his family, saw the number of commercials the man was cranking out, and listened to the speculations of his rumored wealth among the sports commentators, Tyler knew where to find the golden egg. Therefore, the second phase of a master plan began to fall into place.

After Tyler's Houston associates had picked him up at a gas station less than a mile from the Jobe house, Tyler formulated the third phase of a master plan on the ride back to Los Angeles. While others slept through the night, he imagined a new life in Costa Rica where he had scouted out the possibilities of expanding the business while he was there on the church mission trip. "Go to the source and secure the supply," he had told the leadership, and because of his sales pitch and the impressive work he had accomplished in Houston in such a short time, the leadership offered to fund the new venture without Tyler even requesting it. The cash he had stolen from the Jobe home was a bonus, and he would not be in a hurry to transfer a portion of the Jobe millions from the security of a Bahamian bank to one in Costa Rica. The LA leadership never queried Tyler about the Houston murders, several of them offering support to Tyler's alibi when interrogated by the detective, and they regarded this aggression as an asset.

With such a versatile combination of entrepreneurial risk and ruthlessness, Tyler could one day transform this street gang into an international cartel, something the leadership had never dreamed of happening.

It was a win-win for all parties, so with a new identity, new venture capital for a new mission, a new Rolex sold to him at a discount by a gang member, Salvador Alverez arrived in the new world ready to begin his new life. When the woman appeared on the front porch and began to kiss his neck, trying to lure him back inside the bungalow, Tyler produced an envelope with twice the amount of pesos she had asked for, including extra for cab fare. He sent her on her way with the promise she would return and bring a couple of her friends, and then he showered and dressed and drove his motorcycle into the jungle for his first rendezvous with a potential supplier, a meeting that had not taken long to establish since the international language of money, spoken all over the world and even recognized in the Costa Rican jungle, had secured the appointment.

Detective Hathaway had his feet propped on his desk while nursing his favorite bourbon and staring at a list of numbers on the sheet faxed to him early in the day. He was not drinking on the job, though he was no Puritan. His shift was over, but he had some paperwork, and there was no reason to go home to an empty condo and drink alone.

The detectives on the next shift provided some white noise while he sipped his drink and studied the numbers. There really was not much to study. It was not like trying to break some mysterious code. It was the SWIFT code ABA routing numbers of an offshore account the geeks in the lab were able to retrieve from the Jobe computer, all of which had been set up the day of the murders. Were it not for an old buddy at the Treasury Department in Houston, he would not have known the code was a Bahamian account, and for the price of a couple of bottles of Johnnie Walker, he would be told if and when there was any movement and to what location. *Friendship and payola were beautiful things*, Hathaway thought as he dreamed of all those millions floating in cyberspace just waiting for arithmetic summons.

Hathaway could not settle on this case. The knot in his gut still had not relaxed, in spite of the evidence, in spite of the tunnel vision of the district attorney, in spite of public mindset, and in spite of the opinions of his colleagues. Hathaway paid Dewayne a brief visit in the hospital and asked what had been the last thing he remembered before waking up. Dewayne said falling asleep in the car while being driven from the airport to the Stars' practice facility by his alleged paramour, a bit of information that had stuck with Hathaway. Why would this young man in mint physical condition, who was about to leave the country with the young woman with whom he was having an affair, fall asleep in the car? Of course, he could have been lying, but if it was the truth, it seemed odd. In addition, Dewayne Jobe's character just did not fit the profile for this type of murder, this type of methodical plotting and premeditation. This man did not seem the type to calculate this much destruction. Hathaway had studied the Jobe bio: raised by a single mom in small-town USA, good kid growing up, great ball player in high school and college, an NFL career that seemed to have no limits, and millions of dollars flowing in from national brands just for his endorsement. It wasn't as if Hathaway was a football fanatic wanting to prove the innocence of one of his heroes—he watched the Stars on game days as a casual fan—but the Jobe background profile did not a murderer make, and Hathaway was finding it difficult to believe no one else in his world or in the world at large was willing to cut this guy some slack, especially now when Jobe's health had taken such an out-of-the-blue turn for the worse. It was a lynch mob mentality with blatant overtones of racism, and he had said so to the DA, who did not seem to balk when he threw the accusation in his face.

"I have two letters for you . . . O.J.," the DA said.

"So is this what our judicial system has become, a way to settle racial scores?" Hathaway retorted. "Is this your idea of affirmative action?"

"This is about money and lust. Those two things can corrupt anybody and drive him to do insane things, I don't care what color of skin he has."

Hathaway knew this was all about the DA's political campaign. If he could get Jobe tried, convicted, and with any luck at all from Blind Lady Justice, moved to death row, or better yet, executed before the fall election, this should assure his appointment to the U.S. Senate. After all, this was Texas, known for the swift and severe finality of its justice.

However, there was one problem. Dewayne Jobe was not cooperating. Without doubt, he was slowing the process down. They could not conduct the trial with the accused in absentia. He was a national figure, and his presence in the courtroom was critical. The jury needed to see each day the lawful proceedings of the DA proving beyond a shadow of a doubt that behind the mask of a beloved sports star was a true antisocial psychopath with brutal tendencies that, when unleashed, would create the domestic carnage inside the walls of his own home. Dewayne was frustrating the DA, preventing him from doing his job and advancing his political aspirations, and this had kept the case open. Hathaway had more time, thanks to Dewayne, to keep studying this case, to keep watching the account numbers, to curry favor with his police chief for anything that might help him prove this was not the slam dunk the DA touted. So he sipped his bourbon and stared at the numbers and prayed for some activity before Dewayne died by lethal injection or disease.

He lay on his back stretched out on a cold block of marble, shivering with only a sheet covering his naked body. He felt an immense weight on his stomach and legs, and when he opened his eyes, he saw a muscular figure of angelic magnitude standing on top of him, holding a glass vial containing a murky-colored liquid. He heard weeping and looked around to see people kneeling as they surrounded him, their faces buried in their hands as if bereaved at his current situation, a condition about which he could not determine the cause or the outcome. There was a light fading into an incalculable distance, but it was enough to illumine the sky of black clouds so profuse and grave that they appeared at the point of bursting. The figure on his chest began to levitate above him, but the pressure of the weight remained, and the creature was able to grasp one of the bulky clouds and pull it down around them, hiding them from the faceless mourners.

With choreographic moves, the being released the cloud, removed the sheet, and poured the contents of the vial over his body before disappearing into the cloud, leaving a faint trail of laughter pulsating in his ears and replacing the invisible lamentations. He could see his skin was turning blotchy, and he felt as if his bones were burning with white heat.

Hands rose from beneath the marble slab and lifted him to his feet. Through no act of will of his own, he moved through the cloud, the sizzling skin dripping off him, his bones heating to the point of ignition. He could acknowledge these sensations of flight and of burning, but there were no accompanying feelings of fear or physical pain. He moved through shadowy space toward another figure similar to the first but with arms extended in anticipation of an embrace. Perhaps this creature would explain all things to him, but as he approached, the arms of the creature rose not to enfold but to strangle, and his neck slipped right into the creature's outspread fingers.

Now there was fear. Now there was pain. Now there was no hope for explanation or escape.

Dewayne nearly sprang from his hospital bed as if the mechanical remote had a catapult button. The only thing keeping him from flying off the mattress was the set of handcuffs linking his wrist with the bed. The length of the chain was longer than usual to allow Dewayne to stand and stretch and take a few steps, but the excess had caught in the leg of the bed, preventing him from going airborne. He looked around the room, knocking back large gulps of fetid air between coughs, relieved not to be floating through dark clouds with his skin and bones on fire or strangled by a mythical creature.

It took a few seconds to be sure what the here and now was for him. A police officer stationed outside his door stuck his head in and asked if he was okay and then announced he had company, a rarity considering his new life status. Other than check-ins from medical personnel, he did not see anyone but attorneys and officers. So it was a great surprise when Sly appeared at the door.

"How the mighty have fallen," Sly said, marveling at the corporal deterioration of his best friend.

Dewayne continued to cough, and Sly advanced to the bedside table and poured him a cup of water, but he hesitated handing it to him.

In between gasps, Dewayne read Sly's expression and was sure he knew his thoughts: his friend was choking, but maybe it would be easier for everyone if he refrained from giving him this drink. Maybe everyone would be relieved if an intentional act would squelch his breath altogether.

"Help me, Sly," he said, his voice a garroted plea, and Sly offered the drink.

He washed down the strangulation in desperate swallows, then dropped the plastic cup and held on to the bed, feeling its soft warmth, thankful it had no tangible resemblance to icy marble. When he recovered, he leaned back in the bed and gazed at his old friend.

"On second thought maybe you should have let me choke to death," he said, and Sly admitted he had deliberated on the idea confirming to Dewayne that his suspicions were correct. "Then you could have had my jail cell."

"No, my man, I'd be a hero. Nobody would lock me up."

Sly stared at Dewayne, feeling nothing but incomprehension. Was this the man with whom he grew up? Was this the man whose mother had been his mother, her funeral he had of late attended? Was this the man the world condemned, tainting all he had touched with a brushstroke of evil? His fall from grace had bruised the conscience of a nation. Yet Sly felt drawn to this hospital room like the pull to the sideshow of a demonic carnival, and nothing could have prepared him for this. Nothing could have prepared him to look into the eyes of a lifelong friend, one he had known longer than anyone else now left on this earth, and see the alteration from man to beast. It was the stuff of sinister, medieval tales told as morality plays in an attempt to hold in check the evil residing in a man's heart.

"This room sucks. It stinks like a backed-up toilet in here," Sly said, waving his hand beneath his nose.

"What did you expect from a prison hospital? We criminals don't get much selection," and Dewayne raised his arm with its restraint.

It was an ancient room in an ancient hospital from an ancient era when the practice of medicine for criminals and the insane was austere, on the level of care given to neglected domestic animals with little hope. Sly went over to the window and looked through the bent and crooked blinds. All he saw beyond the twenty-foot fence topped off with razor wire was the industrial county penal complex.

"Like the view from here," Sly said, swiping the greasy dust off a blade with his finger and then wiping the grime on the cracked plaster wall.

"It's why I keep the blinds closed."

Sly turned back and really took in Dewayne.

"You've lost some weight." Sly noticed a withered look of aging in his face and a hairline losing its claim on his scalp.

"I've been on the radiation/chemotherapy diet. I don't recommend it."

"So, you really have a brain tumor, my man?" Sly asked, his tone obviously incredulous.

"It's a little octopus at the base of my brain, spreading out its tentacles like the fingers of God."

"That explain why you went crazy . . . killed your family?"

"You work for the DA now, my man?" Dewayne asked. "My best friend has gone over to the other side, gone and bought into the lies. You take what you've heard from the world and pass

271

your guilty verdict. A despairing man should have the devotion of his friends, no matter what they say he has done."

Sly felt contempt rising in him. He thought he had come to find answers, but he now knew he would not have believed any answer he heard. "Let me tell you, my man, you don't have any friends."

There was the truth. Dewayne was alone, and he felt the weight return to his chest, the weight he felt in his dream, the weight of God crushing him, cutting him off from all comfort, all hope.

"Why have you come?" Dewayne asked, his voice a whisper.

"How could you do it? How in God's name could you do it?" Sly asked and bowed his head and stretched his arms over the railing at the foot of the bed. He raised his hand to mute any statement Dewayne was about to make. "I went to Springdale for the funeral of your mother." Sly pounded the rail of the bed. "I buried her . . . Jake and me. I can't believe we buried our mama and you weren't there. I can't believe our mama's dead. I can't believe she's gone from us and you . . . you . . ."

Sly did not finish his accusation. Dewayne had already accepted the culpability for the death of his mother. It was not necessary for Sly to point his finger of blame at Dewayne with one hand and pound his fist on the bed with the other. Dewayne dreaded facing his mother on the Day of Judgment more than he dreaded facing God. In fact, he looked forward to facing God, to standing before God in the boldness of his innocence and confronting him for his indifference, for his terrors against a man who had done nothing to deserve such malevolent attention. But his mother was a different story. From the grave how would she ever know of his innocence? Who would tell her?

Who would plead his case and convince her that her son, her only son, would never, could never, do all he had been accused of? Facing Sly was only a prelude to the moment he would face his mother, whom he had killed. That was the one death, the only death, to which he would plead guilty.

Dewayne dropped his head back onto his pillow, the chains from his arm rattling as he raised his hand to cover his eyes. Grief incapacitated him. He wondered if Sly was capable of feeling real empathy for him.

When the door to the room opened, the familiar voice that spoke her greeting made Dewayne pull his hand from his eyes, and he looked into Rosella's exhausted face. She too had lost weight. She too had physically aged, her face drained of its perennial brightness, and her body appeared to have shrunk inside her loose clothes. Dewayne watched as Sly stepped toward her, and she fell into his arms, both of them weeping, oblivious to the man lying in bed, watching their every move, listening to every sob and moan.

Dewayne felt as though this could have been a scene performed for his benefit. Perhaps it was; perhaps it was a conscious action long held dormant within the hearts of Rosella and Sly, who were, given the circumstances, free to respond to their true feelings. And perhaps this was another in a series of God's humorless jokes, another of his razor-sharp daggers thrust into Dewayne's soul, forcing him to watch his wife being comforted in another man's arms, comforted for the horrendous crimes the couple in the scene believed he had committed, crimes that had rescinded his right to touch his wife or be touched by her. Why couldn't the brain tumor have shut down his mind or at least taken his sight and hearing? Another of God's jokes, forcing Dewayne to be the helpless observer.

All he could do to interject himself into the moment was

growl; he would fight back, even if it were only with primal instinct. Although the sound caused the pair to release their embrace, the two actors did not give him their visual attention. Instead, Dewayne had to continue to watch as they never took their eyes off each other or made a full break from their physical contact—tears were wiped from faces, hands were held. He listened to their inquiries into each other's well-being, of how Rosella was holding up, of where the children had been buried, of how a distraught Bonita had once again fallen off the face of the world, of the tragic funeral of Cherie Jobe, of the doctors' reports and their bafflement over Dewayne's condition, of the media attention and the upcoming trial and her plans to avoid both, of what Sly could do to help her—anything, he said, anything. When it came to her immediate plans, Dewayne was finally recognized.

Rosella had not seen her husband since the episode at the glass booth. She preferred the solitude and protection her parents could give her after the private funerals of the children. At last, her eyes took him in, and his contracting bodily state shocked her. Life had been eating away at him, and he was disappearing from sight, a disappearance that could not happen soon enough or could not be painful enough to suit her.

She had planned to stay only a second, to pass on some information and run, but Sly had slowed her down. She was grateful for his unexpected visit. His presence would make the business quick and professional. She would inform Dewayne of her plans and be gone, and perhaps Sly would go with her.

Rosella reached into her bag and removed some legal texts. She did not hand the papers to Dewayne. She did not want to be that close to him. Instead, she set them on the table.

"For you to read," she said. She had steeled her heart. She

would make it through this. "The house is going on the market. I've signed the papers for a Realtor to start showing it. The other document is . . . ," and here she stumbled, here she encountered the emotional obstacle she dreaded. Divorce was not a part of her vocabulary, had never been an option. Of course, she never considered the recent tragic circumstances to demolish her life either. In her mind, it had all been out of the realm of possibility, but to her surprise, she had not been immune to evil.

She had opened the door to evil, slept with evil, birthed evil's child. No prayers had protected her, no signs of warning given, no holy heads-up to the potential dangers lurking just below the surface of her perfect little world, and she had lost all trust in anyone and anything, including herself. "I want a divorce. Those are the papers. I've signed them; now you sign them."

God seemed to have an endless supply of daggers, Dewayne thought. *How many more plunges of the knife can I take?*

His wife turned to leave.

"Rosella, please don't leave. Don't leave me. I did not do this. I could not. You must believe me. Please don't do this. I need you. I need you."

She hesitated as if reconsidering, then she turned back, but only halfway.

"I want nothing from you," she said, her voice hard, bitter. "I will take some personal items from the house, but that is all. I want no money, nothing. I just want to start my life over."

She made her exit.

The choice must have been easy for Sly. He knew whom to console, and after a brief hesitation, he began to make his departure while Dewayne had his eyes buried inside his malnourished forearm.

Dewayne dropped his arm, the skin damp from weeping, and his words caught his friend at the door. "I've lost everything, Sly, everything. Am I gonna lose my best friend too?"

He reached out his empty hand, but like Rosella, Sly did not hesitate. He was looking past the police officer at Rosella stumbling down the hall, her hand braced against the wall.

"Do me a favor," he said, looking back inside Dewayne's room. "Take my name off the short list of people you wish to see."

And he was gone. The abyss beneath which Dewayne's arm was poised began to widen, the darkness within streaked with an occasional lightning flash, revealing a wasteland of erosion. If only he could cast himself into this gulf. If only there was a force strong enough to pull him into this expansive grave, to lay him out and cover him from the pervasive sight of God and man. But when he heard from the cavernous hallway Sly's voice calling out for Rosella to wait and the faltering sound of her stumbling footsteps, he felt the surprise of hatred seeping into his bloodstream, hatred toward those who had abandoned him. A second surprise followed; a small funnel of strength, dissolving the abyss of self-pity, provided a tension against the urge to cast himself into the chasm of his vision.

22

Salvador Alverez was ready to upgrade. The beachside bungalow did not provide the space needed for business purposes,
and there was not sufficient room to entertain in the lavish
way he was imagining. His tastes were changing as well, more
refined, more educated, more in line with the lifestyle in which
he intended to grow.

Tailored clothes became the norm, vehicles were test-driven,
restaurants with wine lists replaced outdoor cafés and noisy
bars, art galleries replaced the ambles through outdoor flea
markets. Women who frequented his home were attempt-
ing to increase their value by refusing payments in hopes of
persuading Señor Alverez that one of them was worthy of a
more permanent union, as permanent as something could
be for someone with the evolving tastes and commitments of
Salvador Alverez.

It was now time to think about property strategically located
far enough from the big city of Dominical so as not to attract
suspicious attention, equidistant from the suppliers so as to
avoid incriminating association, close enough to the beach for
his legs to carry him, and secluded enough within the flora of
a jungle terrain so outsiders would not have easy access. And
when he procured the property, it would be time to look for

investment opportunities in the commercial infrastructure of the local community. It would be easy for the locals to lose their hearing, their speech, their sight, and their memories when they were confident their financial prosperity was secure through generous payoffs. Once again, the international language of money would be able to satisfy the needs of everyone.

The money Tyler brought with him to Costa Rica was about to tap out. He had invested the advance from the leadership into initiating contact and building relationships with three separate drug producers, each capable of manufacturing a respectable number of kilos of marijuana and cocaine. The producers also had associations with established shipping routes into the U.S. and Europe, and yet were still small enough to be low-level, mom-and-pop suppliers, inconsequential by large cartel standards.

Tyler did not want to draw much attention to his growing industry early in the game. Before he became a serious competitor, he needed the muscle to back it up. He did not need the big dogs to get a whiff of his intentions, and the best way to do that was to fly under the radar of the conglomerates and local law enforcement until he had become a reckoning force. He had proven his business acumen by securing the suppliers in different locations but all within a fifty-mile radius of the jungle terrain outside of Quepos. If for any reason one of the producers were incapacitated, the supply would continue to flow.

Tyler looked forward to giving the LA leadership the full tour of the three production facilities in their remote jungle locations. He would awe his homeboys by what he had been able to accomplish in such a short time. He would fly them down, first class, and not only would they get to see firsthand the innovative ways he had parleyed their development capital, but they would be able to taste the firstfruits of their investment. Tyler had not squandered one dollar, and the leadership would see he had vision, determination, and a developing skill to handle the multilayer drug business. Once they had bought into the capitalist dream of what their puny investment had procured and what luxuries a successful business could provide for them back home, they would all succumb to his submission.

Although Tyler was quite capable of being cold-blooded, out of respect for his roots and recognition of the need for a qualified and trustworthy U.S. distributor, he would not foolishly wield his power. Slowly, beguilingly, he would draw in the leadership first and then the gang's regular members, making them feel a part of his organization, a part of something greater than themselves. If any of them showed separatist tendencies, however, they would become expendable. In the normal course of running a company, Tyler expected he would have to make an example of a few independent thinkers, but believed when his associates saw his capacity for ruthlessness, those times would be rare. It was all a part of his plan.

It was time to invest personal capital. Tyler selected a Realtor, and after an exhaustive search of virtual online tours and a dozen-plus on-site palace tours with the leading contender for number one courtesan in the Alverez harem attached to his arm—Tyler liked the feminine touch in picking a house and the level of legitimacy it gave him to the outside world—he settled on a $2.5 million mansion on a thirty-five-acre plot just outside Quepos. It came equipped with a fence and security system, a winding quarter-mile drive from gate to mansion through dense jungle, a quarter-mile hike along a path through the manicured gardens and down a cliffside opening onto a private beach, a view from the house high enough above the landscape and ocean to observe miles in all directions, and a servants' bungalow housing an older Dominical couple who spoke no English but could provide all domestic services from landscaping to preparing dishes of local cuisine.

The final step was for the Realtor and Alverez and the number one courtesan to go to the bank, do the necessary paperwork, and make the financial transfer. Around $5 million from his Bahamian account was enough to begin with. That amount would purchase the house, stock the kitchen, buy a couple of vehicles, secure the initial funds for the three suppliers to begin production, schedule flight plans for the leadership to come in from LA, including paying back their investment with a nice profit, and allow the number one courtesan to furnish and decorate the rooms. He should not need any more than this initial investment. He fully expected to be turning a profit from the business within six months or less. He might not have to touch the remaining millions for a long time. After writing multiple signatures on the appropriate documents establishing the Sea Breeze Corporation with Salvador Alverez as CEO and president and a few minutes on the computer punching in the numbers on the account, Señor Alverez had instant access to his money. He shook hands with the bank executive of the Costa Rican National Bank and his assistant in charge of offshore account transfers, amidst smiles and laughter on all sides, and Salvador Alverez received the keys to his kingdom before the ink was dry on the Realtor's contract.

The e-mail announced "For Your Eyes Only." When Detective Hathaway opened the electronic message, it read, "Funds moved . . . Costa Rican National Bank, Dominical, C.R., $5,220,000. This is how we catch tax cheats and terrorists. Good luck." Hathaway hoped to add a murderer to that list.

Because of Treasury's relationship with the international banking community to trace suspicious accounts, his pal at Treasury had been able to come through with the information, and if he could catch this guy, he would send his friend a case of Johnnie Walker. The date of the transfer was four days ago. Hathaway began to rub his stomach when he realized the gut feeling he had from day one was beginning to ease. This should be enough to go on, but was it enough to change minds, to authorize a new investigation, to perhaps divert the attention of the powers that be from their prime suspect and open their minds to other possibilities?

Hathaway made an appointment with the police chief that morning. He played on their partnership of years before, on his reputation for being a pit bull with difficult cases, on his outsmarting too many bad guys, on his gut belief that the man now in custody would possibly die without ever exercising his legal right to the due process of justice.

"Besides, I'm due," Hathaway said. He stood. He was tired of sitting. Standing made his argument feel stronger.

"Due?" The chief swiveled back and forth in his desk chair.

Hathaway took a chance. "When you and Mary were breaking up, who bought you the shots of bourbon?" They were friends, former partners. Buying shots of bourbon for a friend whose marriage was breaking up was what Hathaway did, the only kind marriage counseling he understood. Playing the friendship card was almost like he was pulling rank.

The squeaking in the chair stopped and the chief dug his fingers into the soft leather of his armchair. Maybe playing the friendship card was not a good idea.

"Now you're getting personal."

"What we're doing—when is it not personal?"

The chief eased up on his grip of the leather arms. He made all the arguments the DA would make against playing this hunch, but with a lesser degree of passion about what the embarrassment might do to his political career.

Hathaway detected his friend was weakening. "The DA stuck his head on the chopping block at the press conference, giving Jobe last rites in public. You just stood behind him and smiled for the cameras. You can still run for mayor of Houston and this not be held against you."

"Is it wrong to have ambition?"

"If not for ambition, the world would still be flat."

Sure, it would be risky to authorize Hathaway's intuition, as good as it was; he would be sanctioning the mission behind the DA's back, and though Hathaway would fall on his own sword if he failed to nab the suspect, there would still be hell to pay that might imperil the police chief's political ambitions.

Hathaway understood what he was asking of his friend and sweetened the proposition with a reduced risk factor.

"I'm due some vacation," he said. "I'll cash it in on Costa Rica, but you pay the expenses, and if I bust the guy, you have to double my vacation time."

The chief did not think long about that offer. If need be, Hathaway could cover the true nature of his visit in the guise of a Panama hat and Jimmy Buffett shirt. The chief had access to discretionary funds to finance the trip—Hathaway swore to keep every receipt—and if the detective was successful, everybody would win except for the DA. All's fair in love and war, and as slick as the DA was, he might get some political mileage out of a surprise turn in this open-and-shut case.

By the time the sun was setting in the west, Hathaway was sitting in the middle seat between a woman who snored like an asthmatic and a teenage boy who beat on his tray table with his fingers to whatever percussive tempo he was hearing on his iPod. He studied for the umpteenth time all the evidence that went into the making of the Jobe case.

What he did not know and would never know was that in a few hours he would be going through customs in the San Jose airport the same time as the LA leadership.

The leadership stared at an array of treats displayed for them on the large glass table in the dining room of Tyler's furnished house. There was a punch bowl of cocaine, a tray of prerolled joints—both examples of the quality of merchandise the local producers would be able to generate—individual jars of condoms with each member's name inscribed on a card tied around the neck, and stacks of cash that Tyler proudly pointed out were the leadership's original investment plus 25 percent interest for the short time the gang had been separated from their principal. Tyler stocked the bar like a five-star restaurant, and he provided enough food to have eased the starvation of a small village, and the full Alverez harem had turned out in force.

It was difficult to concentrate with all of the distractions, but the host got everyone's attention, and before he lost them to a night of revelry, he wanted a preemptive strike to begin the process of establishing his alpha male status. Before the leadership knew what hit them, they would become Tyler's lieutenants or be expelled into the outer darkness. But tonight after business, it would be all smiles and pure indulgence.

While leaving the leadership to wonder about the funding source for his palace and all the toys that had come with it, Tyler told them that with his connections and their LA distribution center, the gang had the unique opportunity to be elevated to the title of cartel. That designation would give them great power, but with great power would come great responsibility. He would invest his own capital to get production started; tours would be set up to each of the three production facilities.

The leadership should begin using the Houston model to establish outlets in major cities all over the United States. He had already been laying the groundwork for the routes they could use to get the product into the country, but not every shipment could go through LA. He mentioned other cities chosen to accommodate the different shipping lanes.

Maintaining security was vital, and recruiting new blood should begin once they were back on their native soil. He would require gang members to become a part of a rotation system that would send them to Costa Rica and other parts of the world to serve as soldiers to protect product and personnel as the business expanded. All of this would require initial outlays of cash he was prepared to invest, but within a short time of operation, he believed all balance sheets would be in the black.

"Gentlemen, the risks are great, personnel and product will be lost from time to time, but the rapid growth potential is global and the profit margins are astronomical. The question is, do you have the courage and the commitment to live the dream?"

The leadership looked at Tyler Rogan, a.k.a. Salvador Alverez—CEO and president of Sea Breeze Corporation and perhaps a future underworld kingpin—and bowed to him in reverence. They would align their future with him, and Tyler opened his arms to his brothers.

"Welcome to my home."

23

Dewayne's eyelids felt glued together. He was sure his fingers were rubbing away the crust, but he could not get his eyes to open. There were voices in the room. He heard medical jargon, all too familiar language. This was soon interrupted by the arrival of the next meal, perhaps the last meal; whatever the number, any meal would be another wasted effort. All meals, for how long he could not remember, returned untouched. Then everything was silent, which was his preference. If he was going blind, the sound he cherished most was silence.

His eyelids trembled at the cool drops of liquid, which began to loosen the hardened seal. A damp cloth was dabbed over each lid. He was surprised by the gentle strokes, but more surprised his own hand had not initiated them. He thought the doctors had left. They always flitted in and out like darting birds, barely civil in their daily diagnosis, and always left their patient with a prognosis of physical and spiritual condemnation. He thought an attendant had taken pity . . . must be new.

After a few more strokes, his eyes were able to take in the first rays of sunlight coming through the window, but they were too potent, and he turned his head away. The damp cloth plopped onto his chest. He heard footsteps, then the pulling of cords, and the rays of sun replaced the shadow. He straightened his head on the pillow and prayed the hand would reanimate the damp cloth and remove the rest of the coating dissolving on his eyelids. How wonderful; answered prayers—he had come to expect no prayers to ever be answered—and the cloth brought its healing coolness to his eyes.

He could not remember when he had last opened his eyes or what he had last seen. Dreams and reality had concocted a strange potion of corporal images and the specters of nightmares. When the fog partially cleared, he perceived a subliminal form of angel and man holding the wet cloth and studying the effects of his work.

"You don't look so good," the angel/man said. "You don't smell so good either." The angel/man spoke no words of comfort. Just like all the others. How many others had there been?

"How about a bath?" the angel/man asked.

Dewayne could not resist the impulse to chuckle, and a smile creased his flaking lips. The offer was too ludicrous. He had become so accustomed to the smells of his corroding flesh, the dank room, the medicines pumping the poisons into his system, all mixing in with the rancid smells of human and industrial deterioration coming from the great penal complex, that he assumed these smells could be in preparation for his future eternity. Could there ever be any other smell besides his putrescence?

"I'll take that as a yes," the angel/man said.

Dewayne watched the creature, carrying a sack in one hand, go to the nurses' station just outside his door. He heard him smack his fist on the counter to get the nurses' attention off their manicures and social lives, and demand the ingredients and equipment for a bath. When questioned as to who was making such an adamant request, the answer was sharp.

"An uncle, a friend, a former coach, and don't waste my time with any more of your stupid questions," the angel/man said. "Put these smoothies in the refrigerator. I'll feed him after I've given him a bath. And bring me some clean sheets and a new hospital gown too."

The voice had provided a clue to the identity of the angel/man, but when its tone had changed to a bark with the nurses, Dewayne instantly knew who had arrived. For the first time in a long time, Dewayne's flooding tears had laughter in its flow.

The nurses must have believed the authority of the angel/man and all three connections he claimed to have with Dewayne because the bathing paraphernalia arrived soon after the second smack of the fist on the counter, ending the brief Q&A between the nurses and the angel/man. Dewayne soon felt the warmth of the water and listened to the hiss and bubble sounds of liquid cleanser rubbed into his withered body.

"I bet you've lost fifty pounds," the angel/man said, rinsing the soap off Dewayne's thigh.

"Jake Hopper, what are you doing here?"

"I think they really believed me when I told them I was your uncle."

Jake Hopper was angel/man. Jake Hopper had cleaned his eyes and made it possible for him to see. Jake Hopper was washing the decaying flesh off his body. Jake Hopper was smearing the cleanser on the silver-dollar-sized bedsores on his bottom and back. Jake Hopper was cursing under his breath, while he scrubbed around the metal handcuff on Dewayne's wrist, about the medieval conditions of the hospital and the Neanderthal treatment he was receiving.

"It's like we're in the Stone Age," he said as he scrubbed Dewayne's bald head. "What is this place? Auschwitz?"

He went from mumble to shout, which prompted the closing

of the room door by the head nurse right after she dropped the clean sheets and hospital gown on the floor.

"Finally they've done something useful," Jake said as he rinsed the suds out of Dewayne's ears.

"You know you're bathing a corpse," Dewayne said.

"I'd heard that, and now my eyes have beheld you," Jake said. "Looks like you're going to deny the state of Texas the pleasure of executing you."

"The medical consensus is, it's too dangerous to operate, so the tumor is being shrunk to an acceptable size to keep me alive long enough to stand trial and coherent enough to hear my death sentence."

"Sounds like you've got a plan."

Jake marveled at Dewayne's weakened and degenerating shape. When he saw him last, Dewayne had come into his store with the strength and height of a Corinthian column. Now Jake was looking at a candidate for an eating disorder program. Jake worried he might be scrubbing too hard, but Dewayne assured him it felt good, almost like the massages he got from the trainers. It had been so long since he received this kind treatment, so long since someone had touched him in kindness, so long since anyone recognized he was still human.

"Jake, tell me about my mother. What happened?"

This bridge had to be crossed, and it was best to be swift and honest with his words.

"They said cardiac arrest. When I got to her, she was gone."

Dewayne imagined Cherie crumpled lifeless on the floor and he began to sob, but his eyes did not supply him with any tears. He emptied his sorrow in dry heaves, and Jake paused from giving Dewayne his bath and put his arm over his frail shoulders to support him until he had spilled his grief.

In the midst of his weeping, Dewayne marveled that the one man who had shown him kindness by burying his dead mother was the one he had been angry with and rude to the last time they had seen each other.

"It was a nice funeral," Jake said. "I cleaned her house and closed it up and left the keys with the neighbors. I stayed drunk for several days and got sober long enough to sell my barbecue business to the first offer with hard cash, a barbecue chain with eyes on a franchise in Springdale. Then I went back to drinking and watching the news—it is a deadly cocktail—but I got so mad watching reports about you, I couldn't seem to stay drunk. I drank, but it did no good."

"Why did you come to see me?" Dewayne's voice was desert dry.

Jake sat on the bed and dried off the water and suds on Dewayne's chest. He pushed gently on Dewayne's skin, mopping the excess water, and each time he applied the slightest pressure of the towel down onto his chest, it felt as if he were pressing into mush.

"To give you a bath, I guess," Jake whispered, and Dewayne laughed at the absurdity of the answer. But Jake continued. "And for the memory of Jesse Webb. I turned my back once. Won't do it again."

Dewayne's laughter turned to sharp tears, and he covered his eyes with his bare arm.

"You keep crying, I'll never finish your bath."

"I killed my mama," Dewayne said and lowered his arm from his face.

"Cherie Jobe didn't raise a boy to kill nobody," Jake said, a sternness rising in his voice that neither man wanted to hear. "Now I've been sober for a week, maybe a few days longer, hard to tell, but it's been a good stretch since I've had a drink, so I'm grouchy if you haven't noticed. Patience is for monks, so don't make me lose mine with stupid comments."

Jake stood and draped the wet towel over the railing at the end of the bed. He collected the stuff he had used to give Dewayne a bath and left the room. A few moments later, he returned with a smoothie.

"They don't know how to feed an athlete around here." Jake set the cup and spoon on the windowsill. "When's the last time you've been out of that bed?"

Dewayne just shrugged his shoulders.

"Then it's time to breathe those bed sores."

Jake hoisted Dewayne's naked body out of the bed and helped him position himself against the windowsill, the dangling chain connecting him to the bed as a constant reminder of his prisoner status. The air flowed around Dewayne's body like a cool, soothing breath. His first taste of smoothie burned his raw mouth and tongue, and he had to spit a portion of it back into the cup, but he swallowed the rest. For the first time in weeks, he felt the pleasure of something flowing down his throat.

As Jake finished making the bed, he fought to control his anger about Dewayne's appalling condition. He squeezed ointment on each bed sore and then fanned the application with the new hospital gown until it dried. He helped Dewayne put on the gown and guided him back into bed.

"So now you've seen firsthand God's little morality play," Dewayne said. "Hope it was worth the drive from Springdale."

"Is that your way of saying thank you?" Jake asked.

"You can do me one last favor before you go. You can finish this now. You've cleaned me up for burial; now send me to my Maker."

"That must be the smoothie talking."

"The door is closed. You've driven everybody out. I'm ready. I'm chained up like my ancestors so I won't run off." Dewayne jerked the pillow from beneath his head and tossed it to Jake, belying his admission of weakness.

Jake felt a jolt of alarm. He knew too well what despair could do to a man.

"Put the pillow over my head. Finish it, Jake. Finish it. Finish me."

"I never thought I'd be asked to play God," Jake said, kneading the pillow.

"Why not? Why not play God, Jake? You're as good as anyone. The God I believe in has gone AWOL. 'Surely goodness and mercy shall follow me all the days of my life, and I will dwell in the house of the Lord for ever.' Who would write such a thing? Why would God want that lie written about him?"

"I wouldn't presume. I don't know that much about—"

"You know what I know? I'm universally hated for something I didn't do, but the funny thing is, I despise myself more than anyone ever could. I despise myself for ever being born. I despise myself for believing God really cared about me, for believing he watched over me. I feel like a fool, and I'm going to my grave without hope."

"None of this is over till it's over," Jake said.

"Well, there's the quote for the day." Dewayne yanked hard on his prison bracelet. "Look at me, Jake. You may be the last person outside these walls who ever sees me again, who ever hears my voice. Take a good look. Listen real well. I'm never going home again. I'm never going to see my wife or my child or my mama again. I'm never going to play football. I'm going to one place, my grave, and taking my bitterness with me. Do you know how scary that is? Do you know how frightened I am?"

"I can only imagine . . . I can—"

"No. You can't imagine. You haven't the capacity to come anywhere near imagining the horror I feel. I think about what happened to those kids. I dream about them so much, I sometimes think I actually did what they accuse me of, and that's the worst horror of all. I actually can imagine doing the crime. So I feel like I deserve all this . . . this punishment. Why didn't I just die at birth? Why couldn't I have been born with half a brain or without arms or legs? I could have lived and died without ever knowing God went around looking for targets. Who is safe with this kind of God lurking about in the universe? Who is safe? My child wasn't safe . . . my niece and nephew. Who is safe? Not even my innocent mama was safe. Her only crime was bringing me into the world. Do you know how much I hate God for letting her die with the last thought in her heart that her son had killed those children? She went to her grave believing her son was a murderer. I've never done anything . . . anything to hurt my mother."

Jake began to think this suffering was too much for one person to bear. It would be merciful to see this pain end. This was beyond human capacity to accept as life's offering with no way to fight back.

"Have pity on me, Jake . . . have pity. The hand of God has touched me, and this is what is left of me. I'd just like to know what God has against me . . . and if all that's happened brings him some kind of perverse pleasure. I can say I'm innocent all day long, but who would believe me?"

"Maybe me," Jake whispered. "Maybe me."

As Jake began to shuffle toward Dewayne with the pillow

pressed against his chest, an uncanny eagerness mounted within Dewayne, an eagerness to see the end.

Maybe Jake is going to grant my wish after all, he thought. *Maybe he will take pity on me.* There would be such relief by so kind an act. For all the bluster from the outside world demanding justice and revenge, there would be more relief than disappointment were he to quietly breathe his last.

Jake raised the pillow toward Dewayne's head. It was coming. Jake was going to do it, and Dewayne closed his eyes, prepared for the soft synthetic folds to conform around his face. He was calm. Fear had departed. He felt Jake's hand slip in behind his back. The agony was about to end. He resisted the instinct to preserve his life and blew out all remaining breath. This would make the passing quicker.

But the course was reversed at the last minute. Jake's firm hand eased Dewayne forward and wedged the pillow behind his head. Jake placed his hands on each side of Dewayne's face and kissed the top of his head.

"Find someone else to be God," he said and walked toward the door.

"Jake . . ."

Jake paused at the door and turned around to face Dewayne. "You had strength enough to toss me the pillow and strength enough to rail against God. Those are signs that let me know you have strength enough to live."

Jake slipped out of the room, allowing the door to close on its own.

24

Hathaway sat in his rental car in the parking lot of the Costa Rican National Bank in Dominical and checked his appearance in the mirror. Appearance was important when dealing with bank executives, especially when he was including them in a criminal investigation. Not only was appearance important but also timing. Surprise the executives early before the day gets started, and they cannot blow you off with the excuse of tight schedules. So Hathaway gave one last glance in the mirror—tweaked the tie, brushed the dandruff off the suit coat, cocked his hat just so—before he walked toward the bank entrance just as the doors were being unlocked for the first customers.

The bank executive who handled all international transactions was not a gracious or accommodating man and did not appreciate unannounced visits to ask troublesome questions regarding clients he knew very little about. All he cared about was holding and managing their wealth. When the executive's assistant informed him a Detective Hathaway all the way from Houston, Texas, would like to see him regarding a recent transfer to his bank of a significant sum, he bluntly told her the detective would have to wait. When Hathaway asked how long the wait might be, she smiled and offered him a seat, a selection of beverages, and his choice of reading materials, including English language magazines and newspapers. So much for Hathaway's theory of appearance and timing giving him an advantage, but he turned this minor obstacle into an opportunity—all a part of the constant need to adjust to any condition of the job. His line of work was not for the faint of heart, the impatient, or the easily frustrated.

For Detective Hathaway it was time to use the charm offensive on Ms. Rachel Almendarez. It began with the verbal appreciation for playing the hostess when he accepted the coffee she handed him—she must be way too busy for such niceties—and then moved to the plea for knowledge of the interesting places one should visit while in Dominical, which then flowed into questioning her about where she and her husband went when in the mood for entertainment. There was no Mr. Almendarez or significant other, and with this discovery, the charm offensive intensified. He did not go beyond the good taste of complimenting her youthful appearance, which he purposefully estimated to be well below her actual age, but it got the desired response of a blushing smile and a sly admission he had been well off the mark. If he couldn't read clues better than that, he must not be a very good detective, she told him, and Hathaway went right to the edge of going overboard when he laughed at her good-natured but personal jab.

The door of the bank executive's office opened just as Hathaway and Almendarez were finishing their enjoyment of her joke. After a brisk handshake, Hathaway saw the executive would not indulge in chitchat nor was he about to invite him to bring his coffee into his office. He had hoped to be able to show the executive pictures from the crime scene and one of Tyler, always a good motivator for compliance. But this was not to happen, so he had to make his request in front of Ms. Almendarez. His conversation with her had been frivolous and flattering. His words now turned to murder and thievery, and he hoped this might work to his advantage since he was forced to raise this subject in her presence.

Hathaway handed a piece of paper to the executive with the exact numbers, date, and sum he had received from his friend at Treasury and asked if the executive could verify the accuracy. He could do this without compromising international law; however, he knew the executive did not have to acquiesce. When the executive asked why, Hathaway explained the importance of such a transaction to his murder case. The executive remained disinterested in Hathaway's explanation, but he handed the paper to Ms. Almendarez and instructed her to fulfill the detective's wish. While Ms. Almendarez typed in the correct information, the executive spent the time looking alternately at his watch and objects on his assistant's desk, feigning interest in personal trinkets he had long since forgotten even existed.

Once the computer screen verified the accuracy of Hathaway's information, the executive considered he had finished his obligation and denied the detective's plea to reveal who had received the funds and where he might find him. Hathaway took one last stab, showed both a picture of Tyler, and asked if they might have seen him in the bank at any time. The executive was quick to respond with a curt no, but Hathaway was not looking at him. His eyes fixed on Ms. Almendarez.

"His name is Tyler Rogan, but he's probably using an alias," Hathaway said. "He's wanted for triple murder in Houston."

The executive took the picture of Tyler out of Ms. Almendarez's hand and gave it back to Hathaway. He was very sorry, but to his knowledge, this man had not been in the bank. With international law behind him, he bid Hathaway good luck as he escorted him to the bank doors. Hathaway watched him return to his office and close the door, then he turned on his heels and exited the bank.

Still fifty feet from his car, Hathaway pushed the beeper unlocking his front door.

He heard his name called and turned to see Ms. Almendarez waving as she approached him in the parking lot; she wanted to give him his hat. He might have one more shot with this ploy. She placed the hat in his hand and, without saying a word, began marching back to the front entrance.

"How can I thank you, Ms. Almendarez?" Hathaway said. A woman walking away from him was something he had become accustomed to, but usually for relational missteps and rancorous arguments. He must have too high an opinion of his charms. Almost without breaking her stride, she made a 180-degree turn as she spoke: "I hope you enjoy your time in Dominical, Detective Hathaway."

Then she disappeared through the double doors of the Costa Rican National Bank.

He ran his fingers around the edges of his hat, reviewing in his memory the scene inside the bank for any clues about where he might have tripped up, when he noticed a card stuck inside the silk fabric wrapped around the crown. The fact his charm had not failed him was as important to him as the information written on the card.

Mr. Mendoza entered the study to clean the room from the aftereffects of the previous night. Tyler jerked his bloated face from behind the safe, a cigarette dangling from his lips, eyes red and rheumy. He could not close the safe door because in each hand was a large stack of cash.

"What are you doing in here?" Tyler shouted.

Mr. Mendoza did not need a translator to interpret the wrath of his master. His startled ancient body began to shake, and he instinctively tried to explain himself with exaggerated gestures and rapid speech, which only infuriated Tyler more than the pounding hangover and the surprise interruption. Tyler slammed the cash down on his cluttered desk and began rummaging through the debris searching for his handgun.

"When I find my gun, you are one dead . . ."

Though Mr. Mendoza could understand the viciousness of intent expressed for his intrusion, he did not understand the specifics of the language. He remained in the room, compensating by raising his volume and hastening his explanation.

"You idiot," Tyler shouted, his search for a lethal weapon turning up empty. In frustration, he grabbed a paperweight and hurled it at the old man. The paperweight splintered and cracked the study door, and Mr. Mendoza crossed himself in appreciation for Tyler's inaccurate throw. But his gratitude was short-lived. The flower vase was next, and it shattered against Mr. Mendoza's head, slicing a gash across his crown. The old man smashed into the back of the damaged study door. Holding his head, blood seeping through his fingers, he managed to scramble out of the room before another missile could make physical contact. Had Tyler's weapon been in the study and not in the master bedroom, Mrs. Mendoza would have become a widow.

Mr. and Mrs. Mendoza had been married for forty-seven years. They had no children, but in each of the homes where employed as domestics, they had always been surrogate parents and grandparents to the children whose families they had served over the decades. When the last family for whom they had worked needed to move to another part of the country and wanted to take the Mendozas with them, the elderly couple felt they had reached a point where they could no longer make such major life transitions for reasons of age and health. They worked out an arrangement with the Ocean View Realty Company and the former owners. The Mendozas would be an all-inclusive part of the package. The former owners would maintain their salaries and living expenses until the new owner took possession of the property.

The Mendozas regretted their decision the first day Tyler and his entourage moved in. In the short time they had been in Tyler's employment, they had witnessed more hours of debauchery and human depravity than they ever thought existed. The couple knew they could not survive in such hellish circumstances but were lost about what to do. They needed a home and employment. They went about their duties as unobtrusively as possible, trying not to disturb anyone, above all the new owner, as they cleaned the destruction from the revelries of each night before the crowd awoke from their slumbers in the late afternoon for a repeat performance.

Tyler never allowed the two of them to go off the property together. He always kept one Mendoza home and in sight, assuring their silence. On the day Tyler decided to celebrate the agreements with all parties involved in his business, Mrs. Mendoza had to go to the market to purchase the food. Mr. Mendoza paid for the taxi waiting for her outside the gate, ready to take her to the market to collect the items on her long shopping list. Each time they parted, the pair embraced as if it could be the last time they might ever see each other.

She never shopped anywhere else but the outdoor market in the center square of Dominical. All one needed to prepare any dish could be bought at this bustling commercial center. She loved to shop for food, and now, it helped to distract her from the present nightmare she and her husband were living. While selecting some ripe avocadoes, she heard her name called, and when she saw who had spoken to her, she burst into tears.

Danny Boyle was an American expatriate who had lived in Costa Rica for the last eighteen years. He had made some money in the stock market and wanted to escape to an underdeveloped tropical area where he could stretch his modest wealth. He married a local girl, and after beachcombing had become tedious, they decided to go into business developing properties for well-heeled foreigners and created Ocean View Realty Company. He did not discriminate. He took anyone's money and never asked why someone with a vast amount of wealth would come to Dominical and spend millions of dollars on a second or third home. He was just happy some of those paradise seekers came to him. They had made Danny Boyle a rich man. But trouble had come to paradise when Detective Hathaway stepped into his office.

Mrs. Boyle was not friendly. How dare an American detective intrude on her business? How did he know anything about a wire transfer that took place a short time ago at the Costa Rican National Bank, and who had told him that Ocean View was the agency that had closed a deal on the property whose buyer might be involved in untoward circumstances? Hathaway had met his match. No charm offensive was going to work in this instance. Had Mr. Boyle not heard the heat in his wife's voice and her tongue slipping in and out of English and Spanish—Spanish when she needed to swear—the detective would not have known what to do.

Danny Boyle came out of his office and looked into the perspiring face of Detective Hathaway. Boyle's entrance offered both parties a chance to catch their breath, and he opened a refrigerator and pointed to a variety of cold drinks Hathaway could choose from that might lower the temperature. Hathaway took a seat and swiped the cold exterior of the soft drink across his forehead.

Mrs. Boyle turned away when Hathaway displayed the first picture of the Jobe crime scene, and Danny did not need to see but a couple more to agree to help in any way he could. The local papers had given the event some coverage early on, but the story had dropped off the radar. Danny said the owner's explanation for being able to buy such an expensive property was his success as a producer in the music business, and once the bank declared the money sound, Mrs. Boyle had handed the buyer his keys and they had had nothing else to do with him. Mr. and Mrs. Boyle nodded their heads in unison when they looked at the record mogul's picture. He had purchased the house.

Since the banker had refused to tell Hathaway who was in possession of the account number, he was hoping for some incriminating behavior the realty company might have witnessed, which could then justify bringing in local law enforcement. The Boyles had known the Mendozas only a short time. They had become acquainted when the former owners of the mansion were ready to sell and signed an exclusive Realtor's contract with Ocean View. The family had to move before the new owner took occupancy, so the Boyles took it upon themselves to watch over the Mendozas until the property sold. On more than one occasion, the Boyles had enjoyed Mrs. Mendoza's cooking when they came by to check on them and the property.

Because Mrs. Mendoza was such a creature of habit, Danny knew they would find her at the outdoor market around the same time each day. When told Hathaway's purpose for coming to Dominical and upon seeing the picture of her employer, she again burst into tears. Even though she feared for their lives, she and her husband would do anything to escape the tyranny they had been enduring.

Were it not for Danny Boyle's credibility, the police would have missed the small window to catch Tyler and his associates. Since he had been a longtime resident of Dominical and he operated a successful high-end real estate company, Danny was on good terms with local law enforcement. His clients and their multimillion-dollar homes required special attention, and he knew what it took to grease the wheels to secure that kind of first-rate surveillance. But he also knew who could be trusted with this unusual and dangerous information.

Hathaway presented his evidence, but the police captain was not inclined to act with the speed Hathaway knew was necessary to catch Tyler until Boyle described what had been going on in the house as told to him by Mrs. Mendoza. She had not come in person because her long absence might endanger her husband's life. This was not only an opportunity to apprehend a murderer and thief but also a chance to arrest significant local drug suppliers. Even if Hathaway could not find the evidence he needed to convict Tyler of the crimes against the Jobe family, Tyler would at least see jail time in Costa Rica for drug possession. It might not save Dewayne Jobe's life, but it would be some consolation.

The police captain ordered the raid. Danny produced pictures and blueprints of the property so the Dominical police team could study and plan for what would prove to be a bloodless takeover of Tyler's property, though the incursion was not without pain. The police bashed a few heads, and those who tried to escape had their bodies bruised and scraped when tackled. It was unusual for Hathaway to be without his weapon, but he was unable to bring one into the country and not allowed to carry one on the operation. However, that made him feel more like a general who had helped create the plan of attack and stayed behind the lines until it was executed, a feeling he thought he might grow to love the closer he came to retirement.

The benefit of having the schematics of the house also helped Hathaway locate the safe. When the authorities had corralled Tyler and the others at the opposite end of the house, he slipped into the study. He did not bother with trying to crack the safe. He brought along an expert with the right equipment to remove the door without collateral damage to the room. Hathaway was not interested in the stacks of cash. Once he found what he wanted, he left. Before returning to the police station where the Boyles were waiting for him, he stopped to thank the Mendozas, hiding in their bungalow, offering them a sufficient reward that guaranteed the couple a peaceful and comfortable retirement.

He took pleasure in seeing Ms. Almendarez once again, even though the hour was late and the atmosphere unappealing. The lineup room behind thick one-way glass had not been a suggested attraction in Dominical. But after tonight she might at least allow him the pleasure of buying her a drink. He took greater pleasure in seeing the surly and now disheveled bank executive who had been roused out of his bed, driven to the police station, and forced to identify the man who had given him the SWIFT account number, the same number Hathaway held in his hand from the list he had taken from the safe. But he took the greatest pleasure after the mechanical voice instructed Salvador Alverez to separate himself from the others and step forward, and he heard the Boyles, the bank executive, and Ms. Almendarez all say Tyler was the man.

25

Dewayne struggled to recall Hathaway's first visit. It seemed an eternity had passed. On his second visit, Hathaway presented a photograph of Tyler Rogan and asked for an account of his involvement in the Jobe family. Dewayne told the detective the same story that Rosella had given the day before, after Hathaway faxed her Tyler's mug shot and interviewed her via videophone in Los Angeles. Their synchronized stories, including Tyler's history of violence and incarceration, sealed his fate.

Hathaway returned a third time to Dewayne's hospital room, carrying a brown sack and wearing an uncharacteristic smile. The smile appeared when the four witnesses in Dominical identified Tyler Rogan. The smile remained throughout his return to Houston and became brighter as he wrote the report of his trip and included Dewayne's and Rosella's testimonies. Fellow detectives had never seen Hathaway in such a state and accused him of getting a new girlfriend or hitting the lottery, both of which he denied. When he and the police chief entered the district attorney's office and presented him with the body of new evidence, including videotaped interviews with the Mendozas and members of the LA leadership, his smile went radiant. This third meeting would be his final time to see Dewayne in the county prison hospital.

Jake was asleep in the chair next to the bed, but awoke at the first sound of Hathaway's knock on the door. Jake and Dewayne had tacitly agreed not to bring up the subject of Dewayne's earlier request to finish his life. Nature would take its course, and Jake would stick by his side to the end . . . subject closed.

Hathaway did not say a word when he entered the room, his lips preoccupied with whistling. He set the sack beside the bed and went for Dewayne's wrist, lifting it in the air with one hand and producing a key from his pocket with the other. While Hathaway unlocked the handcuff, a nurse came through the door, wheeling a television on a stand. After plugging in the cord, she slipped out.

"Thought you'd like to watch a little TV," Hathaway said as the key opened the lock and Dewayne's gaunt wrist dropped free onto his stomach.

"What's going on, Detective?" Dewayne asked, looking in amazement at the chain and handcuff lying unoccupied.

Hathaway paused from his tune to smile and hit the power button on the television. "I think the DA can explain it best," he said as he checked his watch. It was straight-up noon, and as soon as the commercial was over, the local station would go live to the Houston courthouse.

Hathaway was curious about how the DA would spin these undeniable details after having been so adamant about Dewayne's guilt. He had enjoyed watching him squirm in his office as he presented each detail in the case against Tyler Rogan, and then took extra pleasure in the semi-tantrum the DA had thrown when he realized the walls were moving in. The vindication was so sweet, who could blame Hathaway for whistling a happy tune?

The district attorney was pleased to announce startling new developments in the Dewayne Jobe murder case. Unanticipated and compelling evidence came to his attention proving Dewayne Jobe was not the perpetrator of these awful crimes. Pandemonium broke out, and the reporters assaulted the DA with questions, causing his lip to curl into a scowl for interrupting his train of thought. Hathaway laughed aloud, but his glee was short-lived when he heard weeping and saw Dewayne's face buried inside his blanket. Jake turned off the television's sound. They had heard all they needed to hear.

Dewayne wiped his eyes and looked into Hathaway's sympathetic gaze.

"Thank you," he said and covered his face again with the blanket. "Thank you. Thank you. Thank you."

Jake patted Dewayne's head, and then extended his hand over the bed to Hathaway.

"You responsible for this?" Jake asked, cocking his head toward the television.

Detective Hathaway gave an affirming nod.

"Then we're forever in your debt."

"Am I free? Am I really free?" Dewayne's supplications were as pitiful as those of a menaced child unexpectedly removed from his abuser.

"The DA closed the books on your case. The taxpayers no longer wish to pay your medical expenses or foot the bill for your incarceration. You are free, sir." Hathaway laid a hand on Dewayne's shoulder. "I suggest if you can, you should leave before the media descends," he said, pointing to the ongoing interview on television.

"What about it, Dewayne?" Jake asked. "You feel up to it?"

"Right now I could walk on water," Dewayne said.

"Then let's get out of here." Jake clapped his hands together in a loud whack. "I'll deal with the doctors. What about the warden?"

"Before I came to your room, I turned the papers in to the warden signed by that talking head on the screen, authorizing the release of Mr. Jobe. I will escort us out of here when you're ready to go."

The moment Jake was gone, Dewayne began to laugh.

"I've got nothing to wear but this raggedy old hospital gown," he said.

"Temporary solution," Hathaway said, producing the sack. Inside was a cheap red running suit. "Didn't know size or color preference, but—"

Jagged laughter escaped Dewayne when he beheld the first physical sign of freedom.

Jake returned with a wheelchair, and after a quick elevator ride down to the first floor, he wheeled Dewayne to the loading dock of the back entrance, all the better to avoid as little contact with other humans as possible.

Dewayne lay down in the backseat of Detective Hathaway's car, and Jake covered him with the hospital blanket he had grabbed from the room. Were Mr. Jobe to pursue treatment beyond what the prison hospital had done, the hospital would ship all records to the appropriate medical facilities, the doctor said as he signed his name to the forms fed to him by administrative personnel. Because the tumor was inoperable and the chemotherapy and radiation had not eradicated it, consensus was that it would be best if Mr. Jobe found a good hospice to finish out his last days.

Jake had been amazed at how the world had just discovered Dewayne was an innocent man, but the medical staff expressed no repentant conviction about their treatment of him when they thought he was a criminal.

"This place is right out of the Dark Ages," Jake said. "Whatever happened to 'first, do no harm'?" He had told them he was taking their blanket, and they could send the bill to the Texas taxpayers.

Jake followed Hathaway in his car as they pulled out of the county prison hospital parking lot. Hathaway suggested Dewayne ride with him until they had gotten well away from the prison property. If the press should pursue, then Hathaway had the means to lose them, and as he had predicted, a caravan of television trucks and company cars of rag publishers was barreling down the road in the opposite direction with a couple of helicopters buzzing overhead before they were two miles down the highway.

"Did you kill him?" Dewayne asked as Hathaway drove him away from his nightmare.

"He's locked up with his buddies in a prison in Costa Rica," Hathaway said.

"His buddies?"

"Rogan was building a drug ring with a gang out of LA and local suppliers. It was a major bust."

Dewayne was silent for a while, listening to the vehicles whiz past them headed for the hospital in hopes of capturing images and recording words of a man just resurrected. But he felt like Lazarus when Jesus had brought him back from the dead. He was just going to have to go through the whole process of dying all over again, and for Dewayne it would be sooner rather than later.

"Was he hurt? Did he get shot, bleed, get bruised, anything?" Dewayne asked.

"None of the above, unfortunately."

"That's not good enough," Dewayne said.

"I understand what you're feeling," Hathaway said.

"I don't believe you do," Dewayne said, and Hathaway conceded the point with a nod. "He needs to die."

"He'll get his chance once we get him back here. It will take some time to work through the extradition process with Costa Rica, but—"

"In the meantime he just sits in a cell with his homeboys."

"Trust me, the place you've been in is like a Ritz-Carlton compared to the prison system in Costa Rica."

"Still not good enough," Dewayne said, and he fell silent.

Hathaway knew he was fighting a losing battle trying to satisfy Dewayne's desire for revenge. He decided it was best to let Dewayne rest as they covered the miles back toward Houston.

Once they were back in civilization, Hathaway pulled into an alley behind a deserted strip mall and helped Dewayne out of his car. Dewayne put his arms on Hathaway's shoulders as much for support as a show of affection.

"What can I do for you?" Dewayne asked.

Hathaway looked over at Jake, who sat in his car waiting for the two men to say farewell. Jake nodded for him to answer Dewayne's question.

"See you play in a Stars game one day" was the first thing that came to Hathaway's mind for some unexplainable reason.

"Don't know if I can pull that one off."

"I'm counting on it," Hathaway said, and he helped Dewayne get into Jake's car.

"I can never repay you." Dewayne extended his hand to Hathaway one last time through the window of the car. "In another life I'd like to get to know you."

Hathaway squeezed Dewayne's hand. "I hope we get that chance."

"One good thing I can see in all this," Dewayne said, pulling his hand back inside the car. "At least I can die a free man. Things are looking up."

As Jake eased the car back onto the street, Hathaway looked at his watch. He had no idea what he would do with the rest of his day.

Jake nudged Dewayne awake when they arrived. He was opposed to the idea, but Dewayne insisted. Dewayne gave Jake directions and then fell asleep, exhausted by the dramatic turn of events. He hoped Rosella had not remembered to tell the Realtor about the key in a glass jar underneath the back deck. The FOR SALE sign was in the front yard, but given the circumstances, the house had not seen much activity. The two men sat in the front seat staring at the house, a house very much like every other house in this upscale neighborhood, and the exterior did not reveal in any way the horrible crimes that had occurred inside its structure.

Dewayne had never owned anything in his life until he and Rosella bought this house, their first home together, the first home for his first child, the home that had sheltered his niece and nephew from the cruelties of the outside world. But the outside world had wormed its way inside, turned malevolent, and he had done nothing to stop it.

He had been such a blind fool. He had opened the front door to his home, opened his heart, to the outside world, and it had turned on him with a viciousness he never could have imagined. No security system could have alerted him to the danger. Even God, who was supposed to have parted the Red Sea and raised his Son from the dead, could not or did not prevent the outside world from acting out this bloody micro-apocalypse inside his home, inside his heart. And what about his son? Why was there

310

no power to raise him from the dead? God was on the opposite side of the universe, silent, and dare he believe it, pitiless.

"One last walk-through and then we can leave," Dewayne said.

Once it was no longer a crime scene, professional cleaners had come in the house, scrubbed away the aftereffects of the crimes, and restored order. Dewayne limped from room to room, using an umbrella as a cane for support. It was just as he remembered it a few minutes ago, a few hours ago, a few centuries ago.

He climbed the stairs, praying that one day his wife, his niece and nephew, would no longer blame him. He went into Robert Dewayne Jobe III's room and picked up little Robert's pillow off the bed and brought it to his face. It still smelled of the wonderful combination of a baby's life, but it was the faint whiff of Rosella's favorite perfume that brought him to his knees, bellowing like a mortally wounded beast, for he knew she had performed this same ritual. No more laughter. No more tears of a child demanding his father's attention. No more cooing and gibberish. No more son.

He prayed his son, his only son, did not blame him. He prayed God did not blame him, for he blamed himself. He blamed himself for all that had happened. He blamed himself for every wicked act ever done in the world now and forever. He blamed himself for God turning his back on him, for forsaking him, and the pit of his gut did not go deep enough to contain all the torment blistering inside his soul. It rose, expelled a glut of grief, and pierced his heart again in vindictive strikes of lightning.

He crumbled to the floor, and his soaked eyes caught sight of a blue teddy bear lying beneath the bed. He had brought it home for Robert from one of his trips. He reached out and drew it to him, pressing it against his heaving chest.

Jake backed his car out of the driveway and drove along the avenue past the homes of happy families in the midst of their routines. Dewayne tried to think of routines. What was the routine of his family before all hell had broken loose? What were those mundane activities that are established early in the life of a family, giving them definition and character and certitude? He could not remember as he ran his finger over the furry eyes and ears of the teddy bear, hoping for recall.

"How much money have you got, Jake?" he asked.

"I've got some savings, should be enough to get us through, buy your medicines. The hospital gave us enough pills for a few weeks till we set something up back home."

"You got enough money to get us to Costa Rica?"

Jake came to a stop sign. Turning east would head them in the direction of Mississippi. West would take them to the airport.

"Just a slight detour is all I'm talking about," Dewayne said.

"Don't you think the law should have time to run its course?" Jake asked.

"It's time I don't have, and I don't trust the system to do the right thing."

"What is the right thing, Dewayne?"

"I'm dying, Jake. Why am I dying and Tyler Rogan is living? Is that the right thing? Is there justice in that? So drug me up, Jake, and let's go kill him."

A car pulled up behind them and the driver blew the horn. Jake rolled down his window and waved the vehicle around. In Springdale, most people would have stopped to ask if they needed assistance when they passed. Houston was not Springdale.

"Killing is what he deserves, but given your condition, I'm

afraid I'd be the one to have to do it, which I wouldn't mind. It might drive me back to the bottle, which some days I wouldn't mind either, but I'm kind of getting used to being sober. I might enjoy it again if I can keep my wits about me and can stay with it, but I need you to help me do that . . . help me keep my wits about me."

Dewayne's large hands gripped the teddy bear. "Drive," he said, and Jake eased the car onto the highway.

26

Dewayne did not want to go home until he had paid a visit to his mother. Jake helped him out of the car, and they ambled along the path in a predawn shroud of mist until they came upon the modest headstone with Cherie Jobe's name inscribed upon it. She lay next to her husband of less than one year.

"I didn't know what you might want to say, so I just put her name and dates," Jake said. "There's plenty of room to write something if you want."

"Thank you, Jake," Dewayne said, and he knelt beside the headstone and began a slow, easy polish across the granite top with his fingers.

The memories of his mother began to rise and dissolve at random. There was so much to remember, and he straggled behind each image flash, unable to convince it to remain. He wanted to soak each memory of its emotional warmth, but the scenes would not cooperate. The reminiscences insisted on teasing him, taking advantage of his dull wits made slow by the exhaustion of grief, and disappeared unrepentant of their sting to his heart.

"It's done, Mama. I'm a free man, and God forgive me, I'm so sorry . . . sorry." Dewayne held his breath every few words as though he were underwater and releasing just enough air to say a few more.

"You don't have to do this all at once, son," Jake said, resting a hand on Dewayne's shoulder.

It was as if Jake had been able to see the jumble in Dewayne's head and gave him permission to release the sorrow reserved for his mother.

Dewayne would die in his home in Springdale. He had taken nothing with him from the house in Houston except his son's blue teddy bear and a couple of suitcases of clothes; everything else was meaningless possessions.

Before he left Houston, he had made one phone call: to Coach Gyra. He told him his plans and wished him well before the preseason began. Dewayne was still under contract, and Gyra stated without reservation that he wanted him back. Gyra believed Dewayne's presence with the Stars would be a real inspiration to the team. Dewayne appreciated the sentiment but did not think his teammates seeing him in a wheelchair, his body plugged into IVs and looking scrawny as a starving dog, would be much inspiration. Neither man mentioned what both were thinking . . . Dewayne's time on this earth was ending. Before signing off, Gyra told Dewayne that the Stars' insurance would cover all medical expenses as long as needed.

"There shouldn't be much required from now on," Dewayne said. "I'm refusing further treatment. They'll keep me comfortable, and I've got good help. Thank you for this blessing."

When they entered the front door of Dewayne's childhood home, Jake repeated the story of how he had found Cherie, peaceful and still as though curled up for a nap, so Dewayne might feel another layer of closure. Then Jake carried the bags into his bedroom. Dewayne followed behind him, holding the apron he, Sly, and Jesse had ordered for Cherie and then decorated with their crude paintings of football players. It looked the same as the day Cherie had opened it—no stain or sign of use. The only blemishes of age were the flecks of paint that had crumbled off the picture each young man had painted.

Jake unzipped the suitcases on the bed and opened the top dresser drawer.

"Thanks, Jake. I'll take it from here," Dewayne said.

"I'll go to the switch box and turn on the power. Need some air circulating," Jake said. "Then I'll hustle some food from the store and cook us up some breakfast."

"Hang this back up in the kitchen for me, please." Dewayne handed him Cherie's apron. "I don't think she ever used it."

"I don't think that was the intention," Jake said and left the room with the apron.

The room had never changed. Cherie never moved an object except to clean around or under it and then put it back in the exact spot. He shuffled through the room, cradling the teddy bear in his arm, and handled each object. He opened the closet, taking visual inventory of the first eighteen years of his life that had become ancient history in a short time. He set the bear on top of the dresser, gathered a wad of socks and T-shirts from the opened suitcase, and tossed them inside the top drawer, disregarding any order.

He caught a glimpse of a present half the size of the drawer, pulled it out, and sat on the bed. The cheap wrapping paper had faded with age, and the red ribbon tied at the top like a shoelace was disintegrating. He snapped the ribbon off the box with his finger and ripped off the paper. There was a card taped to the top of the box, "To Dewayne, From Coach Hopper." When had he received this gift? He called out to Jake, but he had left for the store.

Dewayne opened the box and removed a tarnished silver-plated football mounted on a black wooden stand with an

316

inscription written in Old English just below the frets on the football: "Without adversity you have no character. Without character, you have no hope. Never lose hope. To the best receiver a coach could ever have, Jake Hopper." The date inscribed on the stand was the date of his departure for college. He stuck the box back inside the drawer, and then closed his eyes, trying to remember when he received this gift until the effort exhausted him.

When Dewayne opened his eyes again, he lay curled around the suitcases, smelling bacon and eggs, and listening to Jake whistling. He could not remember the last time he had felt hungry, and his mouth began to flood with moisture. Jake entered the room with a glass of orange juice.

"I didn't want to wake you, but we're almost ready. I figured you hadn't had a decent meal in weeks," he said, handing Dewayne the glass.

Dewayne rubbed his eyes and accepted the glass of cold orange juice. After drinking the juice, he handed the empty glass back to Jake and raised the metal football resting in his lap. At first he thought he might tell him he had just now opened it, but thought better of it.

"I never thanked you for this," Dewayne said.

"It's as true now as it was then . . . all of it," Jake said.

"Sounds like a quote from the Bible," Dewayne said, running a finger over the inscription.

"Don't know, could be. It's a good source of inspiration last I checked."

"Jake . . . Coach . . . you don't have to do all this, you know," Dewayne said, holding out his arms to include the totality of all Jake was doing.

"Well, there's where you're wrong," Jake said, and Dewayne looked at him with a puzzled expression. "I'm an old drunk and

317

you're dying. I thought maybe under the circumstances that might make us a good team. We've been pretty well forgotten . . . well, I have anyway, but I saw no need for either of us to be alone right now. I confess I need you more than you need me, but we both need hope. I thought maybe if we stuck it out for as long as it takes, we might find us some hope. And if that doesn't convince you, then I have to do it for your mother. I loved her . . . can't deny it."

He'd said it at last. After all those years, he had let someone in on his secret.

Dewayne could not help but smile at Jake's uncommon shyness.

"You ever tell her this?" he asked.

"Came close a time or two, but no, my affections were a one-way street. Her love for you and your father was enough."

Both men gave each other a moment of silent grace to contemplate the what-ifs of a relationship between Jake and Cherie, until Jake ended it.

"Come on. I don't want our eggs to get cold."

Their routine was simple: meals, medication, rest, limited physical therapy to maintain some level of strength—late-night walks were the best so as not to attract attention. Since Dewayne had declined further medical treatment, the local Springdale doctors' group was in charge of attending to his overall care; a home health nurse made routine visits to monitor his vitals and make the necessary adjustments to all the medicines. Jake devoted his time to shielding Dewayne from the public, though the hometown folks were not the problem. In fact, they were protective. After several minutes of concentrated praise for Dewayne and anecdotal stories of his football prowess to any and all reporters who had come to Springdale to interview their hometown hero, they would, with the sincerest of smiles, give convoluted directions to a variety of nonexistent locations where Dewayne could be found. They just did not trust the slant these outsiders would give their boy. He was due proper respect and who best to give it to him. Jake handled those persistent few who slipped through the front lines, hoping for a Jobe sighting.

All of Dewayne's finances would remain frozen in court until after the trial, but Jake had enough funds to provide for their welfare. However, it was rare that Jake went out into the community to shop that he did not return with sacks of donated supplies, and the goodwill and affections of the community. The incomparable citizens of Springdale would allow this football star to live the rest of his life in peace and assure him that in spite of what the world had done to him and how the media had treated him, they would always remember him with kindness and grace.

The honors only a small town can bestow began to flow in during the following weeks. The high school sent Jake home with a letter, informing Dewayne that the team voted to name the football locker room after him and gave him a framed picture of his retired jersey for his wall. The break room at Webb Furniture would also bear the Jobe name. The head librarian and Winston Garfield of the *Springdale Leader* had loaded Jake down with a mountain of newspaper and magazine articles written about Dewayne's amazing football career that had been assiduously compiled, dating all the way back to his middle school years. The mayor of Springdale sent Jake home with a plastic model of the new road signs reminding residents and informing strangers this city was proud of the Jobe Highway that cut through the heart of town. Even though the number of voices raised to venerate Dewayne was many and their praise began to restore his shattered faith, it was not enough to probe and console the shadowed land of his empty heart.

He stirred when he felt the coolness on his bare skin from the absence of the teddy bear he had tucked into the crook of his arm at the start of the Stars' first preseason game. Jake had gotten him set up in the easy chair in front of the television so they could watch the game. But it was the quiet weeping that had pulled him from the slumber he had fallen into before the first quarter was over. He opened his eyes and saw a woman sitting near him on the floor with her back to him, holding the teddy bear and rocking back and forth. She did not notice Dewayne had awakened. Neither of them noticed that Jake had slipped out the front door without a sound.

Dewayne did not know if what he saw at his feet was vision or reality, but he raised his trembling hand off the tattered arm of the chair and moved it toward the dark, sinuous hair. When his fingertips touched the top folds of the hair, he felt a static spark igniting a heat within his blood that dispensed a warm strength into his hand and arm. The current moved past his shoulders into his chest and settled into his heart. He knew he was awake. He knew the sensation flowing through his fingers and into his heart was real. He felt connection to a familiar touch; the hair and the head and the body he knew, had fully known, had given him life, and now it was giving it to him once more. But the body was slumped in shame. The body would not turn toward him.

The body seemed to grow weaker, as if passing its life into him. The body quivered and continued to shed disquieted tears. The body waited. The body waited to hear its name called, to hear words of comfort, to hear forgiveness spoken. The body could not move until summoned.

"Rosella," Dewayne whispered, and her face moved into his fingers as she turned her head around. It was now skin-to-skin, fingertips to delicate cheek and nose and eyes and forehead.

His fingers smoothed out each wrinkle, each pinched line of foreboding, like the sculptor smoothing out rough clay. "Rosella."

"I did not know how I would come back," she said. "I just knew I had to try."

Dewayne nodded like an old soul, wise in the ways of human action. The lowered head beneath his caressing hand remained submissive, her hand resting upon his, not wanting release. But was he able to trust this touch, this reconnection? Could he ever fully trust Rosella again? The heart is deceitful above all else. Could he even trust his own heart in the short time he had left?

"Do you feel like taking a ride?" she asked.

He knew this would be a test. He knew this ride would try the mettle of his soul and could prove to be the beginning of healing, a healing more of the spirit than of the body, but what would the medicine be?

Rosella drove them back to his high school football field in her rental car. She wanted to return to the spot where she had accepted his offer to be his lifetime partner, hoping the memory of her willingness to marry him might curry favor. She had flown into Memphis that day and was prepared to fly back immediately if the situation warranted. She did not know how to interpret the silent ride to the stadium. Was Dewayne indulging her? Was he mystified or coherent? Was he processing venom or forgiveness?

Dewayne was a willing child led through the fresh-cut grass of his youth. He still struggled with the reality of the moment. He knew pulsating life had begun in his veins with the first stroke of her hair back at the house and continued to surge through his system. He believed the outcry from within his soul was for life, and as long as he stayed connected, as long as he maintained this touch, as long as he followed this source, restoration to life was possible. Murderous floods had fallen from the sky on both of them, but that darkened torrent had washed neither of them away. Standing; seeing; touching; expelling air; feeling multiple levels of pain; moving in any direction at any speed; hearing your voice in silence; hearing the breaking of silence by the muscles in your throat praising or cursing or weeping or comforting—all of these and more were signs universally recognized as circulating life. In this moment of twilight, the choice was upon them.

"We're here," Rosella said, stopping their forward progress with an easy tug of the hand on the point of the fifty-yard line where she had stood to receive his proposal of marriage. The memory was fresh, but the time between then and now had slipped into eternity. She opened the palm of her hand, and Dewayne saw his mother's ring, Rosella's wedding band. "I am not worthy . . . I do not deserve these . . ."

"How did you . . . ?"

She put a finger to his lips. "I am not worthy. I do not deserve them. I do not deserve you. When I tore them from my finger, I threw away the only thing that had any meaning to me. A security guard at the prison returned them, a stranger who could have kept them. I swear to you, when they came back to me, before any of us knew you were innocent, it was the first touch of hope I felt. I have raged against everything, beginning with God and ending with myself. I wasn't ready for what happened to us. How can you be ready for something like that? I will always question why our son and Sabrina and Bruce were taken from us. If I could have fought to protect them, I would have. If I could have died to spare their lives, I would have, but I did not get that choice. I have been given other choices."

She opened Dewayne's hand and let the rings slip into his palm, then closed his fingers around them. But she did not let go, clasping her hands around his fist. The tears she shed lubricated his fingers, and with each kiss upon the skin of his clenched hand, Dewayne felt the pulse of life, an exposure to hope, a sign of the dreadful logic of joy.

Rosella laid her head upon their intertwined fingers, a respite for her soul's raw disclosure. "I'm so ashamed, but I had to come to you and beg your forgiveness."

Dewayne's faith taught him to believe what he bound on earth was bound in heaven; what he loosed on earth was loosed in heaven. Could there be that much power to forgive given to a person? Yet the sparks of life that moments ago had splashed off the flint of his soul would not ignite. His breath quickened. His face pounded as if from shock. He nearly choked. There was nothing to draw on, nothing within him, that could fan this attempt to inflame hope.

He began to uncurl his fingers, relieving the pressure from around the rings in his hand. He allowed Rosella's hands to nest beneath his open hand as he stared at the precious tokens, the wedding band and the engagement ring of his beloved mother. He gently rattled the mementos in his palm, then stirred them with his finger like a preparatory ritual for a mystic reading that would provide him an answer. But there was nothing mysterious about the discord in his heart, nothing enigmatic about the quest to forgive. Was he capable of forgiving? That was the question.

"When does the heart stop bleeding?" he asked, and he surprised Rosella by removing his hand from hers and stepping back. "Nothing to this point has been able to stop the constant stream. The hole you made in my heart is too big. You plunged your knife into it that day in the hospital when I woke up not sure of what had happened. What had I done? What had I done? I had no contact with the outside world. I never saw the news. I never witnessed the public's rage. They told me what I had done and kept me in isolation. My only connection to the horror was through you, and when I see you now, I only see the memories of your hatred, you throwing these rings at me, you insisting I sign divorce papers, and worst of all, the comfort you took with Sly right in front of my face. I don't have a memory of the deaths of the children. I slept through all of that, and I will go to my grave bearing the guilt of being unable to save them. My memories are of you, of your disloyalty, of your condemnation, of your loathing."

The strength to support her weight vanished from her legs, and Rosella collapsed to her knees. The judgment she had measured out was returning to her.

"I don't want to be alone when I die, but I've lost my innocence. I thought for a moment it could be as it was, our love could be restored, but I don't know. I'm dying and I want to forgive, but I have no strength, no capacity. Too much blood has flowed out of me, and I'm very sorry."

He slipped the rings into his pocket and hobbled off the field with Rosella's excruciating cries rending the heavens.

27

"Chemo and radiation have shrunk the tumor, but didn't kill it. I propose we would insert the needle here," Dr. Macy said, pointing to the picture of the tumor on the image from the CAT scan with his pen. "We heat the needle with radio waves and kill all the tissue in the immediate area."

Jake stood behind Dewayne, who sat in a chair in Dr. Macy's office. Both studied the small diameter of tissue at the tip of Dr. Macy's pen. How could a man Dewayne's age and in such excellent physical shape grow so lethal a combination of pulp? The University Hospital in Memphis told them up front the operation posed risks; it was only an experiment. The doctors could give no guarantee of a positive result, but the procedure had been successful with liver, lung, and kidney cancers. Dr. Macy and his team would try to "cook" this tumor if Dewayne was willing.

"The first procedure will target the core of the tumor," Dr. Macy said. "We will follow up in a few weeks with a second stage to wipe out any cancerous cells that may have survived around the edges. If necessary, we can go to stage three where we insert tiny capsules of chemotherapy drugs at the margins of the burn zone. By isolating the capsules, it should spare you the toxic side effects of normal chemo."

In the last few months he had not been spared from the worst of evils—the deaths of his mother, son, nephew and niece, fortunes vanished, career over, reputation vilified—so what could the toxic side effects of one more round of chemotherapy do that hadn't already been done to destroy him? When Dr. Macy had tracked Dewayne down and invited him to Memphis for a consultation, he had decided he had nothing to lose. After listening to Dr. Macy's presentation, he was still of the same mind. Dewayne reached his hand toward Dr. Macy, and the doctor shook it.

"Dr. Macy, I will put my tumor into your hands, and what's left of my faith I will put in God."

"Let's hope it will be a winning combination," the doctor said.

There was no reason to return to Springdale. Time was of the essence, and Dr. Macy was anxious to start the pre-op process. University Hospital would absorb all expenses. Dewayne was taking a risk for science, the first brain cancer patient to undergo such an experiment. There would be several days of tests to establish the operational protocol with Dr. Macy's team and build up Dewayne's strength; he also had some time to prepare mentally for what lay ahead of him. Dewayne insisted the room he was given be large enough to accommodate a bed for Jake; he wanted him by his side. He requested the hospital do all in its power to keep this information from getting to the media. If they caught wind of this story, they would descend. Dr. Macy and University Hospital administration agreed to the news blackout, but requested that, if the operation proved to be a success, they could announce the results with Dewayne at their side, and he agreed to the press conference.

There were three calls Dewayne asked Jake to make once he made the decision to have the operation. Coach Gyra was the first. He wanted Gyra to know what he was preparing to go through with all its risks, but its potential for positive results as well. He had no idea what it might mean for his future if the operation was a success, and Gyra relayed the message that there would be nothing he would like better than to welcome Dewayne back into the Stars' locker room.

Dewayne wanted Detective Hathaway to know, and when Hathaway found out, he asked if he could come and see Dewayne. He had some news, and given the circumstances, he would like to deliver it in person. He was owed vacation time, and why not spend a few days in Memphis?

The third call was to Rosella, which Jake argued Dewayne should make, but he abdicated the task.

"Should I return to Memphis?" she asked. "What should I do?"

"I'd catch the first plane out of Los Angeles," Jake told her.

"Is this what he wants? Does he want me there?"

"He has not said those words." Jake could not lie and he could not manipulate, but he did not restrict himself from editorial comment. "I know he's hurt. I know he's scared. And I know I can't do this alone."

"I'll call back when I have my flight plans, but say nothing about this to him."

On his own, Dewayne made a fourth call to Winston Garfield, the reporter for the *Springdale Leader*. Winston drove to Memphis, and after the first battery of pre-op tests were done, they spent the rest of the day together. Should he not survive the operation he wanted Winston to publish his full story. The last call he made was to a lawyer Winston recommended in Springdale. There were some loose ends he wanted to tie up.

Detective Hathaway's first comment when Jake escorted

him into Dewayne's room was about the upgrade in hospital accommodations.

"Yeah, this is what experimental surgery will buy you, but I'd rather see someone else lying here," Dewayne said.

"This may cheer you up," Hathaway said and took a seat beside Dewayne's bed. "A few days before Jake called me, I was contacted by the authorities of the federal prison in San Jose. They transported Tyler and his LA gang from Dominical once we busted them, quite a comedown, going from a five-star mansion to a third-world penitentiary. This was the end of the line for Tyler Rogan. I don't think the boys from LA appreciated being brought to Costa Rica on a vacation and ending up extending their stay a good ten to twenty. His autopsy report shows signs of acute torture; call it the three Bs: burns, bruises, and blunt instrument abuse in places where blunt instruments don't belong. He suffered. He suffered in the extreme, but it was the slit throat that finished him off, no doubt administered without last rites."

"How do you know it's the right guy?" Jake asked.

"Photos from the coroner, and the fingerprints and DNA match from his juvie days," Hathaway said.

Dewayne's face had been expressionless the whole time he listened to Hathaway. The tale was outrageous, too unbelievable, ill timed in its telling. Dewayne was facing the prospects of his own death; his emotions were at peak level, and hearing of Tyler's brutal death brought confusion. Still, one feeling began to rise out of the jumbled mass.

"They beat me to him," he mumbled. "I wanted the pleasure."

Jake and Hathaway looked at him, thinking it was a perverse stab at humor, but the frustrated glint in Dewayne's eyes revealed true disappointment.

"This way you can have all the pleasure and none of the guilt," Hathaway said, hoping to lighten the morbidity in the room, and then he moved on to the next subject.

"With this new turn of events the money stolen from you will be restored. It will still take some time, but you should get back most of it."

"I'll trade you one brain tumor for everything in my account." Dewayne began to laugh at his gloomy attempt at a joke. His laughter continued and became infectious. It drew in the other two men, and when Hathaway said he would only take cash, they laughed even more, and even harder when the stern-faced nurse entered the room and demanded the volume level be brought down, which by that point was almost impossible. Dewayne had not laughed in months. He did not know he was capable of laughter. He did not know how much laughing he would do in the near future, but now was a good time to laugh.

Dewayne asked if he and Jake could eat their last evening meal together on the observation deck before the operation the next morning. He needed a break from wheeling all over the hospital, in and out of different rooms where the medical staff performed every imaginable test. He needed to be outside, breathing fresh air and looking into the night sky. The slight cool breeze felt good on his skin but made the flame of the candle inside the glass hurricane on the table hiss in complaint. Dewayne could not eat much. He sipped on a smoothie while studying the will he had drawn up.

Jake quietly ate his supper and nodded when necessary so Dewayne would think he was paying attention.

"Rosella gets everything," he said. "That is the right thing, isn't it, Jake?"

Jake nodded as he buttered his roll.

"If I'm not around and there's a glitch in the system about getting our money back, you'll take care of it, right?"

Jake nodded, his eyes cast down upon his food.

"And you'll help her decide what ministries to give money to."

Jake held up his hands as if to say, When is this going to be over?

"It's important, Jake. It's important. And you get Mama's house or its monetary equivalent."

Jake stopped chewing and stared at Dewayne. He set down his fork and washed his last bite down with a swallow of sweet tea.

"You deserve it. No argument. The hospital notary is stopping by before the operation tomorrow to notarize it, and we're good to go," he said and plopped the document in front of Jake's plate.

Dewayne leaned back in his wheelchair and looked into the clear night sky. The lights of Memphis diffused the reflected brightness of the vast universe of stars above him, manufactured light and light-years away competing against the darkness. He believed there were more stars than he could see, but he had to imagine them.

"Jake, I thought I knew so much, but I know so little," he said. "I do know this; mercy is not a natural instinct. When Detective Hathaway told me about Tyler's death, mercy did not come to mind. Disappointment that I wasn't the one who took the knife to his throat, pleasure at knowing how he suffered, but not mercy, not forgiveness. I'm about to have this operation, and I don't know how to ask God for mercy when I'm incapable of giving it. I wonder if God's capable of giving it. I thought that was a given, came with the faith package like a bonus, but I haven't felt it in a long time and don't know if I should expect it now. It certainly didn't arrive in time to save my family or me."

"Lay it down," Jake said. "It's one of those unanswerables."

Jake finished his last bite of supper and set his empty plate on the table next to them. He slid Dewayne's will toward him and brushed some crumbs off the top page.

"Rosella know about this?" he asked, tapping his finger on the document.

Dewayne was quiet, the heavens still capturing his pensive gaze, and Jake repeated the question.

"She'll know soon enough," Dewayne said. Sorrow filled his voice. "When was the last time you spoke with her?"

Jake seized the moment. "Son, if you're gonna die, don't die a fool," he said, tossing diplomacy out the window. "Your mother might have loved me if I hadn't been a stubborn drunk. She might have married me if I had spoken up. Instead, I did that crawl-inside-the-bottle thing and kept my self-pity iced and pickled. I can't talk to you about theology matters since I haven't been very good at practicing them, but you do have one last chance for mercy, and that's with that girl. Don't let it be when she reads this will."

Dewayne looked at Jake. He had never seen him angry before. Never. He had seen him in a myriad of emotional states, but never angry. This was not the last memory he wanted to have of his friend.

"What should I do?" Dewayne whispered.

"You need to figure it out. I can't tell you." Jake took his plate and glass, left the last will and testament of Dewayne Jobe resting on the table, and walked away.

Dewayne went back to the heavens. It was vast, populated with stars, planets, and galaxies, all above him, all floating in unfathomable space, all silent. Where would the comfort come from? Where could he deposit his fear, doubt, and anger and be able to inhale that deep-breath peace that surpasses all understanding?

The touch came with the coolness of fingers caressing his cheek. When he opened his eyes, the vision of Rosella almost made him leap out of his chair like someone healed. She placed a finger on his lips.

"I was hoping I would see you before your operation tomorrow," she said. "Jake thought I should try again maybe. I hope you're not angry. You don't have to do anything or say anything. I just wanted you to know I was here if you needed anything, but I would leave if you wanted me to."

Dewayne lowered his head and said nothing. She opened her purse and pulled out the divorce papers she had brought Dewayne back in Houston when he was at his lowest point. She held them up to the light of the candle and flipped over to the last page.

"Jake gave this to me. You never did sign it," she said, and he shook his bowed head. He did not raise it until he caught a whiff of something burning. He looked up to see Rosella holding the top of the divorce document and the bottom third turning to ash. He saw the blank space on the last page where his signature was to have been written give way to the conflagration. He saw Rosella's name and the name of the law firm and the California notary stamp turn black in the intense heat.

When the fire consumed half the document, she rose from the table, walked over to the balcony, and held the flaming papers over the edge. The cremated particles of official divorcement flew into the air, rising into the silent heavens he had been staring into just moments before. When the papers were near incineration, she released them, and the remaining flames dropped from sight, disintegrating into the atmosphere.

Dewayne pushed his body out of the wheelchair and balanced himself by placing his hand on the table. Rosella started to come to him, but he stopped her by raising his other hand. She waited as he maneuvered through the tables and chairs on his slow way to join her. When he got to the balcony, he looked over the edge, and on the ground, six stories below he saw an exhausted flame flicker out.

"I can't pretend any of what happened to us did not happen," she said. "We have horrors that will always be remembered. I've shamed myself with you in ways I never imagined I could do. We can't recover what we've lost, but there's no scorecard. My loss is equal to yours, and I don't want to keep on losing. I want to hold on to something I loved once with all my heart, something I hope I could love again, and maybe, in time, could love me back."

Dewayne looked down over the balcony, then back into the sky. He caught the faint scent of burnt ember.

"I'm broken," he said. "All this dreadfulness has broken me. I have to turn it over. I have to turn everything over to God, Someone whose trust is in doubt, but I don't know what else to do. Whatever happens after tomorrow, I've got to lay it down. I'm not trying to make any deals with God. I just want to be ready to meet him."

He motioned for her hand and reached into the pocket of his robe, pulling out his mother's engagement ring, and placed it in her palm, then folded her fingers over it. "I've been holding on to Mama's ring for good luck. It's been in short supply. Would you hold on to it for safekeeping?"

Dewayne watched as the nurse wrapped his blue teddy bear in protective plastic before reentering the operating room and setting it on top of one of the monitors.

"It'll be here when you wake up," she said, and Dewayne nodded his approval.

His body was scrubbed and disinfected with some foul-smelling stuff that reminded him of the locker room, and he began to imagine his teammates and coaches . . . the stadium, the fans, and the noise such a throng could produce . . . the smell of the grass on the field . . . his running plays . . . the quarterback calling the signals . . . the team spread across the scrimmage line . . . his legs carrying him at superhuman speed . . . the ball sailing overhead and his hands stretched out to receive it . . . Colby Stewart bowing in veneration as he ran past him into the end zone . . . the operating theater being on the fifty-yard line and a stadium full of people hushed and watching. He imagined his mother, his son, Bruce and Sabrina watching . . . Rosella, Jake, and Detective Hathaway pacing in his hospital room. Just before the orderly had wheeled him away, Rosella kissed him. He imagined the kiss, the moisture, the warmth. He imagined the "I love you" he had heard her say as he rode the gurney out the door.

He imagined her words on a continual loop before he imagined himself in peaceful sleep.

28

"Dewayne, heads-up," Jake said.

Dewayne sat in the recliner in the living room. He twisted his head from watching the Stars' first game of the season to the direction of the voice coming from the kitchen. He caught sight of the missile flying in his direction just as Rosella came around the corner carrying a bowl of popcorn. She gasped and almost dropped the bowl when she saw what Jake had done.

Without thought, without hesitation, and although without his former speed, Dewayne's left hand rose in the air and stopped the ball in midflight. The nose of the ball smacked into the palm of his hand, and Dewayne caught it off the bounce, juggled it, but still held on. He had had several of those catches in his football career. He stared at the ball in his hands. He smelled the pigskin. He rubbed his fingertips over the pebbly texture of the orb. He smelled it again. He tossed the ball in the air above his head and caught it. He smelled it again. He tossed the ball from hand to hand and smelled it again. He tossed it back to Jake and returned to watching the game without saying a word.

Seconds later, eyes still focused on the game, he raised his hand in the air and snapped his fingers. Jake hurled the ball again, and this time the catch was one-handed, no juggle, no bobble. He had not looked at the ball. He tucked the pass into his side opposite the teddy bear.

"You're ready for a press conference," Jake said. "I'm calling Memphis."

The first operation had gone better than expected, and instead of waiting several weeks for the second phase, Dr. Macy pushed up the time frame to burn out remaining cancerous cells around the edges that might have escaped the primary heat blast.

Between the two operations, the reorganized family of three had focused their efforts on rebuilding Dewayne's strength and putting some weight on him. His appetite had begun to return, and though he could not eat big meals, he ate three or four small meals a day.

Once released after the first surgery, Jake and Rosella drove him back to Memphis every other day to monitor his condition. This process was exhausting but preferable to staying in the hospital, and for Dewayne, being out in the world even on this limited basis was a boost to his well-being. After the second operation, Dr. Macy told him he could have ten days off before the next visit.

"Jake, are you sure he's ready to talk to reporters?" Rosella asked.

"Doctors need a CAT scan. I've just had my proof."

Dewayne never took his eyes off the television, and when the Stars scored their first touchdown, he flung the teddy bear in the air while tightening his hold on the football and tucking it deeper into his side.

———

Dr. Macy spent the first part of the press conference giving a detailed description of the operations performed on Dewayne's tumor, ending with the announcement that the CAT scans

338

taken that morning showed no signs of cancerous cells in the affected area. It was premature to say Dewayne was cancer free. He would undergo scheduled examinations for an extended period. *Medical history, medical miracle, medical advancement* were terms Dr. Macy used in describing the success of this operation, and given Dewayne's age and physical condition prior to the onset of the tumor, Dr. Macy predicted he should be able to resume a normal life in a short period of time.

"Does it mean he can play football again?" one reporter blurted out.

"We have done our job in giving Mr. Jobe his opportunity to play football or anything else he wants to do," Dr. Macy said. "It's up to him to decide."

When Dr. Macy sat down, the room erupted with questions for Dewayne. The media had come from all over the country, and not just the usual suspects from the world of sports. Reporters who covered other areas of interest from the medical, financial, political, and entertainment fields were present, eager to make headlines for their readers.

Dewayne cast his eyes over the room in search of Winston Garfield for the *Springdale Leader*. Amidst the waving arms, the flashing camera lights, and the shouted demands for Dewayne's attention, the gray-haired gentleman sat in the back smiling at Springdale's favorite son. He did not need to ask a question. He did not even have his hand raised. When Dewayne found him, he smiled and nodded his head in Garfield's direction. Mr. Garfield stood and waited for Dewayne to acknowledge him.

"Mr. Garfield, thank you for coming," Dewayne said. "What's your question?"

"Mr. Jobe, you have been through a great ordeal in recent months," Mr. Garfield said. "You seem to be coming out on the other side. As a survivor, what are your thoughts?"

Dewayne looked at Dr. Macy. He looked at Rosella and Jake standing by the door. He lowered his head, reached inside his sport coat, and removed the teddy bear. He set it on the edge of the table in front of him but did not let go of it. He looked again at Rosella. Her smile helped him release this prized possession.

"It was my son's. It goes everywhere with me. It reminds me of my loss. I never want to forget all that I have lost. A little over a month ago I came in to see Dr. Macy in a wheelchair. I was a broken man. Today I was able to walk into the hospital under my own power, on my own two legs, but the truth is, I'm still a broken man. In some ways, I guess I'll always be broken. I cannot fathom the mysteries of God. They are deeper . . . deeper than the grave that cradles my son. Could I blame God? Yes. Could I reject him? Yes. Could I curse him and die? Yes. There were times when dying would have been the easiest thing to do. But I'm still here.

"Before this time I thought I was powerful, but human power is nothing. I cannot give you an explanation as to what I have survived. No account would do it justice. And I don't have a tangible or logical answer about why. I will never know why. I'm not sure I want to know. I do know were it not for Detective John Hathaway, my friend Jake Hopper, Dr. Macy and his team, and my wife, Rosella, I would never have made it. But beyond the support of these people, there was something that held on to me, something that carried me, something that would not let me go when I was at my lowest point, begging for my life to be over. I don't know what else to call it but a hope that God would not abandon me, a hope that even though I longed to die, I should still trust in him. What I have survived, I wish on no one, and I don't know why I'm still here, but I am. I choose to live, to live the best I can, holding on to my hope in God."

Except for the resonance of dozens of human beings shifting

their bodies in a cramped room, there was no other sound. No camera lights flashing, no conversing, no verbal claims for Dewayne's notice. Mr. Garfield remained standing.

"A follow-up question, Mr. Jobe, if I may," Mr. Garfield said, and Dewayne nodded his permission. "If Dr. Macy says you can play football again, is it possible you might return to the game?"

Dewayne chuckled, causing a slight tremor in his body. He closed his eyes and took a deep breath, the smell of the football Jake had passed to him in the living room still a poignant memory. He opened his eyes and studied his hands, watching his long fingers contract and release, then he focused his attention on Winston Garfield.

"With God all things are possible."

"What's the first thing you're going to do when you leave here?" another reporter shouted, unwilling to wait for Dewayne's acknowledgment.

"Go visit the grave of my son."

Franklin and Joella remained at the car while Dewayne and Rosella walked through the cemetery toward the graves of Sabrina, Bruce, and Robert Dewayne Jobe III. The ride from the airport had been solemn. When they got out of the car at the cemetery, Franklin and Joella exited with them. They poured their hearts out to Dewayne and Rosella, begging Dewayne's forgiveness for thinking him a monster. Three grandchildren had unexpectedly come into their lives, and just as the bonds were forming and they were solidifying their roles as grandparents, life cruelly took those children from them. As for Bonita, they had no idea where she was. Once she learned what had happened, she disappeared, and no amount of searching had brought her back to them. It was just the four of them left. This was the last of their family, and they would do anything they could to preserve it.

Rosella laid the bouquet of flowers at the base of the headstone. "Robert Dewayne Jobe III. Resting in God's hands."

"I'm trying to remember the last time I held him in my arms," Dewayne said. "And I can't. I can't."

He had not cried so hard since the day in the glass booth when Rosella hurled the rings at him and fled the room. Everything came back. Everything flowed through him. He felt himself the conduit for all the sorrow of the world, for his world lay shattered and buried at his feet. Exhaustion and anguish brought him to his knees, and Rosella knelt beside him. Franklin and Joella turned their backs to the scene, unable to watch their son-in-law's grief, their own grief still too raw to absorb another's.

He apologized. Repeatedly, he apologized to the children. Over and over again, he asked for their forgiveness. Over and over again, he pleaded for strength just to inhale. Over and over again, he swore he would never forget them; he would carry their memories with him until he joined them. Over and over again, he begged for the mercy he felt had been so elusive.

When he had spent himself, Rosella helped him to his feet. They looked at the three headstones, the representations of their shared loss, and the empty vessel that was Dewayne Jobe began to fill up.

"Rosella, have you got my mother's engagement ring?" he asked.

"It never leaves my side," she said, opening her purse and retrieving it from a zippered side pocket. She placed it in his hand, and Dewayne turned her hand over and slipped the ring onto her finger.

"I pledge to you before God and Jesus and all the angels and my mama and these precious children I will remain true

342

to you till my last day on this earth. Somehow, we'll start over. Somehow, we'll go on. And we'll do it together."

They held on to each other as though they were the last two people on earth, a new Adam and a new Eve, fresh from the Tree of Knowledge, made stronger through weakness, covered in mercy's clothes, and facing together a new threshold.

Rosella carried the picnic basket into the vacant bleachers and sat down to watch Jake put Dewayne through his morning paces of stretching, passing drills, and wind sprints, and this after an hour of strength and conditioning in the Springdale Tigers' weight room. Jake had worked out a training schedule with the new head coach of the Tigers that would not conflict with the team's use of the weight room or field. While the team was in classes all the facilities were available. Since Dewayne had not made public his intentions about his future, they wanted to keep away from any media attention, and the high school provided safe sanctuary. There was no reason to build expectation only to crash in disappointment. He had endured enough public humiliation without the media reporting on the failures to bounce back. It would be better to discover what he could do without national scrutiny.

Dr. Macy had made it clear it would take years before the medical profession would pronounce Dewayne cancer free, but in the meantime, the focus was to overcome the physical limitations of getting back into shape. Once Dewayne and Rosella returned from Los Angeles with the Caldwell blessing of support for any direction they chose to take, Dewayne called Coach Gyra for his approval. He told Dewayne his locker was empty and waiting, but the team doctors would make the final decision as to whether or not he could go back onto the field. Dewayne only wanted the chance to earn his place on the team, and Gyra promised to give him every opportunity. The next day the retraining of Dewayne Jobe began.

Rosella recognized the swagger of the tall African-American man coming onto the field, wearing sunglasses and cap, and approaching from out of the sun as Jake threw Dewayne some short route passes. Jake did not have the arm to go much beyond twenty-five yards, and Dewayne had not yet built the stamina to venture much farther.

Rosella almost blurted out his name but covered her mouth to allow whatever would happen to happen. Here was pro football's leading passer just five games into the season walking toward his old high school coach. When Jake released his last pass, Sly stepped beside him and whispered for him to tell Dewayne to go for it.

"Go straight for the end zone. I think I've got the arm today," Jake shouted.

The look of shock on Jake's face made Rosella wonder how he'd even managed to speak.

Dewayne released Jake's last pass while still jogging, and without looking back or questioning Jake's command, his legs kicked in and he started running full bore for the end zone. The feeling was so exhilarating he did not care if Jake might have overstated the potency of his arm. He was enjoying the speed too much to care. Over the last weeks, his body had been steadily building in strength, weight, dexterity, and agility, and the thrill of traveling at such velocity was pure pleasure. He had wondered if he ever might feel this sensation again.

Had not a faint familiar voice cried out for him to look back, the ball probably would have hit him in the head. For a moment, he had been absorbed in the act of running, forgetting there had been an original purpose for the sprint, and as he turned his head and raised his arms, the ball spiraled into his hands with a force that carried him into the end zone and an impact with the ground that took his breath away. He bounced for several yards across the grass, and when he came to a stop, he raised the ball in his hand to show he retained possession.

No way could Jake Hopper have thrown that pass unless supported by gale force winds. The second the ball had touched his hands he recognized the passer. No one had ever thrown to him with such power and accuracy. Sly never cut him any slack because he never doubted him, and this was Sly's way of testing him. If he could catch a Sly Adams' pass, then maybe there was hope for getting back into the game.

He lay on the ground, taking time to regain his breath. He knew he had overexerted, but the feat was well worth it. He was not completely ready for this burst of energy, but perhaps just this once his body might not punish him for his eagerness. A hand came into view and knocked the ball out of his grasp, then seized his fingers and lifted him to his feet.

"Show-off," Sly said, and then he ran his hands up Dewayne's arms and over his shoulders, kneading the muscles. The examination continued. He cuffed Dewayne's chest, poked his sides, and did a quick, light jab to his abdomen. He slapped his thighs, ran a finger down each calf, and squeezed his ankles.

"You trade in your Heisman for a policeman's badge?" Dewayne asked.

"No mush, my man. You got no mush." Sly rose from his pat down. "You are a walking miracle."

"I've added over forty pounds since you last saw me," Dewayne said.

"Yeah, about that last time . . . ," Sly started, but Dewayne cut him off at the knees.

"When you scrambled out my door chasing Rosella, I knew then I hated you."

"I deserved to be hated."

"You still deserve to be hated."

"You'll get no argument," Sly said, the absence of cockiness obvious to Dewayne. "Jake called and chewed me out."

"He's gotten a lot grumpier since he quit drinking," Dewayne said.

"So I'm down here to help out," Sly said. "It's my bye week."

"Then throw me some balls and stay away from my wife," Dewayne said and trotted back toward Jake.

Sly stayed in a hotel for the next seven days. Before and after Dewayne's strength and conditioning time, Sly was on the field, the two old friends running passing routes Jake had drawn up. Passes were accurate, catches made, but there was no small talk, no playful banter, no teasing. It was all business, and no invitations were issued to socialize at the end of each day. Sly and Dewayne treated each other like strangers, Sly unable to apologize for fear of seeming phony, Dewayne fearful of hearing an apology and having to accept it. Rosella was wise enough to stay out of the untouchable barrier they had erected. She felt responsible in part just by her mere existence, and she never broached the subject when Dewayne and Jake came home for dinner each afternoon after practice. On the final day, Jake at last plowed a hole through the line they had drawn.

"So how long are you going to punish your friend?" he asked Dewayne.

"I deserve it, Jake," Sly said, opening the sack and dropping in a pile of footballs one at a time.

346

"See? You heard him," Dewayne said, spiraling a football at Sly with a fierce underhand pitch. "He deserves it."

"I call it cruel and unusual," Jake said. "You're on my field. I never would have let you get away with it back in the day."

Sly and Dewayne hung their heads, all the better to take the scolding.

"So have we got us a Mexican standoff or what?"

"That day in the hospital, I thought I was looking at the worst of you," Sly began, raising his head to get into Dewayne's sight line, but his friend would have none of it. "Come to find out I was revealing the worst of myself. I didn't stick by you in your hour of need. I would have tried to hustle Rosella if she'd let me. I tell anyone who listens what a jerk I think you are, and then I crawl in a hole too ashamed to come see you when the truth comes out. Jake's the reason I'm here."

"Yeah, he saved my life too," Dewayne said, the frown on his lips weakening.

"You boys have been caught in my sinister web," Jake said. "You're my sons and I love you. Kiss and make up. We all know life's too short."

Dewayne tossed the ball he was holding into the open sack, and Sly let go of the corners. Their hands were empty.

"I can't hold a grudge anymore," Dewayne said. "It's too hard."

"I can't bear the thought of your hatred." The muscles in Sly's face began to tremble, his tough countenance crumbling. "I'm sorry, my brother. I'm so sorry." Dewayne took Sly into his arms, and their combined bitter weeping echoed off the stadium bleachers.

29

With all his medical records in tow and after one last checkup with Dr. Macy, Dewayne and Rosella moved back to Houston and bought a three-bedroom condominium in a gated community on the opposite side of the city from where they had once lived. With the help of Detective Hathaway and his connection at the Treasury Department, cyberspace had opened up, and their fortunes restored. Dewayne and Rosella were still unsure if they could live in that city again and did not want to make a huge investment in a home. What they were sure of was Jake's place in this new family.

"It's time to hand you off to the experts," Jake said. "I'd be in the way."

"I need you in my way for a lifetime," Dewayne said.

"Rosella is all you need."

"Jake, you're family. I've lost enough family. I don't want to lose any more."

Jake still wanted to protest until Dewayne pulled out the blue teddy bear. "You think I'd leave this behind? How could I leave you behind? You're the only connection to my history, you and Sly. I don't leave that behind."

Jake blinked first, so they closed the two houses and left the keys with a property management service that would care for the homes in their absence. They would make a decision about the properties once they knew what the remainder of this football season would mean to their futures.

The team doctors put Dewayne through another round of examinations before they allowed him to go onto the practice field. He also had to face the media attention his return brought to the Stars. Avoidance was impossible.

"I just want to contribute to the team's success," he told the reporters assembled in the pressroom at the practice facility on his first day back. "I appreciate Coach Gyra's confidence in giving me a second chance."

The team accepted Dewayne back into their ranks like little brothers welcoming home the big brother after a long absence. When Gyra announced the team doctors had cleared Dewayne for practice, there was spontaneous applause in the locker room.

Dewayne did no showboating during the first week. All he wanted to prove to everyone, and most of all to himself, was that he could just hold his own. He wanted to earn everyone's trust. He wanted everyone to know his body was functional, and they could count on him to do his job if called upon. The first couple of games Dewayne dressed out but did not play. They were road games so he did not have to face the Stars fans until the third game, but like the response he received in the locker room from his teammates, when his jersey was spotted by a group of fans close to the bench, they began a rowdy chant of "D-man" that was soon echoing throughout the stadium.

Dewayne had to stand on the bench and wave his helmet, accepting their appreciation, before the game could begin.

Dewayne did not start or play any of the first quarter. By the middle of the second quarter, he went in for a series of downs but never received the ball. He got to run onto the field, run his routes, throw a few blocks, and run off again without embarrassing himself. His groove was coming back. All the instincts were firing, and he could feel his mind and body readjusting to the physical demands of the game. But more important, his heart was growing into the spirit of the game, something that had most concerned him. What if, once he was on the field engaged in real-time play, he discovered that he no longer cared about the game, that, in fact, he was afraid?

In the third quarter, Dewayne caught passes for a couple of first downs, which brought the fans to their feet, but in the fourth quarter, got smacked high and low after snagging a thirty-yard pass. He brought in the catch, but the referee called an official's time-out for the team doctors to escort Dewayne off the field to the subdued applause of distressed fans.

The next day Coach Gyra announced Dewayne had suffered a mild concussion and the coaching staff would take a wait-and-see attitude about his role in the next game. The media jumped on it, raising doubts that Dewayne was not ready to return, that the game was no longer in him.

"You've got nothing to prove," Rosella said that night in bed as she rubbed his chest. "Nobody will blame you."

"I've got everything to prove," he said, taking her hand in his and kissing her fingers. "I just had my bell rung. That's all."

"How many times can that happen and you walk off the field on your own two legs? How many times can your head take the punishment?"

"It's the life, baby. You know the life. I've just come back from a brain tumor. You think I'm going to let a mild concussion—"

"I'm afraid, that's all. I'm just afraid," she said, pulling her hand away and turning over on her back. "Will these concussions bring back the tumor? The doctors don't know that. I'm just afraid."

Dewayne turned on his side and smiled down at his wife. He took the top of the sheet and dabbed her eyes, and then he caressed her face.

"We've been through more than anybody could ever imagine, and we made it to the other side. We'll never be the same, but I can't live in fear. I want to grow old with you and have a houseful of babies along the way, but I can't live in fear. I want the joy we once had to be restored to us, and I believe that can't happen if we live in fear. I promise I will do nothing foolish that might endanger a happy future together, but if I live in fear, I live as half a man, and you don't want that."

"I don't want to live in fear either." Rosella pressed his hand onto her cheek.

"We're gonna make it, baby," Dewayne whispered. "We're gonna make it."

The Stars had to win the final three games of the regular season in order to make the play-offs. In the previous games, Dewayne evaded injury and made positive contributions, including a few touchdowns, which built the confidence factor. He avoided responding to the press, who had placed a high expectation on his game and expressed disappointment in his ho-hum performance to date. Dewayne's own expectations were all that mattered, and those who insisted he should be doing more by this time in the season to help the Stars make it to the play-offs would not distract or discourage him.

Though his strength and speed had returned to first-season levels, he did not play up to those expectations. This forced the team to play with more cohesion instead of relying on one player to be a difference maker and built poise and camaraderie among his teammates.

The Stars won the first of the last three games with Dewayne getting less than eighty yards and no touchdowns. In the second game, he took a hit that would have floored a charging bull, but when the three tacklers peeled off his flattened body, he bounced onto his feet and trotted off the field as if he had tripped over his own shoelace. The Stars went on to triumph.

The third game was against his old nemesis, Baltimore and Colby Stewart. It was do-or-die for both teams, and Dewayne knew Colby would do everything in his power to get inside Dewayne's head. The smack talk began in the pregame warm-ups.

"Well, if it isn't Teddy Bear Boy back from the dead," Colby said as he high-stepped around Dewayne sitting on the thirty-yard line and stretching his calves.

"Colby, how's the weather in Baltimore?" Dewayne asked.

"Cold, and I brought cold with me today. I'm gonna show you cold. I'm gonna hit you like the iceberg hit the *Titanic*, and you're gonna go down. You're gonna sink, and I'm gonna be the one who knocked the hole in your hull."

"Listen to his bad self," Dewayne replied. "Don't you ever get bored by the sound of your voice?"

"How can I be bored when I've got sixty minutes to smack on Tumor Man?" Colby shouted. "Is it true the docs burned half your brain when they cooked your tumor?"

"Yeah, I heard that story," Dewayne said, wrapping his big hands around his shoes and bending forward until his face mask touched the grass. "You read that in the tabloid section, which is about your grade level?"

"Well, the tabloids say you took a nap while everyone died around you," Colby said.

Every muscle in Dewayne's body stiffened.

"Nero fiddled while Rome burned, and you slept while the devil ransacked your house."

It was as though some powerful hand lifted Dewayne to his feet; pure rage popping capillaries, but the hand went from invisible to solid form and held him in place with a firm grip on his shoulder pads.

"Colby, can I quote what you said to my man, so I can show the world what a real jerk you are?" Sly said, sticking a microphone in Colby's face as a camera operator stepped from behind Sly with his eye attached to the lens of his camera. Colby's expression went from scowl to hateful. "Zoom in on Colby and let him do an instant replay of what he just said, then I'm gonna turn loose of my man here and let him do a little Mississippi soft shoe all over your ugly head, something all of America would love to see."

Colby spat in the direction of Sly's shoes before he put on his helmet and snapped the chinstrap in place.

"The devil is loose in your house, and I'll stomp you like a mouse," Colby said and then trotted in the direction of his locker room.

"My, my, Mr. Stewart, you have such a way with words!" Sly shouted after him. "In your next life you can come back as Shakespeare."

Colby never turned around but raised the middle finger of each hand before he disappeared into the tunnel.

"There goes next year's NFL poster child for Miss Congeniality," Sly said.

"I might have killed him if you hadn't grabbed me," Dewayne said, still trembling from the verbal sledgehammer blow. Dewayne was as surprised by his murderous reaction as he was by Colby's attack.

"And I might have let you if we hadn't had a stadium full of witnesses." Sly released his grip but extended his arm over his friend's shoulder. "Take a couple of deep breaths for old Sly, and remember Colby's in a world of hurt."

"I might just break some of that world over his head today." Dewayne released a deep breath of hot air.

Sly patted Dewayne's shoulder pads. "Focus on the win. You get the win, and Colby can go back to his little pit of hell."

"Yeah. Yeah, you're right." Dewayne started jumping up and down, getting the elastic back into his muscles. "Hey, congratulations on yesterday's win," Dewayne said with a slap to his arm.

"I'm counting on you breezing through the play-offs and seeing you in February."

"To what do I owe the honor of Sly Adams coming to my rescue, sporting a suit and a cameraman?"

"All Sports Network brought me in for halftime commentary. Set me up with a cameraman to score a few pregame interviews," Sly said. "I'm trying out this sports news thing. Couple of championship rings on my fingers, and this may be my second career." Sly signaled the camera operator to roll tape. "Are you ready to face down Baltimore?"

"Baltimore is a great team," Dewayne said. "But they'll go home disappointed."

"I've got some insider information from a very reliable source that says you take your famous teddy bear with you everywhere you go. Is that true?"

"He is sitting in my locker even as we speak, and he goes with me on the road."

"What's the meaning of that teddy bear?"

"It reminds me of how precious life is and how wonderful God is for creating every life, no matter how short a stay it might have."

"Good luck today," Sly said and sliced his finger across his throat for the camera operator to stop taping. Sly cradled Dewayne's helmet in his hands. "You be careful, my man."

On the very first possession of the very first play, the Stars' quarterback let Dewayne build a head of steam across the field and dropped the ball right into his hands for the first score of the game. Had the crowd noise not been so loud, Dewayne might have heard Colby reaming out his teammates as they jogged off the field for letting Dewayne slip by them.

With their second series of downs, Dewayne caught two passes in a row, both for first downs, and Colby took the unusual step of calling for a time-out to rewrite the defensive game plan. Colby did not ask for suggestions or consensus. For the first few seconds he browbeat his squad's incompetence, and then he revamped their strategy.

"If we don't stop him, we don't stop them," Colby shouted to the group before he turned to the cornerback whom Dewayne had turned into a chump. "He's too big and fast for your scrawny ass. I'll roll up on him at the line and knock him around. You help with coverage, and we'll own him."

In spite of Colby's being flagged twice, once for unnecessary roughness and a second time for unsportsmanlike conduct, this double-team coverage strategy virtually shut down Dewayne for the rest of the first half, holding him to three catches for only thirty-plus yards. Instead of being a poet in his next life, Colby could come back as a motivational speaker.

"This is a battle royal," Robert Hickman said, sitting in his chair as anchor for All Sports Network for the halftime show. "Colby Stewart and Dewayne Jobe, two titans of the game, are battling it out on the field. Sylvester Adams, who do you think has the upper hand at this moment?"

"Colby Stewart, no question. After the first ten minutes,

Colby and his crew have dominated the game and shut out Dewayne. If the Stars' defense had not stepped up with those two interceptions and held Baltimore to one score, they could be two touchdowns ahead and we wouldn't be looking at a tie game. I heard what went on between those two during the pregame warm-up. It wasn't pretty, and they've taken it to the field."

"Can you repeat anything that was said?" Hickman asked.

"Not unless you want to lose half your sponsors," Sly said.

"Then we'll leave it to our imaginations," Hickman said. "So, Mr. Adams, what does each team have to do to win?"

"Loser goes home today. Winner goes to the play-offs with a powerful momentum working in its favor. If Colby and his boys keep winning the head game with Dewayne, they could go home with their play-off ticket. I've got the three Rs for Dewayne Jobe: relax, refocus, and rejoice. He's been playing conservative. It's time to play his game."

Rosella, Jake, and the entire stadium stood for the kickoff at the top of the second half and never sat back down. The third and fourth quarters were not much different from the first two. Each team got one more score but only a field goal apiece.

Throughout the thirty minutes of play, Dewayne kept silent and let Colby do all the smack talk. He did his best to block out Colby's attacks for the one dropped ball he had, the two underthrown passes, and the diving attempt he made for an overthrown ball. Colby blamed every mistake on Dewayne, accusing him of spooking the Stars with bad mojo. Dewayne found it impossible to shake the double team, and Colby's harassment fueled the demoralized state of the team.

With five seconds left to play and the Stars on the fifty-yard line, everyone including the commentators expected this game to go into overtime.

When the play came in, Dewayne told the front line to protect their quarterback at all costs. He needed time to sprint close to forty yards.

The Baltimore defense set up a nickel package with an extra defensive back standing at the ten-yard line. Colby's screaming mandate to his teammates before the ball was snapped: "You let Jobe get behind you, and I'll make you a cripple for life!"

A "Hail Mary" had little chance of working the way the defense was spread, so it would be up to the receiver to carry the ball into the end zone.

The front line did their job keeping the defensive line from taking down the quarterback, and Dewayne sprinted his forty yards in near Combine time. Dewayne suckered Colby and the defensive back into thinking he was on a dead sprint mission to the end zone, but at the ten-yard line, he slammed on the brakes and cut directly across the field. The ball was already in the air when he made the cut, and it was slightly underthrown, forcing Dewayne to slow down and catch the ball behind him. This adjustment in speed gave Colby time to recover switching directions, and he plowed into Dewayne's side at the seven-yard line.

Time had run out on the clock, and Colby's driving force almost took Dewayne to the ground. Dewayne had only a second or two before the Baltimore defensive backs would be piling onto this Stewart/Jobe duo moving violently in opposite directions. Colby was riding Dewayne like a cowboy trying to trip a stubborn calf while Dewayne's legs churned the ground like a thoroughbred determined to finish the race.

Colby roared, Dewayne howled, two beasts bellowing dominance. A safety arrived, then another, but it was too late. Dewayne had fallen over the goal line, and the official raised both arms in the air. Dewayne rolled onto his side and held the ball for all to see. The stadium burst in a rupture of ecstatic pandemonium. A horde of Stars converged on Dewayne and lifted their resurrected leader into the air. Startled by this sudden launch into space, Dewayne let the ball fly out of his hand. It landed right beside Colby stretched prone on the ground.

Dewayne hugged his teammates before making his way over to his foe. Colby had not moved nor the ball been knocked away, even though the euphoria around them was out of control. Dewayne put his hands on Colby's shoulders, pulled him to his feet, and brought their facemasks together. Colby was still too dazed and out of breath, or he might have thought Dewayne was about to harm him and would not have been so docile.

"You played a great game," Dewayne said.

Colby's only reaction after hot, panting breaths blown into Dewayne's face through the grid of the facemasks was to knock off Dewayne's hands resting on Colby's shoulder pads.

"Colby, I know what misery feels like," Dewayne shouted. "There's real peace out there, and I know who can give it to you. I'm here for you anytime, anywhere."

Colby said nothing. He snatched the ball from the ground and ran off the field.

Epilogue

Jake and Dewayne looked at the large box containing the baby bed leaning against the wall of the spare bedroom as if they were staring at something that had fallen from outer space.

"Come on, you two. This is not like putting Humpty Dumpty back together," she said. "It's just a baby bed."

The birth of their baby was still several months away, but they wanted to get everything in order. The choice to have another child had been difficult. After visiting the graves of their son, and Bruce and Sabrina who became like their own children, it was easier to keep the prospect of having more children in the realm of discussion, not action. They were afraid of getting pregnant. They were afraid of being happy again with new offspring. They were afraid such action was an attempt to replace Robert Dewayne who was irreplaceable. The emotional risks were great.

Franklin and Joella encouraged them without applying any pressure. They knew well the pain of loss, the guilt and fear of risking another child, so they understood their turmoil and told them they would support any decision.

They asked Jake's opinion and his terse response helped them turn a corner. "I'd make an excellent grandfather," he said.

When it came right down to it, passion made the decision; a night when making a run to the local pharmacy was the last thing on their minds.

"Don't we have to go to practice, Jake?" Dewayne asked.

"Yeah, I think they called a special practice today," Jake said.

Once Dewayne had reestablished himself with the team, he kept singing Jake's praises to Coach Gyra—how he had gotten him through his ordeal. Impressed by Jake's willingness to step up, the Stars' management added Jake to the Player Development Department. It was a perfect arrangement for young players to be the beneficiaries of wise counsel.

"You two," Rosella said, shaking her head. "Intimidated by a baby bed."

"We're not intimidated," Dewayne said.

"No, no, not intimidated," Jake said. "We're just . . . just busy."

"Yeah, we're busy." Dewayne looked at Jake, each man appreciative of the other's backing.

"I've read your schedule," Rosella said. "You're both off today."

The doorbell rang, and both men started to exit, thankful for the diversion from the chore of assembling the baby bed.

"It doesn't take two grown men to answer the front door," Rosella said. "Dewayne Jobe, you get back here."

Jake shrugged his shoulders, pretending to be sorry for this summons.

"If it's another neighbor wanting tickets to the championship, tell him he'll have to watch it on television like the rest of America," Dewayne said.

Jake slapped Dewayne's shoulder before he skipped out, and Dewayne trudged across the room to the box and began to place the individual pieces of the crib onto the carpet while Rosella read the instructions. There had been a huge number of requests for tickets to the big game, but Dewayne had declined them all. He had leased a skybox in the stadium and invited a select group: Franklin and Joella; Dr. Macy, his wife, and select members of his medical team; Winston Garfield of the *Springdale Leader*; special women who had worked with Cherie; Jesse Webb's parents; and Detective John Hathaway.

"You prophesied, Detective," Dewayne told him when he called to invite him on an all-expense-paid trip to watch him play in the biggest game of his life.

"Prophesied? I don't remember," Hathaway said.

"You said you wanted to see me play in a Stars' game. You gave me my 'get out of jail free' card, and I'm fulfilling your prophecy."

And, of course, Sly would make an appearance in the suite when he wasn't providing analysis and commentary for the All Sports Network coverage of the game. He would not be playing against his best friend this year.

By the time Rosella got to step three with the instructions, she began to weep.

"I can't do this, baby. I can't," she said, dropping the instructions on the floor.

Dewayne wrapped his arms around his wife and pulled her close.

"All we have in life is each other," he said. "We have survived so much together. We will do this and it will be painful, but I hope God will someday make our joy complete, and it may be soon. It may be soon."

Jake reentered the room as Dewayne was wiping the tears from Rosella's eyes.

"Sorry, but you need to go to the door," Jake said, his face pale, his eyes darting.

"What's up?" Dewayne asked.

"Just go to the door."

Jake stopped Rosella from following her husband.

"He needs to face this one alone," he said, and he diverted her curiosity by rolling up his sleeves and tackling the baby bed assembly line.

Dewayne opened the door and stared at Colby Stewart, his feet shuffling over the stones of the path in front of the condo, hands behind his back, eyes cast down like a timid boy.

"How did you get in?" was all Dewayne could think to say in his state of amazement.

"An autograph and a sob story." Colby revealed the football hidden behind his back underneath his coat. "Told the guard I came all the way from Baltimore to return this."

Colby tossed the ball to Dewayne, and he bobbled it a couple of times before he secured the pass.

"You gotta do better than that next week in San Diego," Colby said, a shy grin forming on his lips.

"I'll have a quarterback who knows how to throw the ball, not a linebacker."

Both men chuckled. Colby continued to perform his agitated shuffle over the stones in Dewayne's tiny front yard.

"This a bad time?" Colby asked.

"No, it's cool," Dewayne said. "You want to come inside?"

"No thanks, I don't feel comfortable."

"How'd you know I wasn't at practice?"

"I have a mole buried in the Stars' organization. I used to work there, you know."

This time a mutual chuckle turned into a real laugh for both of them.

"You must be tired traveling all the way from Baltimore just to bring me this," Dewayne said, shaking the football in his hand.

"That day after the game you said you knew what it was like to feel miserable," Colby blurted, his face pinched tight as though a pair of invisible hands were pressing against his cheeks.

"I do," Dewayne said.

"You said you knew where I could find peace."

"I do."

"What you went through, it was hell, huh?"

"Every kind of hell."

"But you got through it."

"By God's grace I got through it, but I'm not over it. I'll never be over it." Dewayne reached inside the front door and pulled a jacket off the coatrack. "There's a footpath behind the complex. You feel like a walk?"

Colby nodded in approval.

Dewayne threw Colby the ball and put on his coat. The two men started down the stone pathway in the center of the courtyard, their only communication, the pitching of the ball back and forth to each other.

Acknowledgments

First of all, I would like to thank God for the inspiration of this story and putting all the pieces into place for it to come together. Also, for giving me the sense to know that I cannot write—and without that skill, books usually don't get written.

Without Ron Cook, who became a good friend in the process, this story would still be just traveling around in my head, getting revised with each road trip and going nowhere. For all your prayers, hard work, and introductions—thank you.

Chris Sanders not only contributed the foreword and generously shared his life as a pro-football player, but he was also a great encourager. Whenever it seemed easier to give up, Chris would call with an encouraging word.

Our agent, Esther Fedorkevich, believed in this project from the beginning and never gave up. Her advice and counsel have been valued more than words can express.

Things really began to come together when Esther introduced me to Beverly Mansfield. She got the concept and the story and, through her insight and guidance, felt it was time to make the crucial introduction to Henry O.

Despite telling me that my version of the story was bad and my writing horrible, Henry O. quickly became not only a good writing partner but a friend as well.

Before turning over the writing to Henry O., the two of us met in the good offices of the accounting firm of Jennings and Clouse and the missionary team of Mission Discovery, where we hammered out the action of the story. They didn't seem to mind two wild and crazy guys conducting a healthy exchange of ideas in the next room.

Jennifer, Cat, and all the team at Revell have been wonderful to work with, and their enthusiasm for this book has been refreshing. A special note of gratitude goes to Barb Barnes, whose editorial insights raised the quality of this novel to a much higher level. She was a delight to work with, and her literary suggestions never felt like work.

We could not eat dinner at home without thanking our wives for putting up with us through this creative process.

Finally, thank you for reading this book. We hope you enjoyed it.

Henry O. adds his thanks for the generous support of those already mentioned, and would like to offer a special thanks to Bill for sharing his story with him and entrusting him with a dream he has carried for a long time. That took great courage on his part—courage few demonstrate—and thus a team was born . . . a team that promises more compelling stories in the future.

Bill Barton travels the world as a business partner with three companies that develop and sell products to nonprofit organizations, small businesses, and large retailers. He received his MBA from Baylor University. A sought-after speaker, he combines his business experience and passion for the spiritual life to motivate and inspire others.

Bill lives in Hendersonville, TN, with his wife and two sons (who keep him very busy). Even in light of his busy work schedule and passionate commitment to his family and church, he makes time to satisfy the adventure junkie inside—whether it's hiking, mountain biking, or taking frequent family camping trips to the nearby lakes and mountains. He is an avid football fan and can be found at the stadium anytime the lights are on.

Henry O. Arnold has been a professional actor and writer in theatre and film since 1970. He graduated from Pepperdine University with his BA in acting and completed his Master of Fine Arts degree at UNC Chapel Hill. His original film trilogy *The Word Made Flesh*, three one-man shows, received two first-place awards at the Houston International Film Festival and the Columbus International Film Festival. He co-wrote and produced the film *The Second Chance*, starring Michael W. Smith. He wrote the screenplay for the first authorized film documentary on evangelist Billy Graham, *God's Ambassador*. He co-wrote and produced the forthcoming documentary *Kabul-24* for Seabourne Pictures, based on the story of the capture and escape of eight Western aid workers held as hostages by the Taliban in 2001. He is the narrator for the two-CD recording of *Jesus in His Own Words*, released by Total Content. Henry and his wife, Kay, have two beautiful daughters married to two handsome men. He lives in Portland, TN.

Chris Sanders, third-round draft pick out of Ohio State in 1995 and former wide receiver for the Tennessee Titans, served as special consultant for *Hometown Favorite*. Now retired from playing professional football, Sanders focuses the majority of his time on giving back to the community through The Sanders Foundation.

———————————

Visit the authors' website at
www.barton-arnold.com

Bill and Henry would like to hear from their readers.
Email them at contact@barton-arnold.com.